Praise for *The Launch Date*

"Flirty and full of heart, Annabelle Slator's debut is a dream date in book form. With a deeply relatable heroine who recovers her faith in romance amid enemies-to-lovers tension and workplace hijinks, *The Launch Date* has everything."

—Emily Wibberley and Austin Siegemund-Broka, authors of *The Roughest Draft*

"Whoop, whoop! A sensational debut rom-com has landed! This debut has everything you could want: a fabulously funny and relatable leading lady and a swoon-worthy man with just the right amount of brood. Prepare to fall in love with Eric and Grace as they battle it out for a promotion and try very hard not to fall in love. *The Launch Date* is a witty, sparkly, and hilarious book for fans of *The Hating Game*. Prepare to put Annabelle Slator on auto-buy."

—Lizzy Dent, author of *The Summer Job*

THE
Launch
DATE

A Novel

ANNABELLE SLATOR

AVON

An Imprint of HarperCollinsPublishers

THE LAUNCH DATE. Copyright © 2025 by Slator Creative Limited. All rights reserved. Printed in the United States of America. No part of this book may be used or reproduced in any manner whatsoever without written permission except in the case of brief quotations embodied in critical articles and reviews. For information, address HarperCollins Publishers, 195 Broadway, New York, NY 10007.

HarperCollins books may be purchased for educational, business, or sales promotional use. For information, please email the Special Markets Department at SPsales@harpercollins.com.

Originally published in the United Kingdom in 2025 by Penguin Random House UK.

FIRST US EDITION

Library of Congress Cataloging-in-Publication Data has been applied for.

ISBN 978-0-06-338362-3

24 25 26 27 28 LBC 5 4 3 2 1

*To all my fellow imposters,
I can't believe we're still
getting away with it.*

THE
Launch
DATE

1

I take a deep breath, trying to stay calm.

I am enough, I belong here, I deserve to be here.

I silently repeat the mantra I saw on Instagram to myself—the latest in the long line of attempts to overcome my sickening self-doubt.

I am enough, I belong here, I deserve—

A cough interrupts me and I look up from the table to see *him* smirking at me, as if he knows exactly what I'm doing in the privacy of my own head and knows it's completely futile.

It's taken me five years of hard work to get where I am now: Marketing Manager for one of the biggest start-ups in London. I wake up every day feeling as though the rug is about to be pulled out from under me, the mask of competency that I've been wearing about to melt away, revealing my true shitty self to the whole world. But Eric Bancroft breezes his way through.

My CV is overflowing with every minuscule marketing-based task I've ever done, reading like a pharmacy receipt; full of discount offers (will work for 30 percent off!), campaigns for antidepressants and medical-grade hay fever tablets. Bancroft's entire career history is engraved on the gold signet ring he spins around his finger when he's bored.

Even now, he just sits there, across from me at the expansive wooden conference-room table, utterly relaxed. Never doubting for one second that he deserves to be here. The fractured London sun flows through the twelfth-floor conference room window over half of his face. It makes almost icy blue eyes so bright he looks as if he could shoot lasers through the frames of the tortoiseshell glasses I'm sure he only wears to make himself look smarter.

I glare at him.

"Grace?"

The sound of my name asked as a question bounces off the echoey white-brick walls. My boss, the legendary Susie Jopling, stares at me expectantly.

"Yes, sorry." My laptop whirs softly as I pull up the presentation full of my performance and growth figures for the month to project onto the wall. My clammy fingers tap away at the keys as I silently will my heartbeat to calm. "Susie, would you mind just pushing the button to move it along for me? I'll tell you when . . ."

I am enough, I belong here, I deserve to be here.

"Late night, Hastings?" Eric Bancroft's villain-like smirk asks, holding the end of a Catch Group–branded pen between his perfect teeth.

He loves to call me by my last name, as though I'm one of his private school frenemies.

"Some of us actually work late, Bancroft," I reply with a tight smile, eyes fixed on the screen. A light chuckle from his boss, Dharmash, fills the silence as my eyes adjust to my presentation slides projected on the wall. "Next slide, please."

With feigned confidence, I clear my throat and smooth down the pink suede lapels of my lucky vintage suit. Not the most sensible choice for a sweltering summer in the city, but this, styled with a pair of expensive-looking secondhand trainers from eBay, tricks everyone into believing I am totally put-together.

I throw my hand out to the first upwardly tilting graph. "As you can see here: Fate has had a fantastic month of user growth. Our latest 'True Love' campaign hit the exact target demographic we wanted, our twenty-five-to-thirty-four-year-old user base has increased by seven percent month-on-month, which I'm incredibly pleased with."

Bancroft leans back in his chair and crosses his arms over his navy shirt, no doubt designer. Apparently, a gladiator decides he's defeated his opponent before they've even entered the ring, and Bancroft certainly acts as if he's already won this month's Battle of the Graphs.

"Can we see the campaign footage?" Dharmash asks me. "I'd love to see what you guys are doing on the other side of the fence."

The fence being the metaphorical separation between

the infamously polar opposite companies of the Catch Group office: Fate and Ignite, carved into two distinct spaces separated by a floor in the CG high-rise. The remaining ten floors are inhabited by the tech company's various other gaming apps, streaming services and social media platforms. When I started working at Fate, I didn't understand why the company's two premier dating apps were put on different floors, but now I thank the office-floorplan gods that I don't have to run into Eric Bancroft on a daily basis.

"It's on the next slide. Susie?" I look over at Susie, who is engrossed in her phone. Heat rising in my cheeks, I go over to the laptop and hit the play button, trying to refocus my attention as soft, twinkly music plays and footage focuses on two people on a garden porch. A stunning man and woman with clasped hands surrounded by blooming bushes of pink roses, to be precise.

"I never liked the idea of using a dating app to find true love, but I'm so glad I took a chance on Fate." The handsome man in his late twenties is talking to someone behind the camera while taking brief glances at the beautiful woman clinging to his muscled arm with a massive rock sitting on her manicured finger.

"I tried other dating apps, but I never knew who was looking for a real relationship and who was just looking for a quick hook-up," the woman adds. "Fate helped us find each other in a sea of unserious daters."

She kisses the man on the cheek, and he smiles down at her. I try not to let the cringe show on my face.

I've watched this video a hundred times over, making sure every frame is a perfect depiction of a successful Fate-branded love story. A year ago, I would have been fooled by this, but now this sappy brand of "true love" makes me want to gag and rage and cry all at the same time.

Ever since William broke up with me, the idea of finding a true love match seems like a pipe dream, made up with the sole purpose of earning downloads and selling subscription packages. Fate is a monotonous machine of my own making, spitting out cookie-cutter promises through rose-tinted screens to trick users into hoping for their true love story. I spend most of my days curating new ways to package a concept I no longer believe in: breath-catching, life-altering, loneliness-ending romance.

The video concludes with one final musical flourish, and I resume my presentation.

"In addition to these results, starting this evening Susie is hosting a series of panel talks discussing various topics of life, love and careers to onboard high-profile, serious users to ensure Fate's offering is, as always, the best in the city."

Despite Susie's reluctance to give me any positive feedback, it's thanks to events like these that Fate is steadily becoming the number-one dating app for women and men who are looking for classic, fairy-tale love. Unfortunately, Fate's growth rate is more than often overshadowed by Ignite's "swipe first, ask questions later" marketing strategy. I understand why people use their app: it's simple and uncomplicated. But it's the furthest thing from what I want; I've never been able to play it cool and do the "casual" thing. Unlike some people in this room, I haven't got the constitution to jump from person to person like trying out new desserts on a menu; I'd rather accept that I'll be on my own.

I glance at Bancroft, catching his eyes for a heartbeat before they flick back to the screen. He's clearly plotting his taunts for after this meeting. Shit, I should prepare something too. For the past six months, I've spent so much time thinking about him just to try and maintain the upper hand. It didn't use to be like this; we used to be friends. Which is how he knows just where to hit me and make it hurt. Our relative positions have always added an edge of rivalry to our interactions, but now he makes sure his jabs sting for days. Friendly banter turned into a sour visceral taste in the back of my throat. Bancroft runs a long finger across my painstakingly formatted page of growth figures and sighs contentedly. I'll bet he's mentally checking the figures against his own. My skin goes hot and clammy as I realize he's won this month's battle for marketing dominance.

"No, darling, you've got that wrong," Susie chimes in, a patronizing laugh in her tone pulling me back to the room in front of me. "*You're* hosting the panels; I don't have time for that."

"Oh, OK." I scramble, letting out a breathy laugh and tucking my copper curls behind my ear. "I guess

I can make that work . . ." I trail off as I think of the barren wasteland that is the post–6 p.m. section of my Google Calendar. I shouldn't be surprised that Susie is making me cover for her: it's become the norm over the past few years. When I asked if Fate was offering any internships, she took a chance on me. When Fate was bought by Martin Catcher for a bazillion pounds and brought under the Catch Group umbrella, Susie stayed on as the recognizable Girlboss™ figurehead to run the day-to-day. She insisted her core team, including me, retain their current positions.

She is responsible for any and all of my career growth, and she never forgets to remind me of this fact. I'm grateful to her, but ever since Fate was bought out I feel like I'm constantly stepping over trapdoors and she holds the lever.

"It's not like you've got anything better to do, no?" Susie asks.

A rush of hot shame shoots through my veins, heading straight to my pounding chest. Why did she have to say it like that? It's true—but she doesn't need to showcase my utter lack of a life in front of everyone like a circus attraction. Come and look at the Lonely Woman, she markets love for a living but has absolutely no romantic prospects!

"Ummm, not tonight. No." My face feels freshly sunburnt. I move to sit back down, avoiding eye contact with the now doubly victorious smirk I know is waiting for me on the other side of the table. Loser in work, loser in life. Why does this sort of thing never happen to *him*? Probably because his boss actually respects his time. Bancroft will never experience this; he has been worshipped at Ignite from the moment he was handed this role on a silver platter.

He stands up to present, running a hand through his sandy hair and commanding the room with majestic ease, without needing to say a word. He stands directly behind me, meaning I have to turn my chair 180 degrees to bear witness to his inevitable victory. He's tall, probably one of the tallest men in the company, but it's his inherited aura of utter belongingness that forces everyone to shut up and listen before he has even spoken. He looks down at me and uses his eyebrows to gesture that I move.

Get out of the way—the person who actually belongs is here.

I bite the sides of my mouth and push the soles of my feet against the dull carpet, rolling my squeaky wheels across the floor.

"Our objective this month was to boost user acquisition, something we've achieved with ease thanks to a variety of successful projects." He clicks a black button to move his presentation to the next slide.

I look around. Where did he get a remote from? Did he bring that from home or was it always here? No one else seems fazed by it; frankly, they probably haven't even noticed.

"Our mixed-media approach has been integral to the success of our current campaigns. Unlike some of our competitors, who prefer their marketing to stay stuck in the past, we're utilizing AI and VR to reiterate our USP."

He continues on like this for another five minutes, vomiting corporate jargon that I'm sure everyone is only nodding along to so they don't look stupid for not knowing what on earth he is talking about. The most annoying thing is, he doesn't need to do all this. It's not expected of him. He is a face, a brand, a legacy. A white smile and designer hair for users to desire or aspire to. To be him or to fuck him. Yet every month he walks into this room and tries, sometimes succeeding, to win.

It's as if he gets some sort of sick pleasure from entering the ring with me.

As the meeting comes to a close I keep my eyes glued to my phone and head to the door. If I'm being honest I did this to myself, enjoying the months I won way too much, spending the next few days gloating, rubbing it in his face and taking disproportionate levels of pleasure in his loss. I set the tone for this rivalry a long time ago and now there's no way out of it. Yes, the time I sent a "World's Biggest Loser" ice-cream cake to his office may have gone a bit too far. It is entirely possible that it was my actions that created a creature whose sole purpose is to destroy me. My very own six-foot-three, sandy-haired, blue-eyed, fake-glasses-wearing Frankenstein's Monster.

"That's two months in a row I've beaten your growth numbers, Hastings. You're losing your touch," he said, lifting his chin and sticking his full bottom lip out in a sarcastic pout.

I want to take that lip in my fingers and tug it off his smug mouth.

"The only thing I'm losing is my patience with this conversation." I spin on my heel and walk away, making sure my hips sway a bit more than usual as I leave the meeting room.

Bancroft follows me toward the shiny lift at the other end of the hallway. It's difficult to do a good storm off down a tight corridor with a large annoying man taking up most of the space.

"If you're struggling, I'd be happy to help out. Give you some . . ." He tilts his head, scanning me up and down. ". . . tips."

I roll my eyes and suck my teeth while staring at the permanent smirk plastered on his face. He should trademark this look: the Permasmirk, for only the most entitled London pricks. The Permasmirk, no doubt inherited from his notorious father, has been the key to opening doors that I didn't even know existed.

"Thank you so much, O wise one. I'll be sure to get in touch next time I need to throw a rager to get drunk freshers to sign up for Fate. My app is for people who want to find someone of worth, someone who is serious about true love."

"Oh, so . . . should *you* be running the marketing then?" Bancroft retorts with a pouted lip.

I tilt my head to the side and shoot him an incredulous look, unable to come up with a retort fast enough.

He backtracks, realizing he's overstepped the invisible

line. "Come on, Hastings. You don't believe in this fairy-tale bullshit."

I've managed to keep up the facade with most people, so I hate that he can tell my feelings have slowly been souring. "Of course I do. I love love."

He scans me with a laser focus, analysing my declaration before rolling his eyes. "Please, don't insult me. I know you better than that."

"You don't know anything about me. Sorry, but I don't want to just go home with everyone I meet and never see them again."

Slut shaming—not my classiest move but always an easy insult and deflection against *Societeur Magazine*'s Bachelor of the Year.

"Ignite profiles are full of men who refer to women as 'females' or want someone who 'doesn't take herself too seriously,'" I continue. "Translation: 'Don't take yourself seriously, because I never will.' Face it, your app doesn't respect women."

"And that's what Fate is doing? Respecting women? Are you respecting that women might want something other than The One?"

I let out a huff, knowing he's right but too pissed off to admit it. Instead, I say, "You sound like an after-school special. Do you ever even get past date number one, or do the women you date manage to look past your personality to stick around for the press?"

"First dates are better than no dates at all. Or has Susie finally allowed you to find time in your schedule to go on one? I hope you're getting credit for being single and sexless for the rest of your life." His eyes roll as if that would be his worst nightmare.

"Not everything is about gaining credit. It's about gaining favor. Something you've never had to work for!" Sensing our bosses catching up with us, I lower my voice for my closing argument. "Go back down to your floor, Wankcroft, or ideally to hell."

A look of disappointment washes over his face as he presses the elevator call button, but it's gone in a flash, replaced with the usual cool composure. The lift dings as it arrives to take him down to the Ignite office, a floor below Fate's.

"Fine, I will," he relents, stepping into the silver room. The lights from the lift cover him in an angelic glow as he waits for me to join him, but there is no way I'm sharing a confined space with him. Not for one second.

"Good. Tell the rest of the demons I said hi." I smile, waving him off with a brief feeling of pride at getting in the last word.

In a previous life, we were able to sit in a room together without glowering icy stares in computer screen light and rolling eyes over break-room coffee. We used to be cordial colleagues, workmates, peers. We used to be friends. Now, we act like rivals on a battle-field, waiting for the other to make the first antagonistic move of the day, setting off our cycle of slights, jabs and cuts. We pretend this is how it's always been between us. We pretend that talking every day for a year never happened. We pretend a lot of things never happened.

"It's OK, Hastings. I'll keep your secret." Bancroft gives me that smirk one final time as he presses his floor number. "But I think we both know . . . you enjoy being on top of me all day." The elevator doors push together, and I am left with cheeks flaming.

It's pure pissed-off-edness seeping from my pores. At him, at Susie, but mostly at myself. Even when we used to be friends, he was always faster than me. A childhood surrounded by accomplished industry titans and a private school education will do that to you. Now, he exclusively uses said quickness to charm others or leave me flustered and scrambling for words.

I'm pissed off at myself for not trying harder to beat him; I should be doing more to prove I can win. Maybe if I had a square jawline, a playboy reputation and Daddy's money I could be as laid-back about my job as he is.

Remembering the impending panel talk, I frantically press the call button so I can head to my office to spend the next hour learning everything I can about tonight's panelists. It shouldn't be too hard, considering I organized the entire event, but buzzing nerves are taking up more and more space in my brain with each passing minute. My stomach churns at the thought of presenting to one hundred of London's most eligible single women. Fate users are confident, successful high achievers, usually with their own businesses or very senior positions at the top companies in the city. It would make far more sense for Susie to be presenting tonight; she belongs up on stage in front of those women. She's a tech titan who, in her heyday, graced the covers of magazines and had millions flocking to her TED Talks about female empowerment. I'm not even qualified to be in the room. Stepping into the lift, I close my eyes, and take three long, deep breaths.

I am enough, I belong here, I fucking deserve to be here.

2

My whole body aches as I drag myself and an oversize duffel bag of Fate merchandise up the creaky stairs of the old town house to my flat, as quietly as I can, trying to avoid summoning Bertie, the anecdote-prone elderly man who lives downstairs. Usually, I'd quite happily sit on our steps and listen to his often thirty-minute-long stories about when he ran around the city with a group of punk activists, but tonight I need to hold on to the little brainpower I have remaining to create the expenses spreadsheet Susie emailed me about five minutes before I arrived at the panel talk. My eyes can barely stay open in the blue glow of my phone screen.

She wants me to sort through over forty images of receipts into a comprehensive spreadsheet by tomorrow. Of course, she couldn't have told me the finance team needed it any earlier than the night before the deadline.

Finally up the three flights of stairs, I throw the bag and my jacket to the ground and immediately flop onto the pink squishy sofa we found on Facebook Marketplace, its miscellaneous stains strategically covered by a yellow cable-knit throw and baby-blue-striped cushions. I start looking through the images Susie has sent, and my heart sinks. There is a blurry receipt for a plethora of espresso martinis at a Soho members' club (I guess I'll mark that under "client meeting"), a month's worth of lunch receipts and at least fifteen separate receipts from Wilfred's, the fancy coffee shop that Bancroft also frequents. I stop at an invoice for two tickets to an exclusive European music festival with the words "client gift" scrawled at the top. Furrowing my brow, I zoom in to the price: £1,935 for two VIP tickets.

I google the date of the festival and cross reference it against Susie's calendar: she was away for four days including the two festival days and I find them marked as a vague and unhelpful "business trip." I make a mental note to ask her about it in the morning.

My flatmate, Yemi, walks in and sits beside me, nudging the bag out of her way with her foot. She is the Director of Analytics at Fate and my idol. The day she told me she loved nothing more than finding a hidden gem thrift shop and buying a wardrobe's worth of clothes for fifty pounds I suspected that I'd met a friend for life. I confirmed this when, the morning I walked in with pale skin, greasy hair and puffy eyes from a weekend of crying over William, she left the office with me at lunch and helped me pack up my things, insisting I stay on her sofa for as long as I wanted. When her lease was up, we found both our flat and Alice, our other flatmate, on an online listing and lived happily ever after.

"How did it go?" Yemi asks as I curl up into the sofa

cushions. I instinctively lean against her and she puts an arm around me.

"The panel?" I say, then shrug. "I stumbled my way through without any major mishaps. It would have been a lot better if it were Susie though."

I caught Yemi up via text when I couldn't get the tube home with her as usual; the messages hadn't reached her until she was already home.

"You should have told me earlier—I would have come and helped."

I sigh. "It's OK. We didn't both need to suffer."

"Are you doing her expenses now too?"

I'm used to the never-ending last-minute tasks from Susie, but Yemi looks so pained as she strokes my heavy head that Bancroft's words from earlier echo through my head until they reach my lips.

"I should just tell her I'm not doing bullshit like this for her anymore."

I have this thought every few weeks, when the feelings of ineptitude and exacerbation spill over the edges of my willpower. I start tapping out an email to Susie. As I'm typing the third long-winded, groveling sentence about being "on the verge of professional burnout," Yemi bats the phone out of my hand onto the thick patterned rug below us.

"You're not going to blow up your career because you're tired. You know the house rule . . ." She raises an eyebrow at me and points toward the wall at a portrait of a gremlin dressed as a Tudor king we bought from Etsy.

Sinking my face into the sofa, I let the cushions envelop me whole. "Don't send emails after ten p.m.," I mumble through layers of cotton, polyester and padding.

It's a rule we both set so we don't go absolutely insane or lose our jobs.

Yemi's head tilts. "I know you think she's the be-all and end-all of your career, but you need to look for opportunities to get out from under Susie. Don't do anything rash like sending late-night ultimatum emails for a few more months, and I guarantee you something good will come your way."

Over the years I've pitched ideas for expanding the Fate brand; Susie would feign interest at first, but her interest in long-term projects waned as more quick, flashy projects with a celebrity sponsorship came up. The one concept that's nearest to my heart is one I'm too scared to pitch again. Ever After—an in-app feature that helps Fate couples retain the magic through online relationship therapy and daily love prompts. I've been working on it during any spare time for a while now and, with massive help from Yemi, developed a bare-bones beta version. But the idea of it being shot down again gives me stress hives.

"What if nothing good ever comes my way again though?"

Yemi holds up her hands in a meditative gesture. "Let's just take all this negative, anxious energy and put it toward something truly loathsome."

Before I can respond, she jumps up and skips off to

her bedroom. Our flat is a hotchpotch of charity-shop lamps, discounted-on-eBay decor and repurposed furniture; I like the feeling of being surrounded by things with past lives. From the worn and frayed rugs found in a house clearance to the piles of second-hand art books used as a side table to the contrasting decorative restaurant plates stuck to cover cracks in the kitchen wall, this flat is totally unique and totally ours. The perfect combination of Yemi's bold and bright taste, Alice's Scandi cool-girl vibe and my more traditional tendencies. It's cramped but I wouldn't change it for the world.

Yemi reappears, and reveals the latest issue of *Societeur Magazine*. There's a party-coverage article featuring a picture of Bancroft with his arm around a stunning woman, a model by the looks of her impossibly sharp cheekbones and perfectly coiffed chestnut bob.

Sexy, social and seriously available, *Societeur*'s Bachelor of the Year stays true to his moniker, spotted leaving trendy nightclub Weston's with three different women in a week! Son of architectural magnate and notorious party boy, Malon Bancroft, it seems the apple doesn't fall far from the multi-million-pound tree . . .

"They still do these articles?" I laugh, staring at the devil horns Yemi has already drawn on Bancroft's head in black Sharpie. "Why do you even have this?"

"The first rule of war: know thy enemy." She taps the

page with a lilac fingernail. "I also thought we could find you a dartboard and make a collage of his face, so you can de-stress after monthly report meetings."

She shoots me a megawatt smile, which never fails to cheer me up.

"Maybe we can add Susie's headshot to it too?" I laugh.

Yemi nods in agreement, rubbing my arm in silent support.

Alice pads frantically into the living room, sporting a green clay face mask.

"Babe, can I borrow this dress for my date tomorrow?" She's spinning around in a sequin dress that stops in the middle of her thighs and fits her perfectly.

I cock my head to the side, taking in the familiar glimmering garment, recalling throwing it into the large trash bag of clothing I took to the Cats Protection League charity shop over a month ago.

"Yes, OK, you threw it out, but"—Alice guiltily picks at her fingers—"when the bags were in the hallway I saw it sticking out and may have rescued it because I absolutely adore it and I saw this girl on Instagram wearing something similar recently and—"

I interrupt her one-breath monologue with a forgiving laugh. "Keep it—it looks amazing on you!"

"Really?" she squeals, running her hands down the sequins. "Thank you so much, babe. My date is very, very cool and I feel like a literal potato standing next to her."

Yemi and I scoff at the idea that Alice—an absolute goddess; a you'd-be-shocked-that-she-isn't-Swedish, tanned, tall, blonde bombshell—could ever look like a potato.

I smile at Alice. "You look like a beautiful disco ball and frankly whoever she is, she would be lucky to get within five yards of you, let alone in your pants."

Yemi slaps my arm. "Robert and I say the same thing to you, all the time, and you never believe us."

Yemi met her boyfriend, Robert, while working at a coding class that encouraged young women and girls to get into coding and STEM. It was love at first variable. Alice has never been without a date. My eyebrows jump to my forehead in self-defence.

"That's because, unlike both of you, I am practically undatable. I work ridiculous hours and have absolutely no social life outside of this flat!"

"You work for one of the biggest dating apps in the country, for Christ's sake. If you can't find someone, is there any hope for the rest of us?"

Alice has a point.

Catch Group has its fingers in many tech-based pies, including health and fitness apps, content-management systems and online-booking software. I had noticed good-looking guys working on the other floors of the office. Maybe I should start making more of an effort to get to know the people in my building.

Alice gasps. "I have the best idea. Let's update your Fate profile!"

21

My stomach sinks but I fake an enthusiastic smile, having learned the hard way with Alice it's sometimes better to just go along with her spur-of-the-moment ideas.

Refreshing my personal dating experience would probably make me better at my job, but when your date discovers you work for a dating app, one of two questions always arise.

Number One: Can you help me improve my profile?

Translation: The date has not been the explosive "love at first sight" experience Fate promises it will be.

Number Two: Can you see the messages I send other people?

Translation: they are either a creep or have plans to be in the near future.

The only date I've been on since William started with both questions and ended with me bursting into tears and leaving before dessert. Not exactly the palate-cleansing, passion-inducing rebound I had imagined.

Alice swipes through my photos, a gallery of a woman I think I should be and scrunches her face at the screen.

"Oh God, they are all awful pictures, right?"

"No, you look beautiful, but . . ." She trails off and I laugh nervously.

Yemi takes the phone from Alice and peers at the screen. "This kind of reads like a CV, not a dating profile. Aren't you meant to be good at this kind of thing?"

I furrow my brow and peer toward the screen. I take the phone from her hand and check my profile. Photos of me smiling in a bar, with a group of university friends on a camping trip, and the rest are pictures of me at work events.

"I am! In fact, I pride myself on that skill. When I am doing it for other people," I exclaim. "It's like how you can see someone who has a similar body type to you and think they are stunning but then look at yourself and think: I am a blob. I can see other people's skills, interests and fun facts and package them into something sellable—but I can never do that for myself."

" 'Grace, twenty-nine, originally from Wiltshire so obviously a nature lover,' " Yemi reads.

Alice snorts. "Babe, you hate being outside! You like staying in with a book, and if you ever go out it's to a, like, a museum or an art gallery or something boring."

That point is hard to deny; growing up in the countryside had left me with an intense anti-nostalgia for the great outdoors. Instinctively, I look around the room at all the posters and art prints from those excursions, one of the few things I actually brought to our flat from William's.

"Kind of ironic for the Marketing Manager of a dating app to have the most misleading profile ever," adds Yemi. I glare at her despite deep down completely agreeing.

"You just got a calendar invite." Alice puts the phone in front of my face, the bright screen making me squint.

The meeting invitation is from Catch Group CEO Martin Catcher's personal assistant. I press the notification and the ominous title of "Meeting" at 9 a.m. tomorrow is revealed with no other context. My eyes move down to the invitation list, and my stomach throbs with anxiety as I read off the names:

Martin Catcher has accepted the meeting.

Susie Jopling has accepted the meeting.

Dharmash Khatri has accepted the meeting.

Before I have time to process what this might mean, another message pops up:

Eric Bancroft has accepted the meeting.

Shit. I press accept a heartbeat later, not wanting to seem too slow compared to him. As Alice continues to prep for her date, Yemi offers to sit and watch the Keira Knightley version of *Pride and Prejudice*, sensing that I'm in no place to talk about this recent development. It's one of the few pieces of love-centric media I can still actually enjoy without my evolved cynicism leaking through, but I can't focus on it; instead, I find myself refreshing my emails every two minutes, hoping for some indication of what this meeting is about. And whether it means I'm getting fired.

Yemi sighs and pauses on a frame of Mr. Darcy's perfect mutton-chopped face.

"Hey!" I reach my arm out toward the screen. "We were just getting to the hand-flexy part!"

She shoots me a stern look. "Grace, do you think *he* is freaking out right now?"

"Probably—he's in love with someone who thinks he's an arsehole!"

"Not Mr. Darcy, Eric Bancroft!"

I roll my eyes at both the mention of him and the pep talk I know is coming.

"I have no doubt that this is the absolute last thing on Bancroft's mind right now. He's probably out having paparazzi-worthy fun." I pick up the magazine and drop it on the sofa between me and Yemi, not adding that this isn't the first time I have imagined what Eric Bancroft does with his free time.

"Exactly, so you need to just chill and accept that whatever comes tomorrow, you will get through it." Yemi looks me dead in the eyes. "You are amazing at your job, they are lucky to have you and I promise you the sky is not falling, OK?"

I think of the panel, the room adorned with pink-hued floral displays with winding green stems, the guests eagerly gathered to hear the three women talk about their contemporary fairy tales. Jessie Fig, a lifestyle influencer and social media star who focuses on body positivity and self-love; Sonia Armington, sex coach and CEO of an ecofriendly sex toy brand; and Dr. Bernadette Reid, a popular relationship therapist and podcast host. All incredibly successful and inspiring. I remember the laugh I got as I introduced myself as "not Susie Jopling" and how quickly that glow faded once I saw Eric Bancroft slip into the room and stand at the back. His presence is usually noted by the occupiers of any room he walks into, but this time, with a room full of women looking for love, his quiet entrance felt as if someone had set off a testosterone bomb. All eyes were on him, but his eyes were fixed on me. They taunted me, his eyebrow raised slightly as if to gloat that he didn't need crappy jokes on a cue card to command attention.

As Keira Knightley sobs tragically on screen, I wonder how much of the meeting tomorrow I will spend feeling completely inferior.

3

Freshly painted and bitten-down fingernails tap erratically on my knee as the white fluorescent strip lights rain an unflattering glow over my body. Today's outfit is a matching blazer and trousers in a white-and-cornflower-blue check; I once read defendants in court who wear light blue are more likely to be found innocent by the jury. I don't exactly know what I've done, but I can guarantee if I'm guilty it's something to do with the perpetual instigator sitting across from me.

He ignored me as we entered the conference room, leaning back and crossing one pleated trouser leg over the other in a display of disinterest and defiance. I rolled my eyes and ignored him back, instead intently focusing on the glossy framed *New York Times* articles, *Business Insider* profiles and *Forbes* accolades listing the achievements of Martin Catcher and his well-respected umbrella company.

I shoot another glance at Bancroft. A tingle shoots up my spine when I find his emotionless eyes already focused on me, like one of those ominous haunted-house portraits that follow you around the room. I can't quite put my finger on it, but lately it feels as though his one step ahead of me has been further ahead than usual. In an attempt to match his relaxed stance, I lean back in the uncomfortable chair and cross one leg over the other. Dharmash and Susie are on their phones across the table, neither making eye contact with us.

Bancroft looks good, fresh even, considering what he was reportedly up to after the panel talk last night. *Societeur Magazine* posted a paparazzi shot of him having dinner with a young woman who seemed vaguely familiar. She was slim with short, trendy brunette hair and massive almond-shaped eyes. I tapped the tagged username "@irisfender." Her bio told me she's a model with half a million Instagram followers, twenty-two years old and a Pisces. In the photo of the two of them, I noticed he was staring right at the camera. He had the look he gives me when I beat his report numbers. Even in 2D form, that face still puts me on edge.

Mr. Catcher's booming voice interrupts my train of thought. "Thank you both for coming on short notice. Catch Group is launching a new dating-app experience next year to fill a vital gap in the market, Ditto. A platform focused on matching users through the commonality of lifestyles and interests and automatically setting them up on pre-planned dates. Activities and dating: pairing people based on their way of living and hobbies will sit nicely across from our other two platforms that are focused on image"—he gestures to Bancroft—"and on biography"—looking at me.

"Aligning in this way means users stay within the Catch Group family through their entire dating journey."

"Would the user be swiping on the dates or other users?" I ask, intrigued.

"Great question. We'll use the same back-end functionality as Fate and Ignite, but the first interface users will see is a selection of date packages. Once they've swiped yes or no to whatever sort of date they're interested in, the algorithm will offer them potential matches who swiped for the same date packages. When they swipe on someone they like, they are agreeing to attend a time-slot date with that person."

"So there's no messaging or chat feature?"

Catcher smiles at me, nodding approvingly. "There will be for subscription users, but they will get a limited number of messages per interaction. We envision this being marketed as a pseudo-'offline' alternative to our current offerings, which brings me to you two."

We both stay silent, but I catch Bancroft's jaw tensing.

"So, you two have been working together for nearly two years now and you think we haven't noticed?" Catcher asks, his hair plugs bobbing as he paces around the meeting room.

My mind races. I wonder if I should say something before he does, confess to whatever it is Catcher is talking about before he fires us both on the spot.

He sees my expression and laughs. "Don't look so scared, sweetheart."

My cheeks immediately flare from the embarrassment

of being singled out and annoyance at his casual sexism. Out of the corner of my eye, I see Bancroft's knuckles turn white.

Catcher stands still for the first time since entering the room. "Look, I've been in this industry for a while and I know a successful partnership when I see one, and I wouldn't be the successful businessman I am if I didn't capitalize on such a partnership."

I blink, turning to Bancroft for confirmation that I'm not hallucinating; he doesn't meet my eyes, but the lines on his hand relax to a state of only slightly tense.

"From what I've heard, you two light fires under the other, which has led to the highest user-acquisition rates Catch Group has had in years. It seems as though you bring out the best in each other."

Mr. Catcher glances at Dharmash and Susie. Their reactions are like oil and water: the former looks proud; the latter looks absolutely livid, her eyes narrowing at me like a sharpshooter ready to strike.

Why didn't Susie tell me about this? The news doesn't seem like a surprise to her. She scowls for just a moment longer and then moves her gaze to the floor, sucking her teeth and crossing her arms. Mr. Catcher isn't wrong: battling it out with Bancroft does make me work harder and smarter but we worked just as well, if not better, when we didn't see each other as competitors for monthly bravado.

Bancroft lifts a hand. "With all due respect, Catcher, we talked about this being a solo project?"

I school my expression into neutrality, trying to piece

things together as Mr. Catcher strides back and forth in front of us.

"Eric, I appreciate your confidence but it's vital we have a female perspective on this. Grace has proven she can bring in the feminine user base, and Ignite's daily active users are currently sixty-seven percent male. Don't get me wrong, you're great at bringing the women in"— Mr. Catcher laughs, leans forward and slaps him on the shoulder—"but they're not sticking around for long."

He continues to pace the room, ignoring Bancroft's wince. "That's why I need you two to work in tandem during this ideation stage. I want to take this to market in twelve months. Learn from each other's expertise, and use your contacts to get partners on board."

"What about my presentation?" Bancroft questions through his teeth. My eyes dart back and forth between the two men, trying to connect the invisible dots.

"Oh, don't worry. You'll still be presenting your ideas for the launch strategy, Eric. You both will. Individually."

"Why do you need two strategies?" Bancroft is struggling to maintain his cool, professional persona and I stifle a laugh.

"Great question," Mr. Catcher declares, stroking his salt-and-pepper stubble with his thumb and forefinger. "This launch is a vital move in Catch Group maintaining domination across the dating industry. This is a fresh take to capture users who aren't interested in the new online-focused methods of dating, or they've become tired of swiping with no end result. I want perspectives from both my leading apps to make this work. I'll also need you both to log your feedback during the research stage."

Bancroft's signet ring glints in the sunlight as he runs his hand over his face and reluctantly asks, "And . . . the promotion?"

"Still on the table," Mr. Catcher answers swiftly. "However, Miss Hastings's strategy will also be taken into consideration."

My voice quivers: "Umm . . . the research stage? And . . . what promotion?"

He shoots an annoyed glance at a squeamish Susie, sighs and then turns back to me. "My apologies, I assumed you were told. There is an open role at Ditto. Head of Marketing. We want to bring someone who already knows the inner workings of the company on board, so the individual with the favored strategy to launch Ditto will be considered for the new position."

I hold in a gasp as I try to clarify. "So our strategy presentations will also be a job interview?"

Mr. Catcher nods decidedly. "There'll be outside candidates considered, but I want to keep this new venture as internal as possible. Especially at this sensitive ideation stage."

My whole body becomes clammy. So . . . it's me versus Bancroft?

"This will be a collaborative effort," he continues. "I know, based on your experience and backgrounds, you'll have very different takes on a launch strategy, and I'm looking forward to seeing them both. I'd like you to work together on trialing and bringing in potential partners. It will be more impactful to have representatives from Ignite and Fate showing a united front when approaching brands, don't you agree?"

Bancroft, louder than he has been the whole meeting, starts to protest. "This really isn't necessary—I already have meetings lined—"

"I have no problem with it," I answer, shooting a polite smile toward our three seniors. If a few extra meetings with Bancroft is the price I have to pay for a promotion, so be it. I can be civil.

"Great," Mr. Catcher replies. "Eric can catch you up on the particulars."

Susie finally chimes in: "I can't sign off on this if she isn't going to deliver on her usual KPIs for the next six weeks."

I stare at Susie's irritated face and internally wince. I'm going to pay for this, but it might be my only path to a promotion. My only way out of late-night mental breakdowns. Last-minute expense sheets. It's not *just* Susie. The more I think about it, the more I feel the weight of the constant "true love" rhetoric at Fate pressing down on me. I want out, and this is my chance.

I clear my throat and straighten my shoulders. "I can still deliver my normal level of work. Thank you for the opportunity, sir"—nodding my head for emphasis.

"Fantastic." Mr. Catcher claps his hands together

loudly. "We need to ensure that, as always, the UX is second to none. I want you to road-test the dates, get into the user-experience mindset. Your presentations need to include first-hand research and development of these pre-planned dates, and how to promote the concept appropriately."

My stomach sinks, then flops over and over like an old slinky dropping down a flight of stairs as the meaning of this sets in. I have to go on dates . . . with Eric Bancroft?

I try to stop the shock from showing but my body is rapidly going through the stages of rigor mortis. Susie raises an eyebrow at me from across the room as though she's trying to telepathically talk me out of taking Mr. Catcher's offer.

Bancroft gives me a sly smile, and looks at his watch, clocking my time of death. This is my worst nightmare. "It doesn't seem as though Miss Hastings would be comfortable with that."

"Of course. Grace, you don't have to do this if you're uncomfortable." Mr. Catcher gives an awkward laugh. "I'm sure there is another member of the Fate marketing team that would be happy with this opportunity?"

"No! It's fine, totally fine! I'll do it," I blurt out before either of them can suggest an alternative. "I can keep delivering my work on time, and I can go on the dates. Yes."

Mr. Catcher turns to Bancroft, a dominating, defiant smile across his face. "Fantastic! I hope you don't mind a bit of friendly competition, Eric?"

4

Fuck, fuck, *fuck*.

My heart is pounding so hard I can feel it in my skull. *What have I done?*

The consequences of screwing over Bancroft are one thing, but the repercussions of going against Susie's wishes are undoubtedly going to bite me in the arse sooner rather than later. She used to relish my enthusiasm, my willingness to pitch new ideas and go above and beyond my role. Now it's like she resents the fact that I would ever want any form of career progression. The glass door hisses against the green carpet tiles as I push through it and stomp into the Fate office.

I weave through rows of my colleagues' work stations, trying not to make eye contact with anyone until I reach my desk and drop into the squeaky wheelie chair.

The computer screen dings with a new message from Bancroft:

EB: When are you free for a run down?

My stomach starts to roil. The last time we were alone together it *really* didn't end well. I pull out the magazine Yemi shoved in my bag last night and flip through until I reach the familiar face, homing in on a small box in the corner of the article:

THREE THINGS TO KNOW ABOUT ERIC BANCROFT

He is the son of architectural magnate and notorious party boy, Malon Bancroft, and it seems the apple doesn't fall far from the multi-million-pound tree . . .

1. Eric began his university studies in Architectural Design and Technology but switched to Marketing and Advertising in his second year—rumor has it, much to his parents' chagrin!
2. Rumored to be currently dating Margaux Bardin, French heiress and founder of fabulous sunglasses brand Chaleur Lunettes. The pair were first spotted cozying up at the exclusive Matilda's Bar in February over vodka martinis with a twist: his drink of choice.
3. He is lending his social expertise to the dating app Ignite. Downloads hit an all-time high on the day of his appointment as Marketing Manager at the Catch Group Inc.–owned company. Not bad for a man who's never single for more than a week!

Most of this information isn't new to me, even if it seemed as if our former friendship existed at arm's length. I felt that gravitational pull he carries with him wherever he goes when we first met. I'm drawn into the memory of our initial encounter. I can still hear how Jessica, Catch Group's Head of HR, called to me across the lobby, her shiny black hair bouncing as her heels tapped toward us.

"I want you to meet Eric Bancroft, the new Marketing Manager at Ignite." She had presented him like a shiny new trophy. "Eric, this is Grace Hastings."

I'd seen pictures of him before but in person he was stunning. As though Hugh Grant and Jude Law had had a lovechild who was raised by an impeccable stylist.

"Hello, Grace Hastings," he drawled in a whisky-smooth tone. The emphasis on my first name sent a prickly heat through me.

"Hi!" I said, louder than intended, my cheeks flaming as I saw a dimple appear on his left cheek.

"Hi," he repeated at a far more reasonable volume. "Would you be up for a one-on-one once I've settled in? It would be nice to understand the job a bit more."

A polite smile appeared across his lips and I swear his ocean-blue eyes literally twinkled in the fluorescent office ceiling lights.

"Sounds grud," I responded breathlessly.

There was a beat, and then his eyebrows scrunched together in confusion. I stood there, clutching my laptop like a life raft as we drifted into an awkward silence. My whole body turned loose as he looked me up and down, as though trying to weigh my character: a predator sizing up whether I would be classified as friend, foe or prey.

"Sorry, my brain couldn't decide between good and great so I ended up with 'grud,'" I explained limply, wishing the ground would just open up and swallow me whole.

I still remember the moment his smile curved into a smirk.

Jessica finally saved me from further embarrassment and, helpfully, reminded me that I was on my way to get lunch with Yemi.

"And this is Olayemi Musa, Head of Analytics at Fate."

"Call me Yemi." She smiled, stretching a hand out to shake his.

"Hi, Yemi," Eric replied. "I'd love to book a one-on-one with you as well if you'd be up for it."

"Sure," she replied like a normal functioning human.

I don't think my brain even registered the brief conversation after that; Yemi continued to be her fabulously competent self as I silently nodded along, lips pulled tight in a line.

Finally, he smiled. "Well, it was *grud* to meet you both."

Before either Yemi or I could say another word they both strode off toward the row of elevators, Jessica's shoes echoing around the lobby.

Yemi's voice jerks me out of my involuntary trip down memory lane.

"Are you OK?"

"Yeah!" I reply a little too quickly and enthusiastically, pushing myself off the desk.

She hums at me suspiciously, sensing that my reply wasn't at all truthful. "Lunch? I have a table booked."

"Absolutely." I rise, reaching for my bag.

"Darling, do you *really* have time for a leisurely lunch right now?" Susie's piercing tone permeates the space between Yemi and me.

She never fails to notice me even attempting to take my entire lunch hour. The last time I took it all was for an emergency dentist appointment to fix a cracked tooth. After an eye-watering, wallet-cinching sixty minutes she sent a text with her coffee order, assuming I was out running errands.

"Umm, no. I guess not," I say, sinking back into my chair. I swallow the guilt I know I shouldn't be feeling and shoot Yemi an apologetic, tight-lipped smile. "You go, I'll grab a sandwich later."

Yemi eyes Susie incredulously. Being a head of department means she doesn't have to take shit from Susie, but begrudgingly has a level of respect for her as the founder and former owner of the company. She also knows putting Susie in a bad mood will only serve to make my day worse. Sometimes this job feels as if I'm trapped in a cold, dark lake, gripping on to the edges trying to escape. The water-clogged mud slides through my hands and slippery tufts of grass release from the ground when I pull on them too hard. Sometimes my head goes under, and sometimes I manage to stay afloat, but no matter how close I come to getting out, I always end up back where I started.

As Yemi leaves, Susie turns back to me. "There are some things we need to discuss." She clip-clops in her heels toward her office, assuming I will immediately follow.

I do.

Her layered multicolored necklaces jangle as she swans into her beautifully designed office, which looks more like a swanky private club lounge than a place for business. Her thick floral perfume pervades the space, which is full of pastel-toned mid-century armchairs and chic brass lamps that she uses to light the place as she despises ceiling lighting. There are decorative book bundles from some high-end furniture store dotted around on various surfaces, and I'm certain their pages have never seen the light of day.

"I want to talk about the meeting with Catcher," she says, lips pursing.

I nod my head curiously, trying my best to act as if I don't know what she is about to say. She looked surprised and then annoyed when I agreed to his proposal, and one of her few flaws is never being able to keep her opinions to herself. She sighs and flops back nonchalantly in her white bouclé fabric desk chair behind a pristine glass desk.

"I really don't think you're going to have time for it, darling."

I am enough, I belong here, I deserve to be here.

I remain tight-lipped as she continues.

"Your schedule is already so busy: your daily reporting, your evening events, working on partnerships, all your . . . lunches." She pauses for effect and looks me up and down. "You won't have time to do this too, you'll never have a moment for yourself."

Not like I had time before.

"Well, ummm, maybe I could . . ." My fingers tighten around my notepad. ". . . drop some of my . . . assistant-level duties in the meantime. Like submitting your expense reports?"

The silence sits on my chest until it feels as though my lungs are going to collapse and a cold sweat runs down my back.

I am enough.

I belong here.

Susie stares at her pristinely manicured nails as she replies. "Do you really think I would have time to take on your tasks as well as my own? I have so much going on at the moment. All this . . . Ditto stuff"—she waves her hand in front of my face—"it's just a waste of your time."

She pulls a bright pink Charlotte Tilbury lipstick and compact mirror out of her Louis Vuitton carry-all and refreshes her makeup while continuing to talk at me.

"Darling, I'm late for a meeting. While I'm gone, I want you to think about where your priorities and loyalties lie. Let me know when you've come to your senses and see things clearly."

She snaps the mirror shut and looks at me pointedly. My cheeks turn as hot pink as her lips with a swirl of shame, guilt and ungratefulness.

Do I deserve to be here?

I nod so violently my neck twangs.

She pivots on her heels and goes to leave the room. "And those influencer contracts." She gestures at a stack of papers neatly piled on her desk. "Go through those and find that girl we worked with a couple of years ago."

She clicks her fingers, trying to summon the name out of me.

I furrow my brow. "I'm not sure who you mean."

"She had that little yappy dog with her at all times. You'll figure it out, darling." She breezes out the door with a huff.

I guess *this* is the punishment for this morning then.

I wipe my clammy face with an equally clammy hand and mull over Susie's words. She gave me this opportunity. She is the reason I'm here. She took a chance on me when I was nothing but a lowly Fate marketing intern on minimum wage with a weekend job waitressing at a chain restaurant. She brought me under her wing, always giving me the work of a higher-paying role because she knew it would give me the experience I needed to get further in this industry. Susie is the only person I can credit for me getting this far, so I do the grunt work for her, I cover for her. Sometimes I forget how much our relationship has soured over the past couple of years, ever since Catch Group acquired the company. Her brilliant, fiery spirit and powerful but approachable energy was the reason so many people wanted to work for her when she first launched Fate out of a studio apartment in East London. Her willingness and enthusiasm to champion anyone she saw who had "potential" was a rare trait in the male-dominated, nepotistic tech industry. She was an amazing mentor to me and so many others—until she wasn't.

Maybe this project will convince her that I can run things on my own. That I can be trusted, as she used to trust me. I heave the pile of printer paper from Susie's office and drop it onto my desk. If I won the Ditto promotion, I'd never have to work in a tiny overflowing cubicle again. The thought of not being in constant competition with Bancroft is also something to consider. I'd be burning one bridge in exchange for clearing the rubble of another.

A few hours later a brisk melodic knocking sound startles me so violently I give myself a paper cut on the stack of reports.

"Shit," I say under my breath and squeeze my finger until a small edge of blood emerges from the cut. I glance up to find the source of the sound. My eyes adjust from the lamp-lit white pages to the warm sunset glow flowing through the Fate office's windows, gliding up until they perform a full eye roll at the tall figure standing in the dimly lit doorway.

The early-evening light frames Bancroft's shoulders

as he appears at the glass entrance. He isn't wearing his glasses, so his eyes are even brighter, and they carve through me as he leans against the doorframe. In his hands are two black coffee cups with "Wilfred's Cafe" printed across them in embossed white letters. I watch in silence while one of them lifts to his mouth.

"Sorry to disturb you," he says in a soft, unfamiliar tone. How long have I been sitting here? And when did everyone else leave?

"Yes, you are disturbing. What do you want?"

I type something extremely important out on my keyboard, staring intently at the random series of letters appearing on the computer screen. He doesn't respond, just steps into the room and paces toward me, gauging my reaction to his every step. As he approaches, I spot the copy of *Societeur Magazine* open on the page about him. The devil horns and a big arrow pointing to his smiling face with the word "prick" written in thick black ink clearly visible. Leaning over the magazine to hide it from his viewpoint, I use my elbow to slide it off my desk. It lands in my bag on the floor as I shuffle papers to cover the sound. He immediately surveys the desk like a wild cat looking for mice. He looks briefly disgusted as he examines the crumbs, paper balls and old Kind bar wrappers littering my desk before landing on a picture frame showing a Fate success story: a couple posing with their newborn baby; he grins in patronizing amusement. I flip the frame over and scowl in his direction.

He counters with a smirk. "Working late again?"

"No, I just like to stay here for the fluorescent-lit ambience and sounds of Ronnie the janitor singing along to heavy metal," I reply, thudding the rubber end of a green Fate-branded pencil on the desk impatiently. "What do you want?"

He looks so out of place in this fluffy, feminine office. I've never been to his, even when we were friends. I always try, whenever possible, to avoid walking via Ignite's letchy Product team who haven't seen an actual in-the-flesh woman for months. You can always tell when they have recently been in the building's lift because entering the space after them is a full-on assault on the nostrils. Thankfully, when Catch Group acquired Fate Susie fought to keep the two offices separate to "preserve the magic." I used to think Bancroft liked working here with me, and that getting away from the Ignite bubble was for his own sanity. But whenever he comes here now, instead of our late-night must-meet-deadline-panic reporting sessions, it's clearly with the sole purpose of torment-ing me. I've never been in his office, but I've always imagined it looks as though Matthew McConaughey's office in *How to Lose a Guy in 10 Days* had an interior-design child with Don Draper's office in *Mad Men*. Overtly masculine but classically styled, vintage Playboy covers on the walls, quilted leather chairs and smelling like that cologne he wears every single day. Not over-whelming but a distinctive scent that lingers after he leaves the room, as though he wants you to think about him for hours after he's gone. The complete opposite of the developers. Some of the girls in the office have had a bet going on what cologne he wears for close to a year now. Eau de Lucifer most likely.

"You really need to get an office of your own," he declares, his tone back to its familiar sarcastic drawl.

My eyes roll out of my skull into a pile of notebooks and used Tupperware. If it was as easy as he makes it sound I'd have a whole floor by now, instead of this stuffy room with ten white desks slotted together like the most boring Lego set imaginable.

My mouth curves into a sickly sweet smile as I shuffle in my seat, pulling down the skirt of my dress. "When I get this promotion I'll be sure to ask for one."

He lets out a deep, condescending laugh and shakes his head. "Listen, about that . . ." he says, voice softening again, making me instantly suspicious of where this conversation is about to go. "If you're not actually OK with the . . . *arrangement* then there's no hard feelings."

He takes a tissue out of his pocket, wipes the edge of my desk clear of crumbs and places the second coffee cup in front of me, then folds his arms and leans against the glass wall opposite me.

"We don't *have* to do these 'dates' together." His fingers wave in the air, mocking the concept of the word. "I can use my contacts; you can use yours. We don't have to work together at all."

I can tell he's attempting to mask a devious smile with empathy, so I give him a blank expression in return.

"Or . . ." He drags the pause out, his bottom lip pouting as though he's pretending to come up with this idea on the spot. "I can just take this project on solo."

"And why would I agree to that?" I ask in a deliberately innocent tone.

He shrugs. "Because I'm, as you once put it, 'all gin and no tonic'?" His voice takes on a devilish lilt that gives me goose bumps.

I swallow down the nostalgia. "Sure, being in your presence brings me out in hives, but at least I'll be promoted at the end of it."

The one thing working alongside him brings to the table is his family's extensive black book of founders, CEOs and industry powerhouses. I can't compete with generational nepotism on my own and if I agree to work apart I'd be handing him a gold medal before the race has even started.

I watch his throat bob as he takes a slow sip from his cardboard cup. When we used to have our catch-up meetings at the chic cafe looking out onto bustling Charlotte Street, he would always insist on paying for mine too. There's no way in hell I will accept his pity coffee now, no matter how delicious.

"Hastings, you're obviously uncomfortable spending time alone with me after . . ." He winces as if the thought of my discomfort causes him genuine distress. He doesn't need to finish the sentence for me to know exactly what he's talking about. It hangs over every moment of conflict between us like a guillotine with fraying rope. As though he has an invisible ace he never plays, but we both know is up his impeccably tailored sleeve. The threat of him saying it is almost as great as actually uttering the words.

"I don't know what you're talking about," I snap back, eyes fixing on my computer screen as though I've just been sent an email with the subject *You've won a year of free coffee at Wilfred's!*

Pretending I have no memory of it is my only option of defence against him because he usually doesn't bring it up directly, just dances around it. He's bringing out the big guns today, which tells me he must be internally freaking out at the prospect of having his precious project taken from him. Especially by me.

He tilts his head and some emotion I can't place enters his eyes as he looms over the desk. I look away, trying to force aside the memory of how his breath against my cheek felt as he sheltered me from the cold.

"Hastings." The slow, sensual way he whispers the word makes me hate my own name. It hasn't always made my skin crawl. I used to find it almost endearing. Considerably better than the "Gracie" people seem to naturally nickname me. We used to sit at this same desk, scarfing down takeaway Chinese from a place three streets over. Cracking fortune cookies, swapping office gossip and stressing about deadlines. Now, him coming over here always has some nefarious, ulterior motive.

I don't say a word to his cat-got-the-cream face.

Instead, in a move that is way more ballsy than I'm used to, I pick up the receiver of my phone and call the extension for Martin Catcher's office. Pressing the speaker button to slice through the silence in the room with a high-pitched jarring ring.

A now familiar, chirpy voice picks up with a pleasant singsong tone: "Mr. Catcher's office."

"Hi, Harriet, it's Grace."

"Hi, Grace who?"

I falter. "It's Grace . . . Hastings? I saw you this morning?"

"Oh, from your meeting with Eric."

He raises an eyebrow at me and my ears burn in frustration.

"Yes. That one," I say through my clenched teeth.

"How can I help you?" she chimes.

I lean on my elbow and look Bancroft dead in his squinting, icy eyes. "Please pass the message on to Mr. Catcher that I'm *so* excited to get started on this project and already have ideas for some amazing . . . um . . . test runs."

"OK, Grace . . . Hastings . . . excited about . . . the project. Test runs," she says slowly, writing it down. "Got it!"

"Thanks, Harriet," I say, pulling the phone away from my ear and slamming it down dramatically to end the call.

Bancroft unfolds his arms, takes a seat at the empty desk next to mine and places a leather Armani brogue on the white surface. "You've finally become interesting, Hastings."

I would tell him to put his feet down but Hannah, the owner of said desk, would swoon that any of his body parts have been where she sits all day.

"Interesting? I think Mr. Catcher preferred the word 'vital,'" I say in my best attempt to match his easy confidence as I swing my chair to face him, cross my bare legs and rest my chin in my hand. "We both know he doesn't trust you to do this without me."

His jaw twitches as he glances down. I internally celebrate hitting a nerve. I still know all of his tells. Unfortunately, that means he probably still knows all of mine. I subtly move from an insecure forward lean to a relaxed lounge in my chair, resting my hands in my lap triumphantly.

"Let's not speak too soon, OK? You don't know the full breadth of this project yet." He runs a tense hand through his sandy hair, leaning back to match my position.

I gesture to him with a sweeping palm. "Please, enlighten me."

He picks up a multicolored ball of elastic bands from Hannah's desk and throws it into the air, catching it with one hand as he explains: "I . . . Well, *we* need to partner with companies to create sponsored date packages for the Ditto users, based on a range of lifestyles and interests. Creating the dates is one task, but we have to convince brands and companies to work with us. The launch won't land without backing from a handful of strong partners."

Dread lances into my stomach at the idea of taking on such a task on my own. For a second I'm impressed he was already in the process of doing it but shrug off the feeling. He throws the ball higher with one hand and catches it with ease.

Bag over her shoulder, Yemi walks past the glass wall outside the marketing team's portion of the office, most likely to come and pull me from my work trance and force me to go home. But when she notices who I'm talking to, she shapes her hand into a loose fist and shakes it back and forth at the back of Bancroft's head, mouthing the word "Wanker."

Bancroft notices my smile and cranes his neck around just as Yemi resumes walking past the glass wall toward the elevator. He turns back to me, clearing his throat and placing the elastic band ball back on Hannah's desk with a thunk.

"I have something booked with a major hotel chain in a few weeks, enough time to gather a strong list of complementary brands beforehand. And I've already had an initial meeting with a hiking trail company, but I was going to test the route this weekend." He sighs. "So I suppose you will have to come with me."

He's relenting. He knows I'm right: there is no way Mr. Catcher would leave this project in Bancroft's hands alone; the dates would probably end up at a high-end strip club or pheasant shooting at a country estate.

"And, like Catcher said in the meeting, we need to write a brief report for each experience to collate our data. I've already created a spreadsheet with him so he can track our progress. Can you get a date lined up soon, or have you got too much of Susie's work to do?"

A sly smile that reaches all the way to his eyes scans me for outrage. Patronizing prick.

"Of course I can!" I lie again, gesturing to the Google doc littered with a chaotic assortment of vowels and consonants.

He blinks. "Hmmm, sure. We should organize two or three each, to split the workload."

"That's great because I already have at least three potential leads." Tapping the vacant screen with my pen.

"Well, I look forward to whatever they are. But on Sunday morning, we're going hiking. Please wear something . . . appropriate."

Ugh, hiking. Morning hiking. The only thing worse than being outside is being outside in the morning. And the only thing worse than being outside in the morning is being outside in the morning doing exercise. And the only thing worse than being outside in the morning doing exercise is doing it with *him*.

"Why would I have anything 'appropriate for hiking'?" I ask, mocking his deep, well-spoken tone. "Why would anyone sane *want* to go hiking?"

He lets out an irritated groan. "Just suck it up, Hastings. I would quite happily do this without you." His jaw clicks as he pushes off the desk; he's getting agitated with me, so I relent, not in the mood to feel the wrath I've seen his poor-performing team members receive. It's annoying that people actually respect him, and that he's able to put his foot down without being labeled bossy.

"Fine, since Mr. Catcher said you really need my help to execute his dating world domination plan, I guess I'll help you out." I triumphantly shrug, taking my first sip of coffee. "But if you turn up in those weird barefoot toe-shoe things, I'm going home."

He shoots me a fake smile as he stands to leave the office. "I'm so looking forward to it." His fingers curl around the edge of the doorframe. "Open or closed?"

"Closed."

He breezes off, leaving the door wide open.

5

Eleven Months Ago

The only movement I'd done in the past three hours was standing up and waving my arms around to trigger the motion-sensor wall lights in the office. I was meant to leave at 5 p.m. to meet William for dinner, but Susie had the majority of Fate's marketing team working to finish aspects of a full class on female entrepreneurship. She was presenting at a prestigious university's careers fair the following day, including visuals, worksheets and a history of Fate's most successful campaigns to date.

Hannah was putting the finishing touches on the graphics for the presentation, while I pulled up photographs of and statistics on a vegan ice-cream collaboration pop-up event we did in 2016. I'd worked with Hannah fairly regularly for the past few years, and having someone as talented as her on hand had been a lifesaver on several occasions. Katherine, the marketing team's latest intern, sat opposite me looking bored out of her mind. It was monotonous and mentally tiring work, but she didn't have the "if I get fired how will I afford rent" fear motivator. She lived with her parents and had traveled into the city to spend this evening replacing the ink in the printer.

William never liked me working late, but whenever I brought work home it almost always escalated into some sort of argument about not spending enough "quality time" together. Even if that "quality time" was just watching him watch football.

My phone dinged with a message:

EB: Any chance you're still at the office? I'm working on the stats for tomorrow's meeting and need to pick your brain.

GH: Still here. Send me what you have so far and I'll take a look.

EB: Already en route.

My fingers froze on the keyboard. I scanned my desk, taking in the mess littering the gray surface, particularly the remnants of a day-old sandwich I'd eaten for lunch. Using a notepad as a dustpan and brush, I slid the crumbs and the plastic wrapping into the waste bin near my feet. Turning my computer monitor off so I could see myself reflected in the black shiny surface, I smoothed my hair down at the front and ran the back of my forefinger below my eyebrows, wiping off the shadowed mascara prints showcasing a long day of screen-staring. The last time I'd seen Eric before this was at our introductory one-on-one just under a month ago, where I took him through my day-to-day duties. I discovered in the meeting that his job spec list did not match up with mine.

My laundry list of random tasks was double the length of his. I guess that made sense, seeing as I'd been in the role longer. I'd accumulated a lot of other responsibilities without dropping older ones. I assured myself it was a good thing. I noticed, though, that he did ask a lot of questions. Our emails had devolved into text messages when I realized it would be easier for him to reach me with quick one-off queries that way.

The glass door hissed as it slid open.

"Hey," he said as he entered, shooting a warm charm-slicked smile at Hannah and Katherine before finally landing on me.

"Hey," I replied in my most nonchalant voice, not taking my eyes off my screen.

I could feel the confusion practically radiating from Hannah. A wave of guilt washed over me, flushing my cheeks scarlet red. I took a deep breath and sucked down the idea that I was doing something wrong. Eric chose to come here; I didn't invite him. So why was Hannah glancing wide-eyed back and forth between the two of us as if she should have a bucket of popcorn on her lap?

"You're here late," he stated, walking over to my desk.

"So are you," I said, clearing my throat of any tonal inflection. I spun my chair toward him and crossed one leg over the other.

"True, but I'm the new guy, and trying to look good to Dharmash. Surely you've earned a five p.m. cut-off by now?"

I sighed. "Marketing dating apps is a noble cause that waits for no woman."

He looked at me with that same slow, assessing stare he had given me when we were first introduced. I held his gaze for a second then swiveled back around to face my desk, suddenly noticing how much dirt was in the spaces between the letters of my keyboard.

"Sorryyyy." Hannah winced and drew out the word as if she'd just interrupted a G8 Summit. "Grace, can I just get your final approval on this slide before we head off?"

"Uh-huh!" I stood up, turning to Eric. "Gimme one sec."

Becoming suddenly self-conscious about the way my shoes sounded crossing the carpet, I stepped around our cluster of desks to look at Hannah's screen. Leaning across her desk, I barely took in what she was showing me as I could feel Eric's steely eyes continuing to assess me as he stood casually with his hands in his navy trouser pockets.

"Yep, looks great." I shot them both a slightly awkward but warm smile. "Good job, guys. I'll see you tomorrow."

Hannah and Katherine packed up their things and said their goodbyes as I dropped back into my chair and faced Eric. "So . . . what did you need help with?"

My chest tightened as I waited for his response, nervous that he had a detailed, complex issue I wouldn't be able to solve. What if it was Product-related? I had no idea what the inner workings of the app were like, and I'd be totally lost in the layers and layers of code that made up the Ignite algorithm. OK, he probably wouldn't expect me to know that, but what if he needed visuals for his presentation tomorrow? Or some new fancy merchandise mocked up? I looked toward the door, wishing Hannah or even Katherine were still here so that I'd have someone to defer to when he finally asked his inevitably unanswerable question.

"Right." He rolled the nearest black wheelie chair across the green-tiled carpet floor until it bumped into mine. He placed his laptop next to my computer, the red glow from his Ignite-branded desktop screen hitting his cheekbones. "I can't find the daily active-user information anywhere on the data hub. I need it for tomorrow or I am going to look like a moron."

My shoulders sagged with relief as I realized his problem was something I could help with. I took a deep breath, catching the scent of citrus and woodsmoke as he leaned in closer to view my screen.

"You'll have to follow along with me because I can only access the one for Fate."

I pulled up the program and clicked through the criteria, avoiding looking at the veins in his hands shifting as he followed along with sharp, deliberate strikes on his own keypad.

"So for Fate, it's here." I bent a finger against my screen. "Yemi developed this software for Catch Group, so Ignite's version will match. You just need to calculate the average minutes per day."

I glanced over my shoulder to check he was understanding and found his eyes fixed on me. I held his gaze for a second before clearing my throat.

"I also like to isolate the highest time spent by location, like this, so I can make a heat map of usage."

He nodded, moving his hands across the keys on his laptop to do the same. We spent the next few minutes playing a weird, corporate version of Simon Says as I guided him through the mechanics of extracting the data he needed.

Eventually, he let out a breath and ran a hand through his sandy hair. "Well, shit. You're an expert. Thank you, Grace." His icy eyes melted into a blue sky.

For a second a butterfly tried to get loose in my stomach, its wings tickling my edges. I clamped it down before it could escape and responded with a nervous laugh, shrugging off the compliment. "It's no big deal. I'm happy to help."

His eyes scanned mine, as if I was a map and he was figuring out which direction to take.

Eventually, I went back to the class notes I was writing for Susie, jabbing the volume button so my Spotify playlist could keep me motivated. I had expected him to leave, but the chair creaked as he settled fully into it and pulled his laptop close. Eventually, the nervous energy stirring under my skin died down and I relaxed into our quiet tandem productivity. We sat side by side, the sound of my most-liked songs playing on shuffle through my headphones, our keyboards clacking and the air-conditioning unit whirring from the next room the only things punctuating the silence.

We worked like this for about thirty minutes until Eric finally broke the silence. "What time do you usually go home?"

"Did you not see the sleeping bag under my desk? I live here." I raised an eyebrow. "Always on call, like a surgeon but *much* more important."

I still don't quite know why my default response was to regurgitate the joke William made to his friends at my expense. I felt the same twang of guilt as the words left my mouth, but Eric burst into laughter. Warmth swelled in my chest at the first time I'd seen a genuine smile from him, not just a charming smirk.

"Well, it looks like you weren't the only one tonight, so at least there's solidarity in the suffering?"

My eyes flicked up to Hannah's now-empty desk. "True, Hannah was a big help tonight."

"She seems . . . helpful." He pursed his lips.

I scoffed a quiet laugh at his diplomatic choice of words.

"There's no need to be coy. If you're interested in her, she is the reigning president of your fan club. I'm pretty sure she has a Google Alert for whenever *Societeur Magazine* posts about you."

"Oh, thanks," he said, as though I'd just thrown a bucket of ice water on his head. "She's not really my type though."

"What?" I leaned back in my chair and crossed my arms. "She's cool."

"I'm sure she is," he agreed.

"Then what's the problem?" I asked.

He tapped a pen on his thigh. "If someone is interested in me based on what social media posts and cheap articles have to say, then they're not really into *me*."

I barely resisted the urge to roll my eyes. "You seem pretty sure about that."

He hummed his agreement. "I know it makes me sound like a dick, but it's based on experience."

"So, you won't date anyone unless they know *nothing* about you beforehand?" I asked, trying not to examine why I cared so much.

He pressed his lips together. "Despite what *Societeur Magazine* thinks, I don't really 'date' anyone anymore. Casual sex is a lot simpler."

My lips curved into a sly smile. "Well, then you really are the perfect face of Ignite."

We locked eyes again, a silent challenge in them.

The question leaves my mouth like a bullet. "So, what is your type? For casual sex, I mean."

His eyes moved over me. A quick dart to the left, then the right, as if he was taking a quick mental snapshot of my face. A small smile lifted the corners of his mouth and a swooping sensation fluttered through me, warming my core and staining my cheeks.

"Oh. I didn't mean me. I have a boyfriend," I blurted. "Partner. Person. William."

My cheeks flushed hotter as I tried to avoid physically cringing in front of him.

He smirked, clearly trying to suppress a laugh. "Don't worry. I know."

My shoulders relaxed. I wondered how he knew, but before the question could fully form in my mind he continued.

"People who read *Societeur* and their idiotic posts aren't the only ones who know how to online stalk, you know."

Another pause, this one more weighty than the last. I was on the verge of asking an embarrassing follow-up question when he pulled his phone out. "Are you hungry? I could kill for some dumplings right now."

We lingered in the Fate office for two more hours, picking at cold dim sum and talking about how Eric's first few weeks had been going. I gave him the rundown of all the best people to know at Catch Group, (Yemi ranking number one, obviously) who to avoid (Jeffrey, the Product developer, but Eric had already picked up on that one) and showed him a few other ways of finding good marketing data on the internal software. We eventually dragged ourselves away from our seats at 11 p.m., and I realized on the way home that this was the only late night at work I'd ever enjoyed.

6

It's 6 a.m. on Sunday and I never in my wildest nightmares thought I would be here.

Here, at the bottom of a members-only hiking trail no doubt owned by some private equity firm trying to look eco-friendly, waiting for Eric Bancroft. The warm morning air tracing my bare shoulders is comforting but not worth waking up at 5 a.m. and getting the same tube as the Saturday-nighters just coming home.

Fiddling with the fraying hem of my charity-shop bike shorts, I take in the pristine scene around me. There are kiosks dotted at the mouth of a winding trail selling freshly ground coffee, pressed juices and small glass pots of overnight oats. My mouth waters: maybe I could get into this part of hiking if it was at a reasonable time of day. The greenery bracketing the path is wild and full, but well landscaped, and frames the ticketed turnstiles that grant access to the hiking trail. This place is the Soho House of hiking trails. I watch as other early risers start their ascent. They look so at ease at this time of day that it's as if they rise naturally with the sun, wearing matching Lululemon workout sets and carrying the latest expensive status-declaring aluminium water bottles. A few of them give me the side-eye as I drink out of a plastic bottle of Volvic I bought from the twenty-four-hour corner shop on the way here. The last time I exercised was over a month ago, running for a bus that I ended up missing anyway. I buy an overpriced oat milk latte and pain au chocolat from the trendy coffee cart and sit cross-legged on a decorative boulder, already worn out.

"Good morning, Hastings." My body stiffens at his fake-chirpiness. I was almost enjoying myself in the brief chocolatey moment when I forgot the reason I'm here.

Bancroft sports an all-black outfit and Ray-Bans. Matching Nike shorts, fancy trainers and a quarter-zip hoodie all in pristine condition with perfectly tousled hair, looking alert and at ease, as though he's been up for hours.

"You're late," I say, still chewing the last flaky bite of my pastry. It's as though he loves to be the last one to enter a room, creating the illusion that everyone is waiting for him.

"I thought I'd give you enough time to take care of your sugar and caffeine addiction before we got started." His gaze runs over me and lands on the empty grease-stained brown paper bag in my hand.

I glare at him. "It's research," I say, crumpling the bag into a ball and lightly throwing it at him. An old man dressed like a marathon runner tuts at my faux-littering in between pants for air.

I brush the pastry crumbs off my chest and he starts stretching his toned calves on a beautifully carved, moss-covered wooden bench.

"Look, I've already locked in discounted access for users, so all we need to do is check out the trail itself." Bancroft picks up my bag and launches it at a bin several metres away. Of course, it lands perfectly in the center. I'm slightly impressed but feign disinterest as I slide off the boulder.

"Let's just get this over with so I can go back to bed." I place my worn baseball cap on my head for dramatic effect.

"That's the spirit!" he says, patting me on the back as I stand up.

We hike in silence as the summer sun slowly begins to bake the ground below us. The trail fills with more versions of the 6 a.m. women, then the 6.30 a.m. fitness couples in matching skin-tight sportswear, followed by 7 a.m. friends with iced coffees and strollers.

We try to stay out of each other's way: me walking a few meters behind him, huffing sarcastically every time someone checks him out; him keeping a steady pace just ahead of me, which I'm sure is some sort of dominance mind game he's attempting. I try to regulate my breathing as my thighs burn their way toward what I hope is the end of the trail, but each breath makes my head grow heavier.

"You OK back there?" he asks over his shoulder after the first half mile uphill, the sun glistening off the sweat lightly coating his forehead.

"Never. Better. Thanks." I strain between each word.

My legs, my chest and my forehead are all on fire. It would be fitting to die here, like this: she died how she lived, trying so hard to get somewhere but not quite reaching the peak.

He slows down to meet my pace. "We're nearly at the top but we can stop if you need a break."

"I'm fine," I say, pushing against the incline to get ahead of him.

He stops completely, dust brushing his ankles. "I'd rather you didn't drop dead at the top of the trail. I'll just have to carry you back down." His silver bottle glints in the sunlight as he holds it out toward me. "I know exercise has always been a foreign concept to you but can you at least stay hydrated?"

I clench my fists as I turn back around to him. "Why? If I die on the trail you won't have to work for the promotion. Just glide into prosperity as always!"

He laughs, wiping the sweat from his forehead with the back of his hand. "If you die now there'd be no one to ruin later, and where's the fun in that?" He tilts his head to me in question.

"This isn't *fun* for me—this is my entire life." I stomp further up the trail, legs burning.

He scoffs. "That's pretty clear. Is that why you've sucked up to Susie for years despite never getting promoted?"

I stop and turn to him, my ponytail violently hitting me in the cheek as I whirl. I hate that we used to be friends, that he can now use truths I confided in him against me.

"You don't even need that job! You just want it because *I* want it. And now you're going to be fucking handed it." I'm so furious black spots start to appear like flies in need of swatting.

"Are you serious?" he growls, closing the stony distance between us in three quick strides. His bright eyes blaze with frustration. "If you think I only want the job because *you* want it then you're fucking deluded."

His voice quiets as he comes in closer, glaring down at me so I feel three feet tall.

"As much as you'd love to believe it, not every move I make revolves around you. The reality is, Hastings, I don't think about you as much as you think I do. In fact, I don't think of you at all."

My eyes travel up the towering human iceberg and blink furiously. A wave of sweaty embarrassment washes over me at the amount of mental energy I've expended thinking about him, always assuming that he was doing the same.

"Piss off, Wankcroft," is the only thing my foggy brain can think to say as I start back down the rocky hill.

All I care about is trying to maintain an ounce of composure despite the blood pounding in my ears. The gentle morning sun has evolved into a humid beam of heat, making my lungs constrict. I need to get out of here. My feet tiptoe down the steep, rocky hill as I try to not let my frustration turn into teary defeat. I feel a sharp pain in my ankle and before I have a chance to grab on to a nearby branch, person, anything, my foot jerks unnaturally to the side.

My arms flail out to catch my fall as my knees buckle and I land on my side in the dust. A barrage of words too explicit for this early in the day echo from Bancroft behind me, followed by the pacing of designer-trainer-clad feet.

"Are you OK? Hastings?" he pants as he crouches next to me, a look of pure, unadulterated alarm in his eyes. "We should take you to the ER. Can you move?"

"No, it's fine!" I say a little too loud, eyes scanning for the closest escape route. "I'll be waiting hours and it doesn't even hurt. I'm fine."

Trying to stand and scrape back my lost dignity fails as I buckle under a sudden sharp, throbbing pain lancing through my ankle. I plummet toward the ground again—this time intercepted by strong, warm palms gripping my body and pulling me upright. He stands us face-to-face, so close I can feel his heaving chest as he assesses me. Instinctively, he rubs his hands up and down my arms, leaving a trail of goose bumps in his wake. The feeling pulls me away from the pain for a few moments. Our panicked eyes lock, then soften into nervousness as we both recognize the position we're in. Until he breaks the charged silence.

"There's a shorter trail on the way down. I'll order an Uber to meet us at the bottom," he declares resolutely.

I blink as his expression turns into gravely serious,

tight-jawed control but, despite my embarrassment, I let out a breath of relief. "OK. My address is—"

"I don't need it," he interrupts, holding my arm with one hand and pulling his phone out of his pocket with the other.

I furrow my brow at the combination of pain and annoyance. "Are you a stalker or are you kidnapping me?" My functioning foot wobbles as I try and stand on one leg while on an incline, determined not to use him as a crutch.

He sighs, not looking up from the screen. "I don't need your address because it's already in my phone."

He lets that fact sit between us for a moment; the whoosh of memory from the last time he had to wrangle me into a cab overrides my throbbing ankle. "But also because we're going to my place."

His eyes flick up and pin me with a defiant look, waiting for my protest.

"Kidnapping it is, then!" I say loud enough for us to receive weird looks from passersby.

He glances from my face to my airborne foot. "Your ankle is already swelling up. You need to rest it and I live ten minutes away."

My gravel-scraped hand lifts up to intercept his explanation as I hop on one leg, giving him a pleading look to stop.

He steps in close; my heart pounds out a heady cocktail of anxiety, embarrassment and adrenaline as he loops my arm around his and grips my elbow with his free hand. Stabbing pain lances up my leg as we slowly descend the dusty path. We hobble in loaded silence for a few minutes until I finally let out a huff of a laugh when we pass a neon-green metal sign with the words "Beginner's Trail" emblazoned in bold white letters.

"You didn't think to start us out on this route on the way up?"

"In my defence, I didn't think you'd be this terrible at walking. This is the route people take with strollers."

I remember the women with their sporty buggies earlier and wonder if we could borrow one to get me to the bottom of this never-ending hill. A hiss escapes my lips as my foot scrapes the ground.

Bancroft squeezes my elbow more tightly and runs a rough thumb over a raised white scar on my forearm. "You need to distract yourself. Tell me how you got this."

For a moment I'm amazed he'd noticed it during our dramatic morning, but he's probably seen it before and just never asked.

"It was just some accident when I was a kid." I breathe out, concentrating on the pins and needles tingling in my toes.

"What happened?"

"Ummm, I used to like climbing a really big tree at the bottom of our garden because my mum told me fairies lived up there. Even if it was pouring rain I'd be up this tree trying to talk to the fairies that lived there. Eventually, my dad built a little treehouse in the branches with a tire swing." I feel weak at the memory. "I didn't have many friends, so he thought a treehouse would be a good way to get other kids from the neighbourhood to come hang out with me."

"So, one of those kids did this?" he asks.

My throat dries up as he locks eyes with me, light from the warm, glowing sky bouncing off his irises.

My pained grimace curls into a half-moon smile as I recall, "No. I don't think my dad realized at the time that most kids my age had moved on from playing make-believe to playing video games. I had too by the time he had finished it, I just couldn't work up the courage to tell him. So instead, he, my mum and I had a fairy-themed picnic in the treehouse and then decided to test if all three of us could fit on the tire swing. The rope snapped and I broke my arm from the fall."

Bancroft's grip on my elbow hardens. "Ouch."

"Very 'ouch,'" I confirm. "I still don't think he's forgiven himself. The funny thing was though, I was the first kid in my school year to have a broken bone. All of a sudden, everyone wanted to talk to me about it and sign my bright pink cast."

Bancroft arches an eyebrow. "So, in a weird way, your dad's plan worked."

I laugh. "Yeah."

I wait for him to reciprocate with a similar anecdote about the scarring on his right hand, usually half-hidden by his signet ring, but he says nothing.

Eventually, I give in and ask, "How did you get that?"

He examines the white vein running from his little finger wrapping down the side of his hand, jaw tensing for a second and then releasing. "Just . . . dumb teenage boy stuff."

"Right," I concede, instantly regretting my overshare. My chest loosens as we reach a clearing and I see the boulder marking the start of the trail. "The car will be here in three minutes," Bancroft says resolvedly under his breath, fingers gripping my arm just a little bit tighter.

Fifteen minutes later we arrive outside his apartment building and I stumble as I lift myself from the car. He watches me limp two steps toward the door before offering to carry me in. I protest weakly, but when I sway again he rolls his eyes and swoops me into his arms. The uniformed concierge gives us a confused look as we enter the immaculately styled mid-century lobby. He watches as we head to the elevator, taking in my scrapes and foot held at an awkward angle.

"Is your girlfriend OK, Mr. Bancroft?" the man asks as we round the corner toward a row of lifts. "Do you need—"

"I'm fine! And I'm not his girlfriend!" I shout back at the man. "You can put me down now," I demand through gritted teeth as I hear the concierge's chuckle echo, feeling the heat draining from my flaming cheeks as the metal doors slide open.

Bancroft places me down gently and I lean on one leg against the elevator rail, my grazed hands stinging against the cold metal bar. We wait in the thick silence, listening to the hum of the lift. The arrival of his floor is announced with a deafening *ding*, making us both jump.

He crouches down to wrap a supportive arm around my waist as the door slides open. My sore hand rests on his shoulder and I fight every instinct to explore the taut muscles under my palm. He tenses his arm around my middle and pushes up so he's half carrying me down the sleek, carpeted corridor.

His keys jangle as they turn in the keyhole, filling the quietness still lingering from the elevator. Instantly the smell of wood and citrus hits my nostrils as he tugs me down a hallway with dark herringbone floorboards. This apartment is modern but soft. Hazy natural light framed by linen curtains, high white ceilings, walls adorned with vintage film posters and modern abstract paintings. It is so perfectly him. Masculine, but in all the best ways. Sophisticated but easy-going, blunt but charming. It's inviting and unpretentious, not the seedy James Bond–style bachelor pad I had always imagined. As we enter the main living space I notice a pair of small gold hooped earrings in a bowl among small change and keys.

"Did you decorate this place yourself?" I ask nonchalantly.

He smirks, clearly aware of the negative space between my question. "I had some help."

He places me gently on a gray corner sofa and walks over to the kitchen, where he grabs a medical-grade ice pack and wraps it in a kitchen towel. He lays it on the sofa next to my leg. The cool air from the A/C wraps around me as my heart rate finally begins to lower, but it's immediately increased once again as Bancroft tenderly traces his warm fingers around my calf and lifts it to inspect the damage to my ankle. It's definitely a coincidence that the air conditioning makes goose bumps form all over my body at the exact same moment.

"Is this how you usually get women back to your place?" I speculate, sounding more breathless than I meant to, steeling myself through the pain. "Wound them on remote trails and carry them in because they can't object?"

He shoots me a glittering look with those sharp blue eyes. "And here's me thinking this was more of a damsel-in-distress situation."

I suck in a breath, avoiding the urge to find comfort in his too-familiar expression. "I don't need your help."

He cocks an eyebrow and squeezes his fingers lightly around my ankle. My leg jerks and I whimper in agony. "You're a sadist!"

"You're in more pain than you're letting on and your ankle has doubled in size since the trail." His eyes fix on me. "So, you're going to sit here, accept my help and stop whining." His stare returns to its annoyed-with-me neutral state, but with a flicker of concern so faint, I could blink and miss it.

Him looking up at me like that, his large hands steadying my ankle and calf, gives me a feeling low in my stomach that I really don't want to deal with right now.

I let out an annoyed exhale and fall back onto the sofa, arm up over my face to avoid his gaze.

"So you *are* able to do what I tell you? Good to know."

Heat spreads over my chest and I wish I'd just died there in the dust. Sunk into the ground and became one with the dirt, never to be mortified again. Bancroft takes my ankle and begins unknotting the stained laces of my old ratty trainers, sucking his teeth.

"What now?" I sigh. He can't help but be critical of my every breath. Is he like this with everyone or is this a personality trait he saves just for me?

"It's like a child tied these—no wonder you ate it on the trail." He holds up my loosely tied laces.

"Sorry I didn't learn the Queen's Knot in finishing school or whatever." I feel him holding back a laugh. Even when I'm pissed off at him, it always gives me a small sense of satisfaction to break his controlled veneer. He stands and heads back to the marble kitchen.

"Why are you so eager to help me anyway? We're mortal enemies."

He bends down into the fridge, rummaging for something, and I feel my cheeks redden, his fitted hiking gear not leaving much to the imagination when he's in this position.

"It would be boring to beat you while you're down: not a very worthy opponent." He flashes me a megawatt smile as he cracks the cap of a green juice and hands it to me in a way that feels like a brief peace offering.

Sniffing the thick, dark green liquid is like inhaling a boggy marsh.

He watches me crinkle my nose and lets out a long sigh. "Just . . . drink it. It's good for you."

"You don't eat normal people food anymore?" A pang of regret hits me right in the chest as I remember all the food he used to order for our dinners at the office when we had to work late. How I used to take the piss out of his insistence on ordering stir-fries only to pick out half the ingredients and put them on my plate.

"I don't really eat here. I'm either at the office or out with . . . friends." He turns back toward the kitchen and returns with toasted brown bread and two pills on a beige-speckled plate, I raise an eyebrow in question.

"Don't be weird. It's just ibuprofen. For the inflammation. You'll have to stay here for a bit to wait for the swelling to stop." He hands me a highball glass of water and stands in front of me, watching me. I take the tablets and notice his eyes fixed on my throat as I gulp down the rest of the water. "I'm gonna wash off the hike. You rest. I'll just be a few minutes."

"Please do, I think you got some of your stink on me when you carried me down the hill."

He throws a middle finger up over his shoulder as he leaves. I hear the creak of a door followed by the rainfall of a high-pressure shower.

The urge to snoop around his apartment while he is out of the room is almost unbearable. Every wall, counter and square foot tells a story of Bancroft, or at the very least tells the story of who decorated this place for him. It even smells like him, a soft woody scent with sweet citrus that sticks in your mind long after he's gone. I lean to try and see more of the room, but the movement causes a sharp pain to jolt up my leg from my ankle. Inspecting the injury for the first time, I lift the ice pack and press a finger against the golf-ball-size swelling sticking out where my ankle bone would usually be. I decide to stay put. I can snoop without moving too much.

From where I'm sitting, I can see into his bedroom. I take in the cream sheets with brown piping on the edges making up what looks like a king-size bed.

I don't know why I expected there to be a gorgeous woman waiting here on a Sunday morning to cook him brunch, the same person who helped him decorate. I take the opportunity to investigate the personal effects, mostly magazines and TV remotes, within arm's reach to see if there is anything indicating another person's presence.

After a few minutes, I hear the rapid stream of the water stop, replaced by the sounds of bare feet padding from his bathroom into his bedroom.

"You live alone?" My voice echoes across the open-plan expanse.

"It's what I'm used to," his voice projects back through the cracked bedroom door. "I like my own company."

"I guess force-feeding people green sludge when they walk through the door tends to push them away?"

"Only if they're caffeine and sugar addicts," he calls back.

I crack a smile and sip at the earthy sludge juice.

I scan each surface of his apartment, and eventually land on the coffee table. Stacks of thick coffee table books are scattered in a way that makes me believe he might have actually read them: a giant book of David Hockney paintings, Slim Aarons photography, the NASA archives; Bancroft could start a Taschen exhibition from his living room. Using the tips of my fingers to drag a landscape photography book titled *Remote Experiences: Extraordinary Travel from North to South* from the top of the pile to the edge of the table, I grab it and flip through the pages, hoping an explanation of his inner workings is hidden within the text. The flashes of color and smooth stream of paper through my hands is abruptly stopped by the presence of a bookmark. Except, it's not a bookmark. Placing the heavy book on my lap, I slide out the long rectangular card and my hand starts to tremble as the realization hits me.

It's a strip of photos of me and him from the Catch Group Christmas party six months ago. A missing memory of pulling him into the cramped photo booth bursts through my mind as I run my finger down the images, homing in on the last one. Me, gleaming at the camera, glassy-eyed. Him, looking at me with a softness that makes my stomach do a backward flip off the side of the building.

I hastily shove the photo strip back into the book and

slam it shut. "Listen, I have to go. I promised my flat-mate I would help her with her dissertation today," I lie. After a few seconds of silence, a freshly showered Bancroft appears, wearing a short-sleeved white cotton T-shirt and blue jeans. Ignoring his still-damp chest, I inspect my ankle for swelling, lowering it with a wince onto the oak floor.

"Let me check how the swelling is doing." He leans down over me; his chest smells like soap. His usual sandy blond hair looks darker when it's wet; the short curls fall over his forehead like little helter-skelters.

"It's definitely feeling better." I fake a smile. "So, we don't need to do this whole *Misery* act anymore."

A flash of something glints across his eyes and then disappears; he clears his throat and says, "At least let me help you to the door."

I give him a light nod, trying not to make eye contact as my cheeks begin to burn, thinking about the photographs.

His arms wrap around me and I feel his hands hold me lightly but firmly. His scent envelops me like a warm duvet on a cold morning.

"Thanks . . ." I half whisper, as though being grateful to him must be kept quiet ". . . and thanks for the health sludge too—I feel like a new woman."

He lets out an awkward, breathy laugh. "No problem." He's stepping away from me and running a hand through his wet hair. Before any stupid questions come tumbling out of my mouth, I grab my bag, and my pride, and hobble out of the door.

7

"I knew this wasn't going to end well . . ."

I pry my sleep-crusted eyes open to locate the source of the voice above me. Yemi is looming above my bed with crossed arms and a frost-covered bag of peas hanging from her hand.

"I didn't think they'd end up physically injuring each other this early on," replies Alice from down near my ankle with a concerned look on her freckled face. The bed creaks as I sit up, bending my leg to inspect the swelling. It's turned from pink to purple since I last looked at it but at least the swelling has gone down.

"It was just me who got hurt," I confirm in a gravelly voice, rubbing my face in an attempt to wipe my brain clean of this morning. "What time is it?"

I look out of the window at the late-morning sunlight streaming through the blinds; I must have only been asleep a couple of hours.

"Oh my God, what did he do to you?" Alice asks, mouth agape, eyes darting in question between Yemi and me.

"*He* didn't do anything." I sigh, wincing at my ankle.

"The headline is: I fell; he carried me down the hill and then into his apartment; it was humiliating."

"Unfortunately, we don't have a bag of frozen vegetables for your pride," Yemi consoles me, trying and failing to hide a smile as she places the bag on my ankle.

Instinctively, I reach for my phone to check my emails and watch the spinning loop as the inbox refreshes. Sometimes, when I close my eyes I can still see the little circle going round and round, like my thoughts loading for the next day's long list of inane tasks. As usual, there are a bunch of emails from Susie, a few cc's from various colleagues, a newsletter from *AdWeek* and . . .

ERIC BANCROFT MADE EDITS IN THE FOLLOWING DOCUMENT:

"DITTO PROJECT REPORTING."

My stomach drops. Whatever he has written can be seen by anyone who has access—including Mr. Catcher. My ankle throbs as I drag my laptop out from my bag at the side of the bed, flinging it open and frantically clicking through.

I enjoyed participating in this experience:
Disagree.
Additional comments:
The trail is not for unserious people or those who do limited exercise.

So much for waiting for me to heal so I can be a worthy opponent.

My mind clings to the photos in his apartment. What

if he planted them when I wasn't looking with the intention to throw me off my game? I mean, they were right there, sticking out of the top of a coffee-table book, almost *too* conveniently located.

He doesn't think about me at all. That's what he said on the trail. A single strip of pictures doesn't change anything; the person who put them in the book is also the person who is willing to throw me under a bus for a promotion. If I want to win this job, I need to be cool, calm and collected. Serious. The exact opposite of a person who freaks out about one set of planted photographs or replays overheard words over and over until they shred into mental confetti. Perversely, I need to be more like Bancroft if this is going to work.

My fingers slam against the keyboard as I type:

If one user lacks empathy or is more self-involved than the other, the hiking-trail date package has the potential to be disastrous.

Alice joins me on the bed with a bounce and cartoonishly swoons onto the pillows. "So you went on a date with one of the most desired men in London, twisted your ankle like a fragile maiden and he carried you down a hill? Explain to me how this *isn't* the romcom dream?"

I rub my face, trying to think in full sentences. "Because even if he is as desirable as *Societeur Magazine* claims, he's only 'desired' by people who haven't had the displeasure of spending time with him."

"Also, because in a romcom the love interest isn't the

man who calls you a clingy psycho to his colleagues!"
Yemi says. "Shit, sorry." She winces at me.

"No, you're right." I sigh.

For my own sanity, I've been pushing down thoughts
of exactly how our friendship ended six months ago.
Even Bancroft doesn't know the real reason things
ended so badly. He thinks it's because of what happened at the Catch Group Christmas party; he has no
idea it was three days later.

I was a mess at the Christmas party so I was going to
apologize. When I got to his office door it was ajar and
I could hear him talking to someone. I assumed he was
in a meeting until I heard my name.

*Hastings is a clingy psycho . . . She's not worth going
there, not even for a quick shag. That kind of desperation isn't hot. It's just pathetic.*

He tried to talk to me a couple of days later, but I
just froze him out. It was too much; I was already dealing with the fallout from William and I simply couldn't
handle any more confrontation. Two weeks later, after
he caught me alone, some choice words were said and
he stopped trying.

"It's his loss." Yemi smiles softly, as though she
knows exactly what I'm thinking.

Alice stands up with vigor. "OK, you *have* to beat this
fucker." She flings open my wardrobe. "And I'm going
to find you a killer outfit for the next date."

Yemi nods. "You're in charge of what you're doing
for the next one, right?"

I nod my head in confirmation.

"OK, where is it?" asks Alice, pushing clothes from one side of my rail to the other.

"A cooking class at that restaurant we went to, El Turo? But I've barely got any time to organize it."

To counter Bancroft's contacts from big firms and global companies, I've been thinking my pitch should have an angle of local businesses and bespoke dates. Working to create unique, intimate experiences with amazing independent brands and companies, instead of with giant cookie-cutter companies that Bancroft will be talking to, might give me the edge I need to win this promotion.

"Babe, you haven't been on a real first date in literally *years*," declares Alice. "Even though it's Eric Bancroft, you should consider these dates, like, practice!"

"Immersion therapy," Yemi adds with a serious face. "Going on a date with a dickhead will give you the experience you need to handle any future date."

Alice pulls a dress out of my wardrobe: a plunging seventies-style fire-engine-red minidress I bought from a small vintage stall at a market when I first arrived in London. A purchase made with the assumption that William and I would be living life to the fullest in the city, instead of me being too exhausted from work to ever go out, and him continually expressing his dislike of me going out without him.

I shake my head. "Cute but not appropriate for a cooking class. They said long sleeves."

Alice continues her excavation of my clothing until she drags a dress from the very back and holds it out to me.

The black velvet dress swings back and forth for a few seconds before Yemi yanks it off the hanger and quietly tells Alice, "Not this one. That's *the* dress."

"Oh shit." Alice sighs. "Sorry, babe."

"It's fine!" I blurt out. They both look at me with puppy-dog eyes. "Guys, it's literally fine. It's just a dress . . ."

I run my fingers over the soft fabric. I spent a lot of money on this dress. I wore it for a couple of hours before it was tearstained and stuffed in a box with the rest of my clothes when I moved.

"You're right," agrees Yemi. "Just a dress."

"If it's just a dress"—Alice smiles slyly—"maybe I can do something with it to give it a new identity. You look too good in this for it to die a slow death being eaten by moths on a hanger." My eyebrows lift as she continues, "I'm just going to tweak it a bit and you're going to make new memories of looking amazing for your date and locking down your first brand partner for your presentation. Just give me fifteen minutes and you won't even recognize it."

My lips curve and I stick my bottom lip out, trying to stop my eyes from getting misty. I'll admit, gaining an aspiring fashion designer for a flatmate is a huge win.

"You are the actual best." I sigh. "But for the record, this isn't a 'date.' It's practically a meeting."

8

The next morning I wipe the sleep from my eyes and refocus on the camera monitor as Jessie Fig's full lips curve into a wistful smile. She finishes retelling the story of the dreamiest first date as she swoons to the camera, gripping the arm of her beanie-clad boyfriend, Ezra.

He laughs sheepishly. "I never wanted that date to end. I knew she was The One when the waiters had to tell us they wanted to go home, we were the last ones there!"

"I guess it was . . . Fate." Jessie beams.

I internally fist pump as she finishes off the line with a coquettish, yet natural shrug. They look right at home in front of the hot lights. After the panel talk, I pitched her the idea of her and Ezra hosting a new Fate-sponsored dating-advice podcast designed to destigmatize the idea of finding love on dating apps. The set is simple but beautiful, a hyper-styled dusty-pink living room with sage-green accents. These video spots are for a social media ad campaign that will run in the next few weeks to promote the podcast. Compared to when I've dealt with other projects like this, I feel strangely calm. Both Jessie

and Ezra have strong, loyal followings; the advice podcast is a clean, easy listen that's tried and tested; it has
a clear pipeline to retaining users. Practically foolproof.

As Jessie and Ezra redo the last few takes, performing their lines with a slightly different tone and delivery
each time, my attention is taken up by the rest of today's
work schedule. I list each point in my head:

- *Brainstorming ideas with the wider team for
  Fate's Christmas campaign*
- *Summer influencer campaign reporting*
- *Finalizing contracts for pop-up date spot in
  West London*
- *And . . . eventually, working on the Ditto
  project.*

I have a few initial ideas I need to get down on paper,
but Bancroft is probably much further along than me.
His upper hand is so high it's punching through the roof
of his fancy high-rise apartment. He had prior knowledge of the project and a boss that gives him control
of his own schedule. I'm reeling from the news and I
have . . . Susie.

Right on cue, her name fills my phone screen and
it vibrates violently. Sucking in a deep, deep breath, I
place the receiver next to my ear.

"Hi, Susie. How are you?" The fake smile plastered
across my face seems to make the words sound cheery.
"Is everything OK at the office?"

"Darling, I'm not in today. I have a lunch."

I furrow my brow and turn to the clock on the white-painted brick wall; it's 12:30 p.m. "Is everything OK?" I repeat.

"I need you to run the acquisition numbers for last month's UK and Europe events by end of the day."

I hesitate. "All of them?"

There are close to thirty across the country alone and will take hours to put together. Fuck. My palms start to sweat as dread fills my chest.

"I . . . I don't think I'll be able to finish that tonight. I'm on a shoot all day today and have to work on the Ditto project tonight."

She sends a loud sigh down the line, and we stay in silence for a few moments.

"Darling, it's been a week since you agreed to this overzealous project and it's already stopping you from doing your *actual* job. I'm not impressed." My heart begins to pound in my temples. "I need those numbers by tomorrow morning! Who is going to do the report?"

I creep into the corner of the room before I respond. I don't need an audience for what I'm about to say, or the reaction I'm sure to get.

"Ummm, maybe . . . you could do it? After your lunch."

The silence this suggestion receives is deafening. I hold my breath to try and stop words from tumbling out. A long, annoyed sigh blasts through the phone.

"Or . . . if you gave me more time . . ." I offer, wincing at my own inadequacy.

"Fine. I'll give you an extension just this once, but you can't keep shirking your responsibilities like this."

I purse my lips and nod instinctively to no one. "Wow, thank you so much, Susie. That's so kind of you." The sarcasm in my voice is lost, replaced with the gratitude sweeping through me at such a quick resolution.

"You're welcome. I'm sure you'll make it up to me soon."

She hangs up before I can reply.

An hour later, as we finalize one of the last interview shots and wait for Jessie to touch up her makeup, Ezra pulls me aside, his forehead slick with sweat under his beanie hat.

"I was wondering if we could do one last video after we've finished everything you wanted?"

I check the clipboard. "But you guys did great. We have everything we need."

"I have something I want to say to Jess." He shoots me a shrewd smile and wiggles his eyebrows cartoonishly. "Trust me, you're going to want to get this on video."

My stomach knots as I study his face, and I try to think of a million different things I can say to talk him out of what I suspect he is about to do. The blend of excitement and nervousness, uncertainty and hope. The memory of William down on one knee and that very same look on his face hits me so hard I step back.

"So I'll give you a signal and you can just pretend like we have to reshoot our entrance," he instructs while wringing his hands together.

After a few minutes, he gives me a subtle nod, an edge of fear clouding his usually confident demeanor. I clear my throat and lean toward the crew.

"Thanks, everyone. Jessie, Ezra, can we just do one more take for B-roll? I need you both walking onto the set and sitting down."

We reset, and I watch from behind the camera as Jessie walks into the frame and takes her usual starting spot, but instead of sitting next to her, Ezra gets down on one knee, his eyes already glassy with tears. A chorus of "awwwww" radiates from the crew as if they'd rehearsed it. Jessie gasps, her hands covering her mouth as if she's trying to stop herself from immediately screaming her answer.

Ezra's voice is shaky but confident. As though he hasn't practiced but knows exactly what to say. He tells her that he has loved her since they met, and he can't imagine life without her. Blood pounds against my eardrums and a prickling heat creeps up my neck and across my face. I swallow the familiar feeling of panic and try to focus on the camera's red light, making sure it is on and recording. She starts frantically nodding before he even finishes, tears quietly streaming down her face. When he finally asks her to be his wife, she jumps into his arms to a wave of claps, sniffles and whoops radiating from everyone on set. Jessie and Ezra laugh through wet, happy sobs as he slides a ring with a huge, vibrant emerald surrounded by sparkling diamonds onto her manicured finger.

We wrap soon after, Jessie and Ezra practically running out of the building to the champagne-bottle-and-white-rose-filled limousine he had waiting outside to whisk her away for a surprise post-proposal vacation. The crew pack down the cameras and lighting and quickly filter out on to the next shoot. I decide to use staying behind to clean up as my excuse for not heading back to the office. It's 2:30 p.m., and most of the team will be out at lunch or in meetings by now. I can't bring myself to be around other people just yet.

I collect up the cushions from the dimly lit faux–living room. My breathing becomes more rapid as I stuff each cushion into a refuse bag, the soft fabric contorting and pushing against the clear plastic. My hands shake as I knot off the yellow ties, dropping the bag at my feet. My eyes water and I sense the hot sting of a tear escaping down my face. Another catches up with the first, and another, and another, until I can't control the flow and the dam completely breaks. My chest tightens, and I feel like I can't breathe but also am breathing too much. I'm hyperventilating between intense sobs and can't stop.

"Grace?"

The familiar, comforting voice coming from the studio door makes me jump, and I quickly wipe my drenched cheeks on the sleeve of my jacket. Yemi strides over and sits next to me, leaning in and stroking my back.

I angle my face away from her and swipe at the last remaining wet streaks on my cheeks. "Hey, what are you doing here?"

"Thought I'd pop in to see if you were free for lunch. What's wrong?"

"I'm fine . . ." I gasp, my voice squeaking out like the absolute furthest thing from fine. ". . . everything's fine."

Yemi doesn't say anything, giving me space to gather my thoughts rather than scramble in the dark for an answer. I eventually relent, leveling my breathing for long enough to get out a full sentence.

"Jessie Fig's boyfriend just proposed in front of everyone."

Yemi's eyes close briefly, understanding immediately.

"He had everything planned. Then he just did it. In front of everyone, the whole crew and it . . ."

I flop backward and let my neck dangle over the edge of the sofa, as though clearing my airway might clear the emotional weight sitting on my chest.

Her eyes soften as she joins me. "You don't have to talk about it. But if you want to, it doesn't leave this surprisingly uncomfortable sofa. OK?"

I let out a snotty snort and put my hands over my face, hiding the shame seeping out of my pores.

My phone dings with a calendar notification:

3pm: Ditto partnership meeting.

"Fuck, I have to go. I have a call with El Turo about the Ditto project in five minutes." I wipe my final tears on my sodden sleeve and stand up, head aching with a post-breakdown haze. "Urgh, I don't know how I'm going to handle Bancroft on the date test run. I'm a mess.

He's going to sense it and pounce while I'm weak. Maybe I am just better off letting him have the promotion."

Yemi takes my shoulders tightly and twists me to face her. Her eyes are soft but serious. "Listen, Grace, you made the right decision." She shakes me one last time as I steel myself, exhaling anxiety like hot, foggy breath into cold air. "Take a moment. Get it together. Then make the call and get that promotion."

9

Three days later I pick at my freshly painted nails in the dimly lit corridor of El Turo. The hair on my arms stands on end as the sheer black sleeves move over my skin. To Alice's credit, she altered the dress so well it looks like an entirely new outfit and restitched some of the seams to fit me perfectly. The way it hugs my waist and skims over my calves, a slit on one side hitting halfway up my thigh is only accentuated by my blood-red lips and gold dangly earrings. I borrowed a pair of her black leather boots, the only shoes in our flat that covered my ankle and scraped-up calf. The swelling went down after a day and a half of icing but my ankle looks like a toddler has drawn on it in purple and green crayon. The thought of having the injury on display and reliving our last date with Bancroft is worth the discomfort. This is so different from the outfits I wear to work but after the fiasco that was the hiking trail, I need to feel like a different person.

The heavy scent of roasted garlic is only eclipsed by the sound of mingling conversation, knives and forks on plates and clinking glasses covering the tread of Armani brogues stalking toward me.

Bancroft, dressed in a black turtleneck and navy pin-stripe suit trousers, assesses me up and down with an unashamed, indulgent stare. "Hastings, I didn't think you would even own something so . . ."

"What?" I cock an eyebrow and lean against the dark red lime-washed wall, crossing my bad ankle over the good one and waiting for the insult.

His eyes make it back up the dress to meet mine, a deeper shade of blue in the restaurant's moody light. "Devastating."

I suck in my cheeks in an attempt to stop them from turning flame red and stare at a suddenly very interesting patch on the speckled-gray quartz floor.

He clears his throat and changes the subject immediately.

"Remind me again why you thought a cooking lesson would be romantic?" he asks, plastering on the smirk I am so much better at dealing with than whatever *that* just was.

I match his arrogant attitude. "It's like a sport: it's team building, and it shows how you can bounce off each other, follow instructions together and bend to each other."

The last thing I'm going to do is tell him the real reason why I chose this place, just in case he uses it against me later. El Turo is a local institution, run by three generations of the Alberti family. It holds a special place in my heart because it was here that Yemi, Alice and I had our first dinner together after officially becoming flatmates. It's not fully set in stone, but my current plan for this project involves using my local connections to offer experiences Bancroft would never even consider.

Bancroft's arm flexes under his jumper as he pulls the door open. "Some people like losing control. Maybe you should try it for once."

I lift an eyebrow at his faux-gentlemanly act as he gestures for me to go in first.

"What? Aren't you still all weak and injured?" He purses his lips pitifully at me.

"Thank you for your concern." I use my good foot to kick him in the shin as I walk past him and take way too much pleasure in hearing him trying to suppress a grunt, wiping the pout off his stupid lips. I flick my hair as I enter the room. "But I'm healing fast."

Following behind me, he leans down over my shoulder and holds his lips near my ear. "Who's the sadist now?"

His warm breath causes a jolt of electricity to run down my body as I head through the door.

The shiny, distinctly Italian kitchen is filled with people who have signed up for the same class, mostly women and a few men who look considerably less enthusiastic. Maybe they thought they would be among the actual restaurant chefs in the front kitchen, but this space is reserved for weekly classes. A couple of our classmates glance at me and then do a double take at the tall, lean man shadowing me through the door. By the looks of it, all the women want to be on him and their escorting men want to kill him. My chest prickles as some of our classmates briefly give me the once-over.

I instinctively hunch over, wondering whether they can sense the inherent loneliness and fear-of-dying-alone-ness that radiates off me like a flickering lightbulb. Shame and guilt rise like bile as I scan the intrigued crowd, frantically looking for the class chef. A cheery sun-kissed face meets my eye and gives me a warm and open crescent-moon smile.

"Welcome!" she shouts. "I'm Chef Giada!" She holds out her tanned, calloused hands and pulls us both in for a joint hug, squeezing Bancroft's body toward mine like flower stems in a clenched fist. My face is smushed against his chest. Yep, even under the soft cashmere it is still as rock solid as it was the other day. I can hear his heart pounding and try to count the beats to distract myself. As Giada finally releases us and spins around to the rest of the class, I take a deep breath and brush my hands down my dress, avoiding eye contact with Bancroft. "Everyone, this is our final couple of the evening: Grace and Eric."

It's true there are two of us, but there is something about the emphasis on *couple* that makes me bristle. Bancroft shifts his weight from one foot to the other without saying anything. The awkwardness between us is so palpable you could pluck a piece of it and eat it like an apple.

"OK!" continues Chef Giada, herding us to the last empty kitchen island and handing us striped navy-and-white aprons to match the rest of the class.

"What was that? That weird shuffle," I ask Bancroft

out of the corner of my mouth, struggling to successfully tie the knot in the back of my apron.

He throws the neck loop of his apron over his head and ties a quick knot without breaking eye contact.

"I could tell you wanted to say something but we are meant to be experiencing this class as though it's a real date." He creases his eyes, studying me as I continue to create a neat little bow, shifting my shoulders to get a better angle. "We can't just announce we're here for romance reconnaissance," he says under his breath, emphasizing the R sounds.

"Right." I nod and bite my bottom lip in concentration.

"Oh my God, can you just—" He grabs my shoulder and twists me so my back is to him, batting my hands out of the way. I place my palms on the cold edge of the island and my heart pounds as he undoes the strings of the flaccid half bow at my lower back.

He curls the string around his knuckles and lingers for a split second as I feel an unsteady breath on the back of my neck. A familiar heaviness settles in my stomach at the proximity as I resist leaning into it. But before I even have the chance to, he knots the string together properly with a tight tug at my waist. "There, one day I'll teach you how to tie a knot properly," he says to the back of my ear, causing a shot of electricity to run straight down my spine.

"Thanks," I say quietly over my shoulder, giving a nervous laugh and polite smile to the four other couples who have all been watching this exchange with unreadable expressions. The island is relatively small, so when Bancroft moves from my back to stand beside me the sheer mesh on my shoulders and the soft wool on his arm lightly brush against each other. His scent lingers under my nose; the citrus, woody notes mix with the smells of garlic and rosemary in a way I want smothered on a piece of freshly baked focaccia. I shift to add space between us but then second-guess myself; a couple on a date wouldn't be considering personal space.

Chef Giada claps her hands to gain everyone's attention. "On the menu tonight: El Turo's famous Pasta alla Vodka with Homemade Linguine. Let's start with a couple of key ingredients in every Italian dish, garlic and tomato paste!"

The freshly sharpened knife zings as I slide it out of its plastic holder and begin crushing and chopping garlic on the beige wood chopping board.

After a few minutes, she adds, "If you could also please grab a saucepan from the rack and we can begin boiling our water."

Midway through a clove I look up at the pans hanging above us from a curled iron rack. Bancroft beats me to it, reaching over, causing his jumper to ride up slightly, giving a glimpse of his lower stomach muscles. I grip the knife handle harder and blink to shake myself out of the trance as he unhooks the handle of the stainless-steel pan from the rack. Noticing the garlic bulb I've been pulling cloves from has rolled off the counter onto the floor, I lean down to grab it. But as I pull up from the floor and turn back to the chopping board, I collide with Bancroft's constricting torso as he places the saucepan on the hob with a crash and an oomph.

"Fuck!" he exclaims so loudly the couple on the far side of the room notices; his knuckles are white around the handles of the pan as he bends over the counter.

I laugh in confusion as his scrunched face looks down at his stomach. "You drama queen. I'm literally half your weight."

"Are you kidding me?" My quizzical laugh turns into 100 percent pure-grain confusion at the question until he turns to me and I look down at his apron, a round red blotch smeared just above his waist.

I relax my shoulders. "I'm sure your dry cleaner can handle a bit of tomato paste."

"Hastings . . ." he says quietly through gritted teeth so as to not draw any more attention to us, but harshly enough to get *my* attention. He meets my confused stare with glassy eyes. He flicks down to my hand, still holding the freshly sharpened kitchen knife. "You . . . fucking . . . stabbed me."

Pure adrenaline smashes me in the face like a glass of ice water.

"Oh my God, oh my God, *oh my God*!" My voice projects through the room significantly louder than his hushed tone as the knife clatters onto the countertop. My volume immediately grabs the attention of Chef Giada, who hop-steps over to us.

"It's OK, folks!" she announces to the worried faces

around the room. "I'm first-aid trained, and this isn't the first time a cooking lesson has resulted in a knife wound! You should see my cousin Marta: three years running a restaurant and no fingertips left!" She laughs breezily, pulling Bancroft's jumper up and checking the bloodied area around his abdomen. "Phew, we're OK. Just a scratch, not too deep, no need for stitches." Despite her cheery tone, the relief on Giada's face is palpable. She smiles warmly at Bancroft, who eases his shoulders back down to earth.

Standing awkwardly at the workstation while the rest of the class watches my victim being patched up, I try not to look as Chef Giada wipes down the red line with a sterilizing salve. When Bancroft returns back to our station, I whisper a semi-sincere apology.

"So, are we even now?" he replies, inspecting the slash hole my knife cut in his apron. "Or are you getting ready to finish your revenge plot?"

"Revenge for what? I'm trying to remember when you lacerated me last?"

He lands both hands on the island, long arms stretched straight and gives me another of his "are you fucking kidding me" looks. "You blamed me for *you* twisting *your* ankle."

"I did not!" I feign outrage, crossing my arms and trying to stop the corners of my lips from turning upward.

"You did. I heard you in the Uber muttering something along the lines of 'I wouldn't have been walking that way if you weren't being such a "Wankcroft." ' "

He raises a playful eyebrow at me. "I prefer Eric, by the way. Wankcroft is my father's name."

I try and fail to contain a smile, but after a few seconds he bends his chin down to meet me, eyes shining. "So . . . can we *please* be even now?"

I contemplate for a few seconds.

"That seems fair."

We stare at each other, both thinking of the next thing to say when Chef Giada approaches us. I thank the Italian food gods for her interruption because it's clear from even just a few seconds that I have no idea how to actually have a civil conversation with my fake date.

"Now, I don't want to be harsh . . . but you two are going to have to catch up." She looks to the counter at the fresh non-blood-covered knife replacing my weapon of choice and slides it across the shiny surface to Bancroft. "This time, you chop."

"Yes, Chef. I think that's for the best." He flashes her a winning smile.

We work fast and in sync to catch up with the rest of the class and I'm surprised at how smoothly things are going. Bancroft slicing the onions without shedding a single tear and me grating almost an entire wedge of parmesan cheese until my arm feels like a deflated tire. We're even doing better than some of the others—a couple introduced as Derek and Angela have been arguing about what constitutes "al dente" pasta for a solid thirty minutes. Derek is sure he is correct, owing to his one-eighth part Italian ancestry. Bancroft tries to ignore them and meticulously measures out double cream into a measuring jug. I try not to think about how different things might have been if we were on the same team; how we could have worked to lift each other up rather than spending our days attempting to tear the other down.

"So, how come you don't cook?" I ask into the saucepan, where the mixture of garlic, white onions, chili flakes and tomato paste is slowly bubbling away. "You're clearly not bad at it."

He takes a few seconds to respond, wiping a drizzle of cream off the side of the jug with his finger. "I never really thought about it. My family didn't cook or really eat together when I was growing up. We'd either order in because my parents were too busy or it would be some dinner with potential clients that liked the 'family unit' aspect of their business."

As a giant bottle of vodka gets passed around to our workstation for deglazing the sticky concoction in our pans, Bancroft squats down to grab a couple of glasses from under our counter and pours a measure in each. "To deal with Derek and Angela."

I giggle and crouch down beneath the cheese-sprinkled counter, meeting him out of sight of the rest of the bustling class. We clink and down our glasses.

Grimacing at the sting, I ask, "Did the vodka we used to drink in the office taste as bad as this?" The warming sensation as the alcohol sinks into my stomach makes me shiver.

He coughs out a laugh. "I'm pretty sure that wasn't bottom-shelf reserved-for-cooking vodka."

He reaches his hand out to wipe a line of vodka that missed my mouth but hesitates, clearing his throat instead.

"You have a little—" He gestures to my chin and I use the back of my hand to wipe the alcohol before it drips onto my dress.

We study each other for a second, all sounds of metal clanging and knife hitting wood evaporating into the air. He takes the bottle from my hand, featherlight fingers grazing across mine as he says in a low voice, "It's burning."

I swallow, briefly glancing down as he wets his bottom lip. "The . . . vodka?"

His eyes lift up to the counter above us then back to me. "The sauce."

"Right." My thighs tense as I jolt up and splash the vodka into the pan without measuring, the hiss filling the space between us.

10

"Well, I've never eaten dinner with someone who committed a knife crime against me, but I guess there's a first time for everything." Bancroft's face is shadowed by the street lamps outside, the contrast across his skin highlights his sharp cheekbones and squared-off jaw. I scoff as I look up at him, but then, guilt-ridden, my eyes flick to the hole in the cashmere.

I scratch the back of my head and wince. "I really am sorry about it. I didn't mean to. How's your stomach?"

He lifts his jumper to reveal the square white bandage on his abdomen for inspection. "A flesh wound. You'll have to try harder than that if you actually want to kill me."

My mouth twitches into a smile as we wave goodbye to the rest of the class. The couple next to us brush up close and entangle arms over each other's shoulders as they walk down the dimmed pavement.

We walk in silence. The only sound is the rustling of the leaves from the gated residential park across the road and cars driving faintly in the distance. My hands grip my workbag in front of me while his hold the lukewarm brown takeaway box containing our pasta. There is less awkwardness than our last "date," but when my mind drifts all I can think about is the hidden strip of photographs of us on his coffee table, and then all I can think about is the harsh sound of his voice as he said those things about me all those months ago. But then there are times, like when I twisted my ankle on the trail, when he looked at me with the eyes of someone who genuinely cares. I can't decide which version of him is real.

Behind me, I register the scuff of shoes against the pavement and realize Bancroft is no longer walking beside me on the quiet, sleepy road.

Despite myself, I follow him over the road toward a private residential garden fenced off from the public by tall black gates with ornate spiked ends.

"What are you doing?" I ask in a strangled whisper, whipping my head both ways down the street to check for onlookers.

"We need somewhere to eat our expertly crafted meal."

He grips the top of the iron bars, just higher than his head, and pulls himself up until his knees can balance against a horizontal ledge running against the top. He twists his torso and drops down over the bars in a swift movement before catching me staring. "Coming?"

"We're not allowed to go in there!"

My stomach churns at the idea of getting in trouble. But even as I'm protesting, I'm picking up the takeaway box he left resting on the sign that states "Residents access only" and angling it through the bars.

Bancroft leans his arms above him against the bars, his triceps pressed across the black metal as he smirks at me. "Sometimes, Hastings, it's better if you don't wait for permission. You've just got to grab an opportunity when it presents itself."

I don't reply, instead peeking around his body to see a beautiful moonlit garden filled with white wisteria. He shoves against the black iron entrance gate until it creaks open just enough for me to squeeze under the clinking chain through the gap.

The scent of freshly cut grass, warm earth and sweet florals fill the night air as we leisurely pace around the garden toward one of the wooden benches surrounded by sparkling festoon lights. I make a mental note to ask Chef Giada about this place. It would be so romantic to come in here to bask in the private tranquillity away from the city and eat the delicious food from the cooking class. The old bench creaks slightly as we sit and open up the takeaway box, breathing in the smell of freshly made pasta and rich garlic.

My phone dings and I pull it out of my jacket pocket to see a text from Susie. I grimace.

"What?"

"Susie wants a proposal sent to her for a meeting first thing tomorrow."

He knots his brows. "So, it's her meeting . . . but you're doing the proposal?"

"Yeah . . ." I wrench out, running a hand through my hair and letting the artificial glow of the phone screen burn into my brain. I drop my phone back into my bag. "I'll reply later. I'm starving so there's no way I'm leaving you with that entire box."

I pick up the plastic fork and scoop up the now room-temperature linguine.

Bancroft stares at me, eyebrows raised in disbelief. "I don't think I've ever seen you do that."

"What?" I ask, chewing the delicious savory bite.

He leans in, his voice lowering as though he's suggesting something illegal: "Disregard an order from Susie."

He watches me, waiting for a response, but I turn my chin, shrug and take another bite. Overanalyzing my brief moment of insolence is a guaranteed one-way ticket to Anxietyland. He seems to understand not to press the subject, because when he speaks again he is laughing at me.

"No one on earth takes as big bites of their food as you do." He takes the fork from me, twirls a much smaller amount and holds it up to me. "*This* is what a normal human-size bite looks like."

My lips curve at his teasing and, before he can move, I lean forward, take his wrist in my hand and eat the presented ball of pasta.

"Oh my God, Grace!" He barks out a laugh and shakes his head, taking my forearm in his large palm to pry the fork from me. The feeling of his warm skin in the cool breeze sends a shiver over my entire body.

Pausing midchew, I cover my full mouth with my palm to speak. "Did you just call me Grace?"

"Yeah, I guess I did." He laughs nervously as his eyes

follow the edges of the concrete tiles below us. I cock my head in silent question as he scoffs, "Old habits."

An ache lances my chest, remembering how the moment we shifted from using our last names playfully to using them as a social shield had gutted me. Sure, Hastings is better than *Gracie*, but ever since he started using my last name to address me it created an intimacy barrier I never thought we'd be able to break back through.

Deciding playful banter is our safe zone, I reply with "Hmm, feels weird. I don't know if I can still see you as . . ." and hold my finger to my bottom lip to make a cartoonish pout. "Sorry, what's your *actual* name again?"

He raises his eyebrows in a challenge, watching my finger. A flicker of something I don't recognize passes through his eyes. "You know what? I am pressing charges. And I'm having this . . ."

He finally swipes the fork out of my hand and scrapes the final mound of pasta out of the box. I gasp, despite being so full of carbs I want to explode, and use my fingers to pick out the last few pieces of linguine from the box.

He laughs, shaking his head in disbelief. "You're a monster." He turns the fork in his hand.

My phone dings again. "Urgh, I probably should reply to Susie. Can you grab my phone? My hands are all pasta alla vodka-y."

He reaches down to pick up my bag and pulls

something out that definitely isn't my phone. My eyes widen. Oh my God, the magazine, curled around on the page with his face plastered across the glossy paper. My whole body tingles with embarrassment and adrenaline as I try to grab the magazine out of his hand, but I'm frozen. Maybe he can't see the pages in this light?

He begins to read the page aloud, letting out a dry, coarse laugh that doesn't reach his eyes. "'Time to Mar-GO: Notorious party boy Eric Bancroft leaves Chiltern Bistro with yet another mysterious woman despite Margeaux Bardin dating rumors.'"

My cheeks burn as I glance down at the word "Prick" and the hand-drawn devil horns sprouting from his forehead. His gaze leaves the page and a flash of hurt crosses his face. His jaw ticks as he turns away from me and perches on the edge of the bench, letting the magazine curl in his tense hands between his legs.

Swallowing my shame, I go to explain but he speaks first: "You know, I see how people look at me; when they're speaking to me they think they're speaking to this." He rolls up the magazine like a baseball bat. "'London's party boy who has a different woman on his arm every night.'" He turns his chin to me and lifts his eyebrows. "Which is blown grossly out of proportion by the way." He sighs and turns his head back to the ground. "I didn't think, after everything, that *you* saw me like that."

I am about to say something in my defence, but my mind trails off. I've used the rumors to jab at him too many times.

"I didn't use to, but we haven't talked in six and a half months."

He shifts. "You've been counting, huh?"

"Don't flatter yourself."

He spits a laugh with no humor in it. "You know, they don't run the photos where I'm not with a woman, and when they do it's usually one of my sister's drunk or drugged-up bitchy friends I'm trying to help get home safely before they embarrass themselves in front of fucking *Societeur*, who insist on following us."

He drops the crumpled magazine on the bench with a slap. "I'm lucky at least Dharmash has faith in me, because it's clear Catcher only agreed to hire me because of that playboy reputation . . . and the Ditto project solidified that he'll always see me that way. He never trusted me with it; he was never going to let me actually prove I can be good at my job."

The hurt in his eyes is so jarring compared to how he acts at work. It's almost admirable that he's able to portray someone so confident when this is how he really feels.

I look around awkwardly, twiddling my thumbs and sifting through the bowl of alphabet soup in my head for a useful response. This is more honest than he ever was when we were friends. Maybe it's because we aren't anymore. He can finally be vulnerable; as if it doesn't count with me.

"Why don't you do something about it? Get them to stop."

He runs a hand through his hair and lets out a sigh. "I tried to at first, and it worked for a while. But it was like as soon as I started working at Ignite, the press couldn't get enough. Every quick drink with a friend became a headline for some gossip column. I was reportedly partying all over the city, a new woman every night, racking up bills at the most expensive places. Fuck, even my parents believed it. They believe these fucking magazines, Instagram posts and blogs over the word of their own son. They still do. And Catcher couldn't resist the attention it was bringing in. It got to a point where it was easier to go along with the idea everyone already had of me than fight it. Why disappoint them with the real me?"

A twang of guilt reverberates in my chest. His reputation isn't my fault, but I've tarred him with the same assumptions as everyone else, searching for evidence of said reputation like a sniffer dog the moment he welcomed me into his home. *Societeur Magazine* spoon feeds their readers these narratives, but I perpetuated it any chance I got—even when we were friends. Teasing him, calling him the same names everyone else did, and treating him as less than others because of his image. I'm too stubborn to apologize, but the desire to extend an olive branch is overwhelming.

"How about this?" I begin as his lowered head lifts to face me. "Maybe we could *attempt* a ceasefire . . . just for this project."

He raises an eyebrow in question, making me instinctively roll my eyes.

"You're great at onboarding users; I'm good at creating an amazing user experience. You can prove to everyone that you're more than just a pretty face, and I won't spend the rest of my professional life making sure Susie's coffee is exactly ninety-six degrees. If one of us has a shot at getting this job, we have no choice but to work together." I sigh at the final words about to escape my mouth: "Catcher was obviously completely wrong that we work well together—I came this close to skewering you tonight—but he was right about one thing: we do need each other."

"Sooo, what I'm hearing is . . . you think I'm pretty?" His smile flashes triumphantly in the warm, humming light.

I raise my eyebrows and stare at him in carb-fueled disbelief. "That's the one thing you got from my speech?"

"Fine, you're right. No more mutually assured destruction." He shoots me another smile, tight-lipped this time, a dimple appearing on his cheek.

As we sneak out of the garden, we pass an ornate black rubbish bin. I throw the magazine, complete with juvenile drawings into the trash with a dramatic flourish. Bancroft follows suit, splattering the tomato-covered cardboard remnants of our evening on top.

On the bus ride home, I rest my head against the cool glass and begin mentally planning how to weave an El Turo cooking class into my presentation. It's safe to say my first trial date went much better than Bancroft's. If

I keep this standard up, I think I might have a chance at getting this promotion. Eventually, I give in to the morbid curiosity and pull out my phone to check Susie's latest messages. Instead, I am greeted with a text from William:

Hey. How are you? Was wondering if we could get coffee soon, catch up? Will x

The last texts we exchanged are visible just above this one. Messages from me, begging for him to reconsider the breakup and the ultimatum. Scrolling through the pitiable messages I sent in the days post-dumping makes me feel as if bugs are crawling all over my body. This casual message is so jarring against them. As if I'm just a friend he hasn't seen in a while, not someone whose heart he ploughed into, tore up and then left to fester in the dirt. A delicate tea party next to a gory crime scene. It's so nonchalant. Is that how he's been feeling this whole time, while I've been slowly rotting from the inside out?

Please pick up!

We need to talk about this.

I love you, we just need to talk. We can sort this out. Will, please?

I don't know what I'm going to do without you.

As soon as we started dating William put me on a pedestal. I did the same but on a metaphorical white horse. All I'd ever wanted was someone who loved me as much as my parents love each other, the Fairy-tale Ending. When I met William, it felt like my turn. Even the way we met felt like something from a storybook.

Me the damsel in distress, him the dashing hero willing to drop everything to save me.

It was my second year of university and I was spending every waking hour in the library fueled by black coffee and pure unadulterated fear of failure. I was a walking corpse clad in clashing prints who hadn't been absorbing any information for a good couple of hours. I had decided to go home and see if I could shower and squeeze in an hour of sleep before my next exam. I dragged my body over to the exit clutching my laptop, highlighter pens and books, trying to shove them into the canvas bag half hanging off my shoulder.

A fresh layer of winter had settled in the early hours of the morning, turning the gritted steps into slushy piles of doom. I descended the concrete staircase carefully, trying not to slip. As soon as my feet touched the pavement, I breathed a quick sigh of relief and stepped forward, right into the path of an oncoming bicycle.

I braced myself for the impact, the crash, the impending pain, but it never came. A strong pair of hands pulled me back toward the stairs and I fell to the ground with an "umph" sound, a body breaking what would have been a hard fall onto snow-covered concrete. My books and laptop weren't so lucky, flying into the air before smacking to the ground with a loud crack.

"Are you OK?"

My scrunched eyelids peeled open and looked up into panicked honey-brown eyes. Soft lips repeated the question, but my brain didn't register the words. I was too transfixed on the kind face framed by chestnut hair and a dark stubbled jaw as he scanned me for signs of injury.

I relaxed into him as he held me in his arms, making sure I was OK. My face warmed as he touched my cheek with a gloved hand, checking I wasn't concussed.

As he fussed around me, it was as if I was hearing the voice of some heavenly being say: "Grace Hastings, please come to the front to collect your order: one Prince Charming."

Looking back, it is entirely possible I *was* concussed.

Something snapped me back to reality and I caught sight of my laptop, lying upside down in a pile of slush. I lifted it and watched as dirty water dripped out from the middle.

"*Fuck!*" My cry echoed across the dawn-laced street, and he took a step away from me.

"Are you OK?" he asked again, more tentatively this time. He looked at me warily, the way you might survey an unexploded bomb.

"No. I mean, yes. Thank you for pulling me out of the way, but my laptop is trashed and I need it for an exam in two hours. Even if I could get one that fast, I *definitely* can't afford to buy a new one. Maybe I can go beg my professor to let me take it another day but he's absolutely terrifying and I think you have to give twenty-four hours' advance notice to get out of exams and—"

He put a hand on my shoulder, stopping my panic-induced word vomit. "Take mine."

My head jolted up from the cracked screen and I

properly took him in for the first time. His navy university-branded hoodie was slightly crumpled, as though he'd just rolled out of bed and thrown on the nearest piece of clothing.

"Take. Mine." He pronounced both words slowly and clearly. "Give it back after your exam. I'll be in there." He gestured with his chin toward the library doors.

"I can't do that." I looked at him as if he was the crazy one. "You don't know me. This could just be some big ruse to steal your laptop."

He laughed. "That's certainly a risky heist! I think there are easier ways to rob people without risking your life."

He dragged his backpack from over his shoulder and pulled out a shiny silver MacBook, gesturing it toward me as casually as a waiter handing over a menu.

I reached my hand out, then I hesitated. "But you're at the library? Don't you need it?"

He shrugged and sighed. "I'm here for research, so I'll be reading a very large old textbook for the next few hours."

For some reason the image of him looking incredibly sexy with a furrowed brow buried in a book took over all rational thought.

"What if you leave the library before I get back?"

He thought for a second, then he pulled out his phone, typed something and handed it to me. I winced at the bright screen but lifted my eyebrows at what I saw. An open contact form with the name "Laptop Thief" already typed in.

I laughed, added my phone number and handed it back.

"My name is Grace, by the way," I clarified.

"William." He hit call on his phone, and my phone buzzed in my pocket. He gestured with his laptop once again and I finally took it.

"It was nice to meet you, Grace. Good luck with your exam." He smiled at me sheepishly and climbed the stairs into the library.

From that day on I saw him as my hero, my knight with shining Apple products that saved my arse twice in a matter of minutes. I thought it was a dream come true, a story to rival my parents. The fairy-tale moment I'd always wanted. For our first date we went to a bar on our university campus. We'd texted every day since we'd met, and I felt I already knew him so well. By the end of our date, he told me he thought I was his soulmate. Jokingly, I thought at first, but later realized he was serious.

Shaking off the memories and glancing back at my phone, I read the messages I sent the days after we broke up over and over until I feel travel-sick, or maybe just regular sick. The person who typed them feels like a long-lost friend. To think there was ever a time when I felt *that* out of control, attempting to claw back someone so soon after they'd destroyed me. Relentlessly picking at the scab, opening the wound to inspect it over and over again until all that was left of me was scar tissue. The bus thumps over speed bumps as my thumb flicks to Instagram and types in William's user-name. He's barely posted since we broke up, a scarcity much appreciated during the harsh withdrawal period. Not being able to get a fix of the person who broke your heart living their best curated life online is both a blessing and a curse. The utter lack of them a curse in itself, but easier than seeing them doing better without you.

A slow, thick stream of tears escapes down my cheeks until I clock the familiar landmarks of my street. I wipe my eyes and read the message from William approximately fifteen more times as I walk home, hoping to find a hidden message implying something I can print out and frame as proof I'm not destined to be an unloved husk of a person for the rest of my life. Something along the lines of *Hey just to let you know I'm still in love with you and regret everything OK thanks bye.*

"Look!" I'll say to my imaginary guests. "There was *one* man who thought I was worth a multi-year commitment!"

Instead, I find a deep pit of shame I'm still trying to escape. I decide to leave him hanging, wondering, waiting, just as he did to me.

11

ERIC BANCROFT MADE EDITS IN THE FOLLOWING DOCUMENT:
"DITTO PROJECT REPORTING."
I enjoyed participating in this experience:
Agree.
Additional comments:
Relaxed atmosphere, tasty food and great teacher. The lesson is a good opportunity for bonding.

My body sags with relief after waiting for this report to come through for close to a week now. Thank God he didn't mention the knife incident. As I reread his comment, just to double-check, my eye snags on the final word. Surely he doesn't mean *we* bonded; he just means it would hypothetically be a good *opportunity* for bonding. For anyone who isn't us. I pull out my phone, lingering on the empty conversation before finally typing out a message.

GH: *Thanks for not ratting me out.*

EB: *You didn't stab me deep enough to warrant telling Dad.*

GH: *That's a relief, because snitches famously get stitches.*

EB: And luckily for you I only needed light first aid and a bandage.

We don't speak for a few days after that. Maybe with our new shiny truce in place, it's better if we have limited communication. If you don't have something nice to say, then don't say anything at all. That's the healthy mindset I should have adopted when hyperfixating on what William's text meant, the dark underbelly of the casual message. With Alice and Yemi's guidance, I'd decided not to recklessly jump at the opportunity for an in-person meet.

Hey, things are kind of busy at work at the moment. What did you want to talk about?

William read the message almost immediately; he's one of those people who have no qualms about leaving his read receipts on and replying whenever he feels like it. The digital equivalent of living in a ground-floor flat and walking around naked with the curtains open. Despite myself, I kept checking for a reply.

When I wasn't regretting my message, I locked in another trial date. I'd had a pottery class in mind for a couple of weeks now, and had been talking to the owner, Mellie, about a brand partnership.

"So we're here to make a . . . cup?" Bancroft asks as he holds open the door for me and I duck in under his arm.

"My flatmate brought me here a while ago; she calls it 'creative therapy.'" I cartoonishly roll my eyes to avoid the truth of why I know about this place.

Alice claims that when you feel like everything is falling apart, making something out of nothing helps the healing process. While it didn't do exactly that, it took my mind off things for a while during those first few post-break-up months. We made matching polka dot "friendship mugs"; pink for Alice, yellow for Yemi and blue for me. They didn't actually end up being used for liquid, having too many cracks in them and chips around the edges that cut our lips, but they made perfect decoration for our dull, cramped kitchen.

"Hiiiiii!" Mellie exclaims when she sees us lingering by the entrance. Her green resin earrings bob against her cheeks as she walks over to us, hugging me and shaking hands with Bancroft.

I smile. "Thank you so much for having us."

"Yes, I'm very excited about the therapy cups," Bancroft adds self-assuredly with a nod.

Mellie laughs. "I guess you could call them that. I prefer emotional support pots."

The sun-soaked room is filled with the earthy mix of houseplants and clay. Colorful mugs and bowls sit on wooden shelves lining every wall. It's surprisingly calm, considering any wrong move could destroy infinite amounts of handmade treasures. The anxiety I felt when I first stepped into this room mirrored my own mental health in a way that was too on the nose to ignore. My mind conjures that version of myself: pale, red eyes encircled with tired bluing skin. One sudden move and whole thing would come crashing down.

After talking through the logistics of the partnership with Mellie, Bancroft and I slide on dark gray overalls that make us look like a couple of naval deckhands. Well, they make me look like a plumber, and they make him look like the most dashing seaman ever to grace the ocean.

We sit down in front of two stained pottery wheels, each cradling a textured lump of brown-gray clay. Like El Turo, we are two of many in the pottery class, but unlike at the restaurant, this session is a lot more free-flowing. Less "add exactly three garlic cloves," more "go where the clay takes you." Following Mellie's instruction, we dip our dry hands in a bucket of cloudy warm water sitting in between us. The backs of our hands briefly slide up against each other as they're submerged, sending a jolt up my arms straight to my heavy shoulders. I avoid eye contact with Bancroft, hairs from my ponytail falling loose over my cheeks as I focus down on my squishy bundle of joy.

Sensing my lackluster mood, Bancroft rolls his shoulders back and tries to fill the silence. "Do you want to be Patrick Swayze or the ghost?"

"Patrick Swayze *is* the ghost," I say ineffectually, squeezing the clay to test its durability. The wet substance leaks between my fingers as I slowly push my foot down on the pedal to make the pottery wheel turn under my hands.

"Hey, spoilers!" he says.

"That movie is older than me. How could that possibly

be a spoiler? That's like saying the ship sinking at the end of *Titanic* is a spoiler," I say, my eyes fixed on the spinning clay.

Mellie, now dressed in lilac overalls covered in clay, heads over to us. "How are you two getting on?" She leans on the wooden utility shelf full of bowls, vases and abstract speckled sculptures behind us.

Bancroft beams up at her. "I've been told I'm good with my hands but now I'm not so sure!"

Mellie laughs politely at his dumb joke and snatches a glance at me. "Your boyfriend is funny," she says before turning back to Bancroft. "Like everything in life, it just takes practice. You'll get there." She slaps him on the back. "Grace, we'll talk again later, yeah?"

"He's not—" I silence myself before I stop the positive conversational flow with a potential partner. "That would be great, really excited to be working with you."

I shoot her a believable smile and a muddy thumbs-up. If I nail this, it will be my second locked-in partnership opportunity, meaning I'm currently ahead of Bancroft's one. I have no doubt he's going to pull something huge out of his gold-lined bag soon, so I'm enjoying the feeling of singular success while I can.

Bancroft looks up from his wheel, side-eyeing me under his brow. "I like this angle you're taking, having a mix of local and bigger partners, working with female entrepreneurs. It's . . . nice."

I scoff. "You know, a week ago I would have

interpreted the word 'nice' coming from you as 'derogatory,' but since you agreed to a truce I'm deciding to take that as a compliment."

"Wow. Look at us, getting along," he replies with a sarcastic smile.

"Practically besties," I shoot back with a singsong tone, matching his smile.

He clears his throat. "So, since we're attempting a ceasefire . . . I've been thinking about how we can collaborate more efficiently."

"Right . . ." I reply monotonically.

"You need to be taken on a real date," he says resolutely, nodding his head as though it's been said and therefore decided.

My lump of clay spins freely until I take my foot off the pedal and turn to him, blinking. "What?"

"You need to be taken on a real date," he repeats, still focused on his clay, which is beginning to take shape.

"Why?"

"Well, correct me if I'm wrong but have you actually been on a date since . . . ?" He shifts slightly in his seat, his gaze still fixed on his spinning plate.

I realize that he doesn't want to say William's name. A button he doesn't want to press just in case it opens a trapdoor below him.

"Not exactly," I say quietly, feigning concentration on my clay ball, which I set spinning again. There was that one date when I cried about William in the middle of the restaurant. Practically encouraging the guy to pretend to go to the bathroom and leave me with the bill. "I did go on one, but it didn't work out." I barely even consider that a date.

"OK, so . . . how is the research for Ditto going to be effective if you have no idea what dates are like nowadays? You have no contemporary frame of reference." He throws up his eyebrows, opening the space for me to protest. To prove him wrong.

I suck in my cheeks, trying to remember the last date-esque outing William and I had . . . and come up short. "I'm not seventy! It's only been like"—I count the years on my clay-covered fingers—"six years?"

"So you're saying you've gone without a date for the equivalent length of World War Two?"

I side-glare at him. "Surely you have enough experience for the both of us?" The regret hits my chest like a volleyball as I remember his words in the garden the other night.

His jaw tightens and releases. "In your own words, I'm pretty well-versed." He gives me a wink but the usual twinkle in his eyes is absent. "I'm just saying, if we're working together, I need a strong partner. I can't have you dragging me down with your Amish ways and terrible conversation."

I straighten my shoulders. "Hey! I'm on Fate . . . I just haven't seen anyone that's piqued my interest. And even if I did . . . between this Ditto project and my normal job I barely have time to do my laundry . . ." My thumbs press into the middle of the ball, forcing a round lip to appear on the edges. ". . . let alone go on a date where I waste a good outfit and two hours of my life with a person who I'll inevitably discover down the line doesn't match my needs and expectations."

"I'm not saying go find a husband, Ms. Bennet!" He holds up his clay-covered hands in defence. "Fate just takes itself way too seriously; it's not the place for you right now." He pauses, contemplating. "You should create an Ignite profile."

I snort. "Because you think my soulmate is someone with a pet iguana and katana sword collection?"

He smirks, shifting so our legs are nearly touching. "So you can enjoy some casual dating and maybe, God forbid"—he lowers his voice to a mock-whisper, tilting his head toward me—"some sex!"

Our gazes linger; his eyes flick to my lips. The orange glow of golden hour slips through the windows and illuminates his already intense stare. My fingers go straight through my emerging vase, ruining the shape I'd just managed to carve out. Bancroft's lips curve up as I try to play it off as a deliberate artistic choice by poking another hole on the opposite side.

"You've never even thought about it?" he teases, pupils dilated. His voice sounds like a dare.

My cheeks flare: he knows I have. And he knows exactly when.

Sensing my awkwardness, Bancroft switches the subject. "All I'm saying is, you have this idea that seeking out your 'one true love' is actually going to lead to it.

When, in my experience, the people who find something epic aren't looking for it." He swallows, staring intensely at his clay. "Real earth-shaking love can't be forced or sought out. It happens *to* you, not *because* of you."

I arch a brow at him. "Funny coming from someone who doesn't believe in true love."

He glances up at me. "You assume I don't." We sit in silence for a moment, until his smile, eventually, breaks the tension. "You really think you've got my number, don't you?"

I smush my ruined vase back into a ball. "I do, actually. It's saved in my phone under *Spawn of Satan.*"

"Referring to my father as the devil is giving him way too much credit. He's more your run-of-the-mill chaos demon. Anyway, stop changing the subject. You are making an Ignite profile."

I stare at my vase-bowl-jug lump, considering the idea. "What would I even write on it? Besides age, sex, location and whether I'm DTF?"

He licks his bottom lip. "It's not that hard. Just something simple but interesting about yourself."

"Like what?" I push because I, like any normal person with self-esteem issues, can't think of anything interesting about myself on the spot.

He ponders for a second, pouting out his top lip. "Your music taste: it's bonkers."

My cheeks are plump as I try to suppress a smile. The night before our monthly report meetings when we would both inevitably end up working late, Bancroft would take my phone and hook it up to the Fate office's speaker system and press shuffle. Whatever random song title it landed on first would have to be shoehorned into the meeting the next morning. There were some easy ones like Frank Sinatra's "I Couldn't Sleep a Wink Last Night" and the Strokes's "Is This It"; upping the difficulty was Ariana Grande's "God Is a Woman" and Celine Dion's "My Heart Will Go On." We peaked with me managing to drop an "It's Not Easy Being Green" in the middle of a sentence with neither Susie nor Dharmash noticing. The only one we failed at was 2006 Eurovision winner Lordi's "Hard Rock Hallelujah."

I'm quiet, in the depths of nostalgia, when Bancroft offers a more enticing proposal: "OK, how about this? We *switch* apps; try out each other's platforms. Then at our next trial date, we can discuss which features could translate to Ditto. What we liked, didn't like, functionality, clientele, etc. But you can't just be on it, you have to *use* it. Go on an actual date, not a fake date."

"Wouldn't Margeaux Bardin have a problem with you being on Fate?"

His jaw twitches as his eyes flick down and then back to me. "I stopped seeing her a couple of weeks ago."

I blink. "Oh."

"Yeah." He goes to run a hand through his hair but hesitates at the clay on his fingers. "Looks like *Societeur* hasn't caught up to that one yet."

My brow tightens. "Well, as much as I appreciate this digital wife swap, I just don't think I have the right qualities for a casual hook-up. I'm not fun, like you. I like going to museums and—"

"If you say you're 'not like most girls' I'm going to have to rescind your feminist card," he interrupts.

"No, that's not it. I mean I don't have the qualities guys would be looking for in a chilled-out hook-up. I can't be cool or casual and I'm . . ." I stop myself; this is the kind of vulnerability I could show him when we were friends, but not now.

Bancroft cocks his head, narrowing his eyes in disbelief. "Don't give me that bullshit. You over-think enough to know you have plenty of shaggable qualities."

His phone vibrates on the wooden surface between us. The word *Rissy* is emblazoned on the screen. He ignores it, choosing instead to take my face in his wet hands, smearing cold clay on my cheeks. "You, Hastings, are a catch."

"Oh my God!" A teenage giggle-scream forces out of me, turning the heads of the others in the class. I grab his wrists, attempting to pull his hands away.

His hands hold strong as he pierces me with that icy gaze. "Do we have a deal?"

With the first genuine smile I've let slip in days: "OK, OK, OK! I'll do it!"

"Good." His hands slide from my face as he briefly glances at my lips. I wipe the splattered clay from them with the back of my hand, grabbing paper towels from the pile between us with the other. His phone begins to vibrate again, and he wipes his hands off. "I should probably take this." He gets up, shoulders tense.

"Yeah, sure," I say quietly, pretending to be so engrossed with wiping the clay water off my cheeks that I haven't noticed his sudden change in demeanor.

He slips out of the door onto the busy street outside. I watch as he paces in the early-evening glow through the glass facade of the pottery shop. His face is solemnly laced with a flash of frustration, pinching the bridge of his nose with his free hand. I make out the words "stay there," followed by a concerned look as he hangs up and clutches the phone in his fist.

A few moments later he stalks back through the room looking like the slightly disheveled evil twin of the man who was trying to lighten my mood just a few moments ago. "I have to leave."

His gaze drags between his phone and me as though looking at both simultaneously will teleport him into two places at once. His half-formed vase slumps over on the wheel from lack of physical attention.

I look up at him from the pottery wheel; from this angle I can see how tense his jaw is so I try and sound nonchalant: "Everything OK?"

He nods his head. "Yeah. Well . . . no, it's fine. It's my sister," he says, knuckles white around his phone. He's pretending to sound annoyed but there is a clear edge of urgency to his voice that makes the hairs on my arms stand at attention.

"Is she all right?"

He runs a hand through his thick, sandy hair. "I think so. She and her friends have racked up a huge bill at Matilda's Bar. The manager isn't letting her leave until she pays and her card isn't working. She sounds kind of . . . out of it."

He looks embarrassed, as if it's not the first time something like this has happened. Matilda's Bar is one of the more expensive of the trendy London drinking holes. I've never been there but have heard they're more likely to check your follower count than your age upon entry.

Bancroft sighs and pops the buttons on his overalls, revealing a pristinely uncreased white shirt and tightly pleated suit trousers underneath like a stressed-out reverse Superman.

"I'll come with you," I say, yanking off my overalls too; my T-shirt and jeans are a stark contrast to his outfit. We look like a farmer and the guy who wanted to pave paradise to put up a parking lot.

"No." His voice is harsh but has a quality that makes me realize this is actually serious. Previously, if anything was causing him stress at work he would go into charm-bot mode and the Permasmirk would soon follow. Turning his work persona up to eleven to compensate for the panic going on behind the scenes in his brain. It dawns on me that this is the rare version of Bancroft I got a glimpse of after I fell on the hiking trail. Pure panic.

He's saying he doesn't need help but instead of leaving immediately he slides his hands into his pockets and waits for my response. I cross my arms and match his tense expression. "Do you really think you'll be able to deal with the bar manager, your sister *and* her drunk friends on your own?"

One side of his mouth twitches up in faux-nonchalance as he shrugs. "I've done it before."

The overwhelming urge to put my hand on his arm swells inside me but I hesitate, and instead put on my best resolute voice and state, "Well, you shouldn't have to. I'm coming." Not waiting for his reply, I pick up my jacket, fold it over my crossed arms and nod toward the door. "Shall we?"

He says nothing but doesn't protest as I give an apologetic "family emergency" explanation to Mellie with promises to talk further details via phone. She waves me off insistently as I follow him out of the building, into the back of a black cab.

12

Sometimes in life, the universe comes along and metaphorically knocks you in the head so hard you see colors for the first time. This is what happened when I saw Iris Fender, dressed in a sparkling black halterneck dress, sitting in a dark pink velvet booth slumped over a green marble table surrounded by empty bottles of champagne and cocktail glasses. Finally, it clicks that this is who he was photographed with weeks ago. I knew he had a sister, but he'd never mentioned her by name. Of course, discovering information like this is the exact point in time I also notice their similarities: their tall frames, the shape of their mouths and their icy blue eyes. Like cleaning an old, smeared mirror until you can finally see a reflection. As Bancroft sits down next to his sister and gently lifts her floppy body off the sticky table I try to figure out why he seems to be keeping his younger sibling's similar socialite status hidden.

The dimly lit bar glows a deep orange, with gold pleated fabric drapes over the ceiling as though this is some sort of royal circus tent. It's Saturday night and the place is heaving. The scent of sickly-sweet cocktails and salty dark liqueur fills the space. I can't help but also notice the grandeur seeping from everyone's pores, smelling it in the air like a perfume that costs way too much to smell this bad. I physically shrink, attempting to take up less space as tall men and women in perfectly tailored suits and dresses glide by without a second glance; if they could walk straight through me they absolutely would. Bancroft seems annoyed at everyone, glaring at anyone whose eyes shift in his sister's direction. Anybody in the sea of faces could have seen she needed help, but instead, they scrunched their perfectly plucked eyebrows and snarled their silicone-filled lips at the inconvenient mess in the corner booth, and continued to sip on their espresso martinis.

Despite insisting on attending this rescue mission, now that I'm here, I have no idea what I should be doing to help. I feel like an umbrella you bring on a cloudy day "just in case" but end up having to carry all day for no reason. On the way here Bancroft hinted at having been in this situation before, so I stand a few meters away letting him handle things and giving them some privacy. Well, as much as they can get in a bar full of people who all likely know who he is, if not her too. My gaze moves to a group of tall, slim, good-looking people who look like children. One girl (who if I was ten years younger I would be utterly terrified of) sniggers while taking a video of Iris, her head lolling back as Eric encourages her to drink a glass of water. A man in a sharp navy suit with a slicked-back dark brown haircut

I can only describe as "Lego hair" strides toward them. He swiftly hands over a small brass tray with a piece of folded paper on it; Bancroft sucks his teeth resignedly and pulls out his wallet. Iris's head rolls onto his chest with a thump like a bowling ball hitting the gutter.

The girl taking the video is several inches taller than me so I lift my chin to her to meet her eyes. "Hey, are you one of Iris's friends?"

The girl's hazel eyes travel lazily from her phone screen to look at me. Not at my face; instead, she starts at my shoes and scans my entire body as though she has an outfit price-checker in her brain, deciding whether I am figuratively and literally worth a response.

"We're not friends. We're mutuals on Instagram." She turns back to her phone.

"Right. But you're here *with* her? How long has she been like this?" She ignores me, the light from her phone reflecting glassy spots in her eyes. "Jesus, can you stop filming her?" I put my hand in front of the camera lens. "How long has she been like this?" I repeat.

She rolls her doe eyes and lowers the phone. "Like an hour and a half—she's been in and out." Her golden-blonde hair bounces on her bony shoulders as she laughs. "Such a fucking lightweight."

A wave of anger hits me, and before my brain can catch up my feet are already moving toward Bancroft, Iris and the bar manager. Bancroft sees me first, and I can feel the shame radiating off him as I approach.

"Can I see that?" I ask bluntly, holding my hand out

to the manager. He sighs exasperatedly and places the long paper bill in my palm. My eyes run down the list of drinks until they reach the total. Jesus Christ. Three grand: that's more than I pay for three months' rent, spent in a matter of hours.

Bancroft must notice my eyebrows raise. "It's fine, Hastings. I'll deal with it."

He looks so deeply uncomfortable he's probably willing to pay that much money just to get out of this situation. I scan over the receipt again, trying to work out how many drinks Iris could have had before passing out.

"I need another card—hers bounced," the manager snaps, pointing a bitten-down fingernail at Iris.

I quickly scan the bill again, running my finger down the items. "It says here this tab was opened with her card about two hours ago?" My chin lifts to meet the group of spectators. "They said that she's been unconscious for an hour and a half. So did you not notice a girl passed out on a table in the middle of your bar, or were you happy to let random patrons add four-hundred-pound bottles of champagne to her tab without her consent?"

Bancroft matches my raised eyebrows as the manager sucks in his cheeks, flicking his eyes from Bancroft to Iris to me.

His Adam's apple bobs. "She's only been like that for a few minutes. This was all her! You need to pay now or I'm calling the police."

I steady my voice, trying to stay calm against his escalating tone. "Yes, let's! I'm sure one of the people here with their phones out has evidence of her that would prove you're lying."

The manager side-glances at a huge, bald-headed man in a black T-shirt who looks as if he'd be better suited to a career in WWE than this bar. As the bouncer paces over to us, adrenaline starts to pound through my veins, making my blood thick enough to hold up my shaking legs like stilts. Glancing back to her "friends" so I know they can hear me, I point a shaky finger at the manager and double down.

"You've been racking up a bill while she's been passed out. From what I can tell"—gesturing with a sweaty palm to Iris—"this isn't the first time this has happened."

I pause to wait for a response that doesn't come, so instead, I continue with this new self-confident persona: "Do you do this to all your customers or just the young women? I don't think you want a reputation for taking advantage of unconscious girls."

He rips the bill out of my hand with the alacrity of someone who's just been told it's a winning lottery ticket. The bouncer steps between us and I freeze: a deer on a tight country lane about to become roadkill. This guy looks thrilled to be getting into his first big confrontation of the night. I'm briefly sucked out of my righteous tirade and forced into the reality of getting punched by a human freight train. Bancroft pushes to step between us and gives me a gentle nudge out of the way, blocking my body from the bouncer with his.

The manager turns to us and sighs dramatically. "Just . . . get out. Make sure *she*," he spits, pointing a harsh finger at Iris, "doesn't come back."

"With pleasure," Bancroft interjects.

We each put one of Iris's arms over our shoulders. She's a rag doll, half walking, half being dragged through the bar toward the exit, her heels scraping against the wooden floor like chalk on a blackboard. Her "mutuals" are still stumbling around the room, giggling with cocktails in hand. As soon as they see Bancroft, a look of pure wrath on his face, they scatter like bugs, heading toward the door on to the next stop of their champagne crawl. We make it out of the building and into the taxi Bancroft had kept waiting outside.

"That's not Margeaux." Iris's hand flops like a freshly caught fish toward me as I sit down on the other side of the cab, facing them both in stunned silence.

Bancroft's lips push together, suppressing a smile as he pulls Iris's seat belt over her and plugs it in with a click.

"No, that's Grace," Bancroft corrects. My face creases: Is this first-name basis becoming a regular thing now? My name feels new when it's on his lips, as though it's the first time I've heard it from anyone.

Iris lets out a quiet gasp, her hot breath creating a momentary fog against the window. "Oh, *that's* Grace. Hastings . . . like the battle . . ."

A flash of panic whips across Bancroft's face; he runs

a palm across his mouth and the look is gone. Iris's flushed face smushes against the cab window, and she falls asleep. I'm tempted to ask what "*that* Grace" means but decide against it; he's probably complained about me or talked about me behind my back to his sister too.

Instead, I ask, "Not to sound like a dick but . . . isn't your family like *rich* rich? Why did you have to come to settle her bill?"

The taxi pulls out, making all three of us bob in our seats until we turn on to the road. Bancroft sighs, considering for a moment before answering me.

"Our mother likes to cut us off whenever she's feeling 'unloved.' She does it for attention . . . or if she doesn't feel we're being as appreciative as we should be." He looks over at his dozing sister with a mixture of love and pity. "Since I have a full-time job it doesn't affect me much, but it still works like a charm with Rissy."

Thinking of my own mother, I feel a twang of guilt; there have been so many missed calls and canceled visits over the past few years, because life, work or William got in the way. But I've never received anything but love in return.

"Is that why you took the job at Ignite? To stop being controlled by her?"

"Maybe at first, but I like what I do. I'd do it for a lot less." Detecting my awkwardness, he shifts, looking at his lap. "I'm sorry we had to cut your date short."

"It's OK. Mellie seems really keen to partner. I'll call her to lock it down on Monday." Sensing the need to lighten the mood, I lean back in my fold-down seat and cross my legs. My calf lightly brushes against his knee in the confined space, a touch we ignore. "I am livid I didn't get to finish my clay masterpiece though."

"And what were you making? It looked like you were going for a . . ." He pouts, searching for the words. ". . . gray-brown blob?" He takes off his jacket and lays it over Iris's lap, covering her riding-up dress. As he moves his shirt separates between the buttons, revealing a hint of golden skin and a smattering of hair a shade darker than his sandy locks.

I glance at his chest, then swiftly move my eyes down to my hands, examining the clay still residing under my fingernails. "It was a statue of you. I thought it was pretty realistic."

"Of course. Who am I to misinterpret a master?" He smirks at me, eyes weary. "Was this statue for worshipping purposes or are you planning to put a curse on me? Because if it's the latter, I'd love to know in advance."

I laugh through my nose. "I was hoping it would be like that movie *Life-Size* and I would have an enchanted version of you to do stuff for me."

"You weren't concerned about this turning into a *Pygmalion* scenario?"

I fake an excited gasp, raising my hands in revelation. "Maybe that's the solution to my dating dilemma: creating the perfect man out of stone!"

Iris shuffles in her seat, her face pressing against the fogging glass as she falls fully back to sleep.

"And that perfect man would be me . . . minus the personality?" He throws me a theatrically offended look, pushing his hand across his chest as if he's been shot in the heart.

I lower my chin. "Maybeeee . . . I would be willing to take a *few* traits into consideration . . ." I lightly tap his shin with my foot.

The passing streetlights cast Bancroft back and forth from gold to black. "Like what?"

"Well . . ." I pretend to ponder. "The part that felt compelled to order us expensive sushi during late nights at the office?" I point to him for emphasis. "*That* part of your brain could stay."

"Ahhh," he says, nodding. "The tempura lobe."

I snort a laugh and he leans forward, hands clasped between his thighs. "Want to know what part of your brain I would keep?"

I raise my eyebrows in question, signaling my willingness to play ball. His eyes gleam in the dark. "Whatever part turned you into a fucking badass in there."

As he moves closer I catch the soft scent of his cologne; it wraps around me like a warm duvet on a rainy day.

Instead of immediately reacting, I run through the script of my entire life to check, but . . . "I think that's the first time anyone has ever called me a badass."

He grips me in an icy stare. "Maybe you should be like that more often, then."

Iris grunts softly in her alcohol-laced slumber as the taxi lurches over a pothole.

I let out a quiet laugh at the advice I know is 100 percent correct. "Want to know a secret?"

"Always."

I lean forward, meeting him in the middle of the cab, my chest pressing against the seat belt. "I was channeling *you*." His eyebrows raise to match mine as I continue, "How you are in meetings and with your team. It was like I could feel you inside me and I—" I snap my mouth shut, thanking the moon for masking my red cheeks in darkness. The sound of the whirring engine and beeping traffic permeates around us, as though the fabric-lined walls of the cab are slowly pushing us in toward each other.

He licks his lips and then purses them, trying to suppress a smirk. His voice lowers an octave, making me shiver despite the hot night: "You know, a much lesser man would respond to that statement in a very undignified manner."

My stomach feels heavy as his eyes squint at me; they look almost black in the shadowed cab. I have to actively remind myself that we are not alone in this tiny taxi. Actively stop myself from saying *I wish you would* and asking *What would you say?*

My seat belt digs into the side of my neck as my body is drawn toward him like a magnet; for a brief second I imagine the pinch against my skin is the drag of his teeth. The feel of the nylon strap against my waist is his hands pinning me down as his tongue glides up my legs.

I blink back to reality as the car rolls over another bump. "We're soooo past the point of dignity."

When I can make his smirk turn into a full-fledged grin I feel like a master chef successfully cooking deadly puffer fish: turning something that could kill you into something delicious.

"I think we are too," he agrees, scanning my cheeks, my jaw, my lips and then back up to my eyes, making me feel as if I've swallowed a cannonball. We sit in a comfortable silence punctuated by laughter flowing from passing restaurants and our seat belts creaking as we lean further forward in the center of the cab. Two planets slowly drawn into each other's orbit.

If you vomit onto a fire, would it put out the flames? Because in this scenario it does, as Iris, woken up by a wave of hot nausea, violently upchucks into her bag. The heated air building between Bancroft and me turns into regurgitated champagne ash.

13

I arrive at my desk on Monday morning slightly later than usual (9:06 a.m. instead of 8:45 a.m.) to find a pile of contracts from Susie corresponding to the four emails she sent me at 5:30 a.m. and three neon Post-it notes from various marketing assistants with questions about today's meetings. All expected and fairly standard for me to receive within the first six minutes of official office hours. What isn't usual is a gleaming black coffee cup and a grease-spotted brown bag holding a flaky almond crois-sant. I bring the bag to my nose, sniff and sigh as though I'm a mole man and this is my first fresh air in months. Based on the Wilfred's label splayed across the cup, I'm pretty sure who it's from. Twisting the coffee around, my suspicion is confirmed by the note stuck to the back.

"For my Pyg."

Suppressing a smile at him still remembering how I like my coffee after months of barely speaking, I take the note off and sip the deliciously hot liquid, letting it warm me from the inside out against the heavily con-tested office air-conditioning temperature.

My mind slips back to the end of the night, helping

Bancroft bring his sister from the taxi up to his apartment. Iris, despite her state, immediately kicked off her heels and took out her dangling earrings, throwing them down into the bowl on the side table near the door as though she'd done it a million times before.

"Will you be OK from here?" I asked. I would've offered to come in but it felt more of an intimate family moment than one a colleague should be involved with.

"Yeah, I got it." My body tingled as he stared at me a little bit longer than necessary—until he seemed to snap himself out of it, shaking his head and grabbing his phone from his pocket. "Let me get you a car."

"It's OK, focus on your sister. I'll be fine." I gave a tight, closed-mouth smile, which he briefly returned before jumping to help Iris untangle herself from her cross-body handbag strap.

Before I left, I stood in the doorway for a few moments and watched them transform into two kids looking out for each other because no one else will. A trust fund won't help you get home safe and make sure you drink a glass of water before you go to sleep. I thought about them the whole way home, zoning out from the falsely marked *URGENT* emails I'd received from Susie over the evening. The only thing that broke my hazy post-adrenaline comedown was the reply from William.

I've just started a new job and bought a stunning three-bed out west x

My brow furrowed at the message; did I even ask how he was doing? Or did he just offer up this information with no prompt to show off how well things are going for him? I decided to do the same.

That's great. I've been doing great too. I'm up for a big promotion.

To my surprise, this time William replied almost instantly.

Cool, still at the dating app? x

My curved lips faltered as I fought the urge to over-examine every word. *The dating app.* That's what he used to call my career, as though acknowledging it properly would turn it from some abstract frivolous concept into something real. Something solid I could use to support myself instead of relying on him.

Yep! I replied, regretting the exclamation point as soon as the blue bubble popped onto the message thread.

Once again, the three "typing" dots appeared within seconds. My chest tightened; why did this rapid back and forth feel somehow more personal than the "wait a few days then reply" tepid exchange I had been assuming this conversation would be? The three dots disappeared and I let out a breath of relief, clicking my phone into darkness.

A few minutes later, my phone dinged again.

I've been doing a lot of thinking lately . . . about how we ended things x

Fuck.

"What's this?" asks Yemi, appearing over my shoulder and breaking me out of replaying the memory again and again. I choke on my coffee midthought and try to catch it with the back of my hand as the hot liquid drips down my chin. Her finger is pressed into the note as though she's putting her entire body weight on the one digit.

In an attempt to act nonchalant, my shoulders shrug apathetically. "It's from Bancroft, just a little inside joke thing," I state, clearing my throat of the remaining latte.

Her eyebrows rise almost to the ceiling. "Oh, we're doing inside jokes with him now, are we?" she asks in a high-pitched voice.

"Barely inside, more like a conservatory, a shed . . . like an indoor-outdoor dining situation." I shift my palm back and forth in the air to emphasize my super-cool casualness.

"Right . . ." Yemi looks unconvinced but continues, "So it would have nothing to do with this?" She holds up her phone screen, an Instagram post from *Societeur Magazine* showing Iris slumped under her brother's arm as he guides her barely conscious form into the back of the cab. The streaks of a flash bulb bounce off the car's black paint. The back of my head is visible in the corner of the screen as I hold the car door open for them both.

"Shit." I grab the phone from her hand and use two fingers to zoom in on Iris's face. Her eyes are half-open and her head lolls to the side; my gut twists at Bancroft's look of concern laced with anger. You can barely tell it's me in the photo with them, the overexposure of the flash making my curly hair look strawberry blonde instead of my actual auburn shade, but the caption still mentions me:

FENDER ON A BENDER: It Girl rockstar nepo baby Iris Fender stumbles out of Matilda's—after allegedly skipping out on her bar tab—with brother Eric Bancroft and his mystery redhead girlfriend!

My whole body goes cold, the taste of coffee turning metallic in my mouth as I scan the caption again and again.

Poor Iris, I hope she hasn't seen this. Having your worst moments publicized for everyone to see must be awful. And is this what women who date Bancroft feel like? No wonder he's practically famous for never being seen with the same person twice; if turning up in paparazzi shots isn't the goal, who would want this? And if someone does want this kind of attention, do they even want *him*? Dating is hard enough without every private moment becoming public.

"So how was the date?" Yemi leans on my desk with a pointed look.

"It was good, thanks, Mum." Yemi rolls her eyes and gives me an exasperated laugh as I clarify, "And how many times do I have to say it wasn't a date?"

"For the mum joke, I'm commandeering half of this." She rips the croissant in two and bites down on her share. "For your date delusions, I'm giving you this." She slaps down a folder of spreadsheets onto the only clear space on my desk.

"Ahhh, is this the ranking of Paul Mescal movies I asked for?" I hold the papers to my chest. "Thank you so much!"

"Paul Mescal?" Yemi says in disbelief.

I shrug in reply, a small smile on my lips silently admitting it *is* ridiculous but refusing to back down.

"It's numbers, smart arse. Numbers that might actually help you with your *not-a-date* project." She says the last part quietly through gritted teeth to stop nearby gossip hounds from picking up a scent.

"Pray tell, O wise one." I lean in eagerly, sipping my coffee.

She looks at me with a coy smile. "You need prepackaged date ideas, so I took the self-reported lifestyle data from the top one percent of our most active users and cross-referenced it with the basic three-point profile info to create a tight dataset for you to pull from."

Scrunching my eyebrows, I ask, "In non-computer-genius language, please?"

Yemi scoffs a laugh and crosses her arms. "I made a list of serial-daters in the city and their favorite hobbies for you to use in your presentation." She glances around, then she leans in and whispers, "I also got an intern at Ignite to send me their data too."

"Oh my God!" I gush, wide-eyed, flicking through the pages. "This is amazing, thank you so much!" I push the remaining half of my croissant across the desk, shaking my head in awe. "You deserve the whole thing."

Yemi let out another mouth-full laugh. "I do."

"I've needed something to give me a leg-up against Bancroft's Black Book of Bigwigs, and this is perfect. You, my friend, are spectacular and I owe you massively."

"Keep regifting me your expensive 'inside-joke' pastries and we'll call it even."

"If I win this promotion, I will buy you Ladurée every day," I promise, crossing a finger over my heart to seal the vow.

"*When* you win this promotion, you will buy me Ladurée pastries *and* fancy coffee every day." My cheeks turn pink at the idea as she saunters back to her side of the office.

I eagerly scan the information on the pages. This is perfect. There's no way Bancroft would think to attain this sort of ammo. My smugness is briefly nicked at the edges by an aching chest. I want to beat the Bancroft that drives me insane at work, but do I want to destroy the Bancroft I saw on Saturday night? The funny, caring and protective Bancroft? No, I just need to get him off my mind completely. Even with this new data, I need every leg up I can get. Maybe the deal Bancroft suggested at the pottery class, about me getting real date experience, is the best way to get both versions of him out of my head. With a lump in my throat and the feeling of regret already gathering momentum in my mind, I download Ignite.

Making my profile is a lot quicker than my experience with Fate. Ignite asks very little about you, but is incredibly interested in getting you to upload as many photos as possible. I guess Ignite users like to know everything about their matches except what they are actually like.

I upload some recent photos, mostly of me at work events, hoping no one looks close enough to notice a rival dating app's branding in the background to most of the images. The choice to add very little to my bio was partially made out of spite for the brand ethos, but mostly because I wanted to get in and out of this world as quickly as possible. If my world at Fate is fluffy cotton candy clouds in the sky, Ignite is an oil-slick puddle glinting in city streetlights. I hold my breath and click through to complete my profile.

Susie's muffled voice leaks from behind the door: "I don't care what the board wants, this is my company, Martin, not yours." She sounds angry but leaning back in my chair I can see through the glass walls of her office that her eyes are red and prickling with unshed tears.

She purses her lips as she listens to the person on the other end of the line. "If you do that, you'll be hearing from my lawyer." She hangs up and flattens her hair behind her ears.

My head turns back to my desk as I hear her office door click open.

"I assume you received my emails, since your phone is permanently glued to your hand?"

I let out a nervous laugh, holding my immediate response of "It's glued to my hand because you glued it there," instead opting for "Yes, I was just about to reply to them. Sorry I had some . . . um . . . personal things come up." I fiddle with my fingers, debating whether to ask: "Are—are you OK?"

She looks at me; her eyes flicker with some semblance of the Susie who pulled me from obscurity years ago. She blinks, wiping the slate clean of her old self. "Well, since you're here now I presume they've been dealt with?" Her perfectly drawn eyebrows arch to her hairline.

"Mmm-hmm." I nod, straightening my posture.

"Great." She scrunches her nose and gives me a wide toothy smile. "I need everything on my desk by EOD."

She's one of those people who like to abbreviate when speaking even if the abbreviation takes the same amount of time as the actual words.

"Not a problem," I declare through gritted teeth, turning my squeaky chair back toward my computer. Susie stands over my shoulder and glares at the screen for a few seconds, before pressing a long finger on a folder marked EVER AFTER 2.0.

"What is this doing on your work computer?" she asks pointedly.

"Oh, that?" I laugh nervously, clicking her email open to distract her.

"I told you to stop working on that project." She crosses her arms tightly across her chest.

"Well, after you said it wasn't the right fit for Fate I may have started developing the idea a bit more when I've had time. And maybe I could repitch to you at some point?" I close my eyes, immediately regretting my words.

She sighs again, holding the bridge of her nose as though this conversation is another ink blot on her day. "As I've said before, pitching new apps and high-concept ideas . . . it's just a little bit out of your depth, don't you think?"

My stomach drops three floors. "Well, I—"

"That's more for someone in a *senior* position to be concerning themselves with, no?" She blinks. My skin crawls, trying to come up with an answer that isn't throwing the lamp on my desk against the wall.

"I guess, it's because . . ." I swallow. ". . . you once told me I should be working for the job I want, not the one I have. I thought bringing new ideas was part of that." The repressed rage turns liquid behind my eyes. *Do not cry.*

"Yes, but only if the ideas are good."

My stomach drops another flight, the coffee immediately souring as I wring my hands together under the desk.

"Right." I mindlessly nod, eyes going in and out of focus like a broken camera lens.

"Please take it off your company computer, immediately. And don't bring it up again." Susie's lips curve into a sweet smile. "How about you carry on with the things that you were actually hired to do, like doing that expansion report for me?"

"OK."

She turns to leave as I start blinking furiously. "Darling, one more thing?"

"Yes?"

"I need you to stay to supervise the intern packing up the influencer gift boxes tonight—I don't trust anyone else to do it correctly." She scans me up and down again, sucking her teeth. "Do you think you'll be able to manage that?"

14

"What are you doing, Hastings?" Bancroft looms in the merchandise cupboard's doorway, the light from the main office oozing around his angles and trickling into the room.

"Considering strangling myself with a tote bag," I reply from the floor, scanning over the piles of Fate-branded reusable coffee cups, T-shirts, giant foam fingers, baseball caps and fabric totes littered in a circle around me. "How is Iris? I saw the *Societeur* post."

He clears his throat and stares at the paraphernalia scattered around me. "She's OK. How did you like your fifteen seconds of fame?" His blue eyes lance into me.

"Loved it. The back of my head has already been offered a laxative-tea sponsorship."

He huffs a laugh and crosses his arms. "Don't the interns usually handle this sort of thing?"

I tuck a stray hair behind my ear and sigh. "I sent her home thirty minutes ago, I felt bad that this was taking so long." My eyes travel up his body until they meet his face. "What's your excuse for being here so late?"

"Struggling to write the evaluation form for Saturday.

How does one sum up molding half a vase then having to track down your sister while avoiding predatory bar managers and obsessive photographers?"

"Ah. Maybe start with some light commentary on how once you touch wet clay it gets literally everywhere. I found a smear on the sole of my foot yesterday morning, and I was wearing shoes the entire time!"

He laughs and squats down in front of me, the fractured overhead lighting dividing his face into sharp angles. He picks up a baseball cap, inspecting its logo embroidery, and then flops it back onto the pile.

His bemused blue eyes flick up to meet me. "Need some help?"

"I can't subject you to this—it's going to take hours."

"Well, I kind of owe you one and I need to run some Ditto project stuff by you anyway, so I might as well help with whatever it is you've got going on here."

I shake my head. "You don't owe me anything. Seriously, it's fine. I don't want you to suffer too."

He tilts his head and smirks at me. "If I tell you a secret will you let me help you?"

He must be desperate to talk about his plans. My eyebrow crease deepens. "You're really keen to sit on the hard floor with the weird lighting that makes you go cross-eyed and pack boxes of merchandise with me?"

He takes my question as acceptance of the deal. "My parents used to travel a lot for work, and when I was eleven they sent me to boarding school in Hampshire . . . to provide me with 'childhood stability,'" he says with finger-quotes. "For a while I was the only new kid, so naturally I was the bottom of the pecking order and became the resident punching bag for the other kids in my dormitory."

Continuing to pack while he talks, I add, "I'm finding it hard to imagine you being bullied. You seem unbullyable."

"Then hopefully you can't imagine me with a bowl cut and adolescent acne either."

I snort a laugh. "Oh, *for that* I can certainly try my best."

He picks up and throws a trash bag of foam fingers at me. "Can I finish my story?"

I smile and nod as he continues, "The only coping mechanism I had was organizing the suitcase full of things I was allowed to bring with me. I would alphabetize my books, trading cards, organize and reorganize my clothes in this tiny little half wardrobe. Or pack everything neatly away in my suitcase and pretend I was going home for the weekend like the other kids. Then I found a book in the library about laundry and folding clothes and spent *hours* folding and refolding my school shirts until they were perfect."

"Are you still like that now?" I ask, and then immediately cringe at all the times I made my desk messy deliberately when he's around because I enjoyed the pained expression it brought to his face.

He wrings his hands between his legs, twisting the ring on his finger. "It's definitely not as bad now. One

157

of my teachers saw me obsessively counting in class and reported it to my parents. They made me see a child psychiatrist, which I guess . . . helped."

"Did they ever ask you *why* you were doing it?"

"I don't think they cared that it was a coping mechanism."

"So when did it stop being so intense?"

"When I started punching back." He huffs as though it's a joke but I don't laugh. The furrow of my brow deepens.

"How long did that take?"

"Two years." He sighs. "Until I broke someone's nose and got kicked out. My mum brought me out to New York to stay with her there."

"That's how you got that scar," I say, glancing at his hand, remembering how he glossed over it when I asked. "Why didn't you just tell me?" I hurl the trash bag back at him and it crumples as he catches it midair.

He smiles that same smile he gave me in the cab. "Your treehouse story was just so cute, with your parents and the fairy picnics, it wasn't the right time for a villain origin story."

I smile back grudgingly.

"So, will you let me help you?"

"I guess with your expert knowledge we can get this done a lot faster." My lips curve and I point to several piles of custom T-shirts, phone cases and cup holders. "These, these and these need to be in those boxes."

He grunts as he squeezes down next to me and crosses

his legs, our knees just touching in the small room. We work in tandem, neatly arranging the packages like a military-powered pink and green Santa's workshop as he explains his potential brand partnership lead with a cool hotel chain and how he thinks it could play out.

After a few minutes I freeze. "Shit, the tissue paper."

"What tissue paper?"

"We have to top them off with Fate tissue paper."

"Why?"

"You know"—I flap my arms—"for the grand reveal!"

He stares at me, trying to contain a smile. "The grand reveal?"

"If you can just see the gift, what's the point? It's all about the mystery and then the reveal. It's about the slow build of intrigue, the tension!"

He laughs. "OK, you've sold it to me! No wonder you work in marketing." I try my best to avoid blushing. "So where is the tissue paper?"

My neck cranes as I stare at the top of the silver industrial shelving unit. "In a box up there."

He stands up, wiping his hands on his trousers to smooth them down. He assesses the shelf, towering over even his tall frame.

"Let's hope it's bolted to the wall," he says, straining as he grabs the edges of the top shelf and pulls himself up. "Which box is it?"

"Ummm, a little brown square container?"

"You're describing a small cardboard box in a sea of small cardboard boxes." He jumps down with a thud, his hair now so out of place I want to run my hands through to fix it. I want to smooth each strand down, and rake it so that it frames his face.

"You know what, they'll be fine without it," I say breathlessly, my voice barely above a whisper.

Hands on his hips and slightly out of breath, he raises his eyebrows. "But what about the grand reveal? The mystery? The intrigue?" He throws a hand out at me, eyes wide with a mischievous gleam. "You've sold it to me now. We're finding it. Get up."

"If you can't reach it, I definitely can't."

"Get up!" he repeats, pressing his back against the shelving unit. He squats down a little and then holds out his palms, one placed on top of the other.

"What are you doing?" I ask, arms crossed.

"You'll know it if you see it, right? So let me give you a leg up."

I close the short distance between us and slowly place my hands on his shoulders. The muscles are thicker than I imagined, not that I *imagined* them at all. My heart rate triples as I grip him with my fingers and place a foot in his hands.

"Ready?"

I nod, my lips sealed together in a tight line.

He pushes me up with ease, as I let out a nervous laugh. As the top shelf reaches eye level I lose the ability to process anything in front of me, all my brain power has zeroed in on the tingling sensation of his cheek pressed against the outside of my thigh as he lifts me up higher.

After a few seconds he clears his throat. "Any luck?"

The question snaps the boxes into sharp focus and I spring into action. After rummaging through box after box I finally spot it pressed up against the far wall and throw my arm out like a fishing rod.

His strong hands grip into my calves. "Hastings, if you don't grab it now I am going to drop you."

"I can't reach it." The tip of my middle finger touches the serrated edge as I flick it in an attempt to roll it toward me.

"Hold on." Eric shifts his weight as he grips my foot in one hand and grips the back of my calf with the other. My left leg is still floating in midair as a counterbalance as he pushes me up higher.

I strain as two more fingertips wrap around the box's edge, my calf burning under his touch despite the denim skin barrier.

"Got it! Thank you, God." I shout with glee as I seize the box between my thumb and forefingers, dragging it toward me.

"You're welcome," he says through a slightly labored breath. I can hear his smirk as he starts to lower me down.

Holding the box in one hand, I use the other to hold on to the shelves as he slowly lowers me down; to stabilize me on my descent his hands move slowly up my legs until—

"Shit!" My hand slips from the metal edge and I swing backward and down at the same time, waving my arms around like a cartoon bird learning how to fly. My eyes squeeze close as I drop the box, grabbing at the metal rails for purchase and preparing for injury.

The impact doesn't come. Bancroft drops my leg and catches me with both hands on my waist, effectively slowing me down and keeping me upright. His grip tightens as the soles of my feet hit the floor with a thump.

My clamped eyes eventually open and find him looking down at me. I realize all too suddenly how small the room is, how long we have been in here, and how comfortable we've been in the cramped but somehow cozy space.

"You OK?" he asks, scanning my face.

"Yeah," I reply breathlessly. He swallows hard as his eyes flick to my lips and then back up to my eyes—so fast, I could have imagined it. He breaks our stare and rests his chin on my forehead, sighing—or maybe lightly panting from the effort of lifting and then catching me, I can't tell. I don't pull away because the feeling of warm hands tight on my waist is sending electricity into parts of me I thought previously dead. The bottom of my Frankenstein stomach twists in a way it hasn't done since the night we refuse to acknowledge.

"For someone who basically used to live up a tree you'd think your balance would be better," he says, chest vibrating with each word.

"Just out of practice, I guess." I breathe, only now noticing how my hands grabbed the fabric of his shirt during my rapid descent.

He looks down at me, eyes heavy and face shadowed in the light behind him. The metal shelving creaks as I release my fingers, causing him to straighten. Not knowing where to put my hands, I rest them on his arms, still tense from my fall. The muscles relax, along with his fingers as he exhales, gliding his palms across my waist so delicately my legs turn to liquid. A sliver of memory seeps in between us; his darkening blue eyes flash with it as he draws his lips together and then apart to say something.

The entire metal shelving unit vibrates behind us as his phone, sitting next to a box of Fate-branded bright pink sunglasses, starts ringing. We jolt out of the moment, retreating across to opposite sides of the tiny room as my face burns red hot. A quick glance at the phone shows *Mum* on the screen. I pretend not to have seen it and stretch my arm out to pass the handset to him.

His shoulders tense when he realizes who is calling. "I should take this," he whispers, his chest still heaving.

"Mmm-hmm." I nod, smoothing down my shirt and unable to look him in the eye.

"I'm going to be away for a few days," he adds over his shoulder.

I stare intently at the piles of nearly finished boxes scattered on the floor, resisting a glance up at him. "Cool, good."

No, not good. Why did I say that?

"Yes, *grud*," he says in a slight trance as he swings open the door, the fluorescent light streaming in from the outer office. The warmth his gentle tease gives me is immediately dampened by the realization that he thinks I am happy he'll be gone for a few days.

By the time I get home, it's nearly 10 p.m. In between having a quick five-minute "power cry" in the toilets after Susie's flippant dismissal of my Ever After idea, marketing team meetings and running around the city to find a pop-up Lebanese restaurant for Susie's lunch, my own work didn't start until 5 p.m. Then, of course, I had to fill the boxes. Thankfully, Alice had a glass of our favorite rosé, the one we refer to as "the chicken wine" because of the drawing on the label and our lack of French pronunciation skills, waiting for me as I walked through the door.

We lounge on the sofa, bitching about our bosses for an hour before I'm tipsy enough to admit I had joined Ignite this morning but am too chicken to start swiping.

"You've got to be kidding. You swore on your pink suit trousers that you would *never* join a dating app like Ignite, no matter how dire things got."

I put my hand over my face, hiding my blushing cheeks.

"I knooowwww," I drag out, "but I have to find a *real* date or I'm going to be so underprepared for my presentation. It's in three weeks—I need to do field-work!" I laugh, realizing how ridiculous it sounds. "But I can't bring myself to look at the profiles yet."

Alice gives me a scrupulous look, holding out her palm. "Hand it over."

I roll my eyes like an inconvenienced teenager and slap my phone into her enthusiastic little hands. I wonder if Bancroft is this reluctant to create a profile on Fate. At least I can hold this over him if he doesn't hold up his end of our bargain. My mind slips back to that look on his face. The same look he had at the Christmas party.

"Hmmmm, let's see," Alice narrates to herself with a singsong voice, pursing her lips as if she's perusing a restaurant menu. "What about this guy? He's cute."

She holds the phone to me like a waiter displaying a bottle of wine, flicking through the photos with a manicured finger.

I wiggle my hand around like a fish out of water. "Would be OK if his first photo wasn't him with a giant bottle of Grey Goose."

With a shrug she flicks to the next profile. "Wait." Alice scrunches her face at the screen. "Is this your ex-boyfriend?"

She rotates the phone and the world turns in slow motion as my eyes land on the very familiar face. The face whose text messages I can't escape.

The words ring in my mind as a heavy, sticky rage clings to my chest. I flick through the profile; most of the images I've seen before on his Instagram. Him at a football game with his mates, at a fancy restaurant, topless on a recent holiday, but one makes me stop in my tracks.

"That's my dog," I say to the picture.

"What? You don't have a dog," Alice says.

I look up from the screen. "No, sorry. I mean that's my family's dog."

"Awww, cute. What's his name?"

"His name was Archie, but he died years ago. Why would William be using a photo of him and my dog?"

I remember it so clearly. I took the photo of him and my family's honey-gold cocker spaniel on a beach holiday when we were celebrating our one-year anniversary. It was freezing cold but we wanted to watch the sunset over the sea. The taste of salty air and Bailey's hot chocolate dances across my tongue for the briefest moment.

"It's such a weird picture to dig up and use after getting out of a long-term relationship." I take a screenshot of it before Alice pulls the phone away from me.

"This is an ex-boyfriend-free zone," she says sternly, replacing the phone with my glass of chicken wine.

I fake a laugh, my suspicion lingering like a bad smell. Hoping to drown out the intrusive thoughts.

"OK, NEXT!" Alice bellows toward the ceiling. "What about this guy: *Active, determined, adventurous, excitable, usually hungry.*"

I narrow my eyes. "That's literally just a list of adjectives."

Alice lets out a breath and rolls her eyes, shouting at his photo, "You're right, and we're not here to read!" and swiping left on the profile. "Oooooh, OK, this one is interesting: *Jack. Twenty-seven. Aficionado of comfortable bar seats, love hearing what other people are obsessed with and spending more time in pajamas than a suit.*" She looks up at me with hopeful eyes. "That's kind of you, babe. And look, he has a cute dog! Who is probably alive!"

She shows me his profile; he's certainly attractive. Dark, curly hair with olive skin and a well-maintained beard.

"OK fine, he seems nice. Yes, to him."

Alice swipes right and my phone immediately pings: *Grace and Jack, it's a match!*

"Finally!" Alice lets out a sigh of relief and triumphantly digs into the next profile. "OK, with this one, hear me out . . . *Student by day, DJ by night—*"

"Aaaaaaabsolutely not!"

"He's hot!"

"No offence, but in hindsight, I don't think you're the most equipped to be swiping on *men.*"

She gasps in feigned outrage. "Who told you?"

We cackle in unison as she starts speed-swiping through more profiles. "Listen, just because I date women doesn't mean I can't appreciate a good-looking man . . . like this one . . ."

She tries to hide a fiendish smile as she reveals the phone screen.

"Oh my God, I can't escape you," I say to a picture of Eric Bancroft's face.

I have to admit it's a good photo, one I've not seen before. He's dressed in a sharp black blazer with an undone white shirt underneath, sitting at a table covered in dinner candles and half-full wine glasses. He's laughing and looking at someone across the table just out of frame; his genuine smile gives me a low ache in my stomach, which I quickly suppress, distracted by the fingers wrapped around one of his arms. The person is cut out of the picture, but the slender digits and pointed red nails are enough. Is that Margeaux Bardin, or someone else?

Alice notices my fixation on the image and starts reading from his profile. "*Eric Bancroft, thirty years old, Marketing Manager at Ignite. Please don't ask me to rate your profile.*"

I flop back against the cushions. "Urgh . . . see? He doesn't have to try at all yet still has a constant stream of women lined up to date him. This app is nothing but a parade of beautiful people trying to shag each other."

"Are you saying you think he's beautiful? I think that deserves a swipe to the . . . right!" Alice flamboyantly drags her finger across the screen before my wine-blurred mind can process what she's doing.

"No no no no no no no!" I yank the phone out of her hand and stare down with wide eyes at the screen. "Fuuuuuck!"

"Why was he even on there? You live on opposite sides of the city!" Alice laughs in disbelief.

I shake my head. "I created my profile in the office this morning so it must have picked up our proximity earlier and—" My panicked explanation is cut short by a pinging sound; I watch open-mouthed as an animation appears on the screen.

Grace and Eric, it's a match!

Bancroft's and my smiling faces gaze up at me, surrounded by fire emojis. *Shit shit shit.* My whole body floods with sweat, as though the flames from the phone are real.

"Wait, it's a match? So, he already swiped right on you too?" Alice doesn't even try to hide her excitement.

I beg the app to reverse the decision, but I know it's pointless. He will have received the fiery notification too. A second, different pinging sound emerges from my phone.

Message from William:

I know my text probably seemed out of the blue, but could we meet up to chat about us? I can't stop thinking about you. I want to talk about giving things another try x

I launch my phone to the other side of the sofa as if it's actually on fire.

15

It's been four days, ninety-six excruciating hours of waiting for a message, a taunt, a plane leaving writing in the sweltering sky above my flat acknowledging that Bancroft and I swiped right on each other. Well, technically *Alice* swiped right on him but I seriously doubt he also has a lesbian flatmate slash dating surrogate looking for potential matches on his behalf.

In his defence, Bancroft's communication with everyone has been limited since he said he was going away. I heard that he hasn't been in the office for a couple of days. Apart from the Google Calendar confirmation of another trial date tonight he's been completely MIA. And after that weird moment in the merchandise cupboard followed by an Ignite match I certainly was not going to be the first one to reach out. I just hope he doesn't stand me up on a date *he* planned.

Twiddling my thumbs across my phone screen, I wait for him next to a lush green public park and listen to the birds singing at the oncoming orange sunset. After enjoying nature for about thirty seconds, I flick to my notes app and run through my "long-term tasks" to-do list:

- *Ditto outreach.*

I have a couple more ideas to make my presentation shine.

- *Refine Ever After concept.*

Despite Susie rejecting my idea I just can't stop thinking about it.

- *Find a therapist.*

Once I deal with the whole can-barely-make-rent-on-current-salary thing.

When Bancroft finally arrives, he looks preoccupied. The evening sun bounces off his light stubble, which looks a couple of days old. Not that I'm keeping track of his facial hair, or his face in general.

"Everything OK?" I ask as our shoes crunch against beige gravel.

We pace slowly outside a huge white building with columns and arches making up the facade. A world away from the last two places we visited. This place looks gladiatorial, but we're walking into battle together while being on completely opposite pages.

"Yeah, yeah . . ." He trails off, scratching the back of his wavy hair. I squint, trying to see the truth in his face but he averts his gaze. "Let's go in."

He walks up the stone stairs to the entrance of a stark white room flooded with fake natural lighting. He takes in another deep breath and rolls his shoulders back. I watch as the shiny veneer he wears at work washes over him, and just like that any hint of vulnerability is gone. Pushed back down into the depths where he keeps it, a sunken treasure chest crushed down by the pressure of a vast ocean.

"Mr. Bancroft?" asks a tall, thin woman with square glasses and a slicked-back dark ponytail that makes her look like an expensive sparrow. "And this is your girlfriend?"

"Colleague!" he almost shouts. He clears his throat and shakes her hand, transforming into his usual suave self. "This is my colleague, Grace Hastings."

The woman turns her attention to me and holds out her jewel-adorned hand. "I'm Valentina. Welcome to Calico Gallery. So nice to meet you."

"Thank you. Nice to meet you too." I smile graciously and take her hand. I'm sure I've seen an influencer wear that gold bracelet before, and I'm also sure it costs around £15,000.

My unmanicured, un-bejewelled hands feel naked in comparison. This is Bancroft's world, not mine. His pristine navy-blue suit, caramel-brown silk tie and perfectly tousled hair give him the air of effortless belonging that I could never even dream of.

"Thank you for taking the time to meet with us after hours, I know how busy you are." Bancroft shoots her a dulled version of his schmoozing megawatt smile.

"Oh, it's no trouble." Valentina waves away the notion with her fifteen-grand hand, not noticing the lack of feeling behind his words. "Your mother is a generous patron; we always have time for the Bancrofts."

I cut a sideways glance at him, catching his jaw tighten and release.

"We appreciate it," he says, quickly changing the subject. "The gallery space is amazing. You have multiple shows running at the moment?"

"Yes, isn't it fabulous?" she gushes. "Your users are going to *adore* our latest exhibition."

She places her hand on his forearm and laughs. I'm oddly satisfied when he doesn't respond to the touch, instead giving her a tight, closed-mouth smile.

"I'm sure they will."

"Well," she sighs out contentedly, clapping her hands together. "You're right on time for this evening's showing! If you'd like to join the group, our tour guide will take you through the exhibition, finishing in our bar with curated cocktails inspired by the works."

I smile enthusiastically at her, feeling kind of bad she isn't receiving the famous Bancroft charm.

"Thank you." With a polite nod and smile he strides toward the group of a dozen art enthusiasts.

Trailing a few paces behind, I debate whether to start a conversation with him. He seems to be more interested in headbutting the wall than talking about whatever's going on with him. Before I'm able to get a word out, we are stopped in our tracks by the huge sign with the words *The Art of Self Love* embossed in neon lights. My fingers shoot accusatorially out toward the sign as if it says *ENTER WITH EXTREME CAUTION IF YOUR NAME IS GRACE HASTINGS.*

"Is . . . this . . . what we're seeing?"

He doesn't meet my panicky eyes. "Yep, it's their sold-out exhibition," he says in a stony voice while reaching for a glass of wine left out for guests. "Ditto users will have exclusive access to the most sought-after ticket of the year."

The chasm inside my stomach is briefly filled by warm, gooey admiration.

"That's an amazing perk for the users . . . And your mum got you in?" His brief, proud smile is quickly covered by the sullen look from earlier. I hold both my hands up to the optical firing squad aiming right for me. "Hey, I would use those kinds of contacts if I had them."

"Yeah . . . well, her social prowess is about the only benefit to having her as a mother, so . . ."

My eyebrows meet in the middle as I open my mouth in question but am immediately distracted as we turn the corner into the exhibition. Heat rises up my neck straight to my cheeks as I stand frozen at the entrance. Confidently striding forward to meet the rest of the group, Bancroft looks to his side, stops and turns around to find me standing still, taking it all in. The white room is filled to the brim with wall installations, statues on plinths and sculptures winding their way around the room. My eyes flit from a black and white photograph of a naked woman looking at her genitals in a handheld mirror, to a giant inflatable penis hanging from the ceiling with words like "inadequate" and "be a man" graffitied on it in black Sharpie, to a marble sculpture of a woman in a floral dress hugging a young girl in the same dress.

His hard face softens at the sight of me, his lips twisting into his infamous smirk. "You OK there, Hastings?"

"Fine!" Straightening my shoulders, I stomp into the room, trying to avert my gaze from the wall of clay vagina molds.

I grab a glass of wine from a marble plinth by the entrance and down it. We join the dozen people gathering around the tour guide who introduces us to the exhibition.

"Self-love is the first step in giving love out into the world. To love oneself is to see our true selves and not shy away or criticize. To look into the void through the lens of acceptance. We asked some of our favorite artists-in-residence and a few up-and-coming creatives to show us their version of self-love and self-expression. Some physical, some psychological and some metaphorical: we hope each piece brings you closer to their vision of vulnerability and internal acceptance."

We split up, wandering the exhibition on separate sides of the room. I can't help being aware of where Bancroft is at all times. It felt as if after that moment in the merchandise cupboard something had shifted between us, but now I'm second-guessing myself. A series of twelve self-portraits catches my eye. They span an entire wall, a spectrum of black and white flowing into bright bursts of color. The title card says the artist painted one every month after getting out of a toxic relationship. I stare at the first one, seeing something of myself in those eyes, wondering if this is what I looked like? It's certainly how I felt: a numbness and heaviness that felt almost ironic considering I'd had something ripped from me so harshly. The text messages I sent William after he dumped me ring in my mind like a sad, desperate song. Acutely aware of Bancroft's presence pacing closer, I blink the glaze from my eyes and cross my arms.

"I like this one." I nod my chin to the seventh painting in the series. Colors bursting out of the bleak contrast in wide brush strokes like flowers blooming in fast motion.

"Hmmm," he replies emptily, his mind clearly back to whatever has been bothering him.

I want to stomp my feet and smash through the awkwardness like an angry kid bashing through a Jenga tower, but settle for a softer approach. "Is your sister doing OK?"

He studies the matte white heart pattern painted across the shiny parquet wood floor.

"She was kinda shook up by the whole thing." He pauses for a moment. "And *very* hungover . . . but I'd choose her vomiting into my ficus plant over her being sat in a jail cell."

We both let out shaky laughter. His shoulders release some of their tension like a geyser letting off steam, instantly relaxing me by osmosis. I briefly hate myself for letting his mood affect mine so easily, resenting how connected I feel to his well-being. He turns to face me, meeting my eyes fully for the first time this evening. "Thank you again, by the way. For your help. It was . . . nice not to do that alone."

"No problem," I mumble as we move to the next painting, inching closer together, adding a cushion to this lumpy sofa of a conversation. My body braces as I ask, "Do you think your mother will change her mind about cutting Iris off?"

He downs the remaining wine and places the empty glass on the tray of a passing waiter with a nod; then he puts his hands in his navy cotton pockets and studies the floor once again.

"Hopefully, it's been dealt with."

He's tensing more with each question but I push on. "Is that where you've been the past few days?"

He sighs a reluctant surrender as if he knows that now I've made a dent in him I won't stop until I've hit gold.

"Yes. My mother has been in the country for the week and I had to go and convince her to restore Iris's bank account, so she doesn't end up moving in with her shitty friends."

I resist expressing an opinion on what kind of mother would put their children through that, instead settling on a more tame question: "Why does she do it?"

"I think it's her latest husband; he's a banker in Dubai and has been talking to her about cutting Iris off for good. Our mother is more concerned about the headlines involving us than what's actually going on in our lives."

It's hard to feel pity for someone with a trust fund, but I can't help but feel sorry for them both after seeing how bad Iris's situation was the other night. It's as if she never had a chance to become a fully functioning adult, since she is always surrounded by people who take advantage of her.

"Could Iris live with you?" I tilt my chin up toward him.

"She's staying with me for a few weeks but she doesn't want to be 'babied.' She's trying really hard to work things out on her own, to not have to rely on our mother anymore. But it's hard not to still see her as a kid that needs looking after, especially with friends like *that*."

After some late-night googling I already know the answer to the question I'm about to ask. Iris's father is Lars Fender, a famous rockstar and lead singer of The Shags. A band that was huge in the nineties but has since been better known for their wild antics than their music.

"Is her dad around much?"

"Iris's dad is always on tour. He's fine but not exactly the strong, stable parental figure she needed growing up, or now. When she was younger our mum didn't like her going out on the road with him, but she also didn't pay any attention to Iris when she was at home. So, it was mostly me and a series of nameless nannies looking after her."

I don't know what to say so I choose silence. That's a lie—I know what I want to say. The question that's been eating at me since the night of the pottery class.

"How come you don't mention her often?"

Why did you never tell me anything about her? About your family?

A muscle in his cheek twitches as he gives a light shrug. He runs a hand over his face before answering, "I love Rissy, but I don't like to shout she's my sister from the rooftops. She already has her own shit to deal with. She doesn't need mine as well. Most of the time I don't feel like explaining all the family drama. A few people know but it's not common knowledge. It's almost the only part of my life I've been able to keep private."

The thought that he didn't feel close enough to me to mention Iris leaves a crater-size hole in my gut.

He shifts under my gaze and I realize I'm not hiding my thoughts well.

Bancroft continues, "Our mother and Lars were a whirlwind relationship while my parents were still married. So when my mother found out she was pregnant she disappeared for a while to have Iris. Thankfully the press never really caught on." He lets out a dead laugh. "I guess that's a silver lining of never being actively involved in our childhoods."

We move so that we are standing in front of a minuscule phallic statue draped in clear cellophane with a placard about size not mattering.

"And *your* dad?" I ask, wide-eyed.

He laughs but it doesn't reach his eyes. "What about him?"

I'm a lion tamer creeping around the ring, waiting for the clawed swipe. "What's . . . he like?"

He cuts me a sideways, narrow-eyed glance. "If you've read a magazine in the last twenty years you know what he's like."

"I've read some *stuff*." I draw the words out; the headlines were always something along the lines of: "Architectural Tycoon Malon Bancroft breaks ground on new skyscrapers and a new wife." "But what is he really *like*, you know, as a dad?"

He cringes. "Imagine Lex Luther as a father and go from there."

I don't laugh at the image, just expressionlessly hold his gaze until the Fabergé egg cracks open.

"I'm not a reporter. You can trust me," I say, less confirming and more reminding him of the obvious. "You can pat me down for a wire if you want," I offer with dead seriousness, trying to lighten his mood the only way I know how.

Bancroft smirks, amusement finally reaching his eyes. "Hastings, we're in public."

He eventually relents with a sigh. "As you probably already know, my dad has a reputation for getting around. When I was growing up my parents tried so hard to put on this facade of a perfect, family-run business, but they were barely living in the same house. My mother was my dad's secretary, their relationship started as an affair, so I don't know why, even after fifteen years together, she expected it to end any differently."

I start to ask another question but he turns the

spotlight onto me. "What about your parents—what are they like?"

I push my hair back and prepare to tell my rehearsed story. "They met in a pub on Christmas Eve. They were both from out of town but happened to be in the same place at the same time. They saw each other from across the room and it was instant, love at first sight." I shrug my shoulders and look up to the ceiling as though Cupid is sitting there on a little cloud, ready to corroborate my story.

He tilts his head to me with a smirk. "This is *very* on brand for you."

I respond with a sarcastic smile, choosing to ignore his completely correct comment and continue. Since I could comprehend full sentences, the story of how my parents met and fell in love has been told to me at least three times a year. When I moved away for university and then for work, if I ever wanted to put people in a feel-good mood I told my parents' story. It's my go-to real-life fairy tale, drilled into my head as the standard I should hold any relationship to. It might be cliché, but sharing the story makes me feel as if I'm slipping into fresh bedsheets. Familiar but somehow indulgent.

"They shared a kiss, but my mum's friends dragged her out of the pub soon after—they didn't even know each other's names! The next year, he returned to the same pub with a secret hope of seeing her again. She was there, but she told him she now had a boy-friend. They talked all night, and danced, but nothing happened. Then the same thing the next year. That time, she was single, and he wasn't. This happened again and again, over the course of *five years*. Each time something was in the way. Dad says he started imagining he'd seen her on the street, at the supermarket, at work; like he was going insane, but he knew it meant she was The One. By the sixth year, he'd decided enough was enough. He had a lot of liquid courage and confessed that one night a year with her felt better than three hundred and sixty-four days with anyone else. From that day, they never spent more than a week apart." I take a breath, preparing for the big finish. "The pub where they kept meeting was known locally as the Grace."

I wait for the usual reaction of swooning over my story. Instead, Bancroft scans me up and down, a robot analyzing how and why humans feel emotion.

"Cute," he says simply.

I purse my lips, feeling my cheeks prickle. "I wouldn't call destiny 'cute.' "

"That's not destiny." He turns nonchalantly to inspect the next piece of art.

"Then what is it?" I demand, glare fixed on the light bouncing off his cheekbone.

"Two people who decided to leave it up to 'the universe' and be apart for five years instead of just admitting their feelings to begin with." His gaze remains fixed on the oil painting in front of him.

"There were, like, hardly any phones back then. It's epic and romantic!" I exclaim with a scoff.

"It's naive," he concludes, moving to the next piece.

I follow him, mouth open in disbelief. "You're saying you wouldn't wait five years for the love of your life?"

His jaw flexes as he goes to say something but stops himself, considers, and then says, "I would wait as long as it takes, but I'd still be a fool for putting myself through that kind of torture. I don't enjoy waiting for something I want."

"So, you're just impatient," I surmise flippantly, overtaking him across the floor.

"It's not impatience. It's practicality. If the opportunity arrives and you don't take it, you could lose it. Gambling with that is risky." He meets my eye. "Waiting for the stars to align perfectly could leave you with nothing."

Leaning closer to him until our shoulders brush, I ask, "So you've experienced this sort of thing before?" I cock an eyebrow.

"Something like it." He licks his bottom lip, eyes fixed on an iron statue of two naked bodies entwined. "It didn't work out."

Before I can ask a follow-up question the tour guide encourages us toward the next section of the gallery, which is filled with dramatic sculptures. We rejoin the group and collectively shuffle with them. I pretend to look enthusiastically at the pieces of stone, glass and metal.

"Is that what you had with your ex? A 'grand love story?'" he asks, interrupting my processing of the weird, twisted shapes in front of us.

"I thought so, but then I was unceremoniously, post-ceremoniously dumped." He crinkles his brow in question, so I translate, "He broke up with me at my parents' thirtieth anniversary party."

"Yeah, I heard . . . It was just before Christmas, right?"

The night at the Christmas party and the days that followed fill the space between us.

He clears his throat. "You never actually told me what happened."

It's not quite a question, more of a lingering statement of unfinished business between us. We're playing conversational chicken, daring each other to pull back, to be the first to shy away from the oncoming trucks carrying our emotional loads. I take in his expression, the sharp curve of his tense jaw as he waits to see how much of myself I'm willing to reveal. I take a deep breath, and start speaking.

"He proposed in the middle of my parents' party, in front of a hundred guests, got on the microphone and everything."

The air around us shifts as Bancroft's gaze grows more intense, as though he's trying to make out the blurry memories as they replay in my mind.

"I had just finished the speech I'd been nervous about for days. About my parents, their love for each other and how true love is never really knocked off course." I sigh. "I made people laugh in the right places, tear up a little bit, and I even had a whole slideshow packed with pictures of them from over the years. I was done and everyone was clapping. I felt like I could finally relax and enjoy the party. Only, William caught my hand, taking the mic from me—"

The gallery falls away, and I'm back on the raised platform with everyone staring up at me, smiling, sobbing, clapping. My parents were in the center of the room, wrapped around each other with such happy grins. My dad's expression was filled with pride; my mum was dabbing at her eyes.

"I'm sorry to interrupt, guys," William said with a wide, cheesy grin. "I'm just so happy to be here with you all and celebrating this inspiring occasion. Diane and Emmett, you have what any person wants: a teammate, reliability, someone to come home to after long, hard days at work. I only hope in thirty years' time that I have that with your daughter."

A chorus of empathetic noises echoed around the room as he continues, "Which is why I can't wait any longer."

He sank to one knee and looked up at me with hope shining in his eyes.

"Gracie, will you marry me?"

Every eye in the place was on me, but now waiting with bated breath; the warm atmosphere dissipates. I stood completely still, beetroot-red and wide-eyed. A nervous laugh from somewhere in my throat escaped me, and I pressed a hand to my chest where my heart was thudding so hard it threatened to burst through my rib cage. Before I could even register it happening,

William hugged me and turned my face away from the crowd as the clapping and whoops began, shouting that I said yes.

"Did you?" Bancroft's voice beside me makes me jump; I'd almost forgotten he was there.

"Did I what?"

"Say yes?"

"No!" I say firmly. "There was no ring, no discussion, no planning. He made this huge decision for the both of us in the moment, then held a gun loaded with societal expectation to my head, ensuring I said yes."

Fury wells inside me as I remember how I wanted to leave, to have time to process, to think about my answer. Instead, I got bombarded with more questions. When would we be getting married? Where? What kind of wedding did we want? Could they come to the wedding? I hadn't had time to even think about planning a wedding and all of a sudden I was discussing which of my cousin's children would be my flower girl and what our firstborn son's middle name would be. I couldn't wrap my head around why he had done it there without discussing it with me first, or warning me. He knew I hated surprises, let alone a surprise life-altering decision made in front of my friends and family. A decision that would've ruined my parents' thirtieth anniversary party they'd spent ages planning and spent so much money throwing had I not agreed to it.

"When we got back to my parents' house after the party I confronted him about why he'd done it in such a public way, especially when we'd barely discussed the idea of getting married." I chew my bottom lip. "He got annoyed, completely disregarded my questions and said I'd have time to figure out the wedding and plans for our future myself because now we were engaged I could quit my job and we could start a family."

Bancroft's brow scrunches in disbelief as his head whips to me. "What?"

"That's what I said! He suddenly declared that me 'running around the city playing career woman' was a deal-breaker for him. I don't know how he did it, but he turned the whole thing around on me. When I refused to bend he dumped me and told me to move out of *his* apartment."

It was a flat he'd purchased when we moved to London together but he had always claimed it was mine too. His first job in the city earned him triple my intern salary, but I spent time, energy and the little money I had making it into our home. Then he kicked me out the moment I didn't fit into his plans.

Bancroft's jaw tightens as we drift with the group to the next painting. "How come you didn't tell anyone when you got back to London?"

"Because even just my family knowing what happened was so humiliating. My parents have a beautiful love story and I literally went from engaged one day to single and homeless the next. The break-up was tough enough and I couldn't hide it from people in the office. We work at a company that preaches soulmates and true love; I didn't want people pitying me even more . . . so I just left out the *actual* reason we broke up. I couldn't talk about it. It was too much."

As the truth flies out of my mouth I can't help but feel a burning sensation in my pocket where my phone is sitting. Where William's texts are waiting.

I see the question trying not to leave Bancroft's lips; it's one I've asked myself too many times: *If he'd asked you in private, would you have said yes?*

"I get why you didn't want to tell anyone . . ." Bancroft says instead, stepping in closer and touching my forearm, forcing my eyes up to meet his. ". . . but I need you to know I would never have pitied you. I just . . . didn't realize it was that bad."

He briefly glances back to the art and we move in unison to the next sculpture: a hammered metal sheet turning our reflections into shadowy figures. I shrug, staying put as the rest of the group moves to the next piece of art.

"It's not like you and I were on speaking terms at that point."

Hastings is a clingy psycho . . . not worth going there.

"No, we weren't," he confirms.

I hold my breath, waiting for the air to leave my brain so I'm dumb enough to ask, "What would you have done if we were?"

He huffs an empty laugh and stares at us both reflected in the carved, distorted surface. "Made sure it didn't destroy you the way it did. Protected you from it. Tried my hardest to make sure you didn't fall apart, and if I failed . . . kept the pieces safe until you were strong enough to put yourself back together."

My entire body covers itself with goose bumps like a chameleon trying to blend in with the pointillist painting next to me. Eyes stinging, I turn to face the wall.

A hand lands on my shoulder as he takes a deep breath, the heat from his body radiating through my thin cotton shirt as he comes in closer to whisper, "Grace, I—"

"Everything OK in the back there, folks? You're lagging behind!" The tour guide laughs as the entire group turns around to inspect and glare at the stragglers.

"Uh-huh!" I reply immediately, wiping the moisture from underneath my eyes.

Bancroft's hands slide into his pockets and he takes a half step backward, his head down. "Just so moved . . . by the work!"

I laugh nervously and nod, confirming Bancroft's cover story.

"Oh!" The guide waves a hand and laughs gutturally. "Not the first time—take as long as you need."

"It's fine. I think we've recovered now." Bancroft gives me a tight smile as we follow the group to the next painting.

16

My heels click on the travertine marble floor as I step into the ground-floor lobby. I wave and say "Happy Monday" to Dave the security guard as I head out in the heat to pick up Susie's lunch from the upmarket Asian-fusion restaurant around the corner. I don't particularly enjoy going there, as it reminds me of all the times Bancroft and I used to order takeout during our late nights working together in the office last year.

"If you believe in Fate so much, you should act on whatever the fortune cookie decrees," Bancroft announced one winter's evening after two pints of miso soup and a mountain of dumplings.

"Of course," I agreed. "I would never disrespect cookie law," I said, cracking open the sugar-coated parcel and pulling out the white paper ribbon.

I held it up to read it in the dimmed office light: " 'The usefulness of a cup is in its emptiness.' "

Bancroft nodded and stroked his chin. "You know what, I've always said that."

I laughed. "What does it mean, then?"

"I think it means . . ." He took an old plastic

water-cooler cup from my desk and topped it with a measure of the room temperature vodka, which at this point had become a staple for our after-hours meetings. ". . . you have to clear this cup."

I chugged the contents, shivering from the aftertaste as though a ghost had just paced straight through me, then I placed the cup upside down like a paper crown on my head. "Your turn."

He cracked open his cookie and cleared his throat. "'Follow what calls to you.'"

"Very deep. Pray tell: What calls to you currently?" I leaned forward like a producer interviewing someone for a heart-wrenching documentary.

His eyes twinkled as he considered, smiling to himself as he matched my position. Our faces' proximity made me hesitate but not move away.

"Right now?" he asked, his voice slightly lower than usual.

I held steady, blinking away the flashing vision of him taking my face in his hands and pulling me closer. Did I want that?

With hooded eyes he pointed to the pile of crispy wontons littering my desk. "Mostly those."

I pushed myself back into my chair, letting out a fractured laugh before coming to my senses and shaking off the electric feeling lingering on my skin. *Stop being an idiot.*

"Do you think someone actually writes these?" he asked, mouth half-full of crunchy shrimp.

"I like the idea that there is an old woman in the fortune-cookie factory bestowing the wisdom of her life on humanity," I said wistfully.

"Writing her memoir one vague mass-appealing sentence at a time?" He smirked.

I clicked my fingers at him. "Exactly! Like a commercial Confucius. If we collect every single one, we can line them up and we'll have a new literary classic on our hands."

"Sounds like we'd be doing the world a favor," he agreed.

After that challenge, this became our go-to late-night takeout spot, though we never followed through on collecting the strips of advice from the cookies.

My phone buzzes, pulling me out of the fond memory. I've been avoiding looking at my phone since I finally responded to William's admission when I got home from the gallery:

I don't think meeting up right now is a good idea.

"Grace!" A voice echoes across the space. My head whips around to see a tall, stunning girl leaning by the glass door entrance and waving frantically in my direction. Iris.

Shit, she's most likely here to meet her brother. I haven't prepared myself to see Bancroft so soon after our conversation at Calico. Things felt different after the tour ended. Not bad, but like by becoming more familiar with each other's lives, we were stepping into unfamiliar territory. Glancing at the door as if it's the emergency exit of a plane that's about to start plummeting, my palms begin to sweat.

"Hi, Iris!" I grin involuntarily as she gets closer.

Her ethereal smile is so contagious, I can see why people are obsessed with following her every movement online. She is like a magical party fairy dressed in a deliberately oversize hot pink jumpsuit that looks so good on her stick-thin frame and has blue and green glitter clips in her shiny chestnut hair. Walking over, she embraces me in a tight hug you reserve for loved ones you haven't spoken to in years but are so happy to see. Her warmth is welcoming and invigorating at the same time, like a fire pit at a party everyone unconsciously gravitates toward throughout the night. A stark difference from the helpless girl collapsed across a table at Matilda's.

"How are you doing?" I ask.

She glances down at her boots for a split second then back up to me. "I'm OK." Her electric smile dulls slightly. "I feel bad dragging you guys into my . . ." She waves her hand around flippantly. ". . . stuff."

"That's OK," I assure her, squeezing her arm lightly. "I don't want to sound like a guidance counselor, but you never have to feel bad about needing help."

"I think I just need to start looking for better friends." Her smile lifts. "Like how Eric has you."

I sputter, trying to find the right words: "We're not friends, not exactly, we're colleagues."

"Well, I've never been introduced to *any* of his friends

or . . . 'colleagues.'" She uses her long purple nails to put quotes around the word.

My phone begins to ring in my hand. Even though it's likely Susie asking why her food hasn't magically appeared on her desk by now, I relish the opportunity to get out of this topic of conversation. But when I go to press accept, the name says *William*.

"You can take that if you want, I don't mind." Iris smiles politely, fully intending to carry on this conversation after I'm done.

I let out a nervous laugh, feeling the heat rise to my face. "It's fine." I press reject on the call. "It's just my ex."

Iris's gasp echoes across the marble as I instantly regret my words. Iris has a way of making you feel like the most interesting person in the world, immediately making me loose-lipped.

"No, it's not like that," I clarify. "He just wants to talk."

Iris's already massive saucer eyes widen further. "Oh my God, so exciting!" Passersby in the lobby look over as her reverberating squeal reaches them. "Will you be getting back together?"

"No—I don't know. It's not exciting!" I splutter and shake my head. "It's just texts. It's nothing."

"What's nothing?" asks a smooth, low voice behind me. Ice enters my bloodstream.

"Grace's texting with her ex," Iris immediately confirms over my shoulder to the looming figure. I close my eyes and run my tongue over my teeth, trying my hardest

194

to keep my mouth shut. Rolling back my shoulders I turn around, steeling myself before I acknowledge him.

His hair looks disheveled compared to its usual effortless bounce, but his eyes are still that unnatural blue that laser through my own.

"Helloooo!" I say in a singsong voice that I immediately regret when I see the confused twitch of his eyebrow.

Bancroft's eyes move to my red lips, then flick up to my gaze as he gives me a devastating look of disappointment and asks his sister if she's ready to go. As if he couldn't bear to interact with me at all.

"Yep, bye, Grace!" Iris beams, oblivious to the shovel she just passed to me to dig myself further into a hole. She kisses me on both cheeks. "So lovely to see you. We should grab a coffee soon."

My heart tugs at her genuine sincerity.

Bancroft breezes past me without a second glance and I watch them walk away, reminding me of how different things had become since the first time I saw them together. An ice-cold poker slams through my stomach at the thought of Bancroft and me being thrown back into how we were before the Ditto project began. I wait a cursory thirty seconds before leaving the building, hoping to avoid the pain of a classic goodbye-but-we-need-to-go-in-the-same-direction moment. But I didn't need to worry. As I step out onto the scalding pavement and wander down to the depths of hell to catch a tube, I watch Bancroft open the door of a town car for Iris and close it behind them.

17

Nine Months Ago

EB: Are you free right now?

GH: Just got out of a meeting, what's up?

EB: Meet me at Wilfred's in 15 minutes, I have something incredible to show you.

The bell tinkled as I entered the busy coffee shop, and the sweet smells of vanilla and hazelnut immediately flooded my nostrils. I scanned the crowd, finally landing on Eric, sitting at a table in the corner. He raised his eyebrows and gestured hurriedly for me to sit down.

"What's going on?" I threw my bag down on the spare chair.

He gave me a bemused smirk. "No 'hello'? 'It's been a while'? Nothing?"

"I've only been gone a week." A rare "family" vacation with William and my parents. I'd ended up working most days anyway, much to William's chagrin. I rolled my hands in front of me to hurry things up. "But hi, hello, it's been a while. How are you?"

His smirk grew into something more devious. "Coffee?"

The porcelain saucer ground across the wooden table as he slid it toward me.

"Oh my God, can you just tell me what is going on?" I grabbed the coffee from him, ignoring the spark lancing through my hands as our fingers briefly brushed.

I took a sip; he'd ordered my usual down to a T but I was too frustrated at his teasing to say thank you. Being outside of the office together was strange enough, but not knowing the reason for being here was causing a tingling anxiety in my stomach. Did he need to talk about something that wasn't safe to discuss at work? To tell me something he didn't want anyone overhearing?

After another few seconds of smirking suspiciously, he finally gave in. "OK, look over there, but be subtle . . ." He gestured with his chin at a table behind me.

I spun around and gasped dramatically. A milk frother behind the counter hissed steam, covering the sound.

"Jesus Christ, I said be subtle!" Eric threw a palm over his face.

I placed my fingers on the back of my wooden chair to steady myself as I turned my head back to face him. "I don't have a subtle bone in my body and you know it."

He let out a rare laugh; the sound sent warmth through my chest. "Well grow one, and fast. I'm trying to be incognito."

"But that's Jeffrey," I replied.

"Yes," Eric concurred.

"With a *date*," I said.

"Exactly." Eric took a sip from his mug. "I'm here for her protection."

I scoffed a laugh and then glanced back at the woman sitting opposite Jeffrey. She had a pretty face, a blonde bob and was wearing a simple white cotton shirt and dark blue jeans. She delicately sipped at her paper straw and she seemed to be nodding politely at something Jeffrey was explaining, her expression unreadable.

"I just can't believe someone agreed to a date with him, let alone someone seemingly normal."

Eric lifted his eyebrows in agreement. "He hasn't fully confessed, but I think there was some algorithmic manipulation going on at Ignite for these star-crossed lovers to match."

"Holy shit, that is *really* unethical."

He hummed in agreement. "Hence why I felt the need to be her silent bodyguard."

The sound of a wooden chair scraping across tile pierced the air and I whipped my head around just in time to watch Jeffrey's date throw an iced latte in his face.

The whole room went silent for a few seconds; even the milk frother stopped hissing. The only sound was her shoes clicking against the floor and the ringing of the bell as Jeffrey's date left the building. My mouth agape, I turned back to Eric.

"Well, maybe I didn't need to bother," he said. "She can clearly handle herself."

Jeffrey flicked a soggy paper straw from his soaking wet shoulder and ran a napkin over his face.

"I've never seen that happen in real life," I said, still in shock at the blonde bob's ballsiness.

"You clearly aren't forced to spend time with creepy arseholes."

I settled back into my chair and took another sip of my coffee. "No, just rich bitches like yourself."

He cocked an eyebrow at me. "Enjoying that free latte?"

Our lips curved in unison as we fully locked eyes for the first time in a week. I would never tell him, but he was on the shortlist of people I missed talking to while I was away.

"How was your vacation?" Eric asks.

Our little bubble burst as my mind left Wilfred's and returned to Greece. Less beach and museum tours, which I would have preferred, more of an activity-based holiday followed by dinners with my parents. Early-morning jaunts, pedalos in lakes, climbing one million white stone steps to find the perfect sightseeing spot. William's dream holiday, but not exactly mine.

I lifted my cup to my mouth and shrugged. "It was good, but I had to work a lot."

"Susie gave you vacation work again?" he asked, brow furrowed in annoyance.

"Yeah, but I wanted to use what little time I get off to work on that Ever After idea I told you about."

He nodded as his lips caressed the edge of his coffee cup. He knew how much the opportunity to pitch to Susie meant to me.

"Did they mind that?" he asked, eyes laser-focused on my face.

I knew he didn't mean my parents. For some reason, it felt weird to offload the past week onto Eric. It felt like crossing a line into "confidante" territory. Really, to tell anyone about the series of arguments William and I had had in the confines of our hotel room so my parents weren't witnesses, all stemming from me having to answer emails and take a couple of phone calls when we were all meant to be "out of office," felt like a breach of trust.

Working on personal projects, development that could only be done outside of work, was also completely out of the question. My concept plans for Ever After, a potential in-app feature to retain Fate's user base after they had found love, had been relegated to a pipe dream scribbled in discarded notebooks.

Words William said to me had started echoing in my head since we'd touched back down in London.

"Clearly, you're not good at time management or organization if you can't take a week off work without the place falling apart."

"Yeah, they were fine with it," I lied into my latte, glancing away.

Eric's brow scrunched for a second, scanning his icy eyes over my face like an emotional X-ray. I cleared my throat, quickly changing the subject: "So you haven't been tempted to do some immoral algorithm-twisting like Jeffrey then?"

"I don't need to." He shrugged, following my lead into the new topic.

I scoffed a laugh, holding my hands up defensively. "OK, Mr. GQ, I didn't realize you were in *such* high demand."

I'm lying. I knew he was in high demand. I could see why: his looks were only superseded by his personality. According to my single friends, handsome and funny was a hard combination to find in a city of finance bros and personal trainers with the conversational aptitude of a cardboard box.

He stroked the edge of his mug. "I don't need to . . . because I'm seeing someone."

"Oh . . . ummm . . . congratulations," I said, forcing a tight smile.

Eric smirked and tilted his head to the side, the light bouncing off his cheekbone. "Congratulations? I didn't win a Nobel Peace Prize."

My cheeks flushed as I scrambled for something positive to say. "No . . . I just mean, you know, yay." I waved my hands in celebration, then cleared my throat. "I'm just surprised. I thought you 'didn't date.' " I imitated his low tone. Mockery, yes, that would cover whatever else was going on in my demeanor.

I forced myself to swallow the barrage of questions sitting on my chest. I had absolutely no right to know what she looked like, how they met or if she had any interesting hobbies. I didn't have a right to know anything about his personal life, but it didn't mean the lack of knowing wouldn't eat away at me.

"I guess I'm more nuanced than you thought."

More nuanced for the right woman? I blinked rapidly, refusing to question why I cared.

I pushed my confusing feelings down and settled for leaning into his rumored reputation. "Is she an heiress or model?" My lips curved; this was a comfortable place for us; this was the Venn diagram overlap between sincerity and artifice where our friendship lived.

He huffed a laugh and rolled his eyes. "Fuck off . . ." And he sank into his chair. "Both."

18

EB: *When you're done texting we need to talk through tomorrow's Heimach meeting.*

The message pops up on my screen the literal second my arse hits the chair. Seriously, does he have a tail on me or something? I scan the words three times and blow out an overdramatic breath, rolling my eyes as I push myself away from the desk, pick up my laptop and stride purposefully to the reception of Ignite, face-to-face with Harriet, Mr. Catcher's assistant. Catch Group's CEO likes to have his office next to the Ignite offices to safeguard his flagship app.

She glances up at me and then back to her computer. "Welcome to Ignite. Name, please?"

I study her in silence. "Harriet?"

She looks up again, a smile spreading across her face and pure, unadulterated joy in her voice: "Oh my God, snap! I'm Harriet too."

"No, my name isn't Harriet. It's Grace. From Fate? Grace Hastings?" I clarify.

"Oh, hi, Grace." She looks disappointed to have not met a name twin. "You don't have a meeting, do you?"

"Um, no." I give her a polite smile.

"Then what are you doing here?" She looks down at her keyboard and starts typing, back to being uninterested in our exchange.

I lean on the desk and speak in a hushed voice: "There's a rumor going around the eighth floor that Ignite is run by aliens in human suits. I've been sent to confirm."

She blinks at me, expressionless.

"Never mind. I'm here to see Bancroft. Is His Majesty available?" I ask.

"Right!" She laughs. "Eric is in his office. I'll let him know you're coming."

"Thanks."

She beams. "You're welcome!"

I spin on my heel, opening the door to the main floor before Harriet calls me back.

"Oh, Grace?" I turn around expectantly. "Could you be a doll and give this to Jeffrey? You'll pass right by his desk on the way to Eric's office."

She holds out a thick wedge of papers with perfectly manicured fingers. Jeffrey is the epitome of Ignite culture and he gives me, and just about every other woman in the Catch Group, serious heebie-jeebies.

"I'd love to," I say sarcastically.

She doesn't catch my tone but shoots me a thankful look.

Walking into the Ignite office always feels like stepping into an alternate universe where feminism never existed. I never understood why they put the Product and Development teams at the front of the office. Maybe it has something to do with their complimentary coffee and snack bar being an arm's reach away, but the first impression it gives off is awful. They all adopt a uniform of stained meme-based T-shirts paired with baggy jeans or sweatpants, finished off with the most expensive trainers I've ever seen. Nothing says "I get paid a ton but don't care enough to shower" like drifter on the top, party on the bottom.

Conversely, the women of Ignite are all immaculately styled from the highest point of their sleek ponytails to the lowest point of their stilettos.

"Gracie Hastie!" Jeffrey points finger guns at me as I walk toward his desk, making myself as small as possible.

"Jeffrey . . . Schmeffrey," I wince out.

"What brings you to my . . . humble abode?" He holds his arms out and gestures to the four computer screens creating a glowing semi-circle around him.

"Codes to the nuclear missiles from Harriet," I say, flopping the papers in his direction. I keep my hand as close to the edge of the folder as I can without throwing it at him the way you throw a flip-flop at a cockroach.

"Thanks, babe. You look great by the way—got a hot date?"

I look down at my outfit, a black blazer and jeans with a vintage Rolling Stones T-shirt.

"Funeral," I respond in a deadpan tone.

"Oh, right . . ." He purses his lips, studying me. "Must

be my funeral, closed casket because I'd be upright at the sight of you . . . if you catch my drift." He winks.

"Good thing they take your eyes out first when they embalm you."

He laughs. "You're feisty today. If you need a shoulder to cry on just let me know."

"Will do!" I reply sarcastically across the rows of desks; then I hesitate, feeling the hmmm of my phone searing a hole of curiosity in my pocket. "Actually, I could do with your help if you're not too busy?"

"Never too busy for you." He winks again.

"Great." I flash a breezy smile. "Could you find an account for me?"

I try to keep my hand from shaking as I hold the screenshot of William's profile out to him like a "Wanted" poster.

"Sure." He shrugs. "For a price."

My stomach sinks as I mentally check my bank account. "How much do you want?" I sigh, trying not to fiddle with my necklace.

He shakes his head. "Not your money, beautiful."

I cross my arms. "Then what?"

"Four words: me, you, lobster dinner." He grins, mouth full of coffee-stained teeth.

"How about . . ." I say seductively, leaning in and lowering my voice. He creaks forward in his seat to meet me. ". . . you do this for me and I won't tell all my female colleagues you still live with your mother and her six cats?"

His face blanches. I don't tell him that everyone at

Fate already knows this fact, but that's not the reason they avoid him.

He clears his throat and returns to his keyboard, not meeting my eye. "I need the phone number attached to the account."

I pull up William's number and read it out loud.

We remain in an awkward post-blackmail silence for a few seconds while Jeffrey's software filters through millions of Ignite users to find the right account.

"William . . . Salter?" he asks.

I nod my head. "How long has he been a user?"

"Looks like he's had an account for a few years." His beady eyes continue to scan the account information. "Is there anything specific you're looking for?"

My heart begins to pound so hard I can feel it banging against my rib cage. I try to keep my breathing in check, not wanting to give Jeffrey the satisfaction of seeing me squirm.

"He must have just set it up and forgotten about it," I say more to myself than Jeffrey.

"Mmmmmm." He squints at the screen. "Nope . . . he's been pretty active since he first created the account."

I hear the sound of a door clicking open. Jeffrey glances up briefly as Bancroft strides over to us.

"How 'active'?" I manage to get out in a tight tone, ignoring Bancroft's intensifying stare.

"Give me a second. His account has some extra permission barriers on it, which is unusual for this subscription level."

"Do you have authority to get through them?" I ask, leaning toward the screen and trying to keep my tone steady.

"Grace," Bancroft says in a soft tone over the computer screens separating us; his voice barely registers over the ringing in my ears.

"Hmm, he's been active almost daily for about four years, aaaaand . . ." Jeffrey drags out the word as he scrolls down further. ". . . his account has been flagged multiple times during that time for sending lewd images."

Goose bumps erupt across every inch of my skin as I stare at the lines and lines and lines of documented logins from William's account. The ringing intensifies, a wind-up monkey banging cymbals relentlessly between my ears.

"Wait." Looking up from his screen at Bancroft: "Isn't this the same guy *you* had me look up? Couldn't you have just sent her *your* file?"

The ringing stops suddenly, replaced by a deafening silence.

I turn slowly to find Bancroft, grim and stone-faced, standing a few paces away. He ignores Jeffrey's questions and fixes his creased gaze on my prickling eyes.

"We should talk, privately." He stalks off, hands in his pockets.

We enter his office in complete silence and he gestures for me to sit on the burgundy leather Chesterfield sofa tucked into a corner. That's right, he not only has his own office, but an office large enough to have specific areas for business and more casual conversation.

The whole space gives off a reserved but sensual vibe that makes total sense for his brand persona. The walls are lined with matte-black cupboards and shelving. The floor is a dark brown wood, part covered with a brown and black printed rug that complements his modern wooden desk. If this room was wearable, it would be a black cashmere turtleneck. Professional but not taking itself too seriously, and very comfortable. I want to question why he used to spend so much time at my cramped, crumb-covered desk when we could have been in here, but his cool voice brings me back to the bitter present.

"Do you want a drink?" he asks, taking a seat next to me. He stares at my arm and flexes his hand, then tucks it under his own leg.

"I want you to show me whatever it is that Jeffrey was talking about," I say, eyes fixed resolutely on the chasmic dark walls.

It feels as if I'm having an out-of-body experience but my body is also being slowly crushed by a steamroller. I'm somehow not present yet hyperaware of every speck of dust floating in the streams of harsh sunlight piercing the windows.

"I don't think it's a good idea." His voice softens to melting butter.

My head turns toward him, trying to gauge how bad it's going to sting. His expression is dancing back and forth through guilt, pity and fear all while wearing a half-functioning mask of neutrality. My face creases as

I try to remain calm despite the clarifying fury rising to the surface.

"I don't think you're in a position to decide what is or isn't a good idea right now," I snap. "Show. Me," I repeat slowly, the *or else* silent, but heavily implied.

His pupils constrict: lasers building with energy before unleashing utter destruction.

He sighs and clears his throat, standing up and smoothing his hands down his navy trousers. His shoulders are stiff as he pulls out a light brown folder from a tall gunmetal filing cabinet in the corner of the room. He drops it down on the glass coffee table in front of me and puts his hands in his pockets, jaw ticking as he nods to the folder. "Everything you want to know is in there."

I stare at the Folder of Doom and then flick my eyes back up to his face. His mouth is tight, and his eyebrows creased in the middle. Maybe if I hadn't just received a slew of messages from William about why breaking up *wasn't the best thing for either of us*, I could have let this go. Could have picked up the folder, thrown it in the nearest shredder and lit the pieces up into ash. I know it would probably be better for my mental health in the long run, but that doesn't stop my hand from flicking open the elastic clasp and letting the papers fall out across the table.

Messages, pictures and arrangements spread out over the table like photographs from a crime scene. A timeline of betrayal and deceit laid out over almost our entire relationship. Bancroft silently perches against his desk staring at his hands. The pages blur in my foggy brain into meaningless letters and skin until they start to resemble a word salad with breasts, lips and dick pics sprinkled on as dressing.

Eventually, my eyes snag on a timestamp: three days before he proposed. I rip the page from the table.

Laura: Last night was great x
William: Next week will be even better ;) x

The page drops from my shaking hand onto the floor. Bancroft and I watch it fall; then we stand in sync to meet each other. All I can hear is the giant gong banging against my brain.

I step toward him, head spinning, and with a hoarse voice that doesn't even sound like mine I ask, "How long?"

He strides around the desk toward me, bringing his arms out to touch mine. I jump back, crossing my hands over myself. Bancroft takes a step backward and holds his hands up.

"How long have you known?" I repeat, louder this time.

The dark walls feel as if they are moving inward, pressing against me, trapping me here, but it's my body pressing up against the hard surface of the wall.

He looks at the floor, then up at me with hooded eyes. "I found out after you'd broken up, a couple of months after we . . ." He pauses, trying to find the right words. ". . . when we weren't on speaking terms. His account was flagged multiple times for sending unsolicited pictures and I recognized the name. I didn't want anyone else to connect the dots and bring it up to you, so I buried it."

I swallow the hard lump in my throat. "And you didn't even have the decency to tell me?"

"You weren't talking to me. You told me you didn't want to be friends anymore," he says matter-of-factly. "The last thing I wanted to do was cause you more pain."

"Well, congratulations. You did an *excellent* job." My voice wobbles.

I feel like a handbag being shaken upside down, everything important falling out at once and rolling under the sofa never to be seen again.

His voice softens as he looks at the ground. "I just—I didn't know how to tell you when you could barely stand to be in the same room as me."

"And what about now? You could have told me when I was talking about him at the gallery, *or when Iris told you he'd been texting me!*" The words emerge through gritted teeth.

"I'm sorry," he continues. "I thought . . . I was trying to protect you." His usually bright eyes fill with a dark storm cloud glaze as they flick back and forth between me and the papers.

I spew out a laugh, emotion constricting my throat. "That's what you've been doing? Protecting me?"

"I didn't want you to get even more hurt than you already were. I wanted to tell you, but it just felt like I would be kicking you while you were down," he blurts out, running a rough hand through his hair.

"Oh, so you talking shit about me in your office *wasn't* doing that?"

Hastings is a clingy psycho . . . She's not worth going there, not even for a quick shag. The words ring in my head, overlapping his current words like some sick chorus.

He blinks, halting his pacing. "What?"

I open my mouth and throw my hands up in disbelief, leaning against the wall as my knees begin to shake.

"Great." I gesture to him, trying furiously to blink away the hurt from my eyes. "So you tell your whole office I'm a psycho, I'm desperate and pathetic and you don't even fucking remember. Just . . . great."

I cross my arms, cradling the part of me that feels like taking its first breath after being punched.

He furrows his brow and shakes his head in confusion. I just stare at him until, finally, his expression softens, and he steps closer.

"Grace . . . I didn't know you heard that." He rubs the back of his neck and then brings his hand to hesitantly touch my arm, the warmth searing into my prickled skin. "Would you believe me if I told you that wasn't what it sounded like?"

My mouth is clamped shut as I stare to the side. Now that this is out there, I know anything I say will come out jerked and teary. I don't want to give him an answer or the satisfaction. I pull my arm away from him.

"I'm so sorry," he says, his head lowering.

"Sure you are." I sniff, turning my head to avoid his intense stare, knowing that it will only take one look at his pained expression for me to burst.

Bancroft looks at the ceiling, curses to himself, then lowers his gaze back to me. "Jeffrey heard about your breakup and said he was going to try it with you. I didn't want you to have to deal with his sleaziness on top of everything else, and I panicked. Admittedly, it wasn't the best idea I've ever had but I said those things to put him off you. I swear to you, Grace, I didn't mean a word of it. No one else was ever meant to hear it, I promise."

I meet his soft, regretful gaze and sigh, feeling almost hungover from the conflicting emotions coursing through me. "That doesn't mean it didn't hurt." I turn my head to wipe away an escaping tear clumsily with my palm.

His brow furrows as he takes my chin between his fingers and lifts my head to meet his eyes. "Is that why you refused to talk to me? Why you blocked me out?"

I nod, the ghosts of the shock and betrayal vibrating through my skin as though it was yesterday.

"Fuck, Grace. I thought it was because you were embarrassed about what happened with us. This whole time, we could have— Fuck, I'm so sorry."

We stand in silence for a few moments, our heavy, panicked breathing mixing in the small space between us. I release my crossed arms and let them hang by my sides. His hands fall with them, slowly drifting down my arms as if they're magnetically fused to me. My body heats as he takes a deep breath. "By the way, you never had to be embarrassed. Grace, if things were different that night at the Christmas party—"

"Don't . . ." I interrupt, pressing my hands against his warm chest. "I don't need your pity. I just—I need some time."

I know I need to clear my head because I can't fully comprehend what I'm upset about, whose betrayal hurts more. The person who tried to force me into a life he wanted or the person who kept secrets from me under the guise of "protection." I can't work out why Bancroft lying to me feels just as bad as William's betrayal.

Susie has gone home for the day so I'm free to leave the office without attracting suspicion. When I finally reach my flat I let out a sigh of relief I've been holding in for months, but before I drop my bag on the floor I feel a hot tear roll down my cheek. Everything comes to the surface. William, Fate, Bancroft, the crushing pressure of this promotion, the betrayal, my stupidity and blindness to the obvious truth. My chest cracks open and I let out a deep sob. *Just let it out,* my brain says to itself, to my heart, to my entire body as it shakes and drops to the ground.

19

"Should we order pizza?" Alice asks, seeing me nesting in fleece blankets on the sofa for the second night in a row. This woman has the metabolism of a grizzly bear. She could eat a seven-tier birthday cake and then still go out in a skintight dress to get burritos.

"Shouldn't we have had that first, then the mountains of ice cream?" Yemi questions, pointing to our stacked speckled bowls littering the scratched wooden coffee table along with tear-stained tissues and half-empty wine glasses.

"The ice cream was an emergency protocol and should be stricken from the record," Alice explains.

"Would you like to include the massive bag of crisps and the double G&Ts too, Your Honour?"

Alice hums wisely. "Dismissed."

"I don't think I could eat another thing ever again," I say, laying my hands on top of my protruding stomach like a proud mother of a most beloved food baby. "Thank you for this, guys. I really needed it."

The doorbell buzzes and Alice rolls off the sofa to push a manicured finger into the intercom button.

"Hello?"

"Delivery," replies a loud metallic voice.

"Third floor, thanks!"

"Oh my God, Al, did you already order the pizza?" I laugh.

She flings her hands up to her face, palms facing us. "I swear I didn't!"

A knock at the door echoes down our cramped hallway and she frantically pads over to answer. A man with a beard and Cockney accent asks her to "Sign here please, and here, and here." Then we hear our heavy front door slam shut, and the silver chain rattles against the wood as smooth cardboard slides across the floorboards.

"Uhhhh, guys? I'm gonna need some help with this," Alice shouts in a strained tone. Yemi and I throw confused looks at each other as I release myself from my multi-layer fleece-lined cocoon. We reach the door to find Alice half carrying, half dragging a thin square package wrapped in cardboard across the floorboards into the hallway. Each grabbing a corner, we haul it into the living room and lean it gently against the magnolia wall.

"What is it?" Yemi asks, cocking her head to the side.

"The delivery guy didn't say." Alice holds up a small blank white envelope between two fingers. Yemi takes it and pulls out a thick piece of card. She quickly scans it and then gasps, pressing the note to her chest.

"It's from *Eric*!" she announces with a wicked smile.

My stomach lurches with a sickly combination of dread and embarrassment. What in the note could possibly be gasp-worthy? I take the note; the card has an expensive matte texture. The logo on the letterhead says "CALICO" in blocky embossed cursive. The gallery? I immediately recognize his controlled but scratchy handwriting:

Before you even think about it, this is not me attempting to buy your forgiveness. This is an apology for not being a good friend, twice. I should have told you. It was a shitty thing to do and I'm sorry. You deserve so much better.

Eric

The card wobbles in my hands. Alice rests her chin on my shoulder, reading the note under her breath.

"What's in the package?" she asks impatiently. "Can we open it?"

I nod silently, finding it hard to summon words.

You deserve so much better. I keep reading that line over and over.

Better than what? Than William? Than him?

"Holy shit." Alice's exclamation pulls me out of my trance to see a half-unwrapped painting in front of me. A flicker of familiarity hits me as more brown paper is pulled away to reveal a five-foot-by-four-foot canvas. Recognizing it instantly, my eyes widen. Holy shit indeed.

The painting, shadowed by piles of packaging, is the same one we saw in the gallery. The one I said I liked.

"What is it?" asks Yemi, taking in the abstract brush-strokes that form a brightly colored figure of a woman.

My mouth ajar, I say, "I can't believe it. It's a painting I said I liked at the gallery."

"Woah. It looks expensive," Alice adds in awe.

"Very," I confirm with raised eyebrows. Remembering the price on that little plaque next to the piece in the gallery jolts me out of my nonchalant haze. I shake my head. "Too expensive—I can't accept this."

"But do you accept his apology?" Yemi adds, not taking her eyes off the painting.

I sigh, running a hand through my hair. "He didn't need to apologize. I don't think it was ever really about him in the first place. I think it was about me." I rest the note on the counter, reading the last sentence one more time before pouring water into a ribbed green glass. "I'm angry at William for being such an arsehole but most of all I'm angry at myself for falling for it."

I deleted William's number when I got home, I couldn't trust myself to not send him a barrage of angry texts or drunk-scream at him down the phone. My brain feels like a glass being held under freezing cold and then scalding hot water, destined to end up as jagged pieces.

Alice continues to stare at the painting, following the flowing lines around the canvas. "This is gorgeous. He must like you a lot."

"Or feel really, *really* bad," Yemi adds, bringing me back to reality.

"Well, he's not the only one." I sip my glass of water

to clear the shaky voice from my throat. "He's probably just trying to reestablish our truce before his big hotel meeting tomorrow."

You deserve so much better.

Trying to put my thoughts in order is like trying to rearrange a deck of cards while wearing oven gloves. Attempting to find the reason lodged somewhere in the creases of my brain that can explain why I still feel more betrayed by Bancroft not telling me than William actually doing the deeds. More than anything, I feel like an idiot. Was I so fragile that he thought I couldn't handle it?

"As much as I hate to agree with Eric, it sounds like not telling you was for the greater good. He was trying to protect you from suffering even more than you already were after your breakup," Yemi concludes, perching on a metal stool at the kitchen island.

"But maybe knowing would have helped me get over William faster," I say into my glass, my free hand resting on the card. "And saved me the humiliation."

Alice stretches her hand out across the island and places it on top of mine. "Babe, I don't think you realize how bad it got after William broke up with you. You were on the edge. You were barely eating, not talking to anyone, you basically had high-functioning depression."

I cringe at the image of me lying in bed every night crying so hard I wanted to be sick. At the memory of how Yemi would make me dinner most nights and practically force-feed me. How Alice would make me participate in regular beauty nights with her, testing out the latest skin, body or hair-care product her boss had been gifted and discarded. In the office, I was just a more intense version of my usual self, but outside of the work bubble, I was barely keeping myself alive. The realization sinks to the bottom of my stomach like an anchor finding purchase.

Yemi stares at me, a crease slowly forming as she studies me staring at the card. "It wasn't William you couldn't get over all these months, was it? What actually happened that night?"

"When?" Alice asks, her head turning back and forth between Yemi's and my stare-off.

Yemi, not breaking eye contact with me, says to Alice, "Last December, at the Catch Christmas party."

My eyes prickle. "I guess I didn't tell you guys the full story."

I was freshly single, having been dumped by William and thrown out of his apartment just five days prior. The last thing I wanted to do was go to the party, but Catcher had insisted that all employees attend, and Susie specifically said I needed to be there with her. It was a disgustingly expensive event on the top floor of the Gherkin to celebrate the successes and growth of every company under the CG umbrella. My main objective for the night: drink as many festive cocktails as possible to forget all about my gut-wrenching state of loneliness and misery. My main achievement of the night: pure, uncensored embarrassment.

London lights glittered behind the crowd of people laughing, drinking and bobbing their heads along to the beat of the throbbing DJ set. After my seventh or eighth (or maybe ninth) Mistletoe Mojito, my head was spinning, and I could feel the music pounding through my bones. Susie had left earlier in the evening, thankfully missing my turn in the disco-ball-adorned karaoke corner belting out a slurred version of "I'd Do Anything For Love (But I Won't Do That)," doing the male and female parts and doing them both poorly. I was forcing Yemi to take photos of me in the decorative bathtub by the bar because it was filled with ice and expensive champagne bottles. Routinely scanning the crowd in the dark room framed by the London skyline for familiar faces, I watched as the more senior members of the Catch Group teams began trickling out, going home to their families and partners, causing the crowd's shoulders to finally sag and loosen now that their bosses had disappeared. Yemi went to meet her boyfriend and I wanted to leave too, but all I was going home to was sadness. I also had this alcohol-fueled feeling that my night wasn't complete yet, urging me to stay. I avoided my own gaze in the patinated mirrored bar as though catching it would mean acknowledging the self-awareness trying to crawl its way to the surface. The goal of this night was to forget how I was, why I was and who I was. My reflection was merely a snakeskin that would shed and be left on the dance floor to disintegrate.

Leaning against the bar, mostly because I wasn't sure I could stand up without it, I could feel when Bancroft entered the room. Everyone shifted, as though putting their best faces on for his grand arrival. People like him have always fascinated me: what it would be like to arrive late and command a room with a look, a word, a furrow of the brow—which was exactly what he was doing when I turned around. And unfortunately, that brow was pointed directly at me. I met his intense yet playful stare.

"Look who decided to grace us with his presence," I said louder than I intended as he glided toward me, giving the occasional nod of acknowledgment to his colleagues in the crowd. Looking him up and down, I clocked a jacket he'd never worn to work before. A tan leather moto jacket with sharp lapels. He always had an eye for what looked amazing on him, mostly dark neutrals, but I theorized there must be some sort of female influence in his life that kept his wardrobe in check. No straight man could look this good on his own.

"Were you waiting for me, Hastings?" He took the drink out of my hand and took a sip, putting his lips where mine just were, not breaking his gaze.

"You think too highly of yourself." My fingers gripped the cold bar behind me briefly and then swished a rogue hair from my cheek. "I'm having fun."

"For once," he added through a tight-lipped smile.

"You've been having fun elsewhere, I presume?"

"You would presume correctly," he replied with a

wink, and I responded with an eye roll. His eyes were ever so slightly glassy as he held my stare for a second, causing his expression to soften. "So . . . do you wanna talk about it?"

"About all the fun you've been having this evening? Pfft. I'm good actually, but thanks!" I said, swiping my drink out of his hand.

"No, about . . ." He paused, picking his words carefully. ". . . him."

I threw a fake laugh in his direction. "I really, really, really don't."

The last thing I wanted to think or talk about was William. I was miserable but somehow, despite the sky-high levels of inebriation I was reaching, keeping it together.

"OK." He nodded resolutely and leaned over my shoulder to talk to the bartender. A few moments later, a fresh G&T in hand, he resumed his previous position of staring me down until I finally cracked and broke the silence.

"What did you think of me when we first met?" The question was metallic on my tongue, like something I knew I shouldn't try but just wanted to see how it tasted.

He drummed his fingers on the bar top while his other hand swirled the ice in his glass. "Sure you want to know?"

The crowd behind him cheered in drunken delight as the DJ moved a spotlight to hit a disco ball above the dance floor, causing shiny white dots to spin around the room. Turning the party into an alcohol-filled snow globe.

"Uh-huh," I replied, regretting my question, not knowing if I could handle more evaluation from men whose opinions I valued.

He cleared his throat and said, "I thought you were a little Goody Two-shoes."

I burst out laughing, spitting a half sip of my drink onto the floor.

"Who even uses that phrase anymore?" I said, wiping my wet mouth with the back of my hand.

He held his hand up in defence. "Hey, private school education isn't what it used to be!"

I laughed again, staring at my feet. "And what about now?" I asked, unwilling to look him in the eye.

"Hmmm," he mused, forcing my gaze up to his. He pursed his lips for a second, glancing at his drink and then back to me with a devilish, open-mouthed smirk. "Now I know you better. I know you're not nearly as good as you pretend to be." His dimple appeared and disappeared in an instant.

My stomach flip-flopped over itself as I tried to stop my cheeks from burning, mouth opening and closing with an attempt at a cool response. I settled for taking a huge gulp of my drink instead and shifting on my heels. I felt the alcohol reach my system instantly, the numbing sensation flowing through my body down to my legs.

"So . . . ?" Bancroft asked expectantly, burning a hole in my head with his locked gaze.

"So, what?" I sipped at my icy drink and shivered as the cold liquid trickled down my throat.

"So, what about me?" he prompted. A hint of nervousness flashed through his blue eyes but was blinked away in an instant. His five o'clock–shadowed throat bobbed as he took another sip of his drink. "What did you think of me at first?"

I glanced at the tightening fingers around his glass. "I thought you were all gin, no tonic," I said as soberly as I could, straightening my posture for emphasis.

He huffed a laugh and glanced down at his nearly finished drink. "And now?"

I tried to think of anything I could actually say out loud, but the only thing I could put into words was "And now I want to dance."

I slammed my glass onto the bar and pulled his tailored arm toward the heaving crowd, using both my hands to wrap fully around his forearm. His concerned eyes stayed on me as I bounced through our sequin-clad colleagues. My eyes drooped closed as the music swelled and I flung my arms around him; with my highest heels on we were almost cheek to cheek.

The move, in my drunken logic, had been a good one to avoid an awkward conversation, but in making it I'd managed to get physically closer to him than I'd ever been before. It shocked me momentarily, to see his face so close up. The end-of-day stubble on his jaw, the subtle spattering of freckles on his cheeks, the bow of his full lips: features that were usually eclipsed by his penetrating eyes. I archived them, promising to pay more attention to each of them in the future. I felt his large hands smooth around my waist and grip me—in hindsight, probably to keep me upright. As everything else spun and blurred, my glassy eyes could only focus on him. His hands on me felt like a joyride; we were spinning with no direction in mind, just trying to not crash.

"You're so pretty," I slurred, scrunching my brow. "Everyone calls you handsome, but I think you're pretty."

He laughed. "You're not so bad yourself." He lifted a hand and wiped the hair from my sweat-laced forehead. "But I think you paying me a genuine compliment is a strong indicator that you've had too much to drink."

Even when we were friends, our conversations always skirted the edges of seriousness.

I ignored his assumption. I could have a million more drinks! I was the Queen of Mistletoe Mojitos and nothing would ever stop me!

"What's it like having eeeeveryone in the company adore you?" I slurred into his shoulder.

He laughed again but this time it didn't reach his eyes. "Not everyone adores me," he said into my ear, giving my waist a quick squeeze for emphasis.

"Yeah, I definitely just tolerate you." I draped my arms tighter around his neck and swayed to the music, forcing him to move in sync with me.

"I tolerate you too." He smiled a real smile this time.

"But I've got a feeling you won't tolerate me anymore if I let you continue to the point of alcohol poisoning."

"Booooooo!" Right on cue I stumbled on my wobbly stiletto and grabbed a chunk of his hair to steady myself. His hand met mine at the back of his head and laced our fingers together.

"Come on, let's get you a cab." His warm voice traveled from his curved lips over the music to my ears.

"Picture first, then go," I said like a child as I stumbled out of the crowd pulling him with me toward the Catch Group branded photo booth. Ten minutes later, he finally managed to steer me toward the exit.

The line for the lift was several people deep so we left the circular function room via the echoey concrete stairwell, his arm gripping tight around my waist to avoid a festive neck break. It pulled my dress up even higher, but I didn't care, the fluorescent lights made the world feel even blurrier. The icy wind hit my skin as he pushed through the fire-exit door; I huddled close to him to stay warm. Police sirens echoed down the dark London streets, filling the silence as he pulled out his phone and I clumsily tried to punch my address into the bright screen. He read it out loud to make sure I hadn't accidentally sent myself to Brighton.

"The Uber will be here in a few minutes. How are you not shivering right now? Your arms are freezing." He faced me, rubbing his warm hands up and down my bare arms.

"Alcohol blanket." I beamed at him as the lights from

passing cars shone on his chiseled face. I wanted to touch him and couldn't think of a single good reason not to. I put my hand on his cheek and watched as he automatically leaned into it, his stubble scraping my palm. Our eyes locked and he gave me that smirk. The one that made me blush the first day we met. The one that made my blood boil. The one that sent electricity shooting through me so hard I needed to squeeze my thighs together to make it stop.

We stayed like that for a few moments, frozen in this magical, glittering darkness where we could drop the guards we held in the daylight. I leaned into him until our chests touched, the warmth of his body enveloping me. He pressed his forehead to my brow and I closed my eyes. The bridge of his nose gently pressed against mine and I could feel his warm breath on my cheek. Finally, I gave in to the gravitational pull I'd been ignoring for months, turning my face and dragging my lips toward his. The impact of his soft mouth hard against mine sent a shock-wave through me, a clicking into place unlike anything I'd ever experienced as I moved to deepen the kiss.

"Grace . . ." he breathed onto my lips, his voice low and heavy. "We can't . . . I can't." His mouth pulled away from me, leaving a chill in its place. His brow tilted down and he shook his head as though he could hear every thought running through mine.

"Why not?" I gave a pout, eyes still closed. My ego was too drunk for denial and had the overwhelming urge to change this night for the better.

"I can't. Not . . . like this." He seemed to hate himself for saying that, for being a gentleman.

"I haven't even drunk that much!" A poorly timed hiccup immediately followed, ruining my argument.

He shook his head. "We both know that's not true. And anyway, that's not the only reason."

I stared up at him, eyes glassy from the cold and rejection.

"I can't do this with you when you're thinking of him." His fingers squeezed my shoulders as if it was taking all his willpower to keep them there.

For the first time since Eric had arrived at the party, I pictured William's face. Embarrassed, I pulled my arms away from him, crossing them in front of my chest, still trapped in his half embrace. I stared at the chewing-gum-spotted pavement, blinking furiously.

"Hey, look at me." His expression was more gentle than I'd ever seen.

We were never close enough friends to spend time outside of work, and with every mingling breath we shared I was realizing maybe we didn't for a reason. Not because we didn't like each other enough to cross that friendship threshold, but because we both knew what might happen if we did. What I wanted, needed to happen right then.

He took a deep, shuddering breath, but before he could say anything, a car beeped its horn and flashed its lights in our direction.

"Eric?" a man shouted from the driver's seat.

And then, in the blink of an eye, albeit a slow,

laborious blink from my alcohol-glazed eyes, Bancroft had switched back to his usual self.

"My next clear memory was waking up with the worst hangover of my life and his suit jacket wrapped around me like an expensive-smelling cocoon." Back in the kitchen, I finish with an exasperated sigh, taking in Yemi's and Alice's shocked expressions.

I don't fully remember the rest of the night; it's like a terrible nightmare you wake up from but have no memory of, despite your heart racing and body sweating.

"Oh. My. God. I can't believe you didn't tell us!" Alice gasps.

"I didn't want to tell anyone." I press my cold hand against my face.

"And I only suspected *something* had happened because Eric got in touch with me to get her home safely," explains Yemi. "He wanted to confirm the address because Grace was too drunk to tell him."

I shoot her a quick, tight-lipped smile because it's the only way to explain that even though William breaking up with me shocked me to my core, losing Bancroft was a devastation I never saw coming.

Sighing, I say, "I never thanked you both. You two were basically keeping me alive, fed and washed those first few months. Thank you." My eyes glisten with gratitude.

"And our master plan worked. We got you to shower! Mwahahaha!" Alice wiggles her fingers together, spinning on her high stool.

Yemi paces around the counter and hugs me. "Yeah, we mostly just didn't want you stinking up our home."

"How can I ever repay you?" I ask earnestly.

"Hmm . . ." Alice ponders, turning back to the humongous package taking up half the hallway with a cheeky smile. "I'd take a ridiculously expensive painting?"

"Oh God." My hands cover my face. "It's too much. I have to give it back, right?"

I lean against the counter. Tomorrow, I have to be a consummate professional for our big meeting at the Heimach Hotel when everything I want to do and say is against Catch Group's Code of Conduct.

"I think you should sleep on it," Yemi suggests as she shrugs. "You might feel differently in the morning."

"Or when you see him at the meeting," Alice adds.

This is Bancroft's biggest little-black-book partnership opportunity: a meeting about partnering for Ditto users' exclusive access to the Heimach Hotel's gym, cycle class, spa and yoga facilities as well as discounts across the rooms and restaurant. Ruining things by being a no-show will jeopardize both of our shots at a promotion. I rub my eyes with my palms. How do I even start a conversation like that? "Hey, thanks for the multi-thousand-pound painting but also fuck you for keeping a huge secret from me. Are you ready for our career-defining meeting?"

20

"Where's the report?" Susie's sharp voice scrapes the inside of my ear like a long fingernail on a blackboard.

"It's on your desk," I pant down the phone. I scan the blueprint of her desk in my mind, half the time her Chloé Marcie handbag is slung over the entire surface. "It might be under something but—"

"I don't see it." She sounds frantic. "Darling, I'm about to have a very important meeting and I *need* that report."

"It's definitely there, in a blue folder. I dropped it off before I left."

The phone bounces against my face as I half walk, half sprint down the dusty pavement. I left on time, but it's always on the days you have to look your best that you end up stuck on a delayed tube in the middle of summer and having to walk half the journey. At least the breeze from my pace is drying my sweaty forehead.

"If it was 'definitely' here, why can't I see it?"

I internally cringe. Susie wasn't exactly supportive of me leaving the office two hours earlier than usual on a Thursday to meet with Bancroft and the owner of the

Heimach Hotel, so she gave me some extra last-minute work to do as a punishment. The hotel sprouts through the concrete in the distance; I burst into a full jog in heels.

"Maybe try underneath your handbag?"

She's silent for a moment as I hear shuffling on the other end of the line. "This is why you need to book these meetings outside of work hours. It wastes both of our time."

I guess she found the report.

"I'll keep that in mind for next time. I have to—"

"Next time?" she interrupts. "I'm under a lot of pressure right now. I need to know I can rely on you."

"I just mean . . . the Ditto presentation is in a couple of weeks so . . ." I trail off, not knowing how to say "hopefully I won't be working for you after that" in a way that won't end up with my head being stuffed and mounted in her house as a hat rack.

I can almost hear her eyes rolling in her skull like bingo balls circling a cage.

"I expect your *actual* work on my desk by tomorrow morning, hopefully somewhere I can see it without having to search for it?"

"Of course. Have a good evening."

"*Have a good evening!*" I repeat to myself in a whiny high-pitched voice, chastising myself for my attempt at pleasantry with a hungry, rabid hyena.

I reach the hotel's revolving doors, which are nestled between a tall, glossy office building and a Blank Street Coffee. I take a deep breath and wipe my damp hair and face with my sleeve. My navy-blue fitted suit feels very Bancroftian. In sweltering weather like this, I'd usually opt for lighter colors and fabrics, but this meeting is too important to mess up by being underdressed.

I head into the lobby and the cold air hits my skin as if I'm crossing the tundra. Bancroft is standing with a man at the end of a wide expanse of onyx floor, but he hasn't seen me yet. A sign of glowing backlit marble lancing spreads across the hotel reception. The word HEIMACH spelled out in industrial lightbulbs looms over the lobby. Well-dressed staff with slick hair and black jumpsuits rush around holding iPads. This hotel is a hotspot for cool, creative types who can often be found pounding on their laptops on a green leather sofa in the lobby workspace. Alice would fit right in here. I scan the clientele, checking people against the mental list of Ditto's target audience attributes. Unique, young, cool. Seems as if we're in the right place.

My sweat-soaked skin prickles as Bancroft clocks my presence, studying my outfit with a scrunch of his eyebrows so subtle I almost think I imagined it. Yemi was, of course, right. I spent a lot of last night staring at the ceiling, running scenario after scenario of what I should have done and said differently in his office. Before fully drifting off, I came to the conclusion that, even though it hurts, I can understand his instinct to not tell me. Craving his signature smirk, I shoot Bancroft an awkward tight-lipped smile and his eyes flash with something resembling relief before looking away. He's standing with a man with platinum-blond hair dressed in a striped blue-and-dark-green suit and a bright red tie. He must be Christoph Teller, the youngest of the Teller family hotel dynasty. According to *Forbes* and *Vanity Fair* his father is very good friends with Bancroft's father, Malon. They tower over me as I approach, like two marble columns guarding the entrance of a club exclusively for those over six feet tall with an inheritance.

"Ahh!" Christoph Teller claps his hands together. "You must be Ms. Hastings." His voice rings out through the lobby, commanding but warm.

"That's me. Lovely to meet you, Mr. Teller. I'm so sorry I'm late. Tube delays."

"Please, call me Christoph." His perfect smile beams as he speaks. He seems to radiate an infectious warmth and joy, definitely not what I was expecting for the heir to a multi-million-pound hotel chain. "Eric has told me all about you!"

"If any of his stories involve a cooking class, I swear I didn't stab him on purpose," I blurt without thinking.

Christoph bursts into a sharp peal of laughter that echoes off the black stone walls like sonar in a cave. I cut a side-glance at Bancroft, who is staring at me with an unreadable but intense expression. My eyes narrow back at him and he quickly returns his gaze to Christoph, who has stopped laughing and started telling the story of a guest who blinded himself attempting a sabrage on a bottle of champagne. I try to punctuate the story with light laughter in the right places until he suggests we start the tour.

Christoph slides himself in between Bancroft and me, resting an arm against both of our shoulder blades and guiding us through a dark, moody corridor. He has an uncanny ability of not taking in a lot of oxygen between sentences, meaning his anecdotes weave into his guided tour and leave little space for either of us to get a word in edgeways, let alone speak to each other. Talking to Bancroft about our confrontation or the painting today is melting off the agenda like ice cream in this heat.

Christoph leads us to the sun-soaked gym with parquet oak floors where we pitch him the idea of yoga classes as shared-experience first dates set in an enviable location.

"You would like to try the yoga class?" Christoph asks us in ever-so-slightly fractured English.

"Oh." I laugh nervously, glancing at a blank-faced Bancroft for backup. "That's OK. We don't want to put you out."

"Not at all!" he exclaims. "I will tell my assistant to book you in for the next session."

"Really, it's OK. We don't have anything to wear for a fancy yoga class!" I laugh, panic rising.

"I have my gym gear with me. I'll wear that." Bancroft shrugs, the hint of a devious smile appearing on his face. Of course he does. Of course he will. His eyes flick to me. "Isn't the whole point to try before we buy?"

"And we have a partnered sportswear brand stocked

at the gym reception. Tell them I sent you and they will give you anything you need." Christoph beams at me and I have no choice but to beam back.

"OK!" I relent with a huge, forced grin.

Christoph leads us through the equally moody but sophisticated Michelin-starred restaurant and bar where we discuss throwing the most incredible launch event to bring coverage to the app and the hotel, then he gives us a tour of a deluxe king room where users who sign up within the first three months of launch will receive a discounted stay. Finally, he shows us the crown jewel of the Heimach Hotel: the penthouse suite.

Christoph throws his arms up to the vaulted ceilings and announces that it is his favorite place in the world.

"Hard not to agree with that—it's beautiful," Bancroft says, crossing his arms and staring at the 360-degree city landscape. My attention snags on his tall frame, shadowed by the bright light streaming in through the floor-to-ceiling windows.

Christoph's phone rings and he excuses himself to the other side of the suite, leaving us alone in the kitchen overlooking the skyscraping office buildings, piercing the clouds like cotton candy on sticks, the afternoon sun blazing through the gaps.

There's a sense of reluctance between the two of us. I haven't fully recovered from the hurt, but I appreciated his attempt at making amends. I creep up next to him with my best attempt at a teasing, mood-lightening grin. "You probably don't get to see a view from this high very often, no?"

He stares at me confused for a moment until he clicks his tongue and returns to the window. "Because I'm from hell, gotcha."

A pang of guilt pokes me in the stomach when he doesn't smile back. We linger in awkward silence until Christoph abruptly reappears.

"My apologies," Christoph says as he bursts around the corner. "One of our guests has brought her eight Pomeranians to stay with her but the room was not prepared to have dogs in it. Are you OK heading back to the gym for your yoga session while I fix it?"

We follow him out into the warmly lit hallway.

"No problem. It was great to finally meet you." Bancroft reaches out to shake his hand. "I'll call you tomorrow to finalize the details of the contract."

"Of course, and such a pleasure, Ms. Hastings. I do hope we meet again."

"Oh, we will. I just booked a room for me and my twelve cats," I counter with a smile. Christoph lets out a final bellowing laugh and pats our still-shaking hands.

We watch him skip off down the hallway and Bancroft whispers, "I don't think there was a single sentence you said that didn't make him laugh."

"What can I say, I'm a funny gal," I deadpan in a neutral tone.

"You're funny, yes, but not 'funny ha-ha' . . . more bizarre. Must be the language barrier."

My chest warms as the smirk returns; he puts his hands in his pockets and saunters off toward the lift. I'm relieved he's still willing to joke around with me.

"True humor transcends words; you'd understand that if you didn't coast on . . ." I scoff, waving a hand to indicate his general demeanor: ". . . this."

I follow him to the elevator at a quick pace as he steps into the lift and presses the button. Bancroft releases a breathy laugh, looks at the ground and then up to me. In this light, his eyes reflect the flickering golden lamps scattered across the walls, all warmth and possibility. We wait side by side at the elevator door, both listening to the metallic hum as it zips downward. After a brief air of silence, he gives me a look. I sigh and turn to face him.

"I got the package."

His eyebrows rise and maybe it's the recessed lights from the lift but his eyes twinkle with something I haven't seen before. "Penny for your thoughts?"

"Just a penny?" I cross my arms. "Based on the price of that painting, I know you can afford at least a quid or two."

He doesn't respond but the corner of his lips curl upward. I decide to make him suffer a little while longer.

"I haven't decided what I think about it," I say with a sighing breath, flicking a lock of curly hair over my shoulder as the silver doors slide open again.

21

Six Months Ago

Despite his best efforts in the monthly marketing-report meeting, I avoided Eric's gaze as much as I could, including blaming the air-conditioning unit for me moving to the opposite side of the table when he tried to sit next to me. For the past seventeen days since the Christmas party he'd been trying to knock over each brick of my avoidance wall as I'd placed it. Thankfully, there was a brief hiatus for Christmas but as soon as we all trundled back into the office with our new socks and brandy hangovers he started up again. Unread messages asking what I'm doing for lunch, a coffee dropped off at my desk while I was in a meeting, even showing up the night I usually stayed late. I only knew this because Hannah had texted me while I was at the pub's self-described nineties night with Yemi, shouting cathartic Spice Girl lyrics at each other in between two-for-one jugs of Woo Woo.

Eric seemed flustered during his reporting, not like his usual cool, calm, collected self in these meetings. He was more fidgety than usual, straightening his stationery and cleaning and recleaning his glasses every five minutes. Maybe he was feeling a fraction of what I was feeling. When I looked at him, the cocktail of sadness and regret and longing and anger gurgled in my stomach ready to be vomited up onto the conference-room table. I just did not understand how he could say those things about me and then look at me with such dejection.

That kind of desperation isn't hot, it's just pathetic.

Avoiding his gaze was easy, because every time I looked at him the words rang in my ears. I'd spent the two weeks since trying to convince myself it wasn't him; it was his soap opera evil twin, he was under a spell, his body was inhabited by an alien. That he was anyone but the person I'd started to fall for. But then I steeled my resolve, reminding myself that this wasn't the first time a man I'd trusted had betrayed me like this.

"All right, I have a call in five. Thanks, folks," Mr. Catcher eventually announced, already typing away on his phone as he walked out of the door.

For once, I was grateful for Susie not giving me a second to absorb the past hour's worth of information and jumping straight on me.

"We need to add more ROI stats on the special events summary for next month's meeting. Make it clear the strategy is as strong as it was before the acquisition."

It's a fairly simple command to remember but I relish the opportunity to keep my eyes homed in on my note-book, scribbling down the most detailed notes I've ever written in my life as I follow Susie toward the exit.

"Grace?" Eric waited for the briefest of pauses to interrupt our chatter.

Everyone left in the room turned to look at him as my whole body erupted in goose bumps.

"Could you hang back for a minute?" He held up a sheet of paper. "I need to compare something with your campaign results."

My eyes briefly flicked to Susie and Dharmash: Could I say no? It would probably look too unprofessional to tell him to fuck off right in front of our bosses. He plastered on a polite smile for them, but I could see some other emotion was trying to claw its way to the surface.

I gritted my teeth. "Sure."

We stood in silence until they slowly stepped out of the room, leaving the door cracked open. My eyes remained locked on a small black ink stain on the gray carpet tiles. His unshined shoes entered my field of vision as Eric stepped forward, his hands held high as if he was entering a hostage negotiation.

"I know you're trying to ignore me, but we *need* to talk about this." He glanced through the glass wall of the meeting room to the streams of people walking out to lunch. "Outside of work."

I crossed my arms, one hand flopping my phone out and flicking open the Mail app. "I'm very busy. I don't have time right now."

He shifted awkwardly, jaw twitching. "When will you have time?"

I sucked in my cheeks, trying to school my face into

indifference. "I don't know, probably never." *Just make a run for it. It's been working so far. Eventually, he'll just give up.*

Turning away, I clasped the door handle but his hand reached over my shoulder and gently pushed the door closed. I tensed as it clicked shut, my eyes practically drilling a hole in his signet ring. It was duller than usual but I could see his warped golden reflection as his body heat radiated against my back.

I expected his hand to move when I reluctantly turned around to face him, but it stayed pressed against the door above my shoulder. My lungs heaved; my body didn't know whether to press itself so hard against the door it broke through it or lean into him as it had when we danced at the Christmas party.

"Just . . . talk to me, please." A knife slowly sank into my chest as his eyes flashed desperate and searching for answers.

"I don't think there is anything to talk about." I avoided his gaze.

"You've been ignoring me ever since . . ." He trailed off, not wanting to verbalize what happened. As if that night was some telepathic dream we'd both experienced. As if what he'd said about me was so frivolous he'd already forgotten.

I really, *really* didn't want to talk about this.

"It's nothing. I've just been busy," I repeated, too flustered to come up with any other excuse.

"Look, I get if you're embarrassed about what

happened, but I'm not." He tried to meet my eyes, his head shaking back and forth. We locked eyes for a millisecond and the rest of the room drifted away until it was just us on the dark street, so close I could feel the jolt of electricity jumping between us. Eric must have sensed my stance softening as he leaned in closer.

His hand moved from the door to rest lightly on my shoulder. "You were drunk and upset. It doesn't have to be a big deal if you don't want it to be."

I landed back in the room with a crash. He was making it sound like it was all my fault. Not that he was part of what happened and then had chosen to talk shit about me behind my back.

"Hastings is a clingy psycho . . . She's not worth going there, not even for a quick shag. That kind of desperation isn't hot. It's just pathetic."

He kept talking, but all I heard were muffled sounds and drumming rage stirring up inside me. He was blaming this on me. He had no idea I'd overheard him.

He was trying to be friends with me again for . . . what? So I could continue to help him do his job? Something akin to shame crept up my back like a spider. I felt like a nerd in a high school movie: the jock was pretending to flirt with me so I'd do his homework. And I fell for it: hook, line and sinker.

When I heard him say those awful things I knew it was over. I wasn't desperate enough to continue a friendship, or whatever this was, with someone who talked about me like that. All I wanted to do was go back to my nest on Yemi's sofa, curl up in a ball and forget I was ever friends with Eric Bancroft.

I stood in silence and slowly blinked the emotion from my face before finally meeting his eye. *Hurt him. Hurt him like he hurt you and it will make everything easier.*

"Yeah, you're right. It's not a big deal. I just wanted you for the only thing you're good for. And since you made it clear that isn't going to happen, I don't need anything else from you, thanks." I blinked again, trying to remain as neutral as possible.

His jaw ticked as shock flashed across his blue eyes. He removed his warm palm from my shoulder, sliding his hands into his pockets and stepping away from me in one elegant movement.

His voice was low and soft. "Forgive me for thinking it was anything more than that."

My trainers squeaked as I spun around and practically sprinted out of the room, partially because I didn't want to hear his fucking excuses anymore but mostly because I could feel the emotion stuck in my throat like a giant gumball, stopping me from taking a full breath. My heartbeat pounded in my temples, just as it did with William. Except this wasn't the end of a relationship. This wasn't even the end of a *real* friendship.

This was never anything.

22

Omg, I can't go out there wearing these, I type out to the flat's group chat and send alongside a mirror selfie of the leggings given to me by the gym's receptionist.

Alice replies immediately.

What are you on about? You look hot!

I stare at my arse in the women's changing-room mirrors. These yoga pants are the tightest things I have ever worn. I was already dreading doing stretches in public when I noticed the elasticated seam going straight through my butt crack.

I type out: *I can't go out like this.*

Why not, you look cracking!

Not funny! I reply, a smile pushing against my lips.

Yeah, Al, that joke was pretty half-arsed . . . Yemi chimes in.

Sorry, guys, I'll try butt-er next time, Alice replies.

I think this group chat has hit rock bottom, I reply.

Thankfully, the white HEIMACH branded T-shirt they gave me runs to about halfway down my butt cheeks. I head into the gym and immediately bump into Bancroft coming out of the men's changing room. We both unabashedly study the other's outfit choices under the guise of ridicule.

I examine his all-black clinging T-shirt and expensive-looking yoga pants. "Was 'Douchebag Warehouse' having a sale or something?"

"I bought these for *full retail price* at 'Douchebag Warehouse,' thank you very much." He lifts his eyebrows and I try to stop my lips from curving.

Calming flute music and jasmine incense float on the air as we enter the now-crowded gym and sit on the two remaining squishy black mats.

"This must be a really popular class," I say with a giddy smile. After what I'd seen on the hotel's Instagram, there's double the number of people I was expecting.

Bancroft ignores my comment, instead choosing to scan the crowd with a clenched jaw and a wild panic in his eyes. I tilt my head, furrowing my brow at him, but before I can ask what the matter is a woman at the front of the class holds her hands out to everyone. She has curly silver-gray hair and is wearing a lime-green matching bra top and tight high-waisted leggings.

"Welcome. My name is Crystal and I'll be guiding you through today's session. Please, sit. Before we begin, please turn to the side and take your partner's hand."

My head whizzes around as other people in the room turn to one another; rising panic bubbles in my veins.

We stare at each other, both poker-face expressionless as we reluctantly lay alternate hands palm up and place the opposite hand on top. His palms are warm and coated in the lightest sheen of sweat. As instructed, we push our hands against each other like a New Age arm wrestling match. My entire hand almost fits in his palm, his fingers rising over the tips of mine like seafoam waves crashing over rocks. Bancroft's pupils dilate and he conceals a smirk as I strain and try my hardest to win the non-competition, tensing my arms. He's barely making any effort to push against me—he probably finds it more entertaining to watch me struggle. He shifts, not pressing but holding steady as my skin pushes against his. Crystal eventually raises her hands and we stop, returning our hands to our sides on the mats. The echo of his strong palm pulses lightly against mine.

"See how much energy is wasted when we work against each other? In this session, we will focus on togetherness."

Pure, raging panic shoots up my spine and explodes in my brain like a firework.

"Wait, is this . . . couples' yoga?" I whisper, eyes wide.

His jaw ticks as he stares past me toward the exit. "It certainly wasn't meant to be. Christoph must have booked us into the wrong class." His cheek twitches.

I swipe a palm through my hair and huff a laugh. "Or he thinks we're a couple, just like everyone else bloody does."

His face goes stony as he pushes his hand on the floor. "We should go."

"What? We just got here!" I protest.

"We can't do this," he snaps, shrinking pupils darting

around the gym for the most subtle exit route. Maybe out of the window?

My eyes crease as I examine his body language: shoulders tense, jaw taut, wrinkled brow. You would think he would do whatever it takes to make sure this partnership opportunity goes off without a hitch, but he can't stand the thought of crossing the line if it's made out of my stretching limbs? A vision of him, feet up on my desk, telling me I'd be too uncomfortable to take on this project with him, sears its way into my mind. I've gone toe-to-toe with him at every opportunity when I could have been uncomfortable, and he's trying to duck out the moment things have the potential to get too awkward. I could let him walk and take the credit for the partnership by myself, but I can't do this class without a partner. And *I'm* not backing down.

He gets up into a crouch position so I wrap my fingers lightly around his wrist, only encircling half the width but keeping him down on the mat with me. "We just spent the past two hours learning about every lightbulb and doorknob in the building to secure this partnership." Other people in the room start to watch our exchange; him trying to get up, me trying to pin him down. He moves again, trying to stand and assuming I will let go. When he realizes I can be just as stubborn as him, he makes a fist, tenses his arm and lifts me up to him until I'm off the floor, my body almost pressing against his.

He blinks at our closeness but starts to speak: "I don't think I can—"

I swallow, taking in the panic in his eyes. "If we refuse to do this class, we risk offending a *very* chatty German man into reconsidering a partnership with us and who knows who he'll tell the story to," I interrupt him with an angry whisper, wide eyes locked with his, pleading with him to stay. His pulse pounds under my fingers but I ignore it, too annoyed to think about why. After everything that's happened over the past few days, he can't leave me here now.

"First move to get us warmed up, the Bridged Butterfly," announces Crystal, side-eyeing us as the only couple in the room not paying attention to her.

Bancroft's face creases, undecided.

In a state of panic I change my tactic, pulling in closer and tracing my thumb lightly over his skin. "Think about it: the room offer, the restaurant, the launch party. It's all perfect for Ditto," I whisper seductively. "All we have to do is a little balancing and core exercise. You can do that . . . right, hotshot?"

He lifts his head to the ceiling as he closes his eyes for a few seconds. "Fucking hell." Then he sighs: "You want to be the butterfly or the bridge?"

"Dealer's choice." I smile triumphantly, relief relaxing my muscles.

"We'll start by choosing who is going to be the lead—just like dancing," Crystal advises all of us and I watch the other couples subtly confer with each other. I let out a quiet huff of laughter through my nose. Dancing is what we've been doing this entire time. The push and pull. To say it is anything but a dance would be an understatement. Even when we could barely stand being in the same room together, we were still dancing. Aware of each other's presence as we swayed and dipped our bodies, attempting to avoid each other. At Crystal's instruction, we stand up and I turn my back to Bancroft. He places a hesitant, warm palm on my waist so lightly it's almost hovering, leaving room for the charged atoms to rest in between us. Even the shadow of his hand makes my skin heat.

Crystal pads over to us and places a hand on Bancroft's shoulder, lips pursed. "You're going to need a firm grip here, sweetie." He clears his throat awkwardly as Crystal moves his hands onto my hips. "Your girlfriend is going to need the support."

A jolt of electricity shoots up my legs to meet his splayed, twitching fingers and I am so grateful we aren't face-to-face right now.

You are pissed off at him, I remind myself, trying to temper my fizzing blood.

Crystal directs the class to move into the next part of the position: my feet balancing on his bent knees as I lean forward into downward facing dog and immediately regret my insistence on staying for the session. Once my hands are firmly on the mat, Bancroft leans backward and places his hands on the mat behind him. My eyelids are locked closed as my body shakes for the entire sixty seconds of pose-holding. My heart pounds and my palms couldn't be sweatier, but I can't be sure if it's the yoga or the yoga with Bancroft that's causing my body to react this way.

The next position—"For bonding," Crystal explains—involves us standing back to back, bending down as though to touch our toes but instead holding each other's hands through our legs. We both try not to laugh as we make eye contact between our thighs, releasing the tense elastic band in my chest before it snapped.

"Are you feeling bonded?" he mouths quietly, eyebrows up. Well, down. His face still looks perfect despite being upside down.

I stifle a smile. "My arse is feeling pretty bonded with yours right now."

He bumps into me playfully, trying to lighten the mood. "Speaking of, nice leggings, by the way," he whispers.

I shake my head. "I didn't choose them, they were the only ones they had in my size." My face goes red owing to all the blood rushing to my upside-downness, and not because of how the compliment swept through me like a gush of summer wind.

"Remind me to send Christoph a thank-you note," he deadpans and I roll my eyes.

"Maybe send him a painting instead. You love to do that."

"Time to switch into a new position. Please slowly bring your hands up like this until they are above your head and inhale in mountain pose," says Crystal, demonstrating a wide sweeping motion with her arms.

We copy her, breaking our rigid grips on each other's hands, swinging our arms up and turning to face each other. We're standing close, but come on, it is *couples'* yoga. This is fine, totally normal. This close I can make out the dark blue lines in his eyes, chasms of depth in a vast ocean exaggerated by his flushed face. His face is as red as mine feels but somehow he still looks good. We take deep breaths in unison, releasing them slowly.

"I reserve sending paintings to very special recipients." His tone is a cold martini on a hot day.

"Stop it," I plead. Our arms lower and I have nowhere to put them except my hips.

"What?" he says, mimicking my movement and stepping imperceptibly closer.

"*It.*" I look him up and down, leaning forward. "The trying-to-get-back-in-my-good-books Bancroft Charm thing."

"There's a 'Bancroft Charm thing'?"

I raise my eyebrows in his direction, giving him a look that I hope says "don't act like you don't know." He smirks, wetting his lips and confirming he does, in fact, know.

"Yeah, and I'm not gonna fall for it this time."

His chin tilts, eyebrows furrowing in confusion for just a second before softening as he realizes to what I'm referring.

Shit. Why did I just say that?

"Not that I was thinking about when we—"

"Now we move into our penultimate pose." Crystal's

voice bounces around us like an angel trying to save me from saying something stupid.

Bancroft lies on the mat, holding my legs in the air as I plank above him, gripping his calves for support. His firm but supportive hold on my ankles turns my blood molten.

"So," he says with a grunt, pushing my legs higher, "in the spirit of 'togetherness and honesty,' on a scale of one to ten how much do you hate me right now?"

His question comes out in his usual blasé tone but in between the strands of hair falling over my eyes I see his throat bob as he asks. He's not just talking about the fact that he is getting dangerously close to dropping me on my face.

Shifting my hands further up his legs for better purchase, I say, grunting, "Probably about as much as you hate me. Urgh—did you have to be so tall? This position doesn't work."

"Sorry."

I sigh. "I forgive you."

"For being tall?" He pushes and I can hear the smile on his lips.

"I forgive you for William and for Jeffrey but I can still be hurt by how you handled everything. I can be really fucking sorry about the Christmas party and also mortified. They're not mutually exclusive."

"True," he says, straining to hold me in place as I readjust my grip.

"I get why you kept William's profile from me . . ."

but you knew something important about my life that I didn't." My right arm shakes so I move again, trying to get a better purchase on his thigh to steady myself. "It was a huge violation of privacy."

"Ummm, Grace?" His voice is strained, lips twisting inward.

"Yeah?"

"It's going to be a huge violation of privacy if your hand moves like an inch higher."

"Fuck, sorry." I snatch my hand away immediately and my whole body falls to the side. He catches me with his arm, blocking the right side of my body from hitting the floor. With his hand tight around my waist, he pulls me upright and I land in his lap, my hair covering most of my face.

He leans up into a sitting position, swiping my hair behind my ear in a movement so delicate my limbs feel liquid. "I'm sorry too, again. About everything." His arm holds steady around me as we both swallow air, trying to recover. "I haven't been able to sleep knowing I let you down like that," he admits, eyes creasing as my breath hitches.

"Me neither," I agree, wiping a bead of sweat from my forehead. "I think we need to work on being better friends."

Crystal clears her throat. The sound brings us both back into the room, blinking: the room full of people where I am sitting in Bancroft's lap, his arm around me, both panting heavily.

"You good?" he asks, looking anywhere but at me as he launches me off his lap.

"Yep!" I reply quickly, keeping my head up and focusing on the suddenly fascinating multicolor tapestry on the wall as I leap to my feet.

We balance in silence for a few moments, heat growing in my cheeks as I try to avoid cataloging every place we're touching. We switch into the final cooldown position, sitting cross-legged with knees touching the floor, our faces inches apart. I avoid eye contact, choosing instead to stare intensely at the evaporating imprint my sweaty hand left on the mat.

"I can't keep the painting. It's too much. You should return it to Calico."

"Hastings!" he mocks, appalled, breath caressing my cheek. "You'd take a large sum of money out of the hands of a starving artist because of your own pride?"

I want to grab him by his face and shake him. "Urgh, fine. But why don't you put it in your apartment?" I compromise.

His lips form a smooth line as he considers for a second. He finally shrugs. "Ah, you know, I'd love to, but I just don't have the wall space."

I meet his stare, eyes gawking at his stubborn insistence. "Buy a bigger apartment, then!"

"How about this? I can technically *own* the painting, but you can keep it as long as you want?"

I lift a suspicious eyebrow. "You're not going to give up, are you?" I let a half smile form on my lips.

"I doubt it." He shrugs, lips matching mine.

"OK," I sigh. "New truce. I keep the painting if we agree that as *friends* we have no more secrets."

I hold out my hand for a cartoonish "put 'er there" shake as something flashes behind his eyes. He takes my hand slowly, tracing his fingers along my palm before squeezing the side of my hand with his thumb.

"No more secrets," he repeats, keeping his soft grip on me while mulling over the idea. "Friends."

23

A dark-haired woman with a name tag that says "Hello, I'm Janice. Ask me about our Bratwurst" waves at us from the hotel lobby's concierge counter. "Mr. Teller left this for you." She hands me a note: "*Wunderbar* to meet you both! I cannot wait to begin a fruitful partnership. Our penthouse suite is free for the evening. Please enjoy the best Heimach Hotel has to offer!"

As I finish reading aloud, Janice slides two key cards across the onyx desk with a dramatic flick of the wrist. Everything finally starts to click; is this why Christoph booked us into the couples' yoga sessions?

"Ummm, I think there's been a misunderstanding. We're not together, we're just colleagues," I clarify, glancing briefly at Bancroft for backup.

"I'm so sorry about that," says Janice. "Maybe just one of you could take the suite for the evening? Mr. Teller put room service credits on the room." Her head flicks between Bancroft and me.

Bancroft smirks, dragging a bronze key card across the shiny black surface toward him. "Remember when you said Egyptian cotton sheets were ostentatious and pretentious? You wouldn't want to go back on your word, would you?"

I slap my hand down on the other card. "Someone recently told me I should start being open to new experiences."

My mind drifts to the thought of being spread out across a super king bed, soaking in that huge bathtub, and having my own space for the night to work on my Ditto presentation in peace.

Janice backs away as we stand off, both with a hand on one of the key cards. Half joking, but also completely serious. This has always been our way. We are like the same person in two very different bodies: we want the same things and we can't help but compete. We're dancing again, both refusing to admit you can't *win* a dance.

He looks at me under hooded eyes. "As much as I would love you to have this . . . I think we can both agree I secured this opportunity."

I meet his stare, eyebrows raised. "And *I* think we can both agree that I was the one who won Christoph over."

"I had the contact," he says.

"You wanted to back out of couples' yoga," I say back.

"Don't you have work to do for Susie tonight?" he guesses.

"Don't you literally live five minutes away in a gorgeous apartment?" I guess back.

Bancroft holds his hands up. "OK! Neither of us is

going to win. So, in the spirit of our truce . . . maybe neither of us should take it."

I consider for a moment and then nod. "Equal misery—seems fair."

"It famously loves company, so I think that works with the friends thing."

We both step out of the glass revolving doors onto the gray-speckled pavement, and I watch Bancroft walk away for a few seconds before a rumble from the sky tells me it's time to go home. Dark clouds loom like marshmallows forgotten on a bonfire, spitting tiny droplets of rain on my cheeks as I descend the slippery stairs into the tube. My post-yoga thighs shake lightly as they hold my weight down each step. Commuters lower their umbrellas as we hit the cover of the station, causing a torrent of liquid to spill onto the cracked and faded tile floor. The smell I can only describe as fresh mildew wafts around the turnstiles. Water has already seeped through the mesh side panels of my trainers; I hope I can get home without contracting trench foot.

There's a weird sort of camaraderie in weather like this; instead of fighting the sweat and heat everyone lets it wash over them and we all become one giant breathing organism, arms intertwining and grasping for purchase. For a few minutes a day, we're just cells tucked in tightly and swaying in tandem, hurtling through the city bloodlines.

When William and I first moved to the city we would commute together for half the journey and then separate, him joining the suited masses while I continued with my bright, patterned peers. I loved spending time imagining everyone else's lives. *Where are you going? What is your job like? Do you want to add a redhead with self-esteem issues to your friend group?*

I didn't have friends, but when I was with William, I felt as if I didn't need to create space for those kinds of relationships. Of course, that idea was brought to a screaming emergency stop when he left me. When I realized he liked me needing him and only him.

My phone dings with an email notification.

ERIC BANCROFT MADE EDITS IN THE FOLLOWING DOCUMENT: "DITTO PROJECT REPORTING."

How does he do these so damn quickly? I fling open the document to add my feedback before I lose signal on the tube, quickly glancing at his section.

I enjoyed participating in this experience:
Strongly agree.
Additional comments:

He left the comment section blank. So he *strongly* enjoyed the experience but doesn't care to comment? Or maybe he just hasn't completed it yet? My hand fumbles around my jacket pocket for my debit card. I mindlessly pull it out and slap it onto the yellow sensor, moving forward with the queue like a sheep being herded into a muddy field. My body bumps against the closed barrier and I slap the card again. The barrier beeps and I look down to see not my card, but a shiny bronze card in my hand, the overhead lights of the underground bouncing off its slick surface. It's one of the key cards Christoph left us for the penthouse suite.

"Miss, if your card's not working, you'll need to buy a ticket," a large bald man in an official-looking vest says to me in a monotone voice.

"Sorry," I mumble instinctively, squeezing back past the hordes of nine-to-fivers boxing me in. I wind my way through the crowd, the words *strongly agree* replaying in my mind as I scowl at the card—until the realization dawns on me. We never declined the reservation, and I left with the key card in my pocket. The empty room is still there. Standing in the middle of the moving crowd like a boulder in a raging river, I stare at the thin piece of plastic. Parts of a plan fall into place like a Jenga tower going in reverse.

Would Charlie Bucket just hand back his golden ticket if one of the other kids renounced theirs? Bancroft's words after the cooking class swirl around my head like lukewarm vodka in the bottom of a paper cup.

"You've just got to grab an opportunity when it presents itself."

If he didn't have a quiet, comfortable, luxury apartment with air conditioning and an ice machine in his fridge, would he *really* have gone home? He is used to that kind of lifestyle, so it probably means nothing to him. It's barely a special occasion for him to stay in a penthouse. For me, this opportunity is presenting itself in the form of the words "TAKE IT" repeating over and over in flashing neon lights. *And* Christoph would probably be upset knowing he'd booked us his "favorite place in the world" for the night and neither of us took him up on it. Really, I should stay there for the good of the partnership. Go above and beyond to accommodate the prospective client's requests.

Maybe I'll bump into Christoph and continue some individual discussions to add to my presentation. The idea stews inside me as I mull over my options and the consequences.

Door Number One: spend thirty minutes wedged in a hot tube carriage until I'm coated in a stranger's sweat, drink rosé in my tiny bedroom and trawl through Susie's emails and go to bed too drunk for a Thursday, feeling bad about myself.

Door Number Two: spend the night alone in one of the most beautiful hotel rooms I've ever seen, with pre-paid room service and a giant bathtub, possibly adding to my growing black book of contacts by making a good impression on a powerful and influential hotel-owner.

Spinning on my soggy trainers, I run out of the tube and back to the hotel.

By the time I arrive, the rain has subsided. Lances of summer are trying to break through the rolling clouds, and I'm taking this as a sign from the gods I made the correct decision. The evening sun warms my face as I stare out over the city from the gold-soaked penthouse balcony: the sounds of beeping horns, scuffling feet and commuters talking about their day rising like ivy up the edges of the building. Blues, oranges and pinks pile up like a Rothko painting in the sky. The hotel room, or I should say the series of interconnected hotel rooms, is a glorious meld of cozy patterned cream rugs, buttery brown leather sofas and shiny onyx surfaces. I hadn't truly appreciated the space when Christoph gave us the tour, but now it's all mine for the evening I could cry. Padding through from the living room to the bedroom I resist the urge to jump onto the crisp white sheets like Macaulay Culkin.

Peeling the cotton-spandex-blend cling film leggings from my body, I open the temperature-controlled smoky-mirrored wardrobe to find two white fluffy bathrobes. I hang my clothes to dry and slide into my new sheep cosplay outfit, sinking my sore feet into the doughy cushioned matching slippers, revelling in the new experiences.

It's not as if this is the first time I've ever stayed in a hotel, but this is the first time I've ever stayed in a "capital H" hotel. My first girls' trip to Mallorca before all my friends and I separated off to different futures was in a hostel that smelled different every night but somehow always reminiscent of vomit. The student-friendly long weekends in shitty Airbnbs in the country William and I took when we were at university. Then finally the trips to budget hotels, which in comparison to the shitty rentals of uni days felt like living in luxury. After William and I moved to the city and started careers our schedules hardly ever lined up, and when they did it would always include me having to answer emails at least once a day. My "out of office" autoreply exuded "no worries if not" energy, rendering it pretty useless. This would inevitably turn into an argument with William about how I couldn't be "present and in the moment."

William's job in the finance industry was a cut-and-dry nine-to-five. Every day was the same: clock in, push some spreadsheets, clock out, collect £350 and pass go. When he wanted to drop everything and have some R & R, there was a myriad of similarly suited men in their early to mid-twenties eager to take work off his plate for a few days. There was no one to replace me. There still isn't. Susie was meant to hire an assistant but never did, choosing instead to dump those responsibilities onto my already overloaded plate. Trying to explain to someone who can't or refuses to imagine anything different from their way of life took more energy than it was worth. After a while, I gave up my attempts, instead choosing to hide my laptop and phone away and waiting until he fell asleep to respond to a deluge of emails, tasks and requests; countering my exhaustion by pounding espresso at breakfast with a fake peace-keeping smile plastered on my exhausted face.

My slippers slap against the shiny wood floors and thump on plush wool rugs as I make my way over to the kitchen. Yes, this place has a fully stocked kitchen. Black lacquered cabinets with brass handles and onyx countertops veined in gold and gray span the room, the shiny surfaces reflecting a floor-to-ceiling window's view of the cityscape. I watch as familiar dark clouds begin to block out the sun once again, a rumble crying out in the distance to announce an encore of earlier potent thunderstorms.

I practically dance around with excitement when I see free champagne in the wine fridge, and grab the chilled bottle. Due to the sheer amount of events I manage for Fate, I have become a pro at popping any form of sparkling wine. I sip from a crystal flute feeling fancy as fuck as the bubbles immediately ride down my throat and back up to my brain. Maybe Bancroft is onto something with his whole "grabbing opportunities" mindset? I write a mental note to make it my new mantra.

I check my phone to find an Ignite notification:

Jack: Looking forward to tomorrow :D

Feeling content for the first time in weeks, I reply *Me too :)* and flop onto the bed with an oomph. The combination of a plush robe and five-star bedsheets is better than I ever could have imagined, like lying down on top of a giant soufflé and being enveloped by warm, soft sweetness. Struggling to move, I convince my body to roll over toward the hotel phone and call down to room service. I order dinner and an ice bucket for the champagne, then I flop to the other end of the comfiest surface on earth to run a bath.

While the steaming water fills the marble bathtub in the even more marble-coated bathroom, I pull out my laptop and notebook to assess the state of my Ditto presentation. We're two weeks out from the deadline and it's bare bones right now, lacking the visual flair it needs to pull ahead. I study the notes on each slide, breaking down my thoughts about how Ditto's target users thrive off more than a sit-down dinner and don't want cookie-cutter experiences. They don't want to feel as if they are going on the same first date over and over and over. They don't want massive chains and copy-and-paste encounters that everyone has experienced. They just want dates as interesting as they are, just as varied as their lives are, and just as eclectic as their taste in music, film and art. My thoughts are like kernels of corn in a blazing hot pan.

Maybe that's it? I type out *first dates as unique as you* in bold font, smile at the words and for the first time since that day in Catcher's office think to myself: *I could win this.*

I spend another few minutes flipping through the black and white slides, splicing in Yemi's data from Fate and Ignite in graph form to back up my claims until a noise jolts my head toward the penthouse entrance. I hear what sounds like shuffling feet right outside the door and my mind flashes with horror stories from women alone in hotel rooms. I push the fear down and remember my order. This must just be *very* speedy room service—it is a five-star hotel after all. Pushing off the bed and pulling my robe tight, I see off the rest of my champagne glass, turn off the bath and glide through the mid-century living room. Attempting to flatten my frizzy post-rainstorm hair, I fling open the door to find a familiar black leather duffel bag and Bancroft bent over looking intensely at his shiny bronze key card, as if trying to work out which side to swipe first.

My mouth immediately opens wide to chastise him for going back on his word. That is until I descend from my high horse into my white robe–clad body and realize I'm standing *in* the penthouse suite of the Heimach Hotel half-drunk on one glass of very expensive champagne when he has just arrived. His narrowed eyes gather a glint of amusement as they slowly make their way from the key-card scanner up my fluffy torso, over my just-emptied glass and land on my sheepish, beetroot face, soaking up the view.

"Fancy seeing you here, Hastings."

24

A dimple appears on his left cheek for a fraction of a second as he fixes me an amused stare.

"I thought the idea of one thousand thread count sheets made you nauseous?"

"Nauseous and sleepy," I say, laughing nervously and pulling my robe as tight as possible. "What are you doing here?"

He sighs, flapping his arm out in exasperation. "The thunderstorm cut out the internet for my entire building. I need a place with decent Wi-Fi to work on my Ditto presentation for a few hours."

"Maybe a cafe?" I drawl half-heartedly, fingers gripping firmly on to the door as a blockade.

He looks at his Moncler wristwatch and then back up to me. "Closed."

"Bar?" I offer.

"This work is confidential." He shoots me an accusatory look, as if I've been hosting a nightly stage show about Catch Group's plans for dating-app world domination.

I sigh, accepting my fate and flinging the door wide

open. "OK, Bancroft! Come on in!" I throw my arm out to welcome him inside.

He studies the room. "You made yourself at home quickly."

My stomach cringes as he moves his gaze over the contents of my bag strewn across the living room, clothes thrown over the bedroom armchair and laptop open on the bed. Pieces of the champagne bottle top are littered across the kitchen counter; with one arm I wipe them all into the sink.

Bancroft tries to stop the corner of his mouth from tipping up as he crosses his arms. "What did you do— hide in the bushes until I left the building then sneak back up here?"

Picking up my stuff and throwing it onto the bed, re-establishing my territory for the night, I say innocently, "I was on my way home and then I recalled some advice about taking opportunities when they present themselves."

"Hmmm, good advice. What stunningly intelligent person told you that?" he deadpans, pivoting on his heel as he watches me frantically move from room to room.

"Some guy at work." I shrug. "A colleague."

He cocks his head to the side, pouting slightly. "Sounds like more than just a colleague."

I fling my sports bra, Ditto notebook and trainers into the bedroom and stride back to him, slightly out of breath. "You're right, but former friend slash worst nemesis slash current friend doesn't quite have the same ring to it."

He thinks about this for a second, mouth opening and

then closing again as though he's rethinking what he was about to say. After a moment of silence he speaks.

"So, where can a 'former friend slash worst nemesis slash current friend' work on their master takedown plan?" Eyebrows raised, he looks around the room, strategically avoiding a glance at the bed.

Maybe I should go home—cower at this surprise appearance and slink off back to my flat—but my pride stops me. We are friends now and I was here first. Also, if I leave now he'll win, and that is so much worse than having to deal with his presence for a couple of hours.

I study the room too; then I point to the sofa. "There."

He nods silently and paces over.

"Don't let me disturb the rest of your evening," he says sarcastically, looking me up and down.

"You are *always* disturbing," I mutter as I tighten my robe again.

He lets out a chuckle. I wonder if he remembers the last time I said that to him: when he was trying to put me off taking this project, telling me I'd be too uncomfortable. It's crazy how far we've come since then. I would never have believed you just a few weeks ago if you told me I would be alone, half-naked, in a penthouse suite with Eric Bancroft.

Alone. Half-naked. With Eric Bancroft. I swallow an audible gulp.

He kicks off his shoes and peels off his damp jacket, gently hanging it over a chair, then pads over to the sofa and begins to work as I try to edge my way subtly into the bathroom. Once inside, I shut the door and droop over the marble double sink.

"Get it together. We are over this. This is *not* a big deal," I insist to my reflection. "It's no different than when we were alone in the Fate office together."

Except, it is different. Now, I'm not with William or struggling through heartbreak, and unlike working in the office, there is no chance of a colleague or boss walking in on us alone together. Bancroft and I are alone together. Oh my god, I need to stop overthinking this.

He's just studiously working on his presentation, not thinking about anything but securing the new job, and I've trapped myself in a bathroom freaking about how the touch of his fingers during the yoga class feels practically imprinted on my hips. I shake my head and splash my face with cold water.

Trying to find something to take my mind off the man on the other side of the door, I peruse the free soaps, gels and creams neatly littering the sink counter. I freeze as its contents come into focus on the marble countertop. In front of me is a basket of amenities so extensive I can imagine Alice screaming with excitement. Hair masks, face creams, body oils, something called snail serum and a HEIMACH-branded black velvet pouch, which I can't help opening and tipping out onto the counter. It's a sex bag. A sex bag packed with everything you might need for a steamy night in a penthouse suite. There is a vial of organic massage oil, a travel-size bottle of vanilla-flavored lube and an assortment of vegan condoms. Christoph wasn't exaggerating when he said the team thinks of everything here. I try to put each item back in the pouch, but it's all so tightly packed it quickly dawns on me I can't put it back the way I found it. The moment Bancroft sees the strewn-out basket it will become painfully obvious I've been hiding in the bathroom playing with sex paraphernalia. I shove the condoms, lube and oil into the deep pockets of my robe and rearrange the marginally less stuffed basket until it looks untouched. Bancroft already thinks I'm a prude; the last thing I need is a lube elephant-in-the-room screaming "this is a *sex* penthouse" from the bathroom to give him ammunition. I take a breath, safe in the knowledge that he'll be gone in a few hours and my body will be free of this weird butterfly tension.

I turn the bath taps back on and blast hot water into the tub. Hardly the relaxing experience I was hoping for, knowing he's on the other side of the suite. I lie in the bath, hot, sweaty and uncomfortable. I should just get out. After a few minutes I stand, pulling the fluffy white towel from the rack. It unravels and my stomach sinks as I realize the fabric wrapped around me barely reaches my midthighs, and soaking wet re-curling hair is dripping around my shoulders and back. In my urgency to escape a potentially awkward moment, I didn't even think to bring my clothes in here either.

"Close your eyes!" I shout through the cracked door.

I wait a few seconds with no reply.

"Are they closed?" I ask.

"Yes," he calls back, voice slightly strained.

I take a few tentative steps out to make sure his eyes are actually closed; his hands are also over his face as an extra precaution. Satisfied, I fling my body out of the bathroom past the doorless opening between the bedroom and living room, cursing this room's chic open-plan design. Hiding in the furthest corner of the bedroom I dry off and throw on my underwear and the now dry T-shirt, layering my robe on top so only my bare legs are visible. My wet hair sits in a fresh fluffy towel on my head.

"Are you done?" he asks, hands still over his eyes.

"Yeah," I say, trying my best to sound nonchalant.

"Your food arrived—I took the liberty of checking it for poison," he states, nodding to the plates of Wagyu burger with truffle fries and Caesar salad with grilled chicken on the coffee table. The burger has a huge bite taken out of it. I lift my eyebrows in outraged question. "In my defence, you ordered two main courses for yourself and used all the room service credit, so it was that or starve."

"No worries, buddy! Have as much as you want—perhaps some fries with that?" I say sarcastically.

He either does not note my tone or ignores it and grabs a handful of truffle fries as I slowly slide the warm plate toward me, letting out an involuntary moan as I take a bite of the burger. I cover it by lounging on the chaise longue across from him and watching him as he stares intently at his laptop screen.

Popping a fry in my mouth I ask, "How's your presentation going?"

"Good," he says blankly. "Yours?"

I suck in my teeth, disappointed by his lack of information. "Finished."

His brow crinkles. "Then what are you working on now?" He gestures to the laptop on the bed.

I shift awkwardly, readjusting my robe. "Ummm, you know that side project I told you about ages ago? You probably don't remember . . ." I trail off.

"Ever After." He says it matter-of-factly, as if we'd discussed my idea a day ago instead of nine months ago.

"Yeah." I try to subdue a smile but fail. "I'm reworking it from a Fate feature to a fully fledged app. Yemi created a beta for me."

"Oh yeah?" he asks, something in his expression softening. "I thought Susie said no to it?"

"She did . . ." I agree, looking down at the rug.

"But you can't help yourself," he finishes for me.

I scoff a laugh and tilt my head, unable to think of a witty reply.

He leans forward. "You should keep going—it's a great idea."

My chest warms more than I want it to. "You think?"

"I did back then, didn't I?" His eyebrows raise.

"I've added some more features since then, like the monthly check-in date prompts." I shrug in an attempt at nonchalance. "It was kind of inspired by the reporting we've been doing." It feels strange talking about this with him, crowbarring open a door we'd both boarded up months ago. "But Susie will probably just reject it again anyway."

"My advice, not that you asked for it, is don't waste a good idea on someone who doesn't want to hear it." He leans back, placing one leg over the other. "When I'm Marketing Lead at Ditto you can pitch it to me instead." He smirks as I roll my eyes.

We sit in silence for a few minutes, punctuated by the sounds of my chomps and the clicking of his keyboard.

"Do you have to do that?" he asks.

"What?" I ask back.

His lip curls in disgust. "Chew so loudly. You sound like a velociraptor."

I put my hand over my mouth, finishing my bite.

"Sorry, you're probably not used to being around women who actually eat food, right?" I tease.

"Yeah, we usually just split a vitamin IV bag," he says, running a hand through his sandy hair.

It has more of a curl than usual owing to the rain, which, combined with his undone shirt collar and rolled-up sleeves, gives him a casual, laid-back look I don't think I've seen before. He looks up from his laptop screen, catching me staring.

I clear my throat and look down at my fries. "Is that what you're going to do on your Fate date then?" I swirl a fry around in sauce.

"No . . . I was thinking dinner and a movie then heading over to the nearest town hall to sign the marriage license. That's a usual Fate date, right?"

"Har-har," I say bitterly, mouth full and trying to figure out how it's even possible to not chew loudly. I throw a fry at his face; it bounces off his forehead and lands in his lap.

He snatches it up and tears it in half with his teeth. "What about your Ignite date?"

My shoulders roll as I adjust my posture. "I'm actually going on a date tomorrow morning—a breakfast date."

Bancroft shifts, left hand pressing wide against the sofa. "Oh?" He finally looks up from his laptop and the sofa creaks as he shifts again. Vein-like creases appear in the leather as he tries to relax. The setting sun coats his side of the room in a warm pink glow.

"Yeah, he's taking me to this historic pancake coffee house place before work." My Bancroft emotional index scans his face for a reaction.

Why do you even care what he thinks?

"Breakfast. Veeery seeexy." His monotone voice draws out the words, eyes flaring wide for emphasis.

My smile drops. "I'm really looking forward to it. He says I'm going to love it," I say, eyes squinting, scanner zooming in closer to record every minute movement of his face. His eyes are laser-focused on a point on the table.

"I'm sure you are," he echoes shortly, interrupting my train of thought like a paper plane to the skull before returning his gaze to his laptop screen. "Going to love it, I mean."

"I am!" I repeat, placing my empty plate back on the coffee table, on top of one of his stupid leather note-books, and stomping back to the bedroom.

There is no door between the living room and

bedroom, just a sliding double partition that sits in between two mirrored wardrobes. It feels weird to make the specific effort to block off the two rooms, so, lounging on the end of the king-size bed, I place my laptop on my bare legs and begin typing.

We both work in silence for two hours, the faint beeps and shouts of the city outside giving it less of a "alone in a hotel room together" and more of a "coworking space" vibe. I finish an "urgent" event-data report for Susie in thirty minutes and swiftly move back to my Ditto presentation. I don't know how we used to get any work done together: I can barely concentrate with him sitting in what is technically a separate room. We're facing each other from opposite ends of the suite, our laptops acting as shields. I've felt his eyes on me multiple times over the past couple of hours, but whenever I spare a glance over to him his eyes are superglued to his computer, face stern and deep in concentration.

Finally, I give in and cut through the silence. "You never told me what you're *really* doing for your Fate date." I copy his intense stare in an attempt to seem nonchalant.

His laptop closes with a soft click. "Why do you want to know?" He tenses his jaw, then gets up and paces to the kitchen as I consider my reason. He lifts the champagne bottle from the half-melted ice bucket and pours two glasses. Both flutes dangle leisurely between his long fingers in a way that's oddly sexy. Like drawstrings on sweatpants.

Something in my body twists, making me hold my breath as he stalks toward me and hands me a glass.

"Morbid curiosity?" I finally answer, closing my own laptop.

Our fingers briefly brush as he looks down at me, warm against the chilled flute.

"I haven't booked one yet," he admits, polishing off half his champagne in one gulp and pacing back to the living-room sofa.

"Well, well, well . . ." The self-righteous thrill travels up my spine and into the pleasure center of my brain as I shoot him a devious smile from the end of the giant master bed.

He looks up at me from the sofa and slants his neck to the side. "Well, well, what?" His voice lowers an octave.

"Mr. 'Bachelor of the Year' can't get a date?" I tease, lips pouted.

"More like Mr. Bachelor of the Year is too busy going on fake dates with his annoying 'colleague' to have the time." His tongue draws out the word like a curse.

"OK, buddy, you keep telling yourself that." I match his huge sip and I fling myself off the bed toward the bathroom; my robe flicks outward briefly to expose my upper thigh.

He calls out to me as I pace: "Oh, sorry. I forgot we're not colleagues, we're archnemeses slash work friends." Even from the other side of the room I can see his eye roll—astronauts in the International Space Station can see his eye roll.

"Former friends, and I'm seriously considering if we need to go back to being worst enemies!" I correct in a loud singsong shout, my voice bouncing off the marble tiles as I try to maintain our quickly unraveling truce.

I smile smugly to myself in the bathroom mirror at his lack of retort and pick a hair oil worth more than a week's rent out of the basket, running it through my nearly dry curls. The scent of coconut and vanilla wafts under my nose as I close my eyes and drag my fingers over my scalp.

I jump as an oddly clear voice cuts through the air.

"When are you just going to admit it?" Bancroft leans his bicep against the door, a freshly topped-off glass of champagne in hand. My blood heats at the image of him silhouetted like that, how the crown of his head nearly hits the top of the doorframe.

"Admit what?" My voice trembles lightly as my oil-slicked hands glide out of my hair and land on the cool stone counter.

"That when we were friends, we were never *just friends*." His expression is laced with something I can't place.

Why does this feel dangerous?

"What are you talking about?" My narrowed eyes meet him through the bathroom mirror. The bottom of my stomach tightens into a knot as he takes a step closer, towering behind me in the mirror. I try to school my face into neutrality as the memories of his fingers rage against my bones.

He scans my face, jaw ticking as he mulls over his next words.

"We were allies." The champagne bubbles flatten in my stomach as he continues, voice hoarse: "And now, you put so much energy into maintaining the fantasy that we don't work well together. We could be—"

He stops himself at my confused face and clears the end of his glass. "Never mind." He leans over me, the side of his hand grazing mine as he places his empty champagne glass on the counter with a clink; his other hand is a fist tight by his side. Goose bumps run riot over my limbs while my heart pounds against my chest as if it's trying to break free.

He squeezes his eyes shut for a second, shaking his head before he says, "This Ignite date. Is it a real date? Or just for research?"

I swallow. "Real."

He flicks his eyes to the reflection of mine and then, without warning, walks out of the bathroom. Leaving me alone. His cologne lingers; without thinking I follow it out of the room like a cartoon dog smelling a windowsill pie. I find him packing up his laptop, curling the white charging cable around his taut hand.

"What are you doing?" I ask, knowing exactly what he is doing.

"I should go." He stuffs the wound cable into his leather bag. "You're right: you charmed the pants off Christoph, you deserve to enjoy the room on your own."

The words come out of my mouth before my brain

comes to its senses. "It's nearly midnight and chucking it down outside. Just sleep in the living room." I scratch the back of my head, eyebrows knitted. The rain pounds against the window as hard as my heartbeat.

He stops with one arm in his bag and looks up at me, eyes bright. "You want me to stay?" He raises an eyebrow, just as shocked as I am at the words coming from my lips.

"No!" I blurt defensively, arms crossing tightly across my chest. "I just don't want you to go."

He doesn't respond, but a slow smile spreads across his face.

I throw my arms in the air. "The room was a joint gift. *Mi casa es su casa!*" I say, mouth dry.

"I really don't have to—"

"You can sleep there," I interrupt, pointing to the sofa. He stifles a smile as I throw a pillow of confirmation at him. "But I'm going to bed. Goodnight."

He turns away and my eyes clamp shut. *Why. Why. Why.* Why did my stupid brain do that? I know I should send him home but I just . . . don't want to. I could already feel the empty hole his absence would carve out. A yawning chasm of disappointment. And all I would fill it with would be overthinking and what-ifs.

"OK, I'll stay. Goodnight, Grace." He holds the pillow to his chest, eyes glinting.

I call back, "Sleep tight!"

25

I do not sleep tight. I sleep scattered, my limbs thrown across the sheets, searching every inch of the king-size bed, trying to find fresh pockets of cold like an octopus on acid. I gave up a while ago. The thunderstorm outside isn't helping the feeling that I'm stuck inside a bubble that's about to burst. The air seeping in from the city crackles with energy. I'm not a good sleeper at the best of times; after I moved to the city it took me months to get used to the sounds of ambulances, drunk people and horny foxes all having street-side screaming contests every night. But the intermittent thunder—which seems so much louder up this high—and Bancroft's naturally overwhelming presence in the room mean there is absolutely no chance of me having a restful night.

"We were never just friends."

I debate whether to cancel the date with Jack. It's 2 a.m., the date is in six hours. I'll be so tired. I'll have to wear yesterday's work clothes. Susie will be pissed off if I get in a minute past 9 a.m., so it's barely worth going.

The only thing stopping me from canceling is the fact I've already, stupidly, told Bancroft about it. If I cancel, he'll assume it's because of him. Because of what he said.

His voice replays in my head like some lust-edged ice-cream truck circling the block over and over and over. *"Is it a real date?"*

What does that even mean? And why did he try and bolt the minute I confirmed it was?

Shifting slowly so the bed barely makes a sound I look over to where Bancroft is sleeping soundly. His existence in the room is so . . . loud. He always commands attention but now it's as if some otherworldly being is bellowing "Helloooooo, do you see that stunning man sleeping meters away from you?" directly into my skull. The warm glow radiating from the expansive living-room windows gently caresses him as he sleeps. I'm pretty sure he's just in his boxers under that blanket. His exposed chest rises slowly up and falls gently. It's not fair. Why couldn't the person I am set to destroy be some annoying, unattractive oaf without an ounce of charm? Not the smoky-woody-with-hints-of-lemongrassy-smelling Adonis who's so tall his bare legs are dangling out of the blanket over the edge of the sofa. Urgh.

I bite my lip as my hand rubs in long, drawn-out circles over my belly, tracing the edges of my underwear. I'm just frustrated; it's nothing to do with him. But why can I not stop staring at his jaw, thinking what it would be like to trace my fingers over it; his chest, what it would feel like pressed against mine; his mouth, and what it would whisper to me in the dark? Something curls in my stomach as I remember his lips feathering against mine in the winter lamplight, his eyes hardening and throat bobbing as he tried to comfort me in his office, the ghost of his thumb lightly tracing my ribs during the yoga class. My hand trails up and down over the lace of my underwear in rhythm with his moving chest.

He shifts onto his back and throws a muscled arm over his face. My fingers stop dead.

My eyes scrunch closed as I mirror his movement, lying flat on the bed.

What are you doing? Snap out of it! This is Bancroft. You hate him. You are currently plotting his professional demise!

Sighing, I reach through the darkness to the side table for a glass of water, only to bump my hand against an almost empty champagne glass. The round base teeters back and forth debating whether to fall and break. Punishing me for my indiscretion, it decides to topple. My hand lurches out and I screech through gritted teeth as my finger touches the edge of the glass. The flute hits the edge of the side table and splits cleanly in half against the wooden surface. I thank the universe it didn't completely explode into tiny shards of expensive crystal all over the rug, or cover my notebook in flat champagne. Glancing back to Bancroft, I check if the sound woke him; thankfully, he's still asleep, arm taut over his face. I quietly untangle myself from the sheets, rubbing my eyes.

With a piece of champagne-coated crystal in each

hand, I creep on tiptoes like a Scooby Doo villain through the living room, praying Bancroft doesn't wake to see me in a T-shirt and underwear inching past him with a shard of glass weapon in hand. I let out a held breath as I round into the kitchen, gently placing the two pieces of glass into the copper sink. My head feels heavy as I look out on the sparkling city skyline. Purple, blue and red lights from passing boats bounce off the river, piercing through the rows of twinkling high-rise buildings. This time of night has always filled me with an eddying comfort. It's like being stuck between waking and dreaming, in a world where anything could happen, but none of it seems real.

My body jolts as my peripheral vision catches sight of a figure in the kitchen entryway.

"Thirsty?" the shadowed specter asks with a smirk.

My entire body turns into a canvas of goose bumps. "Parched," I confirm, swallowing.

"Same." He stalks toward me, the light of the city pulling him from the shadows.

It is, of course, Eric Bancroft, standing in just black boxer briefs.

I suck in my cheeks and stare intently out of the window, avoiding dipping my eyes anywhere below his neck. If I did, I'd see rounded pecs with a smattering of chest hair darker than the hair on his head, at least six abs just surfacing on his stomach, and taut, defined Vs dipping into his underwear like a runway. And right next to them: the healing scar I gave him at El Turo.

I shuffle out of his way, letting out a stuttered laugh as he opens a cabinet. His back and shoulder muscles shift like tectonic plates as he reaches for two wide-rimmed tumblers, every movement smooth and deliberate. He clears his throat, snapping me out of my sleep-deprived trance.

"Water OK?" His normally bright eyes look almost navy in this light, city lights blinking in them like constellations.

I nod silently and he fills the two glasses at the sink, not acknowledging the broken glass in the basin. Did he not notice it, or did he already know it was there?

"Sorry if I woke you up," I test.

"You didn't. I've been awake for hours." He glances up from the sink to test me back. "Light sleeper."

My cheeks heat as he hands me one of the glasses, not breaking his dark gaze when his fingers trace the edges of mine. I can't even think of the words, just look into the bottom of the glass wishing I was a hundred times smaller so I could jump into it and never come up for air.

Sensing my discomfort, he shifts, returning to the default cockiness I know and loathe.

"I know that's probably a shock to you, seeing as most of the time I look so well rested." He shoots a confident smile while taking a step back from me.

In an attempt to ease the familiar sensation building between my thighs, I lean against the counter and try to match his sarcastic tone.

"What, sleeping on your usual one-million-thread-count

emperor bed isn't good enough for His Highness?" I stare at him, eyebrows creased in confusion. This version of him is so different from the man in the bathroom earlier, as though the moment the words "real date" loosened themselves from my lips a switch flipped in his head.

A dimple appears on one cheek as he takes another step forward. "You seem *very* invested in my bedroom setup." He takes a nonchalant swig out of the carved tumbler, attention fixed on me. I cross my arms over my breasts to cover my hardening nipples. He's considerably more naked than me but I can't help but feel as though I'm the one exposed.

He frowns because I won't play whatever this game is. "Why did you ask me to stay?"

He takes a step closer, leaving an arm's length between us.

I parry, pushing my exposed backside against the cold onyx countertop. "I pitied you."

He steps back, ending our dance and leaning against the floor-to-ceiling window. The skyline frames him in a white humming glow, a devil masquerading as an angel.

"If that's what you need to tell yourself so you can sleep at night. But . . ." He pauses as if he's deliberating something, turning his gaze to his glass and then flicking hooded eyes back up to me. ". . . you weren't sleeping either, were you? Show me what you were doing."

"What?" I ask, the word coming out more breathlessly than I had intended. He relaxes against the window, crossing his muscled arms over his stomach.

"Show me," he repeats.

The bottom of my stomach throbs with a heavy mix of shame and excitement. He stares at me with sure eyes as he gestures with his chin, slowly trailing his eyes from mine, down to my underwear just poking out underneath my T-shirt. The way his gaze moves isn't like a question . . . more like a challenge. A dare leaving his eyes and landing straight between my thighs. It takes every ounce of confidence in me, emboldened in the dark, to meet his eye. We grip the drawn line with both hands and twist in opposite directions. A defiant smirk flickers to life across my mouth as I accept the dare.

He will not win.

My left hand remains laid casually on the counter as my right gravitates toward the top of my thigh. I steady my breathing as my fingers gently move across my skin, getting higher with each stroke until they reach the hem of my T-shirt. Shifting, the worn cotton fabric pushes up, exposing my underwear to him. I am so glad I'm not wearing the old pair of Muppets-themed pants I usually wear to bed. My hand moves under the seam of dark pink lace until my fingers reach where they had been just minutes ago. Breath hitching, I meet his gaze. My cheeks flush to match my underwear as I realize that while I've been focusing on my hand, he's been staring at my face. Watching my throat as it bobs, swallowing gulps of nighttime air.

He shifts, readjusting against the window pane and pulling my attention from his hardened face to his hardened . . . body. One side of my lip curls in satisfaction, knowing that my rising to this kind of challenge will be his undoing, and make him do the same. The surging wave of power in making his cool exterior break and unravel into something he can't control triggers a jolt of pleasure to run down my body and land between my thighs.

I swallow, mouth dry. "Is this what you think you saw, *Friend*?" My voice comes out deeper than I'd intended, thicker as I remind him of our truce. Bancroft doesn't respond, just lets out a breathy laugh and smirks back.

His eyes blaze as my shaky hand returns to the countertop; it takes everything in me to stop my knees from buckling. My foggy brain reasons that we should stop now before we do something we can't take back, as though touching myself in front of a colleague is just some non-event. My eyes dart between him and the arched doorway to the living room. I could simply go back to bed, and we could pretend this never happened. He dared me, and I accepted. Game over. But my bare feet are stuck to the black tiled floor like soft hands wrapped around my ankles.

"Let me show you what I've been wanting to do," he says, eyes softening.

A statement but also an unspoken question: *Do you want me to?*

He's waiting for my response, but words have left me as my mind runs riot. My legs are somehow jelly and rock solid at the same time. All I can do is nod. He leisurely finishes off his glass of water, taking his time to savor the last drop, then pads at an excruciatingly slow pace toward me. I realize he's giving me time. Time to think, time to stop him, to come to my senses and call whatever this is off. To throw up a white flag, with no hard feelings.

In reality, any semblance of sense left the building as soon as I invited him to stay the night. He comes toe-to-toe with me, placing his tumbler on the counter by my side with a soft clink. His hand slides from the cool glass, traveling under my T-shirt to my warm waist. He squeezes his fingers lightly, branding my skin and burning through all the boundaries we set. My hands grip viselike on the counter, holding on for dear life. As though letting go of the edge would mean letting go of everything. Acknowledging the ticking time bomb of attraction lodged between us since the very first day we met. His body presses against mine, the bare skin of his chiseled torso seeping heat through my T-shirt until my skin prickles. His scent fills my nostrils, smoky-sweet and inviting. I close my eyes and lower my chin. *This is torture*. But I've already made the first move. If he wants this, it's his turn.

He glides his fingers in aching strokes across my side as he brings his mouth to my ear: "In the yoga class this is all I could think about."

His warm breath and vibrating chest send a message to my knees to just give up now. I sink a couple of inches, but he steadies me with a gentle hand.

"Is that why you declined to comment on the evaluation form?" I whisper, my breath caught somewhere deep in my chest.

He chokes out a laugh. "What was I meant to say? 'I was barely paying attention to the class because I was concentrating so much on not getting hard'?"

Rough hands trace my sides, dragging down my waist and my hips until they slide toward the outside of my thighs, fingers pressing in lightly and then, slowly, more tightly around my skin. His eyes are laced with roaring desire, but I can see that he's holding back. Every movement, every touch is softer than he wants it to be. Restrained when it wants to be fierce.

"And how's that concentration now?" I ask, whispering it breathlessly into his ear like a statement I'll deny if he ever repeats.

He lets out a low hum, smoothing his hands around my thighs until they're underneath me and lifting me up onto the cold counter. I let out an involuntarily moaning gasp, releasing my hands from the surface and grabbing on to his broad, toned shoulders for balance. He settles between my legs so I can feel the press of his erection against me.

His shoulders shift under my palms as he reaches out and lightly strokes my cheek with his thumb. "Grace, I have never been able to concentrate on anything around you."

Before I can reply, his lips delicately brush against mine, soft and faint compared to the hardness sitting between my thighs. I curl my fingers into his skin, parting my lips for him. He groans at the invitation, and slips his tongue against mine, grinding himself against me and increasing the intensity. Electric desire prickles through every nerve as I match his demanding rhythm. My hands slide up his neck and into his hair, our mouths clash and his sweet taste makes my insides reach their boiling point. His lips drag kisses over my jaw and down until his teeth meet my neck. I whimper, gripping and clenching his hair in my fists like pulling tufts of grass from the earth. The jagged feel of his teeth and tongue and lips and breath make me so lightheaded I'd fall off the counter if his body wasn't pinning me against it. He slips his hand into my hair, matching my light tugs and sending me into a complete spiral of staggering lust.

Finally coming up for air, his chest heaves as our foreheads meet. His brow knits as though he wasn't expecting it to feel *this* good. Eyes blazing, he flicks between my heavy-lidded eyes and my plumped pink lips. I lean my mouth forward, ready to accept his on mine all night, but instead of meeting me halfway, he bends down onto one knee, keeping my gaze as he pushes my legs apart with his overstretched hands.

"Wait." As soon as the word leaves my mouth I feel his steel grip on me loosen. He stays nestled between my legs but pulls back up and moves his hands to the counter. I feel the focused burn where his fingers pushed into my skin. His gaze meets mine, waiting politely as I'd asked.

"I'm not . . . I haven't . . ." I swallow dryly, feeling embarrassed for the first time since he started touching me. "I haven't shaved . . . in a few days."

More like twelve days but who's counting?

I know it's nothing I should actually be ashamed of, but William wouldn't touch me unless I was completely clean-shaven. There were a couple of times where he stopped so that I could go and use an emergency wax strip before we continued. And I certainly wasn't expecting my night to end this way.

He lets out a breathless laugh, a wave of relief flowing over his face as his forehead leans forward to meet mine.

He drags my bottom lip between his teeth and then says, voice dropping an octave lower than I'm used to, "I know whatever I find is going to be perfect. Plus, I'm a fan of the retro look," he admits onto my lips with a curling smirk and a shrug, forcing another nervous breath out of me to mingle with his. My blood pulses around his fingers. I lift my chin to the ceiling as he lowers himself again and pulls my underwear to the side, fearing that the image of his mouth between my thighs is going to make me explode on sight.

"Fuck, Grace. Have you been this wet for me all night?" he growls, sounding almost annoyed at the time we've wasted in this suite. "We'd better do something about that."

His mouth hovers near me, one final question before we march hand in hand over the line. My palm moves from gripping his shoulder into his hair, pulling lightly on the soft strands, circling them around my fingers. He chuckles through his nose, accepting my silent answer.

I gasp as he pulls me into him, dragging me forward, gravity helping him put delicious pressure against my aching center. His biceps harden as his arms wrap under and around my thighs, caging the lower half of my body in place as he slowly, gently, devastatingly licks his way inside me. Every swipe of his tongue, his lips, his teeth pulls me further away from my inhibitions. I grind against him and he matches the rhythm, taking notes on what pulls gasping breaths from my throat and giving me more of it.

A wave of throbbing heat shoots up my body. I bite my lip to stop myself from crying out, as if I'm in denial of the overwhelming sensation firing around my core. Every nerve ending is about to burst into flames as I combust on the cold counter. My legs shake as I arch my back, crying obscenities into the dark.

He comes back up and kisses me hard, drawing breath from my mouth as though I'm his own personal oxygen mask. Before the fog of orgasm fully clears, he grips my thighs again and lifts me until I lock on to his hips. My limbs wrap around him as he carries me through the suite to the bedroom. I catch his bottom lip between my teeth, kissing the smirk right off his face. His throbbing cock rubs against my underwear, sending a jolt of heat up my legs with every step.

As he lays me on the bed among the crumpled sheets, he kisses my forehead, my cheek, my jaw, my neck and it's so tender I briefly forget who we are and everything that's happened between us. A shy smile splits my lips. He notices and traces my lips with his thumb, smiling a full smile back before returning to map my body with his mouth, gliding my T-shirt up over my chest and greedily taking my nipple into his mouth.

After a few seconds like this, he lifts his head as if coming out of a trance.

"We need a condom," he says breathily.

"Do you have one?" I ask.

"Why would I bring a condom to a business meeting?" he asks my rib cage.

My heavy head lifts up off the bed to look at him.

"Don't you keep one in your wallet or something?" I say desperately, trying to ignore the sinking feeling in my chest.

"No, wallets can start degrading the latex after like three hours." He rubs his face with the hand that was just all over me.

"Oh, so *now* you follow the rules?!" I laugh, half-amused, half-exasperated.

He lifts his weight off me, one hand next to my head pressed into the bedding, and hangs his head as if he's just lost his winning lottery ticket, his messy hair flopping onto his face and his mouth pressing against my shoulder.

For a few moments, we stay paused, neither wanting to untangle our legs from each other but both knowing what will happen if we don't. I feel the overwhelming urge to brush his wavy hair back onto the top of his head when I remember the sex bag in the bathroom.

"Oh my God!"

He looks down at our meshed bodies in a panic. My hands on his bare chest, I push him off me and sprint to the bathroom.

"A-are you OK?" he shouts from the bedroom, but I can barely hear him over the sound of me rustling through the two bathroom robe pockets until—

"Aha!" I stick my head around the door and hold out a Heimach Hotel–branded vegan condom as though I'm showing him my most prized possession. "Thank you, Christoph."

I have to stop myself from sprinting back over to him, instead attempting a tantalizing pace, pulling my rumpled T-shirt up over my head and throwing it to the other side of the room as I stride back to him. He's sitting on the edge of the bed and reaches for the condom. I have to stop myself from ogling his taut sun-kissed frame. He sighs, turning the plastic square in his fingers between his thighs.

A line forms between his brows and he lets out a breath that settles on my exposed stomach. "Are you sure you want to do this?"

My heart sinks at his hesitation. The realization of just how *much* I want this dawns on me like a punch to the gut. Like flipping a coin but not knowing which side you truly want until it lands. I brush the loose hair from his face and ask in the most seductive voice I can muster, "Aren't we already doing this?"

He takes my hips in his hands, lightly tugging me closer until I am standing in between his legs.

"No," he replies with a faint smile, the small glimmers of light in the room bouncing off his cheekbones. My stomach turns molten as he kisses the skin above my underwear and looks up at me under hooded eyes. "We haven't even started."

26

We move as one, breathing almost completely in sync while the hot rain pounds against the window like a chorus of ratifying applause. I don't think it's ever been as good as this. Especially not the first time with someone new. It doesn't feel like the first time, it feels like I've been away for years and have finally come home to someone who knows me inside and out.

"Fuck, you're so beautiful."

He pushes the sweat-lined hair from my forehead and slides his tongue against mine, forcing my whole body to shiver on top of him. He must feel what his words do to me, because he whispers into my ear about how much he wanted to bend me over the conference table in my pink suit, about how sad it made him that I didn't want that too—

"I've never not wanted you to do that," I cry breathlessly. My eyes fly open in panic, and I take a deep breath, as though trying to suck the words back inside to wherever they came from.

His teeth drag at the nape of my neck, leaving a trail of simmering heat all over my throat. All of a sudden,

I'm so close, on the edge of a cliff I can only survive if I leap off it again. In between the words "fuck," "don't stop" and "right there" on repeat in my head I make a mental tally, and no, never in my life has a man made me orgasm twice in one night, but after what he did to me in the kitchen I don't question his skill set.

He wraps his arms around my waist, lifting me up with him. He kisses me hard and with a low groan leads me toward the smoky-mirrored wardrobe. I let out an involuntary ragged moan as he spins me around so I can see both of our reflections.

My sweaty hands make prints against the glass and his dark, focused eyes move their attention to mine.

"Say my name," he growls as he takes my ear in between his teeth, his low voice vibrating down my neck.

"Bancroft," I pant out as his forearm tightens around my waist.

His palm snakes around me gently, pulling me up into a firm embrace. "No, *Grace*. For once, I want to hear you say *my* name," he rasps.

I throw my head back so we're cheek to cheek, and the stubble of his jaw scrapes against my skin. I lift a hand and run it through the back of his hair, tugging the strands into a fist. Holding on to brace for whatever will happen when I say the word I have avoided since we first met.

"Say it." He grips the flesh of my inner thigh. "Please." His voice softens as if he's begging for confirmation that I'm even on the same planet as him. Handing me the keys to his undoing just as much as mine.

I'm starting to understand how power corrupts because as the word "Eric" flitters across my lips I feel almost evil. He lets out a rough laugh onto my shoulder before pounding into me again. The pulsing thrusts create waves of pleasure that burst through me up into my throat. We jump over the edge of the cliff together without thinking about where we'll land.

Our heads share a pillow in the moonlight, limbs intertwined like an atom refusing to split. The early hours of the morning feel like another world. A parallel universe where we aren't Hastings and Bancroft: industry rivals. We're just Grace and Eric: two people finally overlapping. The opportunity to be anything and everything. Whatever we want, together.

A small voice reminds me this isn't real; we are both just playing pretend for a few hours and tomorrow we will be back to being uneasy allies until this project is over and we go our separate ways. But the sound of my name on his lips, our heavy ragged breath and moans of pleasure replaying in my mind drown out that voice— drown it out so completely that I'm no longer listening.

His arms wrap around me as my face sinks into his chest, the hairs tickling my cheeks as I take in a deep breath.

"What are you doing?" he asks, looking down at me over the slope of his chin.

"Trying to figure out what cologne you wear," I say, coming up for air.

He chuckles softly. "Why?"

"Some of the girls in the office have a bet."

"About me?" he asks innocently.

"Oh, come on . . ." I wiggle out of his grip and prop myself up on an elbow. "Surely you know they're all obsessed with you? The way their jaws drop to the floor when you walk in the room must have been a good indicator."

"I never really notice anyone else when I visit your office." His eyes are glazed but soft in a way that makes me think he's telling the truth, and the butterflies in my stomach confirm it.

I narrow my eyes and hold my tongue between my teeth, trying to keep in a blush. Slowly, he untangles himself from me and paces stark naked over to the living room. Fucking hell, even his arse is sculpted by the gods.

"Stop looking at my arse," he calls without glancing back, walking out of sight for a few moments before striding back to the bed and handing me a glass bottle of pale liquid.

"Vetiver," I read, spritzing myself with the earthy scent and humming my approval. "Mmmm, I could bathe in this."

"Oh my God, it's not just the people in your office. You're obsessed with me too!" he teases with a cheeky smile spreading wide across his face.

"I think this . . ." I gesture back and forth between

our naked bodies hidden by a bedsheet. ". . . has made you fly up and off the cockiness scale."

When I go to sit up he catches my waist, eyes twinkling with a devilish sheen as he guides me onto my back.

"You're obsessed," he repeats into my ear, caging me on the bed with his large torso. "With *me*."

"I am not!" I let out a squeal, executing an extremely poor attempt at fighting him off by lightly pounding my fists against his chest. He takes both my wrists in one hand and holds them against the pillow above my head.

"Well, then. Clearly, my work here is not done yet."

He leans his head down, taking my lips in his and tracing his free hand up my jaw. My eyes flutter shut, accepting my fate. It's slow this time. As though he needs hours to archive every piece of me for a private collection. Two bodies pressing together like the pages of a closing book.

27

Even though we only sleep for a couple of hours, those 120 minutes have transformed what happened from some blurry abstract notion under the blanket of night to an actual concrete light-of-day event. A car beeping at street level wakes me; the small noise foghorning me back to reality. I reach for my phone, as is my reflex the moment I wake up. I turned it to "Do Not Disturb" mode after the *first* time last night, so I missed a ton of notifications.

An email from Susie sent at 6:34 a.m.

A text message from Yemi sent last night asking if I'm working late tonight or if I'll be back for dinner.

A Facebook message from William, which I choose not to open. I'll unfriend him later.

A calendar notification: my date with Jack, in thirty minutes.

An Ignite message from Jack: *Be there in 20, looking forward to seeing you :)*

Shit.

Eric's arm is lazily draped over my waist, but our bodies aren't touching. Could I leave without waking him up? Sneak out and pretend as if none of this ever happened? Do I even want to do that?

As I inch toward the edge of the bed, his hand curves around to my front and splays across my stomach, slow, circling fingers reaching my ribs. His slow rhythmic breathing doesn't falter as he pulls me in closer. My insides melt as he tucks my back tight to his body, his morning erection pressing against my backside. Still-forming memories of last night come flooding back. I loosen as a newly familiar mouth drops tender kisses over my shoulder, my neck, my jaw, my cheek until a pair of perfect teeth grazes across my earlobe, causing me to boil over. In a moment of weakness, I lean into the feeling, gripping the pillow and grinding my hips against him.

His laugh tickles hot air against my ear. "Good morning." His voice is low and gritty.

"I have to go," I half murmur, half moan, mentally grappling against the gravitational pull keeping me in his arms.

"No, you don't," he insists, almost pleading, pulling me tighter on to his length. "Here's the plan: we both call in sick, I book this room for another night and we can just do this all day."

I avoid doing the calculations of how much an extended stay here would cost and whether I'm flattered he'd spend *that* much money just to have another twenty-four hours with me. He glides his hand over my hips, making light circles with his thumb, building the pressure in my knotted stomach.

Stifling a whimper, I push my face into the soft pillow. I don't want him to stop but I need him to. I need to clear my head. This is Bancroft. Bancroft, my competitor. Bancroft, my colleague. Bancroft is sinking his fingers into my . . . My brain whirs through potential statements until I think of the only thing I know will defuse the tension building between us: "I have a date in thirty minutes." His hand pauses instantly.

"You're still going on the date?" his lips ask against my shoulder.

"Yeah." I breathe out sharply as his body slowly peels away from mine. Cold air seeps in to settle in the space his warm skin has left.

"Right."

The mattress dips as he flops onto his back, hand wiping over his mouth in contemplation.

"Yeah," I repeat, not knowing what else to say. I decide on a word. "Shower."

A second wind of determination seems to wash over him as the soft look in his eyes regains its cool, sexy confidence.

"We could get clean together?" He smirks and nods his head to the bathroom door. "I think that shower is big enough for two. Want to test my theory?"

I imagine him pushing me up against the steamy,

wet tiles but am quickly thrown out of the fantasy. My eye snags on my notebook, my presentation notes clearly visible, on the bedside table. For a split second I wonder, *Did last night happen to stop me going on a date he suggested I pursue? So I don't outperform him?*

Shaking my head, I brace myself and announce, "I think this"—flapping my hand from him to me—"shouldn't happen again."

My gut twists as a flash of pain runs through his eyes before they quickly harden, becoming unreadable.

Surely he knows this can't happen again? He's probably just never had this kind of physical rejection before, and he's not used to it. Our presentations are only two weeks away; if I continue this now it will be over before it starts. One of us will win the job and the other won't be able to handle it. Sleeping with your competitor is one thing, but being with the person who beat you to your dream job is a pill too big to swallow. We can't do this again, no matter how much we might want to—there's no point. It would be over before either of us knew it.

He schools his face into neutrality. "You're going to be needing these back then?" He dangles my underwear from a finger. I swipe them out of his hand more aggressively than intended and spin on my bare heel to the bathroom. When I return from the steamy room in a bathrobe he's fully dressed, packing his bag by the door.

He made the bed, all evidence of last night smoothed out as though nothing happened.

Trying to fill the awkward silence, I ask, "You're not showering?"

"I will, at the gym," he replies, zipping up the duffel bag.

"Ah." I nod my head as though that makes perfect sense.

He shrugs as if this is a normal thing for him: having a one-night stand in a luxury penthouse and then jumping straight back into his standard morning routine as though it was nothing. As though *this* was nothing.

"Well, enjoy your *date*." He lifts his eyebrows, jaw taut as he looks me up and down before striding toward the door.

"Bancr— Eric?" I suck in my cheeks remembering what he whispered in my ear before coaxing me into a second orgasm.

"Yeah?" He almost seems nervous as he looks over his shoulder. His knuckles are white around the handle of the bag.

Fingers intertwined in front of me: "Could you . . ."

Not tell anyone about this?

Do that thing with your tongue again?

Stay so we can figure out what this means for both of us?

". . . leave your key card by the door, so I can return it to the front desk?"

309

His shoulders sag slightly and I hold my breath as he places the card on a side table and leaves without another word. When the door slams shut the bubble of energy in the room finally bursts. I'm standing alone in one of the most expensive rooms in the city, so many thoughts rushing around my brain that they've turned into white noise.

Ten minutes later, including the fastest makeup routine I've ever done in my life, I'm flying out of the door to meet Jack. If I wasn't so flustered from last night and stressed out about being late, I would find it endearing that he arrived early.

"Miss Hastings!" A booming voice bounces off the walls as I press the call elevator button.

"Christoph!" I reply breathlessly. He's wearing a bright red suit printed with white and gray hibiscus flowers. It's hard not to smile when you see him, even under these irregular circumstances.

"I trust you found your stay satisfying, *ja*?" he says with a wink.

"What?" I blurt.

Christoph looks confused; of course, he doesn't know about Eric staying.

"I mean yes, *ja*! Thank you so much!"

Did I have the best and then second best and *then third* best orgasm of my life in one night? Yes. Do I regret it? Yes. Do I want it to happen again? Yes. Wait—no!

"*Wunderbar!*" He claps his hands together. "Also

I'm so sorry for the misunderstanding about the room. I do hope Eric didn't mind giving up the suite to you for the night."

My stomach lurches at the idea of Christoph bumping into him on the way down to the lobby. Here it is: another reason why this shouldn't have happened. We both risk looking unbelievably unprofessional in front of our biggest potential business partner for the Ditto launch, putting the chances of either of us getting the promotion at risk. Sure, *he* has this kind of reputation already, and even if he hates it, it works in his favor. The last thing I would want is a new business contact to assume that about me.

"I think he was fine with it," I insist, eyes wide and head bobbing frantically. The elevator dings open. "I have to run but we'll be in touch on Monday about partnership contracts."

I smile my most enthusiastic toothy smile, which probably makes me look like a crazed extra in *Wallace & Gromit*.

He waves his hand, disregarding the "business talk." "*Ja, ja*, no worries. Talk soon!"

He ushers me into the gilded elevator. I wait for the giant metal doors to slide shut before I collapse against the railing.

I need every single minute it takes to get to the place I'm meeting Jack for breakfast to compose myself, and even then I'm vibrating as I sit down opposite him.

Jack looks like someone you would take home to

your parents, and they would say "what a nice young man." Because that's what he is: A Nice (has kind eyes, politely insisted on buying my coffee and pancakes and is asking lots of questions), Young (more baby-faced than in his pictures but still handsome in an unkempt, rugged kind of way), Man (he is built like one of those men on the front of old romance novels straddling hay or a fainting heroine, long dark hair flapping in the wind).

This is what you need. A Nice Young Man. Someone who isn't going to tell your whole family you're engaged and then leave you less than twenty-four hours later. Or someone who isn't going to make you feel like the most special person to ever walk the earth, while planning to steal your dream job from right under your nose.

The cafe, adorned with exposed brick walls, French jazz posters and four resident baristas all with matching moustaches, is busy but quiet. Not pin-drop quiet but it feels library-esque—as if anything louder than a dull whispered tone would get you ssshhhed by a middle-aged woman with cat's-eye reading glasses on a chain. We're sitting in wingback armchairs, half-empty plates of pancakes on the table, facing diagonally outward as if we're performing the famed stage show *First Date Isn't Going Great* for everyone else in the room.

My still-swollen lips trace the edge of my warm

mug. It's crazy to think four hours ago I was begging Bancroft to—

"—and then he rolled in a puddle of mud and feathers. He came out of the woods looking like a chicken!"

I snap back into the room as Jack belly laughs and holds his phone up to show a picture shining from the screen of a muddy, feather-covered dog in a field looking pleased with himself. Shit, I haven't been listening to a word this Nice Young Man has been saying for the last five minutes. What is wrong with me?

I wonder if anyone within earshot notices the laugh I give to Jack's phone screen is completely fake.

"Do you have dogs?" He looks at me hopefully, as though this question is the deal-breaker on which he judges every potential girlfriend.

"No," I breathe out over the edge of my latte. In my hushed tone, it comes out harsher and more repulsed than I wanted.

"Oh." He creases his brow and pouts.

He looks into the white foam separating in his cup and seems genuinely gutted, as if I've just told him I kill puppies for a living instead of just not owning one.

"But I really like them!" I offer with a tight-lipped smile and raised eyebrows.

"Oh!" He lets out a sigh of relief, relaxing back into the chair. This guy is *really* into dogs. Do I dare admit I'm a cat person?

My phone dings, reminding me to submit my evaluation notes for Heimach Hotel. How the hell am I going to summarize the past twelve hours?

My brain scrambles to find literally any other topic to talk about with Jack. I wade through sticky thoughts of Bancroft's teeth on my neck, his hands in my hair and settle on: "So what do you do for work?"

He sheepishly stares into his cappuccino, swirling the remaining liquid around the mug until it leaves a fluffy coat of brown foam up the edges. "I'm . . . I'm a bartender?"

He looks up at me with puppy dog eyes. I furrow my brow; why does he look so uncomfortable at his answer? Does he think I look down on bartending as a profession or something? Then it dawns on me.

"Shit, you've already said that. I'm so sorry! I had a . . . rough night last night. Hardly slept." I down a huge glug of my latte for emphasis, lifting it in a remorseful "cheers" gesture toward him. "My brain's a bit frazzled this morning."

He perks up at my explanation. "Oh, no worries. I could have rescheduled if you wanted. Is everything OK?" Argh, what a Nice Young Man.

"No, no. It's fine! Everything's fine," I maintain. He's so accommodating he's trying to reschedule the date we're currently on to make it more convenient for me. "Please. Tell me about your job—I'm all ears."

I make a conscious effort at a real smile, focusing on his eyes as he talks. He actually has really nice eyes.

Deep brown with orange-gold flecks like a dancing flame, the opposite to Eric's icy blue stare.

"Well, I work at SALT. The bar downtown?"

"No way! I've been there for a work event. It's so good!"

He lets out a nervous laugh, his crisp white T-shirt lifting as he scratches the back of his dark curly hair. "I've just finished revamping their cocktail menu. They want to do more of those Instagrammable, experimental drinks that have things like dry ice and stuff."

I cross my legs and lean forward as though I'm making a heinous admission. "I think I'm more of a martini kinda girl."

He mirrors me. "I can see that," he says, flashing a perfectly symmetrical smile framed by matching dimples.

My chin rests on my knuckles. "So, do you have a favorite drink on your fabulous new menu?"

"Yeah . . . maybe you could come by the bar and I can make it for you?"

My confident facade falters and my entire body breaks into an instant sweat as though he's just asked if he can extract a few of my teeth.

Blinking furiously, I force out, "Ummm, sure, sounds good," trying to regain my smile.

What is wrong with me? I can go on a million fake dates with my enemy but don't want a second one with this obviously great guy?

We talk for another twenty minutes about places we've been for drinks, for walks, for food, before I notice the time and have to leave, explaining my boss wants some work delivered to her first thing. Jack touches the small of my back as we weave through the tables to the exit. His hand feels like an unwelcome intruder attempting to invade my personal space. I thank my past self for making this a breakfast date; the meal least likely to end in sexual expectations.

We burst into the already baking morning sun, the rush hour crowd brimming with ambitious energy.

"Well, this has been great. I'm not usually up this early but it was definitely worth setting an extra alarm."

I laugh, but then realize he isn't joking. My smile fizzles out trying to imagine me working into the late hours of most evenings and early mornings, him working every night, how we'd ever see each other. Spending our weekends running around outside covered in twigs and bugs instead of leisurely wandering through climate-controlled galleries and museums hand in hand.

Jack leans in and my entire body freezes. *Fuck, fuck, fuck*. Do I let him kiss me? Do I kiss him? I can still taste Eric in my mouth—how is that fair to Jack? Is this what people do on the first date nowadays? Or just an Ignite date? I'm about to thrust my head into oncoming pedestrians when his lips land on my hot, flaming cheek. My shoulders smash back down to earth and as the dust settles I feel absolutely awful. Of course, he doesn't just go in for a post-coffee kiss on the first date. He is a Nice Young Man.

We say our goodbyes and obligatory "I'll text you" promises, then we turn and walk in opposite directions. Him back to bed and me into the office, trying to suppress an instinctive wish that he was someone else.

28

When I'm working on something I'm truly passionate about, hours fly by with me barely blinking. Creating the Ditto presentation, much as when I was working on my Ever After pitch, doesn't even feel like work. It feels like something I am genuinely good at: developing an idea from the ground up and figuring out the puzzle of how to turn it into a real-world scenario. Despite all the unexpected things that have happened during the research and development of the Ditto project, it's the most fun I've had at work in months, possibly years. Susie is out in meetings all morning with strict instructions to "do not disturb," so I've been holed up in her office putting the final touches on my slides, adding flair, cleaning up any rambling sentences and fine-tuning it into a clean list of prompts to back up my verbal presentation.

The shrill ring of her black office telephone makes me jump, but I let it ring out until the answering machine message plays, followed by a deep voice:

"Good afternoon, Ms. Jopling. My team has looked into your request. They retain the right to remove you

from your role, but your board seat remains safe as per the terms of the acquisition. Please call my secretary so we can set up a meeting to discuss next steps."

I freeze. I can't press replay—she will know someone listened to it. Trying to process the words is like trying to remember the license plate of a car going by at ninety miles an hour. Is Catch Group trying to get rid of Susie? My gut twists; during Fate's acquisition, she fought for all of us to keep our jobs. What would happen to the rest of the team if Susie was gone?

A Slack message from Yemi pops up on my laptop screen, pulling me away from the edges of the spiral:

OM: *Free for lunch, dirty stop-out? x*

GH: *Meet you at the elevator in 5 x*

If it wasn't for the dull ache between my thighs and the not-so-subtle bite mark on my shoulder, I would start to think I made last night up.

"What the fuck?" Yemi leans forward in her chair.

"You can say that again."

"No, but what the actual fuck!"

Sitting back in relief at sharing the burden of this problem with someone I trust, I take my first satisfying breath of air since Eric left the penthouse. "OK, let me know when the shock subsides."

"Oh, I'm not shocked you had sex with him," she says into her drink. "Frankly, I'm shocked it hadn't happened sooner. *And* that you still went on that bloody breakfast date straight after."

My iced matcha latte nearly comes out of my nose.

"One: Weren't you the woman who suggested I put his face on a dartboard? Two: I needed the real date experience for my presentation—it definitely cleared some stuff up for me . . ."

"I suggested the dartboard *before* you started going on these trial dates with Eric." She shrugs and sips her iced hibiscus tea, eyes studying me intently. "Ever since you started this project you've been . . . glowing."

My eyebrows touch the ceiling. "Glowing?" I repeat in disbelief.

"Yeah. You seem, like, more assured in yourself. I honestly was preparing for you to completely burn out with this extra work on your plate . . . but it's like you have a new lease on life, or at least your career. There's fire in your eyes again."

I twitch my jaw, trying my hardest to hide how much I love that observation. She's right: the last time I really enjoyed my job was when I was with William. I assumed it was my breakup that had created the ricochet effect on my work—I mean, who wants to promote finding The One when The One just completely screwed you over? But the Christmas party was only a few days later, and soon after that was the end of my friendship with Bancroft. The thought sits there. A seed of a thought, really. That maybe the fire going out really was because of losing Eric, and not William?

"You two light fires under the other."

Was I the only one who hadn't noticed how he challenges me, pushes me, and treats me like an equal instead of seeing me as a threat? I try not to think about how he denied seeing me as an enemy, saying he always saw me as an ally. He always thought of us as being on the same team, despite being pitted against each other at every available opportunity.

I stifle a smile until Yemi sighs. "Or maybe you're right and this is just the glow of three orgasms in quick succession."

"Oh my God!" I throw a scrunched-up paper straw at her. "I immediately regret telling you that part."

"Speaking of, are you actually going to talk to each other like functioning adults or just pretend it never happened?" The ice in her glass clinks as she swirls her straw.

I shake my head, placing my drink on the table with a thunk. "I can't think about it right now, not until the presentations are over. That seems like the most mature thing to do." I nod at my own statements for emphasis. "Thank you so much again for the data. It really opened my eyes to what the user would want out of Ditto."

"You think you've got the upper hand now?" she asks in between slurps.

"Not the whole hand, but maybe like two or three fingers," I say, shoulder blades shrugging against the wooden chair.

"Sounds like that's all he needed," she mutters into her glass.

I bash my head against the table.

Forty-five minutes later I'm welcomed back to my desk by a scratchily written Post-it note stuck to my computer. Susie's calling card is one of my absolute pet peeves, always leaving a sticky residue behind on my screen. I'm sure she does it deliberately. Slapping tasks in the middle of my screen to show what she feels should supersede everything I might be currently doing. Whatever whim of hers it may be it must immediately be given a VIP ticket to the front of Grace's never-ending task queue. This time, the note ominously says: "*My office.*"

My stomach drops as I slink into the room; does she know I know about the voicemail? Seemingly not, because she spends the next few minutes berating me about the quality of my work. The expansion data report I gave her yesterday is apparently no longer good enough.

"You need to redo this immediately." She rubs the top of her nose as though the work she claims needs to be redone is somehow going to cause *her* stress, not me. It took me an hour and a half to put that report together for her. Redoing it with an in-depth analysis will take several hours. I wanted that time tonight to put the finishing touches on my Ditto presentation and start doing a few practice runs.

I swallow my nerves. "I . . . I don't think I'll have time for that tonight."

Susie's eyes blaze as if she was waiting for me to say

the words to spur her into a full-on tirade. She purses her lips and leans forward on her glass desk, her sharp eyes penetrating through any remaining self-esteem I was grasping on to like a cocktail stick through a grape. She speaks low and slow, mulling every delicious word as it hits her lips: "I only had one caveat for you doing this project for Catcher: You continue to fulfil your duties to me. This is a huge disappointment. Huge. You'll stay late tonight until this is finished to a *considerably* higher standard."

My chest begins a shallow heave; I don't have time to do this work *and* start practicing my presentation. If I roll over this easily now, Bancroft is destined to succeed and I will continue in this never-ending cycle of coffee runs, guilt trips and spreadsheets.

Accepting my punishment, I turn on my heels to leave as the words I'm dying to say pile up on my shoulders. Bancroft flashes through my mind, his smug face when they give him the news of his promotion. How would he deal with this situation? He would say something. This is *the time* to say something. If I don't get the Ditto job, do I really want to come back to this working relationship? I steady myself, balling my hands into fists and taking what I suspect might be my final breath.

"No . . . the caveat was I continue to do my duties as *Marketing Manager* while taking on this project, which I have done." Separate from my brain, spurred on by what I can only think is the "fire" Yemi noticed in me earlier, my footsteps carry me closer to Susie's desk. "I know something is going on with you at the moment and I'm sorry about that. But what you're annoyed about is me not having time to be your *assistant*: something I don't have time for and don't get paid for."

She huffs an unamused laugh. "You have no idea what you're talking about."

My voice trembles slightly. I can't believe I'm doing this. It feels like an out-of-body experience. As if someone with some actual self-worth has grabbed the reins and is taking me for a joyride.

"Maybe I don't, but you being under pressure doesn't give you the right to treat me like this."

It's like the rush of adrenaline I got standing up for Iris at Matilda's Bar, but better. Standing up for *myself* is a whole different ball game. With others, I can see clearly when they are being taken advantage of or treated poorly. When it comes to myself, I can't see between the lines as clearly—even if the people around me are screaming it from the rooftops. Maybe that's what happened with William? I finally begin to see the similarities between their two personalities. They called the shots and told me when things were progressing, and I just floated along, carried by their currents instead of swimming to the shore.

I blink furiously and clear my throat. "I used to look up to you. I am still so grateful to you for the chance you gave me but gratitude can only go so far." I hold up the rejected report, which crinkled under my fingers. "As far as disappointing you: this report is fine work. This isn't about the report. It's about you wanting me to be your assistant forever at my own career's expense."

The well of tears, which tend to appear whenever I express any extreme emotion, bubble just below the surface, stinging my eyes. *Do not cry.* I blink back the frustration and take a deep lungful of air.

She adjusts her posture, straightening as if being spoken to like this has woken up her bones. She sighs. "I didn't realize that's how you felt."

"It is," I confirm. "I've felt like this for a while. If I don't get the promotion, and start working for Ditto, things have to change."

She stares at me blankly. "What do you want?"

Shit, she thinks I actually prepared this speech.

"I want you to hire an assistant. I can recommend some people. Not an intern, but a fully salaried assistant. And I would like a pay raise, to the level I should be at if I'd asked for annual raises in pay since working for you. Industry-standard."

She crosses her arms. "OK. Have HR draft a new contract and I'll take a look."

I shoot her a polite smile. "Thank you."

I turn to leave, actively having to stop my wobbling legs from collapsing over each other. The last thing I want to follow a power move is a slapstick topple in heels. High on the release, I try my luck one final time. I've come this far, I might as well go all in.

"Oh, and I want my own office. There's an unused storage room down the hall; I can make that work."

She raises her eyebrows, almost as if she's impressed. "OK."

"Thank you. And—I know it's not much, but if you need someone in your corner, I will always have your back." I nod for emphasis and give her a tight-lipped smile.

She taps her fingernail against her desk, her other hand massaging the bridge of her nose. "You know, just because you run a company doesn't mean you are in control; there will always be people—or in my case, a boardroom full of people—deciding you aren't good enough, that your years of contributions don't matter because you no longer fit their 'vision.' I'm sorry if I've made you feel the same."

"What 'vision'?"

She waves her hand, summoning the reasons. "Apparently, I am too old to be the public face of Fate. It's too depressing to have a single woman of my age representing the search for love. They want me to resign."

My face scrunches in disbelief.

"Exactly," she agrees with my expression. "Do you think Dharmash is getting this kind of evaluation? I get a wrinkle, and I'm on the chopping block. He pays a magazine to stalk an employee and the board gives him a pat on the back."

My nerves stand on end. "I'm sorry?"

She tilts her head. "I thought you knew?"

I shake my head. "Knew what?"

"About Eric Bancroft?"

29

Having finished the slideshow part of my presentation, I am practicing the spoken parts in the living room. Doing so until my throat is sore will be the only thing to stop the plague of locusts raging around my stomach.

"In conclusion," I declare with a flourish, "with this strategy, Ditto will pave a new way to match users and bring a breath of fresh air to the industry. Market research suggests the new generation of potential users has been experiencing dating-app fatigue. Ditto cuts out the awkward preamble and gets straight to the date but in a safe, controlled environment."

My face scrunches with indecision as I ask Yemi and Alice, "Did that last bit sound kinda lame?" I fiddle with the edges of my oversize linen shirt, tucked into frayed denim shorts to counter the lack of air conditioning in our building.

"No, it sounds really good!" Alice gushes, lounging next to Yemi on the sofa, their feet curled up in a yellow knitted blanket.

Flopping down on the tatty gingham-print armchair next to them, I admit, "I want to get across how passionate I am about this idea. I genuinely think it would be great." Warm honey fills my chest. "I haven't felt this way in a really long time."

"Why don't you talk about your passion then? They will be looking for the numbers and data and stuff, but they want someone who will champion the brand. You know, speak from the heart," Alice suggests.

"Yeah." Yemi nods. "The ultimate goal for users is to find someone who shares their passions in life, so it would make sense to speak about yours."

After scribbling down their advice on my cue cards I look up to see both of my wonderful friends stuffing their faces with leftover popcorn. I'm on a high, an adrenaline rush fueled by this rare, precious feeling of self-esteem. Is this what confident people feel like all the time? I take a gratifying breath. "I feel like I actually have a real shot at this."

"Do you think Eric's presentation will be as good as yours?" Alice asks.

"I know it will be, and he's got the Black Book of Dreams to back up his strategy. This could really go either way." I suck in my cheeks. The thought of the decision coming down to that goddamn Rolodex is a very real possibility. Being twice as good as him is a tall order, but it's the bare minimum I need to be to stand a chance. "Now that I've started practicing, I can use the next ten days to refine everything and really nail it."

"Have you spoken to Eric since the, ummm . . ." She mulls the word in her mouth. ". . . incident?" I filled

Alice in when I got home a couple of hours ago and safe to say her reaction was not as subdued as Yemi's. Weeks from now we'll still be finding the popcorn she threw into the air like confetti at a wedding.

"Not properly." I run my hands through my hair, wilder than usual from being towel-dried in a rush at the hotel room this morning. "What would I even say? Hey, thanks for the mind-blowing sex, I kind of want to do it again but I know it won't work long-term. Also, I have some pretty damning accusations about one of the few people you trusted being the person who has been ruining your life and relationships for over a year."

Yemi shakes her head in disbelief. "It's so shady. Surely you have to tell him about that?"

"I feel like I should." I cross my arms as though already protecting my body from the potential blow-back. Would he even believe me? Or think it's some sort of mind game to throw him off before the presentations?

Of course, I could do what he did to me. Keep it quiet to protect him, but maybe like me it would just cause more pain in the long run. Maybe if Eric had been upfront with me about William, it would have hurt but it would have saved me further pain. It would have helped me make decisions for my future instead of dwelling on the past.

"The main thing I need to do for now is clear the air." I purse my lips. "Establish that what happened at the hotel can't and won't happen again."

"Even if you want it to?" Alice's lips curl and I blush.

"Being in competition with someone while having a sordid affair with them is giving major *Dangerous Liaisons* vibes." She wiggles her fingers at me like mini jazz hands.

"But it's going to end the moment one of them gets the job. They're both too competitive to handle something like that," Yemi argues to Alice.

My finger points toward Yemi in agreement. "Exactly! I know my limitations. Might as well rip the Band-Aid off before it even gets put on." *While it's still just a gaping open wound.*

My phone stares at me from across the room, the red circle of seven unread messages like an evil eye of doom. I could make this easy for myself and text him, but something this sensitive needs to be done in person. "OK, I'm gonna go talk to him," I announce. "I'll decide what I'm going to say on the way." My keys jingle in my hand as I pace down the hallway and fling open the front door. My entire body freezes like a deer in icy blue headlights as I see Bancroft walking up the stairs toward my front door.

"We need to talk." His low words echo up the stairwell and land right between my thighs. *Fuck*. He somehow looks perfect despite the evening being so humid it's almost wet. His simple but impeccably cut white T-shirt and jeans manage to look so put together, leaving no doubt he's wearing those subtle designer labels only people in the know can identify. Meanwhile, I'm wearing Daisy Duke shorts, which are slowly unraveling at the seams and a top I found for 50 percent off in a bin at the charity shop.

Yemi's curls bounce as she flips around to a wide-eyed Alice. "Pub?"

"Pub!" Alice confirms, overly enthusiastic about being forced out of her own home. "Text us if you're . . . busy later."

Behind Bancroft, I stare wide-eyed at Alice bending Yemi over the stairway's iron railing and miming spanking her with glee.

I glare at both of them as they skip down the stairs, leaving me alone with a stony-faced Bancroft lingering in the threshold.

"Can I come in?" he asks in an unreadable tone.

"What are you, a vampire or something?" I sigh, attempting to disguise my heaving chest as annoyance. I widen the door for him as his large body brushes past mine. It leaves a faint trail of the cologne that has been haunting my sense memory for the past eighteen hours.

We both make our way into the main living area in silence. A sudden wave of self-consciousness hits me, like stepping out into the beating sun from an air-conditioned building. Nobody beyond Yemi and Alice has been here before, not even my family. His home taught me so much about him I would never know otherwise, and I'm not sure it's a good idea for him to know those things about me. Inviting him in is slicing through a taped-shut box containing precious parts of myself and saying, "Please, rifle through!"

OK, would I have done the exact same thing if I hadn't been temporarily incapacitated while in his home? Absolutely. Do I feel good about that truth? No. What I found just from sifting through his coffee table decor started a chain of events in my head, ultimately leading to the shift in dynamic between us. A swooping sensation takes over my stomach as I remember the versions of us in those photos: tipsy in a Christmas-themed photo booth with cheeks pressed close. The way he looked at me when I was completely oblivious seems so far away from this reality.

He wanders to the carved wooden bookshelf on the far side of the room, shoulder muscles forming valleys across his T-shirt. He runs a finger over the creased spines of romance novels I used to read obsessively. They've been gathering dust since I moved here. I told myself it was because I didn't have time to spend my nights combing their pages anymore, but all I've been doing instead is combing through pointless emails from Susie about what weeks-old TikTok trend she thinks would be good for a paid ad.

I clear my throat, and lean against the kitchen counter, immediately remembering what happened the last time I leaned against a kitchen counter with him in the room. I push off it and pace into the living-room area, leaving an entire sofa's length between us. He scans the room silently, analyzing pieces of me he's never laid eyes on before. The sensation it gives me is oddly reminiscent of him roaming my body with his mouth, cataloging everything he felt and saw when the early-morning sun started to leak into the room.

"Where's the painting?" His face is indecipherable as he studies the art- and film-poster-coated walls.

"In storage," I lie, forcing my eyes to stay fixed on him and not my bedroom door, where the painting is hung above my bed.

"Hmmm," he grumbles suspiciously, gliding a palm over the side of the couch.

He cuts me a faint sideways glance, sandy hair flopping over his forehead. My hand folds into a fist to stop from brushing it back.

"How was your date?" he asks.

"It was . . . nice," I say to the floor.

"*Nice?*" He spits out a harsh laugh.

A line forms between my brows. "You have a problem with 'nice'?"

We're circling the living room now, like two cowboys waiting for the other to draw their pistol.

"I just didn't realize your bar was so low," he scoffs, one eyebrow raised.

I open my mouth to snap back some ill-thought-out retort but he continues, "You deserve more than '*nice*.'" He tilts his head and paces slowly toward me. A wild panther measuring the reaction of its prey. Before I get eaten, I jolt to the other side of the sofa and start frantically folding a strewn-out blanket.

Honestly, I've never considered anything more than "nice" as the criterion of what I'm looking for. I hold the folded blanket in front of me like a fluffy shield, before asking, "What would you recommend instead?" One side of my mouth twitches as I try to underplay the minor revelation occurring in my head. Maybe after William the bar was so low I thought nice was the best I could ever dream of. Someone who didn't try and control me, deciding my future as though it belonged to them.

"Someone who understands you." He dips his head, rounding the corner of the sofa. "Who wants you for who you are, not what you could be."

The air around us goes completely silent. With William, I had to fit within a rigid box. I had to be the sort of person who was worthy of all the love he gave me. He loved me so much, but he loved the version of me he had built. His own creation. But with Eric, I've only ever felt like myself. I can be my most outspoken, ambitious, confident self. I can be the best version of Grace. The Grace who sticks up for herself. The Grace who knows her worth and isn't afraid of the consequences when showing it.

As if he's reading my mind he says, "The best version of yourself."

"You two bring out the best in each other."

Even Mr. Catcher noticed it. But it can't happen. The neon sign flashing "Presentations in ten days!" in the back of my head fills my vision. We will enter the ring together and only one of us will come out. And why is he saying these things now when he's had *all* this time to say them? When he could have told me at the Christmas party months ago; he rejected me instead. I shake my head, his words tumbling out onto the ground like rocks in an avalanche. The only reason for saying these things now is to throw me off my game. This is what we do. We compete. We play dirty until we win. We're the same, and what was I just thinking about before he arrived? How could I throw him off before the presentations to give myself the edge? My head spins like a blade of grass in a hurricane. Who's to say he isn't doing the same thing? That he won't take all of this back the moment I'm too love-drunk to care who wins or loses? Tell me he wants me forever then take it all away in an instant, just like William did.

I school my face into the stony expression he held at my door. "Why now?"

"What?" He places both hands on the back of the sofa, the veins in his forearms becoming distractingly pronounced.

I take a steadying breath. "Why come here and say this now? Why did you decide, just days before one of the most important moments of our careers, you wanted to come here and make me—" I stop myself, blinking furiously and start again. "When you had the entire night to say something. When you've had months to say something . . ." I take a step back, gripping the blanket tighter. "Why now?"

His jaw tenses. Eyes laser-focusing on me. "Because last night changed things."

We both stand in silence, fingers dancing over our weapons.

I take the shot: "For you." It hits him right in the gut, his brow knits as the words seep into him. *Even if the lie hurts now, this is the best thing for both of us,* I tell myself. "It changed things for you." I clear the emotion from my throat. "When we find out what happens one of us will be happy and one of us will be crushed."

He rolls his shoulders back. "Right." It doesn't seem as if he's agreeing with me, just accepting my opinion.

He rounds the sofa toward me but I'm stuck to the ground. The withered romantic buried in my depths bursts a hand up through the dirt and tells me to stop what I'm doing. To tell him the truth. Stop going on the defensive, stop trying to protect myself from a version of events that might not even occur. We can get through anything together because we are and have always been Grace and Eric, pretending to be Hastings and Bancroft.

Moving closer until we're toe-to-toe, his body shadows over mine and I bask in his presence. His jaw ticks as his intrusive gaze flicks from my lips to my neck to my burning eyes. Without saying a word he brushes past me. I listen as his footsteps bounce against the floorboards. The front door opens and clicks shut behind me.

A sobbing exhale I didn't realize was waiting finally bursts free. My palms push against my eyes as every expletive I've ever heard runs on repeat like a siren. How is this possibly the best thing for both of us? If we were the same, wouldn't he have come here to emotionally destroy me? To take a devastating blow at my self-confidence? Not to talk to me as though I can do anything I set my mind to. I've fucked everything up.

Before my brain can catch up, my legs are moving out of the door, down the staircase toward the building entrance. My arms fling open the door to catch up and throw themselves around him, but he's already gone. Along with any shreds of hope remaining between us.

30

"I'm sensing tension between you two."

Iris Fender flicks her sapphire gaze between Bancroft and me.

We're crammed into a round two-person table at the food court of Fair Play, the brand new "adults-only funfair experience." Behind us rows and rows of food trucks decorated with graffiti, glitter and multicolored festoon lights line the edges of the venue. In the next room there's a roller rink, arcade and a dance floor playing exclusively nineties and noughties club music. "Where's Your Head At?" by Basement Jaxx blares from the speaker system as neon flashing lights encase us in a Euphoria-themed snow globe of chaos.

Bancroft says nothing, waiting to see my reaction to Iris's interrogation.

When both siblings arrived, instead of just him, I thought he had dragged her along as an emotional bodyguard. When she briefly left to use the bathroom, he explained that their mum was refusing to talk to her and he felt bad leaving her alone. Him caring so much about her softened my bristled exterior slightly. Her infectious, glowing charisma helps too, so much so that I speak candidly.

"There were some issues recently, but time heals all wounds, I guess." I tear a napkin between my fingers, leaving little pieces of red confetti on the table, in case I need to throw it in their faces and run away like a shitty magician.

Iris leans back in her fold-out chair. "Was this anything to do with that ex you were texting?"

I tense.

Bancroft shifts to face her and pulls out a credit card, holding it up between two fingers. "Why don't you go order us some food. Get whatever you want."

"Okaaaay, but don't you crazy kids ravish each other while I'm gone." She plucks the shiny black card from his fingers and swishes around toward the bar, every single person she walks past turning to gaze at her.

He hunches forward, resting his bare forearms on the sticky table. "Sorry about Iris."

"It's OK. I like her."

He turns his head to check on his sister, who is leaning at the bar waiting to be served. "Me too."

The past four days of radio silence since he was standing in my flat quickly turns sour and sits between us like the last guest to leave a house party.

"So about—"

"I think we should—"

We start at the same time, our unwieldy, clunky attempts at easing into conversation overlapping. My shoulders lower slightly as I watch him squirm, clearing his throat and sipping on his drink before starting again.

"This is a cool idea." He takes in his surroundings. "Have you been here before?"

"Umm, no. I saw someone come here on TikTok and it looked fun so I reached out."

He nods his head, neither of us in the mood to keep this banal conversation going. I steel myself, ready to ramp things up a bit.

"So, I have something to tell you abou—"

"They didn't have any burgers left so I got tacoooooos!" Iris slams a bright orange tray on the table, causing half the tacos to tip over and spill their innards all over the tray. "Shit." She scoops the mounds of lettuce and cheese back into the shells and hands them to us.

I look for an alternative topic of conversation. Maybe I could bring this up in front of his sister, but telling her the real reason paparazzi have been photographing her at her lowest feels like something Bancroft should decide upon himself.

I opt for something easier: "So, Iris, what are your plans after you stay with Eric?"

Clocking his attention pricking up at the use of his first name, I hope he realizes it would just be weird to call him Bancroft in front of his sister, nothing more.

Iris is halfway through a huge bite of a pulled pork taco as she says, "I'm not sure. I might go spend some time with my dad."

"Malon?" I prompt.

"No, my *dad* dad. His band is taking up a residency in London soon." She says it with an innocence that's hard not to love.

"Oh, cool!" I nod enthusiastically.

"Does *he* know that's your plan?" Bancroft interjects, stony-faced.

Iris's pink cheeks are hidden by the red neon light against her face but I can tell by the way she tenses that no, he doesn't. "I don't think it would be a big deal . . ." she says quietly.

Bancroft's jaw tenses and he doesn't reply. It doesn't seem to be out of anger, but caution. From what he told me, it sounds like Iris's dad didn't try very hard to stay in her life, but I could be misinterpreting the situation. Either way, the atmosphere is so awkward I'm almost tempted to restart the conversation about Dharmash. Thankfully, the sound of Bancroft's phone ringing slices through the tense air.

He glances at the screen. "I should take this."

The metal folding chair scrapes along the concrete floor as he towers over us and strides away from the speaker system.

I turn to Iris, a dulled, polite smile holding up her usually cheery face. "Are you OK?" I ask, placing a hand on her forearm.

"Yeah, I'm fine. He's just . . . really protective. It's annoying in a bossy big brother kinda way, but I know it comes from a good place."

"I can see that." I glance over to him, hunched against a wall with the phone to his face and a finger in his ear. His eyebrows are scrunched as if he's trying really hard to hear the person on the other line over the Scissor Sisters blasting around the room. His eyes flick to mine, as though he could sense me looking at him, and I quickly tilt my head back to Iris. "Has he always been this protective?"

"I guess so. I don't think he had a choice—it's not like our parents were looking out for us, even when they were still together. Sure, they kept us fed with the most organic food and clothed in designer children's wear, but I think they expected us to be ornamental little mascots for the family business." She considers, twirling a lock of hair around her finger before tucking it behind her ear. "We had everything we could ever want, but what we actually wanted was our mum and dad. The moment we were old enough to realize how messed up that situation was we both rebelled . . . in our own ways."

We both glance down at Iris's drink, which she specifically asked to be non-alcoholic.

"I wanted to thank you for what you did at Matilda's. For me and for Eric," Iris says into her glass. "I don't know if he ever thanked you, but I know he really appreciated having someone there with him."

A nervous, breathy laugh escapes my lungs. "I don't know. I think I might have just gotten in the way, made a bigger deal of the situation than it needed to be."

"No, the next morning, when he told me what happened, I realized how we both got used to this routine of me partying like crazy and him doing damage control. It wasn't fair to him. I think it just took someone outside of the situation to make us both come to that conclusion." She nods. "I'm trying to do better now."

"That's really good." I squeeze her forearm. "And you don't just have Eric. You have me as well."

She beams. "So, does that mean that you two are—"

"No!" I blurt. "I just mean that, you know, we can be friends too."

Her wide smile turns into a Bancroftian smirk. "You know, Eric talks about you a lot. *A lot*, a lot." She swirls the straw in her drink. "I don't think he realizes he does it."

"Probably because I've been annoying him so much over the past few weeks with this project," I rebuff.

"No, it's more like . . . kinda sweet." She giggles into her drink. "And he's been doing it for *way* longer than a few weeks."

A twang of something lances through me . . . guilt, for not being honest with him? Regret at leaving the hotel room that morning? Relief that I'm not alone in replaying everything that's happened between us? Maybe all three.

I can't get his face out of my head, the look in his eyes when I implied our night together meant nothing to me. Cracking open a walnut shell with two broken fingers would have been easier than getting him to admit what he was really thinking. When he's spent his whole life pushing away the people he cares about under the guise of protecting them. At the art gallery, I persuaded him to open up to me and he's spent weeks slowly showing me the real person underneath the shiny, smirking veneer. Then I told him our night together meant nothing. I pushed him away to protect both of us from the potential consequences. A voice of reason sounds off in my head: *The moment you asked him to stay you knew there would be fallout. You caused the damage. This is your fault and you know it.*

As he paces back to the table, all I know for sure is neither of us are getting out of this unscathed.

31

The sounds of London streets rage as I toss and turn in bed. My shitty desk fan is on full blast to drown out the sound and circulate the hot city air.

It's been five days since I last saw Eric. Since we sat in awkward silence, leaning on stunted conversation about everything except the thing we needed to talk about. We haven't spoken; instead, I've been counting down the days until the presentations and stewing on our night together, his words in my living room, the bomb Susie dropped; they swirl together into one big gelatinous mess until my brain can't occupy anything else.

It's only 9 p.m., the summer sun just settling into darkness, but I forced myself to go to bed early, hoping to get a good night's sleep before the presentation tomorrow afternoon. Forgetting that lying in bed wide awake tends to wrench my mind open and let all the things I can avoid during the day slide out. I need to get this over with.

The phone light glares bright against the darkness of my bedroom as I type, delete, and retype a message. Finally, I close my eyes as I hit send:

Can we talk?

Immediately regretting it, I toss my phone to the other side of the bed and throw an arm over my eyes. *Can we talk?* What do I even want to say to him? I want to come clean about Dharmash, I want to tell him I'm sorry for not being honest with him, that the night we had together meant something to me, so much that I can't stop thinking about it whenever I'm alone. Even if he actually replies, how am I meant to articulate those thoughts via text?

I pick up my phone, typing out another message.

Actually, sorry, don't worry abou

Three dots appear on the screen, quickly transforming into a location pin drop. My chest instantly tightening, I click the phone screen off, as though pretending to not see it makes it go away.

He wants me to come to him? I can't do that. The presentations are in eighteen hours. Seeing him now would be reckless, impulsive and completely idiotic.

I whip off the covers and head out of the door.

32

Forty-five minutes later I end up at a pub on Eric's side of the city. Actually, it's more like a town house than a *pub* pub. Swanky but understated, lit by sconces and candlelight with bursts of laughter echoing around the room like fireworks. I meander through the crowd until I catch sight of a familiar figure. He's at the bar, shoulders hunched as though invisible hands are pushing him further into the red velvet padded barstool.

"Big day tomorrow," I say, sliding onto the empty stool beside him.

"Very big." He doesn't meet my eye, instead slides a fresh vodka martini with a twist over to me, just how I like to order it.

"Thanks."

"What did you want to talk about?" he asks into his drink.

My finger rims the edge of the cold glass and I purse my lips. I decide to go straight in, not giving myself time to chicken out. Taking a huge gulp for courage, I wince as it goes down but push on: "I have something to tell you about *Societeur*. It's Dharmash. I don't know when it started but the press have been following you all this time because he's been paying them out of Ignite's pocket."

I let out a lungful of air.

The dark side of his face flickers in the dim candlelight as he turns to the bartender. "Can I get another, please?" He points to his empty glass.

"You're being surprisingly chill about this."

"I know."

"You know you're being surprisingly chill?"

"No, *I know*. I know about Dharmash."

My mouth hangs open. "What the fuck?"

"Well, I had my suspicions. I just didn't want to believe it. Then I got a call from a friend a few days ago, when we were at Fair Play."

I recall his stony face when he was on the phone, similarly hunched over.

"She said *Societeur* had called her for a quote about our 'secret rendezvous' the night before." Seeing my face, he adds, "She's an estate agent; we met up to discuss Iris's options. Whether I could contribute to her rent or be her guarantor or something if she wanted to get a place of her own. I had it in my work calendar as *Dinner with Isabella*. The only person who has access to my work calendar besides me is Dharmash."

"Have you told him you know?"

"Nope." The bartender places a fresh frosted glass in front of him and he takes a sip; his jaw winces as the spirit hits his tongue.

"Why not? Surely he'd stop if you confronted him."

He sighs as if he *really* doesn't want to talk about this. "Because if I did, I would have to quit. And if I quit . . . who would hire me? Google 'Eric Bancroft' and the first ten search pages are filled with stories about me. The only company who would benefit from that kind of reputation is Ignite."

My shoulders slump to match his. "I didn't think about it that way."

"Yeah, you're not the only one with boss issues," he huffs, gulping his drink.

"I guess we have more in common than I thought." I solemnly clink my glass against his, watching as a dimple makes a faint impression on his stubbled cheek.

He shifts, placing his elbow on the bar and turning slightly toward me. "Did you come all the way here just to tell me about Dharmash?"

I cross my legs toward him. "We said no more secrets, right?" I hesitate before adding, "And despite everything, I still care about you."

His weary eyes soften, traveling from mine to my lips as they graze the edge of the chilled martini glass. I'm unsure whether it's the cold liquid or the icy stare that sends a shiver down my spine. Either way, the feeling keeps traveling until it lands between my crossed legs.

He clears his throat, a slight smile returning to his lips as we inch closer together until his knee is lightly touching mine. "I thought maybe you wanted to meet to tell me you regret going on your date."

"I don't," I reply matter-of-factly.

"So, he's getting a second?" He clears his drink and gestures to the bartender for the bill.

"No."

His knee smooths against mine, twisting me and the swivel barstool until he and I are fully facing each other.

My cheeks flush as I admit, "I don't regret it, because it showed me what I *don't* want."

We hold, our legs grazing as I balance my foot on his stool. Every part of me is on fire under his icy stare. I look down at his silk tie, touch it, let it glide through my fingers, resisting the urge to wrap it around my knuckles.

"I should go soon—presentations tomorrow," I remind him and myself. My eyes lift to his lips, remembering how they tasted.

He stands up, pays the bill and rests against the bar, leaning in so close I feel his breath on my cheek. "Can I walk you home?"

I look up at him and stifle a laugh. "It would take like two hours to walk back to mine."

"I didn't say to *your* home." His lingering look unspools any resolve I entered with.

We walk in silence, our fingers are intertwined. He took my hand to drag me across the road during a quick break in the traffic, and without us noticing our palms had molded together by the time we reached the other side. His apartment building is ten minutes away, but I would have stayed like this for hours, meandering the streets with him in a sweet, blissful silence.

He leads me into the familiar building, past the concierge who nods politely at us with a knowing smile, into the lift, where my chest starts to heave but he doesn't move, just strokes my palm with his thumb. Nothing has ever felt better than his skin on mine. The elevator dings and we traverse the length of the sleek gray hallway until finally, *finally* we reach his door. He lets go of my hand to reach into his pocket; the keys jangle in the lock as the door creaks open.

He walks ahead, flicking on the lamps. Warm light trickles through the room like honey, illuminating parts of his home like synapses of the brain. My mind is firing on all cylinders as I absorb all the facets of his space from a different perspective. I linger awkwardly at the end of the entrance hallway at the threshold of the kitchen as he rounds the central island and fills two crystal highball glasses with water.

"Is Iris here?" I ask, having spotted the telltale sign of her earrings in the key bowl.

His head lifts toward a door further down the hallway. "She's asleep in the guest bedroom."

I wince, lowering my voice to a whisper. "Shit, sorry."

He chuckles, still speaking at his normal volume. "Don't worry. The walls are thick and, to be honest, she'd sleep through an earthquake."

"How long is she staying here for?"

"As long as she wants, but knowing her it won't be for much longer." My heart swells at his protectiveness. Iris seems like the sort of person who wants to be independent, but knowing you have someone who can be relied upon when your parents can't be is something everyone should have. A small voice in my head tells me maybe I could be that person for Eric, but it would be unfair to us both to promise anything until after we know our fate at Catch Group.

He takes off his jacket and pads into the living room, switching on his vinyl player, which already has a record sitting atop it. A live, slow jazz recording quietly fills the space as he paces back to the kitchen island, picks up the glasses and hands one to me. I realize what he's doing. He brought me here, but this time he isn't running the show. For the past few months, he's been the one deciding whether something was going to happen—denying me or daring me. This time, he's waiting for me. We stand there, staring at each other and sipping the ice-cold water. My stubborn nature wants to hold out, play this game of chicken with him all night. But my body wants to do something else. I compromise, downing the water in one gulp and handing him the empty glass. I slide off my loafers and shoulder bag and leave him in the hallway to begin inspecting his apartment room by room until I meet his bedroom.

I'm snooping, blatantly. Something I have desperately wanted to do since I first came here with a sprained ankle. I look at picture frames, books, little trinkets I didn't expect him to have. The same strip of photos I saw the last time I was here is now poking out of a book on his dresser. I feel him enter the room as I slide the pictures out, revealing the mirrored images of my past self and him.

I grip the edge of the glossy strip, lifting it over my shoulder to him. "You knew I'd seen this?"

He lets out a breathy laugh, scratching the back of his neck. "I was fucking mortified when I realized *that's* why you left so abruptly."

"Why didn't you say anything?"

"I thought you'd think I was a crazy person, telling you I never thought about you then using your face as a bookmark."

I run the side of my finger over our happy, tipsy faces. "No crazier than I was at the Christmas party."

He sighs, stepping in closer so his lips rest near my ear and hands rest on my hips. "I know you don't associate that night with good feelings, but knowing something was there for you too was one of the best moments of my life."

I swallow, breath caught in my throat as my neck cranes to feel his touch. Photo-booth Eric looks at Photo-booth Grace with something I thought I'd never seen in real life, but maybe I just wasn't looking. I twist to face him, my back pressing into the wooden dresser. "I'm glad you did it, pulled away. I think if it had happened then, we never would have spoken again."

"I would have tried." He smirks.

I huff a laugh, biting my lip. "OK, fine, but I would have been too awkward to talk to you *ever* again."

"I don't know. Something tells me you would have come back for more," he jokes, the dimple reappearing in his cheek.

My eyebrow cocks as I look him up and down. "Someone's confident." We shift, our bodies inching closer together.

"*Someone* snuck into my bedroom," he counters, placing his hands on either side of me on the dresser. My blood heats as he holds the position, patiently waiting for me to move closer.

"Well, I wanted to see where the famous Eric Bancroft magic happens."

His voice lowers. "It's close-up card tricks, exclusively."

I stifle a smile. "And I was very concerned about your thread count." I furrow my brow and press my hands to his broad chest to push past him.

Sitting on the edge of his bed, my legs dangle over the end of the mattress as I lie back and smooth my hands over the crisp white sheets like a duvet snow angel. "Upon closer inspection, I shouldn't have worried."

He remains silent until, eventually, I sit back up and find him standing in the same space I left him. He's really giving me nothing here. My eyes travel down from his face to his suit trousers. Thick pleats form as he begins to harden under my gaze. I smile triumphantly, as if I've finally won this little game we've been playing since we left the pub.

His lips twist into an embarrassed smile as he tilts his head to the side. "That's not fair."

My eyebrows arch. "Don't be a sore loser. It's not my fault you have a tell."

"When you're on my bed, looking . . ." He clears his bobbing throat as he slowly steps forward. ". . . like that, it's *definitely* your fault."

He places his glass on the side table and slips his hands into his pockets, as if he has to restrain himself to not touch me. I reach out and gently tug on his black leather belt; the silver buckle clinks as I slide it undone.

"Sorry." I pout. "I don't make the rules."

I pause for a moment at the button of his trousers, giving him the chance to pull away, to make everything easier and back out.

He takes my chin in his hand, eyes twinkling in the dim light. "If you are my consolation prize then it's worth losing."

We dance in between kisses, words and touches. Each one featherlight compared to the weight of the past weeks and months. I pull him closer, our foreheads pressing together as though we're attempting some new kind of telepathy. His mouth runs the length of me, reacquainting himself with every curve and bend until I arch my back and see stars. My mouth explores him for the first time, learning what makes him moan and curse until neither of us can stand him not being inside me.

"You're so fucking . . ." he says into the crook of my neck as he mercifully presses between my thighs, his lips parted but unable to finish the sentence as I roll my hips higher to accommodate him.

"Sadistic?" I smirk, running a hand to the back of his head through his messy hair.

He kisses up my arm, leaving a trail of goose bumps. "I was going to say devastating."

"You've already used that line. I thought you were meant to be witty?" I bite his earlobe.

"Well, forgive me," he says, kissing my jaw. "There is considerably less blood in my brain than usual."

I huff a half laugh, half moan as he pushes deeper, filling me completely. "Do that forever and you will be absolved of all sins, always."

"Thank you, God."

"You're welcome."

The moonlight from his bedroom window spills onto our bodies like a blanket of fresh dew. Neither of us have spoken for the past ten minutes, or maybe ten hours, I'm not sure. Time seems to have slowed down as we lie chest to chest, naked and entangled, tracing our fingers over each other's edges.

"What are we going to do about this?" he asks, finally breaking the comfortable silence as he smooths his palm down my bare spine.

Turning onto my back, I let out a sigh. "I don't know."

"Are you going to run off like last time?" He smiles, the mischievous twinkle in his eyes failing to hide his nervousness.

"I'm pretty sure you were the one who bolted first," I challenge, pulling the sheet up and tucking it under my arms.

He turns onto his side, the pillow dipping as he leans his hand on his elbow. "Only because the image of you leaving first to go on a date with someone else would have been burned into my brain forever. I couldn't do that to myself."

"I do have to go eventually." I angle my chin to meet him. "I have to get home," I confirm solemnly.

"It's late—you could stay?"

A solid ache presses against my chest as I say, "All my stuff for the presentation tomorrow is at my house."

He lets out a breath. "OK. I'll get you a car. Just stay with me for a bit longer?" He slides his arms around me and pulls me against him.

My eyes prickle as I press my face against his bare chest and breathe him in, trying to tattoo the smell of him onto my memory. It's painful, physically painful, not knowing if I'm being with him like this for the first or last time, lying here together in total flux.

The words build and build in my chest until they finally pour out onto his: "Let's wait and see what happens tomorrow." I clear the uncertainty from my throat. "We could make a decision now and tomorrow feel completely different. I don't think it's fair to either of us to decide now."

He hums a noncommittal agreement, his chin resting on my temple as he pulls me in tighter.

I lift my head, my face meeting his. "If this ends badly, are we still going to be friends?"

He stares at me for a moment, then brings up a hand

to cup my cheek and kisses me slowly, deeply, as though he's savoring every last slide of my tongue against his. Finally, he pulls away, eyes glassy in the dark. "Grace, I already told you. I don't think we've ever really been friends."

33

The old adage of "sleeping on it" didn't come close to being true about my feelings toward Eric. Sleeping on a conversation over who feels what and who is brave enough to act on it doesn't look any different in the cold light of day. It brings a side dish of emotional hangover to choke down with breakfast. Seeing him last night has only raised more questions. I know his feelings are real, but am I naive enough to think they wouldn't change if I got the promotion over him? Would the way I feel about him now sour if I had to watch him take my opportunity and thrive? The small, lingering voice in my head tells me none of it is real, that I'm a gullible idiot who deserves to fail. Was he being honest? Or was this just all part of some grand plan to try and make me fall for him before squashing me like a bug under his Prada loafers? Maybe I'm just a pushover, as malleable as a wet rag. Twist me in your hands and wring me out. It's something William must have known about me, and used to his advantage until I finally noticed.

The moment I met William he zeroed in on me as someone to mold and manipulate into an empty shell of a person who would be his subordinate in life. Maybe Eric and I have hardly seen eye to eye because we're the opposite of that: we see each other as worthy opponents. Equals scrambling toward the same future. I push the feelings down, taking deep breaths to fill my brain and my blood with oxygen instead of searing self-doubt.

My hand jitters against the waiting-room chair as confidence-boosting mantras swirl in my head, smushing together like fruit in a blender. We were both instructed to send our presentation slideshows over to Catcher's office this morning so they could be pre-queued up on the huge flat-screen. This is both a blessing and a curse: the former is because I can't panic about last-minute changes, and the latter is because I can't panic about last-minute changes. Instead, I panic about what they'll think of me as a person. Will they interpret my nervous energy as care and passion, or immaturity and unpreparedness? My stomach wrenches as I smooth down my powder-blue suit. I put this on thinking it would match the Ditto brand colors. Some subliminal messaging to suggest I should be part of the launch. It's only now I realize it's the same suit I was wearing the day I found out about this project.

My phone vibrates and I flinch, knowing a message from Eric right now will throw me off even further. *Jesus, you need to calm down.* It's probably just a good-luck message from Yemi and Alice. It's neither. It's a message from William via Instagram. Ugh, I can't think of anything worse than talking to him right now. If I continue to ignore him on every platform hopefully he'll get the hint. Standing up for myself with Susie gave me such a surge of confidence and reassured me that, actually, the world wouldn't end if I vocalized my wants and needs. So why can't I bring myself to definitively shoot William down? I've already spent way too long pushing away the someone I *actually* want. I dismiss the notification and roll my shoulders back, trying to stop fidgeting.

We're presenting to Catcher and two major investors for the app. My nerves calm slightly as I enter the room and notice one is a woman. Hopefully, this means I won't be presenting my ideas to a boys' club of tech VCs. Catcher is bad enough. I pray he doesn't call me sweetheart during this interview. My lip curls on one side while remembering Eric's knuckles turning white at the word "sweetheart" in our initial Ditto meeting. I was too nervous to dare correct the CEO of the company on his misogynistic tendencies, but Eric had to hold himself back from punching him. My stomach twists with guilt: his instinct was to protect me even when I was acting as if I hated him.

I sit down in front of a row of impeccably tailored business people. Catcher: his usual wiry salt-and-pepper hair and beard cut so freshly, I imagine he has a live-in barber who trims it while he sleeps. Another man, Angus Glass, is a fairly recognizable angel investor; I've never met him personally, but I know he's invested in a lot of Catch Group start-ups. His red hair is almost as vibrant as mine, but it's cropped tight and short, letting his green eyes do the talking. The woman, who introduces herself as Suma Harada, a transplant from Catch Group's New York office, sports a blunt fringe with long black hair that gracefully drapes over her shoulders in a way I could only dream of achieving. After shaking hands with everyone and introducing myself, I take an audible gulp, which thankfully is covered by the sounds of chairs and papers shuffling. All three of my destiny-deciders study my face as I tap my cue cards straight against the wooden conference table. It's safe to say no amount of mantra-ing in a fluorescent-lit hallway would have ever prepared me for this moment but I do it in my head anyway.

I am enough, I belong here, I deserve to be here.

My hands are sweating, my knees are weak and my arms suddenly feel so unbelievably heavy they might as well be filled with lead. I think I finally understand the realism of Eminem's opening words of "Lose Yourself." My mouth starts to dry up as I answer the first few questions about my current experience; even though most of my work experiences and achievements are not *officially* listed on the piece of paper summing up my career. Doing all the work and letting Susie take the credit seems like a less sensible plan than I previously believed it was. My peripheral vision watches Angus Glass doodle at the top of the page next to my name. Owing to Susie's hectic social schedule and demanding daily task list, I can say with confidence I have essentially performed the role of Head of Marketing by proxy already with relative ease. It's satisfying to think I could step into her shoes at a moment's notice because I have so many times in the past.

Verbalizing this sort of thing has never been my strong suit but maybe spending time with Eric over the past few weeks has forced me to be more of a self-advocate. He always seemed as if he had been born with a head full of subconscious affirmations guiding him through life, when in reality he also has to fight the overwhelming urge to be validated by others to achieve something of which he can be proud. The awareness pulls in me like an elastic band ready to snap. If I had just stood up for myself, spoken up about what I wanted instead of bending to everyone else's will, I could have actually been happy, fulfilled and proud of myself and my job much sooner.

Nerves rake up my spine to fight with my brain as I stand up on shaky legs to present my strategy. The tagline emblazoned across the screen tells me there's no going back now. When I lay out my plan to not only bring current dating-app users to the space but also to attract a new generation of users who are experiencing dating-app fatigue too, the three people deciding my fate seem quietly interested: eyes narrowed intently, subtle unconscious nods and laid-back comfortable demeanors. After announcing my strategy's premise I plow on, laying out my plans for partnering with powerhouse names in the leisure and entertainment industries but also smaller, upcoming, cool businesses; bringing a mass appeal to Ditto while establishing its reputation for authenticity. Something neither Fate nor Ignite has fully managed to execute under Susie's and Dharmash's leadership.

"While Mr. Bancroft and I have been securing larger brands and locations as initial launch partners, I've also been working with independent brands around the city to create truly unique dates. Not your usual axe-throwing, escape-room date fodder."

Catcher raises his eyebrows in approval.

I list some of my example dates:

- Cabaret and dim sum
- Kayaking in hidden gem areas
- Immersive theater performances
- Authentic cuisine cooking classes
- Roller skating in a genuine refurbished retro rink
- Abseiling down the side of a skyscraper, for those adrenaline junkies
- Brazilian nightclub dancing
- Hole-in-the-wall quirky museum tours
- Late-night gallery tours.

An image of Eric in the gallery bursts into my mind, hesitant but willing to show me a part of himself he keeps locked away from others. Him falling into stories of his childhood without even realizing it at El Turo's cooking class. Trying so hard to keep the want from his eyes during our yoga session. The strip of photo-booth pictures hidden in a book he usually had open, but was too scared to show me. The person who, instead of going along with my drunken advances, didn't want me to have an ulterior motive when I was with him. To not be like every person who wanted something from him, to mistake him for someone he never wanted to be. He deserves so much more than that.

My gut twists.

I explain how we'll work with a wide range of influencers to create their own dream dates and promote them via social media. One-of-a-kind experiences that will only be available through Ditto. A curated date from not only brands and businesses they love, but tastemakers who potential users look to for the next big thing.

"In conclusion . . ." I stare intensely at the three suits, mouth dry of words.

I glance down at my notes.

OK, time to speak from the heart!

But where is my heart? It's currently sinking to the bottom of the ocean.

The whole reason I was gunning for this new job was because I wasn't happy with the terms of my current one, but now they've been renegotiated. Eric, however, is working for a snake who has never had his best interests in mind. If I win this and Eric stays at Ignite, he'll never have the relationships and respect he deserves. Despite everything, his options are limited. If I lose this, I know I'll be fine. I know I have value beyond Susie, Fate and Catch Group. If I win this, I will have deserved it, but I don't think I'll be happy.

"In conclusion," I repeat, swilling the words around my tongue until they turn sweet, "you should give this role to Eric Bancroft."

"Excuse me?" Suma's eyebrows shoot up and hide behind her fringe as she leans forward and checks her papers. "Isn't that the next candidate?"

She turns to Catcher for confirmation. My stomach turns to lead but I'm not nervous. In fact . . . this is the least nervous I've been all day.

"Yes. It is," I confirm.

Catcher holds his top lip in his teeth, trying to mask his frustration as he keeps his fiery stare fixed on me.

Sensing an explanation is needed I clear any remaining hesitation from my throat and clarify, "He deserves this job. He's talented, passionate and smart. He's the reason we were even able to get in the door with our biggest partners." I gesture to the collage of logos floating on the screen. "You should give this role to him," I repeat for emphasis to the knitted brows staring dumbfounded from across the table.

"You realize what you're putting on the line right now?" Catcher looks at me in complete disbelief.

"Yes." I lift my chin and answer as assuredly as

possible because I don't think I've ever been so sure about anything in my life.

"OK," he accepts. "That will be all. Thank you, Grace."

He glances at the door, gesturing for me to get out before I waste any more of their time. He sits back in his chair, pinching the bridge of his nose with his thick sausage fingers. The investors to his sides are leaning in, no doubt to discuss the ramifications of my unexpected towel-throwing.

For a moment my body goes stiff. Maybe that was the wrong way to do it. I should have just bombed the entire presentation and then they would have automatically given it to him. I shake the thought from my head. I shouldn't have to make myself look weak to champion someone else. I know I'm enough, I know where I belong and I know what I deserve. I'll be fine. Ignite is slowly destroying Eric and he doesn't believe he deserves any better. Even if he never speaks to me again, I want to do this for him more than I want this job.

The only thing I can think to say as I leave is "Thank you for your time."

Catcher spits out a laugh and I run to the door, dumping my cue cards in a rubbish bin as I exit.

Do you ever get that feeling where you're drunk on your own decisions? Those few moments of exhilaration and relief when you finish a roller-coaster ride designed to have your heart in your throat?

That's how I feel, stepping out of Catcher's office into the quiet hallway. As if I need to scream the final slivers of raw feeling out of me until I'm completely empty. A clean slate. Free of emotional baggage and ready for whatever life throws at me.

34

Eric's presentation is scheduled straight after mine. It was a small miracle I didn't see him as soon as I left the meeting room. When I arrive at my desk my whole body starts to sweat. I should get out of here, and go get some air before I end up bumping into him somewhere in the building.

The consequences of my actions slowly dawn on me. Did I seriously just give up my dream job for a guy? Am I going to be shunned from the gates of feminist heaven for this bullshit? I swallow the dryness in my throat.

Maybe I should go back and rescind my statement. Beg them to give me a second chance. We all make mistakes! Spur-of-the-moment gut decisions that end up being completely idiotic, right?

The elevator flows with people heading out as if it's a normal day. It probably is for them. Their agenda so far includes "go to work," "catch up on emails," "attend a meeting" and "go grab an overpriced sandwich." Not "pour your blood, sweat and tears into a fucking good job presentation then self-sabotage so hard your nervous system feels like loose change clanging around in a pocket." As others start to occupy the lift, I pull out my phone and begin to type out a message. Something casual like *How did it go?* or *So how did they tell you you're the new Marketing Lead of Ditto? In skywriting or one of those giant novelty checks?*

I press delete and watch the letters evaporate into the humid, breathy air of the elevator.

More and more Catch Group employees filter in: some I recognize, giving them a polite smile as though I didn't just blow up my life. The doors slide closed, inches from touching as a hand slams around one of the metal slabs, triggering the doors to reopen with a cheerful ding. I look up and lock eyes with Eric and his unreadable face. His jaw goes taut as his eyes latch on to mine. He must have been in his interview for maybe ten minutes tops. Did they just offer him the job on the spot?

Eric turns around to face the front like everyone else, something I've never thought of as unusual until right now. The lift bundles down a couple of floors, stopping to add even more sardines to our tin. Whoever thought of the stuck-in-an-elevator trope in romance novels must be rolling in their literary grave right now.

The mass exodus of bodies into the lobby moving in the same direction lulls me into a false sense of security until Eric turns around and spots me at the back of the crowd. I veer right and keep moving over the main lobby floor. I can't stop. Interacting with him before we're officially told he has the job will just be too hard, and trying to predict his reaction to what I've done leaves the plains of my imagination completely barren.

He catches up to me, placing a warm palm on my back and gently steering me away from the flow of the crowd. Eventually, we stop, his hands on my arms. Up close, the shadows under his bright eyes are more pronounced than I've ever seen them. His face twists as though he can't quite get the words out.

A lance of unease pierces my chest. OK, this seems bigger than the interview.

"What's going on? Is Iris OK?" I ask, having only ever seen this look of concern once before, at Matilda's Bar.

"Yeah, she's fine." He shakes his head, looking confused, and lets out a curt breath, lips relaxing into something resembling relief. He steps closer to face me as his hand subtly rests on my waist, a magnet finding its opposite.

With a jolt, I realize I've seen this look of concern more than once before. Once when Iris was slumped across the table, and once when I lay on the ground beside the hiking trail. I place a reassuring hand over his.

He clears his throat. "I had to tell you before they do. I know I—"

"Grace!" A booming voice cuts across the marble expanse, traveling along the stone veins and slicing into me. Eric's hand tenses, matching my body. My face feels as if it's trying to escape straight off my skull as I watch his soft lines go rigid with understanding.

I spin to face William, my hand slipping from Eric's.

For a moment I just stare at the former man of my dreams; there is a sheepish smile on his face, partially hidden by a massive bouquet of flowers held over one arm, and a small velvet box in his other hand. My mind returns to the room, and I cautiously walk over to him. The warmth of Eric's hand melts from my side but I feel his presence remaining close behind me as I approach William.

"What are you doing here?" The question comes out more feebly than I had anticipated.

"You weren't replying to any of my texts or calls and I was so worried about you, Gracie. I needed to make sure you were OK." He almost looks confused, as if he expects me to have dropped everything to call him back. "I called you—I needed to see you," he repeats.

"I told you I've been too busy—that I was up for a promotion." I narrow my eyes, shooting the same confused look right back.

"Oh," he says, looking hurt.

I wait for a question; some interest in how it went, how I feel, if I got the job, but instead he awkwardly scans the linear patterns on the wall.

I look at the flowers and sigh at his dull brown eyes. "Why are you here?"

William clears his throat and looks up, wide-eyed, like a terrible actor waiting for his big monologue moment.

He takes a deep breath. "I've been looking at your social media. Seeing you thriving and looking amazing proved something to me: I can't and don't want to live without you. We belong together."

A few "awwww"s spring forth from the growing crowd. My mind slips to their perspective: a man has come to win a woman's heart with a dramatic, romantic confession. Not long ago I would have gobbled up this scene too. This is the thing love stories are made of. Instead, I cringe as what he's doing fully dawns on me.

I know this is nothing but a play: deliver public displays of affection, adoration and loyalty; perform said display in front of people whose opinions I value, making me feel obliged or too embarrassed to protest; then act the exact opposite in private. He's not even offering a rebuttal of his ultimatum. Maybe he thinks time apart from him was "punishment" for not giving him what he wants. For not giving up my entire life to him in exchange for his performative love.

My body trembles with frustration, confusion and exhaustion as I ask a little louder than necessary: "And what about all the women you were messaging while we were together? Can you live without them?"

I used to think people knowing what happened would make me look stupid and weak—as if it was *my* choices that led *him* to make those decisions. The last few weeks have shown me you can't control how people perceive you; the only important thing is how you perceive yourself.

"What?" His face reddens with either embarrassment or anger as he splutters, "I don't know what you're talking about." His brow knits, eyes flicking between me and the crowd as though he's watching the Wimbledon final. He grabs my hand. "Gracie, come on. If it means that much to you, you can keep your little job."

"Don't call me that." I make an attempt to yank my arm free, but his grip remains tight as he ignores me.

"Was it him, Gracie?" His lips twist into disgust. "Did *he* tell you these lies?"

He gestures at Eric, who is moving toward us, jaw clenched like a panther ready to finally take its kill. The crowd must read the tension on his face as they quickly begin to act preoccupied as if they weren't just gawping at us.

"What the fuck have you said to her?" William leans around me to shout at Eric, his words bouncing off the marble and turning more heads toward us.

"I didn't have to say anything. You managed to fuck it up all on your own." Eric's voice is smooth and sly compared to William's flustered tone, I've never seen his face look this deadly.

To stop this from escalating into a full-blown Bridget Jones–style fight, I interrupt the fast-growing tension, turning first to William. "This has nothing to do with him." Then I place my hand on Eric's toned chest, the cotton brushing my clammy palm. "Eric, just give us a minute."

Reluctantly, Eric takes a few steps back. Giving me space to take the reins on the conversation but staying near to support me if I need. Guilt twangs in my chest; even after I couldn't promise him a future, his instinct is still to protect me.

I turn back to William, still standing in the middle of the lobby, the center of attention. My guilt subsides as I look at his pathetic face. "I know the truth so there's no point in lying. I've seen the messages and the pictures. You're just embarrassing yourself."

William lowers the bouquet to his side, petals dropping out as the flowers hang upside down. The look of desperation, shame and annoyance on his face just makes me hate him even more. He lets out a nervous laugh and scratches the back of his neck.

"It's not like we were engaged or anything. I would have stopped once we were married," he pleads, as though this would be a sacrifice he would make in exchange for mine. My face creases as bile creeps up my throat. Sensing my outrage, he gently takes my hand for emphasis and tilts his head. "I will stop, I promise."

I suck in my cheeks, looking at the floor and pleading with my eyes to stop burning.

"Why?" My voice comes out thin and quiet. "Why did you do it?"

"You were so busy with your job. I needed more. It's why I wanted you to marry me and quit." His lips curl into a tight smile. "That's what you want too, deep down. It's the best thing for both of us, Gracie."

I rip my hand from him. "God, do you even know me at all?"

"Listen, just . . ." He wipes a hand over his mouth as frustration flashes across his dark eyes. ". . . just come with me so we can talk about this."

He grabs my arm and tries to pull me through the automatic glass doors out toward the street. There he goes again, dragging me wherever he wants to go, expecting me to silently, dutifully follow. Before I know what I'm doing my hand is up in a fist, flying toward his face. A blast of sharp heat runs through my whole arm and my knuckles bark in pain. William stumbles back, dropping the bouquet of roses so forcefully dark pink petals scatter all over the beige floor like an exploded flamingo, matching the color of his face as blood begins to trickle in a steady stream from his nose down his crisp white shirt.

He holds his bloodied hands out, shocked by what just happened. He takes in the damage, pinching his nose gingerly and then he lunges at me, mouth snarling as the blood lines his teeth.

I jolt back as a hand grabs William's shoulder, balling his shirt into a fist. "I wouldn't do that, mate," a calm but firm voice comes from behind him. My shoulders lower at the sight of Dave the security guard, cool as can be.

"She attacked me! The bitch broke my nose!" William spits, nose still spewing thick red.

"No. You grabbed the nice lady and she defended herself," Dave replies serenely.

"Are you fucking kidding me?" William stumbles, eyes jarringly wide as he tries to release himself from Dave's grip.

"I suggest you leave now, sir, or I'll have no choice but to call the police." Dave guides him like a leashed toddler at Disneyland toward the glass doors.

My heart pounds as I watch William shrink away into the busy London street. The hate and shame and pity swell in my chest like a waterlogged drain as my brain tries to grasp his true nature. He so desperately needed to look like the knight in shining armor when all he really wanted to do was keep me locked up, where he could always find me, my only care to keep him happy. *My* happiness was only important when he deemed it so. People murmur around me and adrenaline races around my body, shaking my limbs like a wild animal slamming against the bars of its cage.

"Grace?" Eric's smooth voice is a balm on my frazzled senses. "We should get you out of here."

Eric looks around at the people lingering in the lobby and then holds a palm out for me. With my still functioning hand, I take it. My eyes are heavy as he carefully guides me past the last audience members into the lift.

A man in a suit strides up to the elevator doors, takes one look at our faces and says, "I'll wait."

The doors slide shut with a clang, followed by a quiet but oddly soothing whirring of the pulleys. We remain in silence until I lean against the support bar and examine my hand, hissing at the bruise already forming. The moment air escapes my mouth he is there, studying the marks, gently caressing my fingers resting on top of his. He brings my hand to his mouth and places a delicate kiss on the knuckle, then blinks his thoughts away.

"Sorry," he half whispers when I blush. "Probably a stupid question but . . . are you OK?"

Everything that's happened between us in the past few days flashes through my mind, and I'm back in the hotel room as he tenderly catalogs each part of me. He straightens his shoulders.

"I think so. It'll heal," I reply, studying the state of my dominant writing (and apparently punching) hand.

"Good." He smiles softly. "But I meant are *you* OK?"

Oh, he means am I going to transform into the shell of a person I was when I was with William? A cracked egg with no pan—broken, messy and useless. I gaze into his eyes, recognizing a depth of care and kindness in them I've never truly grasped before. If I was still a broken, messy, useless person, he would be here. He would wait for me to heal because that's what he has been doing this whole time.

The words come out before I have a chance to catch them between my teeth. "I told them to choose you."

My tone conveys a casualness more in the realm of "I told them you'll have a Diet Coke," not "I told them to give you the job we've both been fighting over for weeks."

"What?" He blinks at me, mouth agape.

I nod. "I told them you were the right choice for the job."

He puts both sets of fingers on his temples and rubs them in tiny circles. "Why did you do that?"

"I don't know," I say, but I do know. My foggy mind can't compute why he wouldn't be happy about getting the job of his dreams.

He sighs. "*I told them to choose you.*"

"What? Why did you do that?" It turns out getting the shock of your life is a great way to alleviate pain from your recently injured hand.

He rolls his lips together and shakes his head, then turns to the metal sheet of glowing buttons on the wall and slams his palm against the big shiny red one. The quiet whirring ceases and I clutch the railing as we jolt to a stop.

Eric paces the short length of the lift until he's inches from me. "You said at the hotel there was no point in this thing between us continuing because whoever lost out on the job wouldn't be able to stand the other person winning." He looks at me wide-eyed, waiting for confirmation.

"Yes!" My eyebrows almost hit the ceiling as I completely agree with him in the most disagreeable voice I can muster.

His head tilts upward as he shoots me a sidelong glance. "Well, you were wrong. I could. I wouldn't just be fine with it. I'd be fucking ecstatic."

I stutter, "B-but you want this just as much as I do."

He takes a step toward me and shakes his head. My chin lifts to meet his gaze.

"I want *you* more. Us being on each other's team, waking up next to you every day, taking you on real dates, watching you realize you deserve the fucking world and being the one who is allowed to give it to you. Being able to tell you every day that I'm in love

with you. That's me winning, Grace. I don't need anything else."

I take a shuddering breath. "Well . . . fuck. I love you
too."

It comes out so matter-of-factly that "obviously I love
you, duh" would have been more appropriate. So bru-
tally honest I don't even stop to think about it.

He takes my face in his hands and kisses me softly,
thumb delicately stroking my cheek until he pulls away
to look at me. "And you probably would have beaten
me anyway. Better to end with some dignity."

He winks at me and I let out a teary laugh, pressing
my forehead against his. He holds my jaw in his palms,
stroking away an escaped tear from my cheek like a
windshield wiper in a rainstorm.

A man's crackling voice bursts from the lift's speaker.
"Everything OK in there, guys?"

Eric presses the call intercom button. "Yeah. But can
you give us like two minutes, please? Just baring my
soul to someone."

The gruff voice stays quiet for a few moments then
states, "I can give you one minute."

"Thanks, man." Eric tugs me by my waist toward
him. "Where was I?" he teases.

"Confessing your love for me." I nod, trying to keep
my beaming smile from blinding him.

"Ah, right." He kisses my lips—"I love you"—my
cheek—"I love you"— my neck—"I love you."

We barely have our hands off each other as the doors

glide open on Catcher's floor, revealing Harriet standing with her arms out in frustration. "I've been calling you for twenty minutes! Mr. Catcher wants to see you immediately."

"What about?" Eric asks, hand out of sight stroking the small of my back as if he'll never fully let me go.

"I have no idea." Harriet runs a hand through her honey-blonde hair. "Have either of you seen Grace Hastings? I'm meant to fetch her too."

Eric shoots me a look of amusement as we step out onto the office floor with bated breath.

35

It's a weird combination of emotions, knowing that best-case scenario you are going to be ripped to shreds by your boss, and worst-case scenario you will be straight-up fired for embarrassing the company in front of its major investors, and yet you're so deliriously happy you know nothing can hurt you. Feeling grateful to be in the sun even if you're about to burn to a crisp. This is how it feels to walk hand in hand with Eric toward Catcher's office. Harriet's raised eyebrows suggested she had caught a glimpse of our private display of affection in the lift, but when Bancroft's fingers interlace with mine in her presence it makes my heart swell. Whatever is coming next, we can deal with it together.

Eric's thumb lightly traces soothing circles on the top of my hand as we pace down the hallway and pass a row of glass fishbowl meeting rooms. The occupants stare wide-eyed and slack-jawed. I'm not sure whether it's because the news of me punching my ex-boyfriend in the lobby has already traveled up to this floor or whether it's because we, the famously mortal enemies from rival dating apps, are floating past on a cloud, looking like two cats who got the most luxurious cream imaginable. Either way, we both have more pressing matters to worry about right now.

We make it to Catcher's office, squeeze, and then release each other's hands. Giving Catcher impassioned, overlapping and entirely unrehearsed explanations as to why we both sacrificed this opportunity for the other would likely negate our very efforts. We did this because both of us deserve to be here on our own merits since either of us would thrive in this role.

We face the doorway of doom; Eric holds his arm out to knock but then hesitates. Instead, he leans into me. "I'm feeling the urge to say something along the lines of 'good luck' . . . but that seems like kind of a moot point now."

"Something like 'nice knowing ya!'"—I mime a tip of my hat—"feels more appropriate."

He lets out a breathy laugh and replies, "Nice knowing you too." Then hits the door with three brisk knocks.

Martin Catcher, founder and CEO of Catch Group Inc. and the man ultimately responsible for our livelihoods, stares in silence as we sheepishly perch on chairs on the other side of his massive carved wooden desk. His office is a clichéd "old rich man who probably owns a boat" style. Red leather–bound books with gold embossing, sparkling whisky decanters arranged neatly in the corner and framed black-and-white photographs of him and every famous businessman of the twenty-first century littered across the walls. His lips are pursed and his eyes narrow, as though he's trying to unravel the master plan we've concocted specifically to ruin his day.

He takes in a sharp lungful of air and places his joined fists on the desk. "You know, I was thinking of just firing you both on the spot after the stunt you pulled."

My stomach lurches, as though the fist that hit William actually went straight through a wormhole, time traveled to this exact moment and punched me in the gut instead.

"It wasn't planned," I state calmly. I glance over at Eric and watch him lean back in his chair as if this is just a casual catch-up. As if he has life-altering meetings like this all the time. I swear I hear him say "Speak for yourself" under his breath. I suck in my cheeks to avoid a shy smirk of my own.

"I should hope not, considering you wasted my and our investors' time." Catcher's eyes flick between us, waiting for one of us to break.

Honed from years of people-pleasing, my instinct is to give him what he wants: groveling and repenting and begging for forgiveness. My lips part, the word "sorry" tingles against my tongue but my mouth closes when I remember I'm actually not sorry. Not in the slightest. If I could have the time again I would do the exact same thing.

At our silence, Catcher continues, "That being said, Suma and Angus were quite impressed by your tenacity." We both shuffle in our seats, the dread and stress shifting underneath us like tectonic plates. Catcher continues, "They thought it showed a 'real passion for the role and the company' "—he finger quotes, eyes almost rolling—"putting egos and competition aside and recommending the best person for the job."

I would give anything to have been a fly on the wall in Eric's meeting. Maybe after this, he'll indulge me with a dramatic re-enactment. That is *after* we both perform a re-enactment of our night in the penthouse.

Catcher runs his tongue over his front teeth and a whoosh of air releases from his nose. "I was clearly onto something when I said you work well together."

I school my curving lips into neutrality. Upon first hearing the conclusion of our relationship I vehemently opposed it, but after everything that has happened it is hard to deny. We found it so difficult to be just friends because we demanded more from each other. When we couldn't give it to each other, we burned out. Working together on Ditto forced us to rise from the ashes and flame together.

Catcher turns his attention to Eric. "You were so certain Miss Hastings would be the best person for the role you didn't even do your presentation."

My head spins to the side, catching Eric's tense jaw. I thought what he told me was an exaggeration. He just walked in, told them I was right for the job and walked out? My heart simultaneously sinks and swells.

"And you." Catcher turns to me, brows crinkled, face taut with restrained irritation. "If you hadn't been so adamant we give the role to Mr. Bancroft, I would have disregarded everything he submitted for the project since he didn't even bother presenting it. However, Suma and Angus were convinced by your words to assess his strategy, and they were very impressed by his work."

I lean forward in my chair and hold my breath, my heart pounding. Did my incredibly poorly thought-out plan actually work?

"So, let's get down to brass tacks." Catcher leans back in his chair, crossing his arms and assessing our tense faces with an odd look of satisfaction. We made him suffer; he wants us to suffer too. "As I said, I've seen your side-by-side potential for a while now. After discussing the matter with our investors and the board, I have made the executive decision to promote you both."

"What?" we say in unison; my heart pounds so loudly I swear Catcher can hear it.

He crinkles his brow in a way that screams "Have you not figured this out by now?" "If my two best Marketing Managers walk into the room, provide equally good strategies with opposing strengths and insist I hire the competing candidate . . . do you think I have any other option but to select them both?"

I mean, firing us both seems like a solid option too, but far be it from me to bring up that alternative.

Eric tilts his head and asks in a low voice, "But what does that mean exactly?" His fingers twitch on the wooden arm of the chair; it takes everything in me not to cover them with mine.

The deep green leather armchair creaks as Catcher relaxes, a man satisfied with his control over the conversation. "It means—pending the funds clearing—our investors are willing to put forward the capital for two Head of Marketing salaries. We think it will bring a bit of gravitas to Ditto. Having a man and a woman managing the launch allows for a more holistic approach to the rollout. You can divide and conquer based on your strengths, then work in tandem for any major elements."

"Based on our strengths?" I ask.

"Eric handles bringing in the big fish, the established mainstream headliners who keep the lights on, and—like you set out in your presentation—you focus on localized brand awareness and the up-and-coming businesses to partner with for unique experiences."

My foot taps the air as I try to calm my body and mind. Not in my wildest dreams did I ever think this would even be an option, let alone the consequence of us both going completely off script.

"That's if . . . you two are happy to continue working together?" Catcher asks, eyebrows raised.

Be cool: he doesn't know you're obsessed with each other. He thinks you're still rivals. Maybe we still are? Maybe we'll always be the ones to light fires under the other. To challenge each other to be the best version of ourselves, to be the greatness we see in each other. To be the greatest things we love about each other.

I look to Eric, my heart beating so hard it's halfway out of my chest. He turns to me and smirks.

EPILOGUE

Eighteen Months Later

"Ready?" Eric asks from the bathroom.

"Yep, gimme one sec," I say, frantically typing out the final words of my email.

He leans against the doorframe, arms crossed and an eyebrow cocked. "They'll be here any minute now."

"I know, I know, I know. Sent!" The chair scrapes as I jump up and slam the laptop shut.

Eric's phone dings and he rolls his eyes playfully at the screen. "You know this whole cohabitation thing means you can just tell me stuff instead of emailing me?"

"We agreed on work-life balance, hotshot," I say, bumping him with my hip as I enter the bathroom and smooth down my hair through my fingers.

"Only because my co-founder is a workaholic." He slips his phone into his pocket, slides his hands over my waist and plants a kiss on my cheek. "Ready now?"

I turn, leaning on the sink. "No, your tie is crooked."

Eric glances in the mirror over my shoulder and then

back to me. "No, it's not." He tilts his head and gives me a confused look.

I run the silk through my fingers and tug him toward me. His eyes flare for a second and then close as we melt into each other. Our own little bubble before the chaos begins.

He huffs a laugh as I restraighten it. "I'm sorry, I must have been mistaken." I grin. "What would you do without me?"

"Have much, *much* more time on my hands," he says, lifting me up by my thighs. I scream-laugh as he walks me back into our bedroom and drops me onto the bed, prowling on top of me until his lips meet my nape and leave toe-curling kisses up my neck.

The doorbell rings and we ignore it for a few seconds, too focused on holding on to these last moments. It rings again, followed by the sound of keys tinkling in the door.

"I gave Iris a key last week," I admit, biting my lip as his hands travel up my chest. "For emergencies."

"Hiiiiii!" Iris's voice echoes through the apartment, the sound of her shoes clattering on the wooden floor as she flings them off.

Eric drops his head onto my shoulder. "You know if she has a key to this place, the only sacred space left where I can have you all to myself is your new office."

I plant one last kiss on him, holding his lip between my teeth for a few seconds before relenting. "The sofa is arriving next week so I'm absolutely holding you to that."

"OK, let's go." He hauls me up and we smooth down our clothes.

"Hey, Rissy." I bundle his sister into my arms and sway back and forth.

"Those were at your door." Iris points to a huge arrangement of orange, fuchsia and violet flowers, birds of paradise sticking out of the top. I know who they are from just by the sheer ridiculousness of the bouquet.

Congratulations on your new venture, let's talk soon. Susie x

My mind conjures an image of Susie sipping on a mimosa in Greece with her other friends dressed in white and beige like a cashmere cult. Susie left Fate not long after me and began a full rebrand into hashtag girlboss-ery. I have yet to attend her women-only networking retreat, but according to Susie the door is always open.

"And Mum asked me to get you this." Iris holds out a shiny black bottle of Dom Pérignon Vintage to Eric. "She sends her love from Dubai."

"She sent her sober daughter to pick up champagne?" he asks, sliding the bottle out of her hand and inspecting it.

"Her maternal instinct remains alive and well," Iris deadpans as he pulls her in for a tight hug.

"How's your dad?" I ask as Eric pads through to the kitchen with the champagne and flowers.

"He's good! His residency is going well and I've been helping the videographer whenever I can." Iris's cheeks blush peony pink.

"Yes, I'm sure you've been very . . . helpful." I try not to smile.

She widens her eyes and shakes her head. "I haven't told him about her yet," she mouths, glancing at Eric.

I mime zipping my mouth shut.

"I have no idea where to put this." Eric holds out the giant bouquet and hands it to me, wiping the water left over on the surface with a kitchen towel.

"Susie is never one for practicality," I reply. I take the flowers to our bedroom, resting them on the dresser behind our framed strip of photo-booth pictures. The door clicks again and the voices of Yemi, Robert, Alice and Claudia fill the space with scattered joyful greetings. I grab a light blue velvet pouch from the dresser and slip it into my pocket.

Fifteen minutes later my parents arrive, each embracing Eric at the door. They bear-hug Iris too, adopting her into the family just as much as Eric.

As my parents take their seats on the sofa, Eric straightens his shoulders and clears his throat. "OK, now you're all here, we have some exciting news to share."

I take a breath. "So, you know we've been working on a project for the past few months since leaving Catch Group. Well, thanks to Eric's excellent schmoozing skills—"

"—and your incredible presentation—" he adds with a smile.

"—we have officially secured funding and have the launch date for Ever After!"

"Oh my God! How exciting!" Iris leaps up to embrace us again, jumping up and down, followed by Robert's loud slap on the back as he hugs Eric.

"I'd like to add it was also the excellent beta created by the one and only Yemi that sealed the deal." I slide one hand into my pocket and lift my glass with the other.

Yemi stands up, does a little curtsey and then holds up her glass. "And I cannot wait to take more credit going forward when my non-compete expires! To the new founders of Ever After!"

I down my glass and announce, "Wait! We need more champagne for the toast!"

"I thought you were going to announce you're engaged or something," says Alice, giggling into her drink.

Eric and I look at each other, beaming, as I reveal my left hand, much more sparkly than it was a few moments ago.

"Well, before we cheers, there is one more thing we have to tell you . . ."

CREDITS

I'm a big believer in giving credit where it's due. The creation of a novel does not just include the obvious author, agent and editor. A plethora of talented individuals have touched this book, a lot of them without me even knowing. I want to thank every single person who has aided in the production of *The Launch Date*.

Everyone who wanted to be included is listed below:

Editorial
Alice Rodgers
Sally Williamson
Asanté Simons
Shannon Plackis

Copy Editor
Richenda Todd

Proofreader
Heather Bosch

Marketing
Deanna Bailey
DJ DeSmyter

Audio
Abigail Marks
Kirsten Clawson
Peter Bobinski

Cover
Yeon Kim
Mallory Heyer

Sales

Kelly Roberts
Ronnie Kutys
Lillie Walsh
Rachel Levenberg
Casey Coughlin
Wendy Ceballos
Donna Waitkus

Publicity

Jessica Cozzi
Danielle Bartlett

Production

Brittani DiMare
Robin Barletta

Managing Editorial

Hope Ellis

Contracts

Tanya Seamans

ACKNOWLEDGMENTS

Thank you to my parents, Karen and Albert, who showed me what it means to be ambitious and take big swings. As well as encouraging me to follow my passion for creative writing throughout my childhood and adulthood; this novel genuinely would not exist without your patience, encouragement, love, open-mindedness, enthusiasm and ever-present support.

Thank you to my husband, Alex. An in-house sounding board on every aspect of this book, from character names to cover art. When we were dating, I saw him making notes on a movie we'd just watched so we could talk about the story on the bus ride home. Now I sit in bed and watch him beta-read my books. You learning how to speak my language brings me daily joy that, ironically, words cannot express.

Thank you to my godmother, Angela Hoyes, who took on the role of "London mum" when I first moved to the city. Every experience that inspired this story and my writing would have never happened without your support.

Thank you to my mother-in-law, Karen McHale, who

was the first person ever to read this book and told me to add more sex. I took the note and got an offer of representation two weeks later. Thank you for always being so welcoming and openhearted. I am incredibly lucky to have gained an extra mum in my life.

Thank you to every one of my friends and family who didn't laugh in my face when I said I was writing a book. When the word "author" was just a taste in my mouth. Thank you to my incredible team of cheerleaders, best friends and proofreaders: Charlotte McHale, Christina Hilton, Emma Burgoyne, Georgie Arnold, Hannah Worth, Hannah Carroll and Kate Urquiola. Also thank you to all the local book club members who have known me since I was a baby and still insist on me signing your copies. Your unwavering support and encouragement mean more than you will ever know.

Thank you to Charlotte Hay for beating me to the coveted Year Six Creative Writing award. Beyond your lifelong friendship and love, it is the twenty-year-old revenge plot that pushed me to the finish line.

Thank you to Annabel Faulkner for being a constant inspiration for the limitlessness of the human spirit. Whenever I think I can't meet a deadline or finish a project I think about how you would get it done, go for drinks then climb a mountain the next morning. You are insane and I love you for it.

Thank you to Kat Grant; I still think of that moment in the restaurant in Paris where we admitted we couldn't think of living with anyone except each other. Thank you for listening to me rant about my job every day, your endless love and infectious joy got me through some of the most high-stress times of my life.

Thank you to my agent, Silé Edwards, for plucking me out of obscurity into slightly less obscurity and allowing me to be my purest Virgo self. But mostly thank you for being the best wrangler, colleague, ride-or-die and confidante during this wild journey. You truly are a dream agent.

Thank you to my amazing team of editors: Alice Rodgers, Sally Williamson, Asanté Simons and Shannon Plackis. It takes a village to produce a novel and I am so grateful for your kindness, encouragement and faith that some random girl from Lincolnshire could produce a half-decent book.

Thank you to the writing community who have provided a soft landing to any stress or query I've had during this entire journey. My 2025 debut group, Lizzy Dent and my agent sibling Simone Soltani for their unwavering support. A massive shout-out to Emily Wibberley and Austin Siegemund-Broka for being my first-ever blurbers!

Thank you to Catherine Love and Jessica Paul for creating an encouraging environment for my love of English to flourish! Thank you to Will Buckingham, Jonathan Taylor, Kathy Bell and Simon Perril. Teaching hungover creative writing students is tough, but you made a huge impact.

Thank you to all my fantastic colleagues and everyone

who has ever hired me to write and create. Experiences, good or bad, mold us into who we are and I'm grateful for every one. In particular, thank you to Emma Dai, Aimee Barrett, Ariadna Morrell Cheung, Jemima Knight and Francesca Perks, who are just a handful of the amazingly talented people who made sitting at a desk working overtime for shitty bosses worth it.

Thanking yourself feels incredibly indulgent but honestly, my penultimate thanks goes to a real one: me. Thank you to the thousands of versions of me who decided to push on each day to write this book without any hope that it would ever be published. Without fully understanding how much it would mean to achieve baby Annabelle's pipe dream.

And finally, thank you to you. Buying a debut author's book is always going to be a gamble, and I am forever grateful that you chose this one and read the acknowledgments, because that's a bloody commitment.

ABOUT THE AUTHOR

Annabelle Slator grew up writing stories in the depths of the British countryside. After achieving a degree in creative writing, she spent most of her late teens and early twenties writing social media and blog posts for startups and tech companies in London. Nowadays, if she isn't spending time writing, you can almost always find her obsessing over niche internet drama, practicing her fencing parry or mooching around vintage fairs and flea markets with her husband and two mini dachshunds, Gruffalo and Gryffin. *The Launch Date* is Annabelle's first book, inspired by her time working at a popular dating app.